Praise for Matt Rauscher's Sensational Debut Novel

The Unborn Spouse Situation

"A stunningly quick-witted and sincere first-person narrative....the introspection of *The Catcher in the Rye*....Stark, passionate honesty coupled with economic, elegant description....With his novel, Rauscher has proven himself a master of first-person writing, taking his reader on a journey that changes form....from simple conversational narrative to stream of consciousness mind-blowing exhilaration....a poetic intermingling of experiences and sensations."

-The Independent Gay Writer
Andrew Barriger, Author of *Finding Faith*

"Rauscher captures the antsy angst of urgent desire with intelligent wit, and the emotional and sexual maturity of his young character with entertaining assurance....*The Unborn Spouse Situation* is a wonderful mix of emotional liberation and soulful melancholy....an engaging debut."

-Books To Watch Out For
Richard Labonte

"This book about college student angst set in the Midwest rocks."

- Instinct Magazine

"When a Jewish boy meets an Indian boy it's kismet."

- Self-Publisher News

The Unborn Spouse Situation

Matt Rauscher

Copyright © 2005 by Matt Rauscher
All rights reserved

ISBN 1-4116-2920-5

This book is a work of fiction, and any similarity to any persons or events is entirely coincidental.

www.mattrauscher.com

www.lulu.com/mattrauscher

For Jessica Benjamin

Book One

It sounded as if the Streets were running
And then—the Streets stood still—
Eclipse—was all we could see at the Window
And awe—was all we could feel.

        -Emily Dickinson

1.

"You're the only faggot in the house," Victor said. "Do you think you can handle it?"

He undid his belt and took off his pants. My stomach turned with excitement; I'd never seen an Indian guy nude before. "I can handle a lot of things," I said, hoping to sound nonchalant. We were staying at the Harley Hutt. There was not an ounce of sanity in the place, or a fragment of normalcy. There wasn't even an air conditioner in a window. I'd just moved in.

"Will you exchange boxers with me?" he asked, standing before me in a baggy pair of blue and white striped shorts, his skin the color of almonds, his nipples surrounded by hair. I wanted to shout, "Yes!" at the top of my lungs and hear it ring out from the Harley Hutt's third floor window and reverberate around campus. Instead I asked, "Why?"

"Why not?" He smiled and ran his hand through his hair. It was blue-black and silky, parted in the middle, and down to his jawbone. He widened his face into a come hither grin and then smirked, as if this scene was an old cliché or taken from a bad movie. His droopy eyes looked amused.

I stripped off my clothes in a second and a half and glanced nervously toward the open window. Anyone could see in, but Victor said, "Don't let that bother you." I tried to obey. I stood across from him in my Valentine's Day boxers, replete with big red hearts, and Victor slipped down his shorts to reveal an enormously haphazard mass of black pubic hair and a horsey, light brown dick. It was disproportionately large, in just the slightest way, like his nose, which was just slightly disproportionately phallic. I thought I might end up with the boner of my life, so I quickly yanked down my shorts and handed them to Victor.

He examined my penis for longer than I would've liked and said, "They're about the same size, don't you think?"

I thought he was a blatant liar, but appreciated the charity, and I grabbed his boxers and pulled them on. They were so baggy on me that I had to hold them up by the waistband. Victor slowly tried to ease mine up over his privates, but the shorts were too small. He turned around and desperately yanked them up but they wouldn't go over his ass, which was big and brown and shaped so perfectly I thought it was worthy of accolades, of commemoration, of statues. My mind began to wander. I felt lust so strong that I wasn't focused on anything but the fine, barely visible, black hairs sprouting from his ass cheeks and the shouts of joy pouring in the window from the partiers on the street.

Eventually, Victor gave up on the boxers and remained naked. I sat down on the bed and grinned, thinking of the coming year, the coming night, the naked man leaning out the window yelling to friends. For I, Augie Schoenberg, 22, fag, aspiring filmmaker at a school without a film school, had been stuck in this mess of a Midwestern college town for four years, and was horribly, utterly single. But all of a sudden in late August with my new roommate Victor Radhakrishna, naked three stories above campus, at one with the obscenity of it, at one with the intimate absurdity of it, at one with each other's cock and balls (and bare, hairy asses), my mind became flooded with so many gorgeous, heady images that I thought I could start planning my movie, my chef d'oeuvre, my entrance into the artistic world. After college, I was going to film the story of my life on this sun-rotted Illinois campus and show everyone what it felt like to experience such debauchery, such anticipation, and such freedom. And the sight of Victor's naked body in front of me was freedom. It was absolute salvation.

I needed sex badly. A day passed. My mind was a muddled, pornographic slur; my body was constantly clammy and full of sweat. I'd been single for three and a half long, bone-dry years, and was starting to feel so lonely and so incredibly cynical about my prospects that I was drinking too much, hoping to ease the urge in my body for sex and to neutralize the longing I felt for someone to just touch me. I thought I could try to push Victor a little further but, as he said, I was the only faggot in the house, and there was no guarantee of anything substantial happening. It seemed useless to set my sights on an admittedly heterosexual guy, but the nude ritual in his bedroom had sparked a gleaming streak of hope in me that I knew I wouldn't shake. I prayed there was more ahead than just homoerotic hijinks: what may be fun and games at the Harley Hutt was real life for me, and it was getting so real I wasn't sure I could stand it. The sight of Victor's massive black bush and huge penis had kept me constantly hard. I had an enormous wet dream that night and woke up sticky the next morning. Victor kept smiling at me mischievously; we shared a secret. I wanted so badly to reach out and grab him by the penis and fuck him against the windowsill. I wanted to lose myself in his powerful arms. I wanted to suck his dick till he shouted. I could almost taste it, his penis; I could almost taste his nut sack as I dreamed of licking it up and down.

Summer would not end. It was hot as hell. My four other roommates looked at me with curious interest, wondering why I was so dazed. I thought I might go insane and become an invalid. I thought I might break.

The Harley Hutt was a campus institution: a ramshackle Victorian mansion, light blue with white trim, falling down and moldy, the wood expanded and warped from all the heat and all the bitter cold, standing smack in the middle of an old farm town as a relic from a time when, as Victor told me, you could stand on the third floor in one of the towers and gaze out at nothing but cornfields. Witness the old iron hitching post in the front yard in the shape of a horse's head, or the remnants of the old well in the backyard. I sometimes stood in the living room, surrounded by turntables, by stereo equipment, by empty plastic cups formerly filled with cheap beer, desperately trying to imagine a turn-of-the-century family in heavy suits and dresses, gathered at a fine cherry wood dining room table, enjoying a holiday feast. It wasn't easy, but Victor told me, "Augie, just look at the woodwork and its delicate shapes or the sculpted design of the banister. Look at the width of the stairway." In Victor's words, I was a believer. In his voice, deep and smooth, I could find anything, even the ability to transpose an old 19th century farmhouse into a dumping ground for intellectual misfits. Suddenly, the graffiti art on the dining room walls became wallpaper with roses; the DJ booth in the living room a wind-up phonograph.

Originally a dorm for ROTC Marines, the house was taken over a decade or so ago by a group of misfit punks with highbrow minds and lowbrow social lives. In years past, no one knows when, someone dumped a pile of broken motorcycle parts in the backyard and had the big idea to turn the house in to a makeshift nightclub. Suddenly, the rambling old shack became the site of the university's best parties. These were the parties where the white chicks had red hair spiked to the ceiling and the black chicks had dreadlocks down to their knees, where half the guys were mod and half the guys were punk, where you couldn't tell who was gay and who was straight if you were paid to do it. Cheap cups of beer were in everyone's hands, hallucinogens were on everyone's tongues, and the music played till five a.m., sometimes on three different levels.

People in our crowd clamored for years to live there, but you had to have some deep connections to be chosen. I'd been lucky: for years I'd gone to parties as a total nobody, but I finally met Ted Demetropoulos, a gay DJ who was my absolute idol and who had lived in the Hutt for three years. It was fast, and it was hurried, and it left my mind spinning, but Ted decided to move to Chicago in July and he promised his room to me. "I can get you in there," he told me one night, and he meant it.

The morning after I moved in, dreams of Victor's boxer shorts stunt still heavy in my mind, I staggered down to the second-floor hallway and passed the modern exit sign above a door that led to a fire escape, left over from the days of the Marines. The bathroom, a vast sun-filled place that was perversely free of privacy, had been converted into a communal-style shower room, complete with a bench and lockers. There, in the sweltering heat of morning, I came across my roommates one by one, naked like it was the most natural thing in the world.

I stumbled into the bathroom and found Paul Veracruz, a Mexican-American anthropology major who usually lived in overalls, standing at the mirror nude putting in his contacts. Jean-Claude Jolie, a Haitian dude in a punk rock band, stood in red crepe-paper-like shorts shaving his head. "Check it out, it's Augie Schoenberg, the man himself," Paul called out in his raucous, booming voice that ensured nobody'd sleep off a hangover with him around.

"What's up, what's up," I said, as if this scene was normal; that every day I walked into bathrooms littered with the occasional naked man.

"Augie, did Jean-Claude ever tell you about the time we went through the Burger King drive-thru completely naked?" Paul asked, looking at me in the mirror. "I was on the passenger side, also nude, with my feet up on the dash."

"It's the stuff of legends," Jean-Claude added.

My peripheral vision took in Paul's smooth, hairless ass, the legs of a Greek statue, the powerful back covered in blue and green tattoos, the stubby feet. His hair had gone wild and was spiked up punk-rock style. There was a ring in his eyebrow and one in his lower lip. He was only threatening on first glance, though, and the night before, he'd backed me into a corner, over beers, and told me, "Dude, we like faggots." It was a defining moment, for sure, that this Aztec Indiana Jones thought gay guys were fun to have around, that he was telling me, "Be yourself."

"So what'd you guys order?" I asked, hanging my towel on a peg, reeling from the realization that every morning would be a locker room peep show with the house faggot trying not to get hard.

Jean-Claude ran the razor over the last bit of shaving cream on his skull and rinsed his razor under the faucet. The back of his head stuck out in such an exaggeratedly rounded way that his head looked incredibly fragile. I wanted to reach out and cup it in my hands so that it wouldn't break. From the reflection in the mirror, I could see his bright, intelligent expression, his nose that angled down severely, making his face look long, and his eyes that curved up in almost an Asian way and made his face look wide. He walked toward the bench. "I ordered a double cheeseburger and onion rings. Paul ordered three packages of condoms."

I laughed and walked toward the showers, which were really just three nozzles sticking out of the wall with small, useless dividers on the sides. Under the water, I had a full view of Jean-Claude as he slipped down his red shorts and strode toward the stall next to me. I'd seen him in English classes and I'd seen him on stage playing bass guitar, but this was my favorite view of him. His chest had small rivets of black hair that looked pinched together in certain select spots, all the way down to his dick hair, which showcased a long, curved, brown stump of a dick that angled to the right and had a thin, fleshy foreskin. I wanted to laugh with delight when I saw it: it was hard to tell, but I thought underneath the foreskin the dickhead was bright pink.

Paul walked by, his tiny, arrow-shaped dick flapping against his nuts, and scratched what little pubic hair he had. "The problem is," he said, stopping in front of me, "there weren't any chicks working. And the guys there refused to serve us." He looked me right in the eye, as if we weren't nude, like we were having beers. I could feel my dick perking up a little and I prayed for it to go down. "We were really quite hungry," he told me. Mercifully, he moved along to the last shower stall. I turned around to face the wall.

"And from what I understand," Jean-Claude said, his face now drenched. "Paul actually was out of condoms, and was attempting to buy them in earnest."

"I was under the impression they carried those, but I guess I had been misinformed," Paul replied.

They were cracking me up, but they kept trying to make eye contact with me and I was trying not look at them below the waist. But how couldn't I? It was ecstasy and torture all at once, and I was a willing participant. I made it through that morning without popping a boner, but the next day was even riskier.

I stood in the shower thinking I had the place to myself, but no such luck. Mark Israel, a lusty, hairy Jewish guy from Evanston that I actually went to high school with but didn't know, slowly strutted in. He wore a pair of old white briefs that were so holey and sagging so badly they must've been holdovers from the teenage years, his stomach hair spilling out the top and his ball hair leaking out the sides. Big-boned with a bulging stomach, he carried himself with an overwhelmingly dad-like swagger that made him look closer to thirty than twenty-three. Even his dark hair made him look old: he'd brushed it back like a TV newscaster. Cursed with a chronic sinus infection, he stood at the bench snorting. "Augie," he said, finally, and nothing more. His face was slightly cocky, slightly pudgy, slightly confused, but with a swarthy, olive tone to it that rendered him alternatingly sexy and frightening.

Tony Valentine, an Italian-American soccer player who was the most clean-cut of the bunch, and who I longed to see naked, even more than Victor, walked in wrapped in a beach towel covered with tropical fish. He had curly brown hair cut short, a large crooked nose, lips that quivered, and beautifully shaped pectoral muscles whose hair made them look shaded rather than hairy. He twirled off his towel and hung it on a peg. His buns were so muscular they stuck almost straight out, but looked a little squishy when he walked. My dick began growing, and I turned around to face the wall. He was like one of those people in high school that everyone's jealous of because they seem to have it all: looks, popularity, buckets of masculinity, and in this case, a huge dick. I told myself that this was getting to be a dangerous experience, but there was nothing I could do.

"So, Augie," Tony said, taking the stall next to me. "We heard Victor pulled the old boxer switcheroo on you."

I could hear Mark cackling a little. I was startled they'd been told. I glanced over at Tony, because I could feel he too was trying to make eye contact with me, and met his eyes just for a split second. Still, I could see his dick: bright white, weighty, uncircumcised, and one of the largest I'd seen in some time. If I'd looked longer, I might have never looked away.

"Yeah, he did," I said, confidently, as if it was a known rite of passage. "Unfortunately, mine didn't fit him."

At the bench, Mark Israel pulled down his briefs, revealing a carpet of rampant, swirly ass hair dotted with lint and nearly hiding his dusky skin. He walked over to the last stall, and I dangerously watched him do it. I thought his dick might not be visible inside all the hair, but there it was, fat and bratwurst-like, with an abnormally prominent circumcision scar.

"Ah, Victor's a big pervert," Mark said. "But he's mainly harmless. Wouldn't trust him with my kids, though."

With three shower nozzles going, it was hard to hear, but Tony shouted, "He's getting fat, though. That's why he does the boxer shorts thing. He wants to still believe that he's the same size as everyone else, when it's totally obvious he's getting huge."

"Victor is not fat," I stated, plainly, like I was his boyfriend and was defending his honor.

"Oh, no, me neither," Mark Israel, who clearly was, called over, his chest hair white-green with soap. "He also doesn't eat like four frozen pizzas a day."

Maybe it was me, but I thought for a second I saw Tony's dickhead starting to peek out of its shell casing, so slowly it moved by millimeters, like in time-lapse photography. As for his upper half, Tony grinned away and massaged his sudsy scalp. "Could be, though, that Victor likes ya," he said, brightly. "Maybe you'll be his new little buddy."

Tony laughed to himself, and I was about to ask what he meant, when Mark yelled out, "Hey, that's it. Schoenberg is Victor's new bitch."

I had been considering asking Mark what temple he went to, or what summer camp, but while Tony and Mark laughed together, I thought that last comment didn't sound like it was all in fun. I tried to shake it off, but it stuck with me. I couldn't tell if they meant Victor made a habit of exchanging underwear with guys or if they were mocking me for being gay. Anyway, we had half a year to sort it out: Mark was leaving for a semester in Israel in January. I could picture him in the Middle East, perhaps as an Israeli soldier: tall, sun-drenched, menacing, carrying a gun.

Days passed, long, late-August days. I showered alone and enjoyed the feeling. The bathroom had three large windows that were always open, and there were no curtains. The second floor of Trailer Trash, a house full of Amazon-like women next door, had a prime view of us, but I was sure they'd already seen all there was to see at parties. I stood under the stream, feeling so out in the open I may as well have been in public.

Then—Victor Radhakrishna padded in wearing plaid boxers. Victor, a South Asian from Downers Grove, which was suburban hell, had a family that went straight from Calcutta to the Chicago suburbs, where they promptly bought a minivan and a ranch house with a swimming pool. Caught between two fucked up worlds, Victor had become an idealist, and was the leader of the campus chapter of Amnesty International, which made him, at least for me, into a practical demi-god: a crusader for justice in skateboarding shoes. I was so intent on impressing him that I was playing it cool, trying not to be obnoxious and annoyingly immature; I'd never tell anyone that late at night I was writing his name over and over in my notebooks.

Under the shower, Victor's muscles rippled from underneath his skin in such a defined, glossy way that I was sure he'd been lifting weights. I could tell he was in no way overweight. It was torture not to be able to join him in his stall, to not hear him say, "Get in here with me." He looked at me once with big, white and brown eyes, as if to say hello, but that was it. Afterwards, he sat on the bench on his towel, dripping wet with his legs spread, and I couldn't help but stare. Starry-eyed, I must've looked like an absolute fool. He caught me looking and wrapped the towel around himself. Then, he disappeared.

And then there was me, the sixth roommate, Augie Schoenberg, half French, half German, latently Jewish, and all faggot. Nude, with crappy well water cascading down my body, I must have looked like an overgrown teenager who hadn't completely finished puberty. My ass was the ass of a fourteen year old boy, round and small, the crack so hairy it looked like I shit myself. My stomach was an oval pot belly, complemented by stick arms and an overly prominent rib cage. My hair, when dry, was black and curly and beginning to fall out. When it was hard, my dick could get reasonably big, but when small looked childish and weak against my oversized balls. When I walked through the bathroom nude, I wanted to slowly strut like Paul Veracruz and think people must be admiring my ass. I wanted to strut like Tony Valentine and feel my horse dick banging against my legs. I wanted to strut like Jean-Claude Jolie and hold my regal head as I high as I possibly could. I wanted to strut like Mark Israel in old underwear and still look like a Mediterranean recruit. I wanted to strut like Victor Radhakrishna and sit on a towel on the bench with my legs wide apart and my dick drawing stupefied gazes from onlookers. But, more than anything, I wanted Victor to be my boyfriend. But that was impossible. And that was my dilemma.

Victor smiled at me in the kitchen, leaning against the refrigerator. "We have shooting contests sometimes. You should come."

I thought he was talking about guns. "Do you go to a range?"

He laughed. "Not that kind of shooting. You know, we jack off together and see who gets it the farthest. We have valuable prizes."

I was stunned. The thought of the five of them with their pants around their ankles, stroking their dicks, floored me. I couldn't wait to see if it was true.

"We do it in my bedroom," he said.

I could just picture myself joining in these insanely homoerotic antics only to find myself desperately, silently longing for more. But how could I not? I was young, I was full of homosexual lust, and I was hurting for a boyfriend. It could spell danger. I thought maybe I should fuck the whole thing and drop out of school and move to Chicago. I thought of Victor Radhakrishna's naked copper body and imagined it all over me in bed, his doe eyes staring at me as I ran my hands in and out of his jet colored hair. Fuck it, I said to myself. The lease is signed. I'm not gonna break it.

It's the big downfall of living on a campus that everyone is constantly moving, everyone is in a continual state of transition. My friend Ted wasn't there to introduce me around, and I was getting a little lost without him. I'd no idea Victor and I would get to know each other so intimately and, after that afternoon of the boxer switcheroo on the third floor, I realized things may be trickier in the Hutt than I'd anticipated. I longed for school to start, so I could take my mind off my body, and my brain, and my need for affection, which went beyond even the need for sex. I didn't think the country could make me so hot; I didn't think I'd meet people this intense, and this strange, and this sexy. I was terrified to think I'd be taunted by a year of rampant nudity and blurred sexuality and still wind up without a partner.

I thought I was about to leave my years of stiff and wooden loneliness behind me and magically become the coolest cat on campus. But I was worried: my expectations were too high.

The anxiety I felt was not out of proportion: these guys were cool as rock stars, they drank Japanese beer and smoked opium, and when they got drunk they kissed each other on the lips. Considering where we were, it meant something: the Harley Hutt was on Cherry Street, just off the abandoned train tracks, in Normal. Normal, Illinois.

2.

Nighttime came, a Thursday night, and the Harley Hutt boys and I congregated around the kitchen table for a game of Truth or Dare. It was still the week before school started, that raucous, charged, free for all of a week when dogs ran wild, when people pushed their sofas out onto the porch to drink hard liquor and watch TV, when there was nothing to do but procrastinate.

I smiled inside and looked around the table. The first time I ever went to a party at the Harley Hutt I was an 18-year-old nerd who was nervous just to walk in the place. All of a sudden, I was really a part of it, and I didn't feel the same at all. I felt like I was transforming minute by sweltering minute. It was 1995, a locust year. They rose from the ground and massed in the trees around the house, belting out a horrid crank of a noise, like a thousand incessant maracas all shaking at once. The sound mercilessly poured in the windows and seemed to add to the heat, which was enormous, especially under my polyester shirt, the flared collar, the heavy jeans. But I couldn't wear something ordinary and expected, not at that house. I wanted to be so incredibly different that to them I seemed normal. I was getting there, slowly.

The game of Truth or Dare took me one step closer.

It was close to ninety degrees that night, even after the sun had set. The heat was so humid, and so all-encompassing, and so practically cruel, that it seemed like we should have gone so far as to shut the lights out, but then I wouldn't have been able to see the five rambunctious and blazing faces before me that laughed and yelled and talked over each other so loudly that it was impossible to tell what anyone was saying. We sat in chairs, but no one was still.

Jean-Claude Jolie was out of breath. Tony Valentine, our resident soccer player, had dared him to run around the outside of the Harley Hutt naked five times. After he made the dare, Tony banged on the table laughing and everyone cried out in mock amazement. Jean-Claude said, "You guys are gonna pay for this," a reasonable voice above the calamity, but I had no confidence that he was in any way embarrassed.

We left our chairs and poured out on the porch to watch. The boards squeaked beneath our feet, and sunk so dangerously low under the weight of the six of us that it seemed a certainty the porch would collapse. There had been precedents: I knew scores of people injured at parties after dastardly porch collapsing incidents.

Jean-Claude marched down to the sidewalk, took one leg out of his pants and then the other, grinning sheepishly, so that eventually nothing was left on him but a red T shirt. The porch light shed what little light on him it could, and I could see the exercise was turning him on. His dick, as brown and long and curved as a smoked sausage, had perked up and arced a little off of his balls, the bright pink head crowning out of the foreskin.

"The shirt, too," Mark Israel yelled, and Jean-Claude turned to look at the street, as if searching for help, and yanked off the T shirt and threw it on the grass and took off running. When he rounded the house the first time, Tony Valentine held a pair of obnoxiously large binoculars to his face and watched with a smile stuck on his face that didn't reveal whether it held voyeuristic joy or sexual longing or jungle fever, or all three.

The third time he passed, scampering by so furiously it seemed he was an animated version of himself, Paul Veracruz said, "Now that is the smoothest butt I've seen."

Victor Radhakrishna agreed. "It is. He puts baby powder on it every morning."

"And lotion," Tony said, "in his bedroom. He squirts it out of the bottle directly onto his ass cheeks and it looks like a load o' sperm."

"Have you watched that through your binoculars?" I asked, but instead of responding he pointed to Paul Veracruz, who ran down to the walkway and grabbed Jean-Claude's clothes. Paul trotted back, the heap of clothes spilling out over the tattoos on his arms.

"Put them inside!" Mark called out.

Then the cops drove by. The black and white sedan rolled up so slowly we almost didn't notice it, but by the time it was in front of the house it was unmistakable with its sinister, faceless facade. You'd think someone would have yelled to Jean-Claude to go in the back door, but instead we all walked inside, Mark Israel and Tony Valentine laughing to themselves under their breath. We went back to the kitchen.

When he arrived, naked and practically red in the face, he said, "Dudes, you guys suck eggs."

Everyone burst out laughing.

"Where are my clothes? The fucking cops are out there! I ran by, my ass blowing in the wind, and you assholes are all gone from the porch."

"What happened?" I asked. He spotted his pants and T shirt under the table and put them on.

"Dude, they took one look at me and I ran in here so fast I fell on the porch twice. I looked out the front door and they were driving away, laughing."

"Well at least you weren't arrested," I said.

"That was not funny," he said. "All right, Veracruz, truth or dare, and be very careful, cause I am gonna get you back."

Paul Veracruz assumed a valiant, show-stopping look of triumph and said, "Dare." The ring in his lip didn't tremble once.

"Go on the porch," Jean-Claude said, carefully, savoring each word, "and moon the first group of frat boys you see."

"No problem!" Paul said and jumped up and ran to the porch. We followed but stayed behind the screen door. After a quick moon to random unsuspecting frat boys, we went back in.

I wanted to play so badly, but I hadn't had a turn yet. I wanted to ask Victor Radhakrishna as probing a question as possible. I wanted to dare him to do something wild, and tactile, and dirty with me. I thought these guys would go for anything. After all, they were playing Truth or Dare and they didn't even invite any women.

Paul Veracruz looked around the table with a look of incredible mischief on his face. Tony Valentine was passing out fresh beers. Victor smoked a cigarette with his chin slightly raised.

"All right, Victor," Paul said, rubbing his hands together. "You know the drill."

"Dare," Victor said, with little emotion.

"I can't wait for this," Mark said.

"Get up and french kiss the man you'd go for if you were gay."

The words hit the room like a slap of thunder. No one called out an objection, or complained, or laughed, or cracked open a beer. After an instant of silence, Paul clapped his hands together and cried, "Ha! You have to do it!"

Victor stared straight ahead, apparently at the refrigerator, his brown doe eyes not blinking or twitching.

"You gotta do it!" Paul yelled.

Mark Israel scrunched up his face, as if a bad smell had permeated the room. Tony looked down at the table, shifting in his chair. Paul cackled. Jean-Claude looked pleasantly amused, but nonetheless wouldn't make eye contact with anyone.

I loved it. With the magic stroke of fourteen words, everyone at the table had been turned into gay sex objects. I smiled at Veracruz and drank half the can of beer in one sip. I prayed to the heavens that Victor would pick me. I didn't care if it showed. I rocked back and forth in my chair.

Still not looking at anyone, Victor rose from the table and shuffled slowly around the back of it in his skateboarding shoes and baggy black shorts and Bad Religion T shirt.

"It's like duck, duck, goose," Jean-Claude said.

"Yeah, but gay!" Paul Veracruz responded.

I looked up at Victor and saw him standing at the head of the table, staring at Mark Israel. Paul said, facetiously, "God, I just don't think Victor likes me in *that* way."

"He doesn't *like* like you," I said.

Noticing Victor's gaze, Mark moved his arms in front of him and said, "No...."

And before I had the chance to even look at Mark Israel and see what might happen, an enormous weight was on my thighs and Victor Radhakrishna's face was in mine, and the smell of him, like graham crackers and beer, was in my nose, and I moved my hands automatically around his waist and held him in place. He had his eyes open, so glassy and full of depth that I got lost in their virtual kaleidoscope of browns. He opened his mouth and planted it on mine, but I didn't notice at all what it felt like. His lips overshot my mouth so widely that they ended up along the stubble on my face. The only thought in my head was, "He's straight." He was trying to overtake me. He assumed my mouth would be smaller than his.

Victor attempted to move his lips around and even stuck his tongue in me for a second or two but his mouth was so close to my nostrils that I couldn't breathe and I almost choked from lack of air. The inside of his lips grated against the stubble on my face but he wouldn't readjust himself. He had no idea what it would feel like. He was accepting mistakes as if they were expected consequences.

There were cheers in the background and cries of, "Oh my god," and there was an unresolved pang of nervous desire inside my crotch that begged for me to do more. Boldly, I pulled away from him and grabbed his cheeks with both hands.

"You're kissing my face. Not my mouth," I said.

"I thought that was wrong. It was so stubbly," Victor said.

"Victor can't kiss!" Paul exclaimed.

Apparently wanting to get it right, Victor didn't resist, and I laid my mouth gently on his and moved my lips around till they matched the two of his and then we really did it. Our tongues slid together like they were old friends and the most perfect amount of saliva leaked out in between our lips so that the entire movement was completely effortless. My dick grew fast and I leaned into his torso with my arms around his shoulders, forgetting about everyone else in the room.

"God dang!" Paul said.

"Enough already!" Mark said. "Get a room."

Slowly, we stopped. My dick was jutting into Victor's leg underneath the surprising weight of him, but it didn't hurt at all. Waves of ecstasy ran through me. I longed for Victor at that table more than I'd longed for anyone. I wanted him then, I didn't care if it was on the table in front of people, or outside on the lawn in front of the cops. It was the heat, it was the alcohol, it was the smell of five guys in the room, it was the thought of Victor naked with his boxer shorts just barely hanging onto my ass and penis, hanging on by a thread.

He returned to his seat and I knew I was in for it. I had a grin on my face that was not for other people's benefit. It was involuntary, and it bespoke all the dirty things going on in my head. He chose me. I didn't think I'd ever forget that, even if I wanted to, which I didn't.

"Augie, you are glowing," Paul said, matter of factly. "You look like you are gonna jump somebody's bones."

"Dude, the look of satisfaction on your face is insane," Jean-Claude said.

"Augie," Victor said, lighting a cigarette. "Truth or dare."

"Truth," I said, immediately. I didn't need a dare anymore.

He exhaled a line of smoke and pushed one side of black hair behind his ear. "Since you are the gay one in the room, who would you have picked?"

There were happy looks and curious stares all around me. They really wanted to know.

"He's blushing," Paul said. "Look at that."

"It's sunburn!" I said, and then my face got hot and I knew I really was blushing.

"Tell us," Victor said.

"That silence is speaking volumes," Jean-Claude said.

"OK, OK. You're all attractive, intelligent, fine-looking young men, but after that kiss it'd be a crime if I didn't pick Victor."

"Oooh, he grades on improvement," Jean-Claude said.

"Or maybe Victor has hidden talents..." Paul replied.

Underneath the conversation there was a whisper of a noise, just barely audible. Tony and Mark had moved on with the game and there was again the comfortable din of male voices. I glanced over at Victor, two chairs to my right and one chair up, and he had his eyes locked on me, his head cocked as if to say something. I studied his face and I saw him mouth something. I shook my head. He looked at me intently and raised his voice just a little; no one was paying attention to us. "Seriously?" he asked.

I smiled and raised an eyebrow. I looked away. "Augie," he said. A whisper, but a forced one. I turned my head back. "Seriously?"

He looked at me with such curiosity that I couldn't resist telling the truth. I had no idea what his motivation was: ego trip, lust, confusion, but I was so fucking horny and so horribly amazed with him that I didn't care. "Yeah," I said out loud. "You."

3.

Campustown had a new Korean restaurant. There was something oddly comforting about its arrival: though it wasn't fancy, and it wasn't particularly accessible to non-Korean speakers, and there were no windows, the restaurant's presence gave off the faintest hint of sophistication. We weren't totally cut off from civilization. Kim chee was available among the cornfields.

I carried my take-out bag of beef bulgogi down the main drag of campus in my down-to-the-knees cutoff jeans and a Queer Nation T shirt. The shirt was a ballsy move: I wouldn't admit to anyone that wearing it made me paranoid to the point of near-exhaustion. I was secretly convinced that some crazed fundamentalist was sure to drive by in a VW van and gun me down. Reasonably, though, I knew most crazed fundamentalists had no idea what gay rights protest groups were accurately named, and I was almost sure the Koreans didn't either.

The students that jammed the sidewalks that afternoon had me concerned. They were out stocking up for the new school year in droves, and had caused a run on the stores that left me wondering how they all could afford to buy so much stuff. The bong store had a line out the front that went down the block. I'd have thought the line would be made up of Harley Hutt-type freaks and slackers and burnouts, but apparently our crowd had enough inventory. Everyone in line was obnoxiously preppy and clean-cut, their polo shirts tucked into their khaki shorts. I passed by the entrance, the stench of incense billowing out as strong as bus exhaust, and saw a muscled, sunglass-wearing junior yuppie stroll out with an oversized paper bag, ready with his car keys in hand for a year of dorm room pot parties.

I passed the used record store, the used bookstore, and the secondhand clothing store, where mannequins sported the latest fashions from the seventies. I supposed you could conceivably live on campus and never buy anything new at all, except for perhaps food and occasional drug paraphernalia.

Through the August heat, warmth rose from the bag to my hand. The trees waned under the sun and the leaves rustled, starting to dry out. The air was empty of birds, as though they'd been exterminated by the heat. Couples strolled out of the ice cream store, licking melting globs of brown on cones.

I raced home. There was a gnawing hunger in me so pervasive that I couldn't tell if it was really hunger or an odd form of irritation. I'd been drunk every night, horny every morning, awe-struck every day, and I needed this food so badly that my insides were punishing me. I ached to spend the rest of the day, and hopefully the night, with Victor, but I'd need energy. Just the thought of him, and that forced, watched kiss was draining resources from me. I needed more.

The third floor hallway was a wind tunnel. Multiple fans on the floor and in my and Victor's bedrooms ran at highest capacity, making the hallway not cooler but hot and windy.

Victor and Mark Israel sat on Victor's bed drinking beer from cans. At the sight of me, Mark crushed the can in his hand, burped and stood up. "I'm outta here," he said to Victor. "What's her face awaits." He walked past me, looking at me out of the corner of his eye.

"Have fun with what's her face," Victor said.

I walked into the room, the plastic bag rustling next to my leg. The room was big and wide, shaped like a pentagon, and Victor had decorated it with all sorts of swirling tapestries and weird lamps, so that it looked like I was in the middle of a Marrakech drug den instead of in the middle of central Illinois. On shelves, there were tiny little Indian statues of deities I couldn't name, and on the floor some psychedelic paintings rested against the furniture. Bad Religion played on the stereo—a warm, high energy song, the lyrics reassuringly deeper and slower than the race of the guitars. Victor wore, like me, baggy cutoff jeans, and an Amnesty International T shirt. A candle with a burning flame was in the middle of his chest.

"Well, look at Mr. Queer Nation," he called out. Maybe it was those heavy eyes, but his face was overwhelmingly serene and wise-looking. The hair, though, wild and rebellious, spilling off his head onto his shoulders, really made the deal for me. "You're lucky you didn't get your ass kicked on this campus."

I giggled and sat on the floor. "Look at Mr. Amnesty International. All you have to worry about are the victim's rights groups."

He scoffed at me, but a flicker of amusement passed over his face. "Dude," he said, proudly. "I have taken on the president of Burma."

I pulled the styrofoam tray and a pair of wooden chopsticks from the bag. "That's good....But you know what that means? You can never again vacation in Burma."

He laughed a little, and a grin stayed on his face. "I like you, Schoenberg. Wanna beer?"

My stomach quivered and my resting knees went weak. I was getting too into him. A stupid offer of a beer felt like a proposal of marriage. "I would love one." I flipped open the container and found a massy collection of diamond-shaped beef chunks. I rolled them around with a chopstick, their luster and shade the same color as Victor's skin.

He pulled back a tapestry, took a beer from a mini fridge, and sat it down on the floor in front of me. I cracked it open and watched as he pulled his hair back and swiftly banded it into a ponytail. The simple act opened up his face. Once his jawbone was revealed, his face had a strength to it, a means of support. His eyes, the sad, quixotic doe eyes, pointed straight at me.

"Whaddaya got there?"

"Beef bulgogi," I said, almost giggling again. I snatched up a few small pieces of beef and a clump of pasty rice with one sharp clench of the sticks.

He kneeled down before me and inhaled. He looked up at me while I chewed. "Can I have some?"

I nodded furiously. I considered searching the bag for a second pair of chopsticks but had a better idea. Trying not to let my fingers shake, I grabbed a small pile of beef with the chopsticks and held it up to his lips. He didn't hesitate at all, but opened his mouth as if waiting for a thermometer to be inserted, and then I slid the beef in and waited while his lips slowly closed around it. Carefully, I eased out the chopsticks, his lips running over them, and I felt, at least via two wooden conductors, the delicateness of him, the fragility.

"It's wonderful. Since when do we have Korean food in this cow town?"

"Since last week, I think." I picked up more beef and fed myself, moving my lips around the sticks as if there'd be a taste to them, or something more than an invisible salivary connection to Victor.

A song ended and immediately a new one started. The music blared and ran as fast as an engine, but the low vocals put me at ease. Victor sat back and stretched out his legs. He hadn't taken his eyes off of me.

I looked around the room. The few open spaces on the walls were covered less with rock posters than with political fliers: stark advertisements for protests, boycotts, the obligatory portrait of Che Guevara. "So what do you call yourself?" I asked. "Are you post-punk? A leftist crusader? A Gen X'er gone wrong?"

I scooped up the biggest piece of beef in the pile and fed it to him. He accepted it eagerly. "Augie," he said, chewing the beef as if it had inspired him. "I am a post-punk, leftist crusader that has gone right!"

I guzzled some beer. "Here, here."

He grinned and looked sideways toward the window. "So what are you? Don't tell me. Let me guess: You are a radical, gender-smashing, commie hipster with overwhelming queer tendencies."

I pulled the chopsticks from my mouth. They were getting warm. "I don't think I'm a commie. But if Congress ever asked me, I'd say yes."

"I like that. Good answer. So what are you doing with these queer tendencies of yours? Do you have some stud of a gay rights crusader waiting for you in Chicago?"

I grabbed more beef and held the chopsticks up in the air. He leaned in slowly, and I fed him with so much precision that I instantly found the center of his tongue. "Ha! I wish. No, I'm one of those single for life types. Nobody likes me."

I eased the chopsticks from his lips. "Nobody likes me, either. I've been single for two years."

"Three and a half."

I drank more of the beer, which was cold but cheap and metallic. I wanted a buzz so badly at that moment—to push me up to the point where I could cross another line and dive further into an already ambiguous intimacy and make it less outrageous and more grounded, as if I'd accomplished something.

"I'm surprised," he said, thoughtfully. "You're a good-lookin' guy. And I've seen all of you. You should have a boyfriend."

"I think you should, too. I mean, I think you should have a girlfriend. Of course, I've seen what you have to offer, also."

He blinked. "I guess I'm always in the wrong place at the right time."

The beef was dissipating. I scraped up the last few remnants. "Maybe this year you won't be. A lot of things can change pretty quickly."

He cocked his head to the side. "Well, I've got a pretty good prospect."

Maybe it was dumb, but I wanted the chopstick feeding incident to be one of life's high moments. If Victor didn't provide it, maybe the beer would. "Anybody I know?"

He got up and threw his beer can in the garbage. "Nah."

"Isn't it funny, though? Some people are in relationships constantly from the age of fourteen and some of us have only had tiny little moments where we could even think of using the word love. I don't get it, really. I don't think there's anything wrong with me."

Victor settled on the floor holding two new cans of beer. "Well, it may be, Augie Schoenberg, that you're too smart. You're concerned more with inward travels than the traveling of your penis."

He smiled and widened his eyes, knowing he'd just offered a complimentary insight that left me almost drooling. "I've traveled a little. Well, at least my penis has traveled a little. Not that it's little, really, I mean that it's traveled a little..."

Victor laughed silently. "It's not little," he said, and he was right, because after he said that my dick swelled up till it was pulsing against my thigh.

"Someone said once that sex is the realm of the stupid. Do you think that's true?"

He snapped open the beers. "Who said that?"

I shrugged. "I don't know. I think I heard it in a movie."

"Sex can be stupid, but not if you're with the right person. Then it can be almost, what's the word? Exalting. No, transcendent."

I wanted to say so badly that I knew sex with him would be terribly transcendent, but instead I gazed at him like a sucker, my eyes big and stupid, and drank from the cheap can of beer like it was nectar from the gods.

"Transcendent in a base way. Isn't orgasm the most base, ignorant thing we experience?"

"No way, Augie. Transcendent in the way that you're instantly at peace with everything that's ever happened to you. Have you ever felt that? It's like cauterization. It seals everything up."

"I think so," I said, nodding. "A couple times."

"With the right person, it could happen every night."

No one knows how much I wanted to take that comment as the biggest flirtation ever uttered, but I was scared of letting myself go, of letting myself feel what I wanted to feel, because I feared in the end I'd be let down.

I didn't answer him, but looked out the window at the heavy old trees swaying in the sweltering air. Evening was coming, and I wanted nothing more than to stay where I was, and let night come, and hope for something to happen. As it was, Victor rocked back and forth a tiny bit on the floor, looking like a question was just busting to get out of him.

"So the thing is," he said, looking at me slyly. "What about these gay guys. Do they like...." He stopped, looking practically embarrassed.

"Do they what?"

"Don't get offended but....like how many of them, you know....like how may of them give blow jobs?"

I laughed out loud so hard that Victor looked confused. It seemed to me that straight guys were almost obsessed with this topic: how much women don't want to do it, how much they think gay guys will, how much they think they're missing out on. "Well, all of them!"

Victor gaped at me with open lips. "Like every single time? Or like, every night?"

"Well, yeah. If I had a boyfriend he'd probably do it every night."

"That's different than chicks, though. They hate doing it."

"Oh, even I know girls that like it." I knew I'd better change the subject. He was hardly asking me to suck his dick, which I gladly would've, and I didn't want him to start thinking sex was all just a breeze to me. I'd barely ever had it. "So, what are you doing with yourself tonight? Any big plans?"

"I'm gonna drink a case of beer with you," Victor said, confidently. "It might take all night. Is that OK?" The thought of an all-nighter with Victor, and the sight of the dark tapestries all around me, and the prospect of getting even deeper inside the thoughts in his head left me so stupefied I could barely spit out the word 'yeah.'

4.

Isabella told me about the rugby party. We sat on the front porch of Trailer Trash, with the Harley Hutt resting uneasily off to the side. From the warped look of the flaking wood, the Hutt looked like it was near collapse. It was just as well: the trees on Cherry Street must have all been a hundred years old, and the branches hung down so low that you had to push aside armfuls of vegetation just to walk down the sidewalk. I rattled the ice cubes in my vodka-lemonade. It was two in the afternoon and Isabella had prepared drinks.

"I know you've heard of it," she said, her throaty voice a witness to how many cigarettes and joints she'd smoked in college. Her straight brown hair fell past her shoulders and the sun had pinkened her alabaster face. "They have a whole house, just for the team. Anyway, I've been to these parties before and it's incredible."

I sipped some of my yellow liquid, but in the afternoon heat it was making me feel more dehydrated than drunk. I'd heard Isabella and friends still partying in their backyard when I went to bed. She must've immediately started drinking when she woke up. It was no surprise: I'd met her years before at a party and she'd been wasted then. Isabella was the one who was responsible for introducing me to Ted, who in turn gave me his room at the Harley Hutt. I'd been standing alone at a party at the Harley Hutt two years before, still a nerd with acne and braces, gazing at Ted while he spun records, lamenting the fact that a gorgeous, bronzed, DJ in black jeans and a white T shirt would never go for the likes of me. Isabella walked up to me, tall with big legs in a pink minidress, and said, "I know. Everybody wants him."

I'd responded with, "That's the man of my dreams," in a drunken slur that probably sounded as stupid as you'd think it would.

I'd no idea who was who: the crowd was different back then; there was no Victor, or Paul, or any of them. When I found out Ted and Isabella were close friends, I was hoping she'd let the comment slide, but instead she brought me over to the Hutt the next week and introduced us. It became instantly clear that she'd told him what I said about him, and though I was mortified, Ted found it all endearing and took me under his wing as though he were my mentor.

So Isabella and Ted were my entrance into this Harley Hutt world, when I jumped from the geeky side to the cool side of campus, and I treated them with a certain kind of reverence. For almost two years, we went out almost every night, but Isabella was always the connection; without her, I wouldn't have ever known about most of these parties, let alone be let into them. I felt like I needed to be grateful to her, but I was getting worried. Now that Ted was gone, she'd lost her own connection, and was hanging out in a crowd full of meatheads that she was apparently using for sex. She also seemed kind of annoyed when I was around.

Nevertheless—on the porch over vodka lemonades—she was robust and animated, and waved one hand around while she talked.

"So what do they do at this rugby party?" I asked. "Are there initiation rituals?"

"Oh, my god, Augie, initiation rituals. Like you have never seen! The entire team is completely naked. For the entire party. Like they walk around mingling with nothing on but sandals and those little necklaces all the jocks wear. Tell me you wouldn't love it."

"I'd love it, all right. Are you sure we can get in?" I had no confidence that any sports team would voluntarily be naked while I was around.

"Hell, yeah. I've got connections." She smiled a little, but I had a bad feeling about her contact. Isabella had recently begun to stray from our group, and was spending time with people I knew wouldn't accept us. Or at least wouldn't accept me.

"Such as..."

"Just a little someone I met last weekend. OK, he's a frat boy, but he's alright. And he has a really nice ass. You know, they all do. Maybe it's in the burritos they're always eating, but god those buns..."

"You can date anybody you want, but I'm used to getting the feminist line from you."

She looked out at the street, as if somehow pained by the mere mention of the word 'feminist.' "I don't go to as many of those Feminist Alliance meetings. The group isn't really the same. Anyway, go to the rugby party, Augie." She shook my shoulder. "It'll be a blast and a half."

I watched her face, but she was hard to read. I had a feeling she was perhaps trying to singlehandedly change the whole frat boy culture by treating the guys like sex objects and fucking them at random, but that was probably more my optimism than it was her intent.

"I'll try to bring one of the Harley Hutt boys," I said, rising to go. "Thanks for the lemonade, sister, it was a real country treat."

"Bring that Tony Valentine," she said and winked at me. "I'd like to peel his banana."

"Oh, no kidding. Maybe Victor will come." Isabella smiled and formed her lips into a smooch. "We will see." I wandered across the grass, pushing aside the tendrils of a weeping willow, and went back home.

"Augie Schoenberg, you're coming to a party with me."

"Who's that?" I asked. I stood in my bedroom with a fan blowing in my face. Tony Valentine appeared in the doorway: brown curly hair, Roman nose, dressed like a soccer player. He looked shiny and new, and ready to go out. In another house, or in another life, he could've been a frat boy. I took it on faith he wasn't.

"It's me. The party's at the rugby house, for the initiation."

Apparently Isabella had gotten to him before I could. "Where's everyone else?"

"They're all out together applying for the same exact job as a bartender at the same exact time. Can you believe those idiots? We're gonna meet Isabella there. It's just you and me, babe."

My stomach burned with excitement. I was nervous enough to go to this thing, but with Tony Valentine, I thought I could get away with it.

Tony and I strode down Cherry Street talking incessantly. Literally every house on the block was having a party and the mood carried over to us. It was a jungle outside that night: the air was humid and thick and we had to fight our way through not only the crowds of drunk people but the branches that stuck out sideways from the bushes. In the distance, there were flashes of lightning and the sound of thunder. Bugs ate our legs.

"Dude," he said. "This is always my favorite party of the year."

"Yeah?"

"Oh, yeah, it's fantastic. Like half my friends are on the rugby team and these guys are nuts. You're not gonna believe what happens."

"What happens?" I was desperate to know the details. I was so excited I'd been chain-smoking the entire way.

"Dude. It's absolute insanity. These poor saps have to strip completely nude and do these totally disgusting things to each other. There's all this hazing stuff and weird rituals and later the chicks start flashing their tits." He put his arm around me. "Dude, you are not gonna believe some of these chicks. They are so fuckin' hot. I don't think I'd know what to do with girls like these. And then if you're lucky and you play your cards right, you may be able to spend the evening with one of them. There was this one chick last year, and her tits were *so* fuckin..." He took his arm off my shoulder. "Oh, wait, I'm sorry. That offends you, right?"

I didn't know if he meant telling me about some girl's tits offended me or if assuming that I wanted to hear about it offended me. "What?"

"No, I'm sorry, I shouldn't have said anything."

"I'm not offended," I said. "Tell me about all the chicks you want."

"No, I shouldn't have brought it up. I mean, if you told me about some guy's dick I totally wouldn't want to hear about it."

Half the excitement I'd been feeling dropped out from under me. I'd always told my straight friends about my sexual exploits, rare as they were, and they always seemed interested.

"It honestly doesn't bother me," I said.

"No," he said. "Just drop it."

We walked a torturous moment in silence and then mercifully came to the rugby house. There was a mad conglomeration of people crammed onto the porch trying to get in.

"Luckily," Tony said, resuming his confidence with me, "you're with me, so we can get right in." He smiled. I smiled back but I felt like I'd been chastised for no reason. I began to wish the other roommates were with us, especially since I wanted to see how Victor would react to the nudity. We plowed through the crowd and walked through the door.

The party was in full swing. One of Tony's friends led us to the back of the living room, where there was a large bar. We sat down and I looked around the room. Scores of people were furiously drinking and talking to each other so loudly there was a deafening roar. I didn't recognize anyone, and for a second I got nervous, thinking everyone there could tell I was gay and they were all gonna kick my ass. I knew that was unlikely and anyway everyone else was there to see dick and ass, too, so what could anyone say?

Two giant steins of beer were slapped down on the bar and Tony and I started gulping them down. I was exhilarated: there was a palpable excitement in that room. It rose from the noise, and the flushed faces, and the glow of beers through clear plastic cups. Everyone was looking over their shoulders, apparently wondering when the action was gonna start. The air was full of testosterone and smoke, of body odor and heat.

"Sorry about before," Tony shouted. "I forgot you were gay for a minute."

"That's OK!" I yelled back.

He leaned in close. "To tell you the truth, I always come to these parties for the chicks. But that's not the only reason." He leaned back and took a dramatic drag off of a cigarette. He blew out the smoke and then leaned in again. He put his lips almost directly around my ear and said, "I'm not one hundred percent straight, you know."

Shock hit me and I tried not to let it show. Did he mean he was ninety-eight percent straight? Sixty percent? For a jaw-dropping proclamation like that, it was fairly vague. I was about to ask for specifics when someone banged a gong, and then someone else started ringing a cowbell. I looked critically at Tony and thought that few, if any, people have ever been saved by the bell in such a huge way. Oblivious to my stare, Tony turned to the bar and ordered shots.

The crowd began to shout and applaud. The lights dimmed. Tony handed me my shot. "To the Hutt!" he said and we drank. Heat poured into me and expanded throughout my entire chest. "Tequila!" Tony shouted and I nodded. I looked at him in his black soccer shorts and his World Cup T shirt and shamelessly pictured myself pulling them off. He shouldn't have said anything to me; my sex drive was about to take off so badly that I thought he might be in danger of finding me to be an unwanted suitor. Or, perhaps, a wanted one.

"Ladies and gentleman!" An overgrown man in a rugby uniform took the floor. The crowd parted around him in a circle. "Tonight is a very special night. Tonight we shall indoctrinate a group of individuals, a group of young men of a very special breed, into an organization we call the University Rugby Team."

"Get on with the show!" a girl across the room called out.

The man replied, "This is the show, sweetheart, so shut the hell up!" The crowd roared.

"Show us your dick!" the girl cried back and everyone laughed. Someone banged the gong again and people cheered and stomped the floor. At last, the overgrown guy yelled out, "The 1995 University Rugby Team!" The crowd went bananas. The lights went totally out and a second later I could see the silhouette of a line of guys descending a staircase and lining up right in front of Tony and me. They were all in maroon-colored rugby outfits. "Those guys are wearing clothes!" I said.

The lights came up and people whooped and hollered and flashbulbs went off. There were about twelve guys of all different sizes: some were fat and balding, others were short and stocky, but a few were tall and virile. I smiled with perverse excitement.

One by one they started taking off their shirts. The crowd went, "Ooooh." Next they took off their pants and to an ear-splitting roar from the crowd stood before us in nothing but white jockstraps and rugby shoes and socks. Their backs were to us, and when I caught my first glimpse of a dozen pairs of rugby men's meaty behinds, my legs went limp and I thought I might fall off the stool. The men turned to show their butts to the rest of the crowd and then to great applause bent over, pulled down their jockstraps in unison, as if this had been choreographed, stood up, stepped out of the jocks and proudly hung them on the tops of their heads.

"Hey, look, that dude with the red pubic hair isn't circumcised," Tony said. I looked down and saw a sideways bulge in Tony's pants. His dick was getting hard.

There was a hush over the room as people tried to figure out what the team would do next. No one dared breathe. Then, in an amazing feat, the naked guys formed a circle and each one put an arm through his legs, and then that arm was grabbed by the guy behind him, so that they made an awkward human chain. They began to slowly ramble around the room like a bulbous, naked line of elephants while people screamed with laughter and poured beer over them.

The chain went around the room a few times and then the entire group collapsed to the floor at once. Tony handed me another shot and I drank it down so fast I almost puked. The bartender tapped me on the shoulder and told us we had to move. We got up and stood against the wall. Then, a mean-looking blond guy slowly walked to the bar, shooting us a perfunctory scowl, and climbed on top of it. The guy with the red pubic hair followed, looking as if he were being marched to his death. He knelt on the floor and the blond guy bent over. Then, a sexy, Hispanic dude wearing a sleeveless T shirt and no pants and sporting more pubic hair than I have ever seen on a person, walked to the bar with a can of beer. He opened it up and poured it down the ass crack of the blond guy and then the red pubic hair guy had to put his opened mouth underneath the stream and lap up the beer that had just traveled over the blond guy's fuzzy anus. The rugby team surrounded the action, chanting something in unison and shaking their fists. Half the crowd screamed in disgust and half shouted in what I thought was joy.

"This is intense," I said to Tony. Another guy stood on the bar. "I'm going to find the bathroom." Tony nodded. He was watching the action so intently he did not look like he wanted to be interrupted.

I wandered through a long hallway that was packed with people and found the bathroom at the end of it. The door was open and two of the players stood inside peeing together. One looked thirtyish, and had a rough, powerful body and a hairy ass with a tuft of hair in his lower back. His dick was long and darker than the rest of his skin, and his calf muscles bulged out of his socks as if they were grapefruits. The second guy was short and muscular and so tan his ass and dick were uncommonly white. His dick was short and fat, and almost the width of a beer can. I couldn't help but stand there and stare.

A woman came up next to me and shouted, "You two are fags!" The guys laughed and told her to shut up. "Bitch," one of them said. I was the only person waiting, so I turned against the wall outside the bathroom with my hands in my pockets, feeling uncomfortable. The guys finished peeing and slowly walked out. They both had cocky, swaggering gaits, and looked around with razor-sharp glares, apparently to make sure no one was staring at them. The tall one looked right at me and said, "Can you believe this shit?" To my horror, I realized he was looking to me for sympathy. With his heaving pectorals and meathook arms, he was at least twice as wide as me, and about a foot taller. I stood meekly below him, after witnessing the ultimate experience in male objectification and humiliation, and thought I may not be able to speak. What could I say without sounding like a complete faggot?

"Yeah," I said. "Be careful out there, it's getting ugly."

The other guy laughed and said to the big guy, "He's a fag."

Dismayed, I retreated to the bathroom and shut the door. There was no lock, so I shoved the door closed as tightly as I could and undid my pants. I wanted to take my dick out and give it a few good pulls till I spooged all over, but that would've been risky, so I tried to think of unsexy things till my dick softened a little and I could pee. People say to think about baseball to get rid of a boner, but baseball turns me on more than any sport, so I had to think about a teacher in high school I particularly hated, and finally the urine came.

Back outside, Tony was talking to the blond guy, who I still thought looked like trouble, so I stood next to them and surveyed the room. There was another pair at the bar doing the asshole-beer thing, but I saw a sight in front of me that was considerably more interesting. The guy with the T shirt and no pants who'd been pouring the beer had apparently been relieved of his duties and was standing in front of me. He was exactly my type. He had a round, energetic face and a buzzcut and a uniformly tanned body. There was a cagey, whimsical sexiness about him, maybe from his affable expression, or his average size, or his little belly. His stomach stuck out just far enough that it made his crotch look like it was pushed slightly back at an angle and ready to fuck. Beneath his T shirt I could see small dark nipples. His dick was compact and looked slightly leathery but there was so much hair around it that it made his whole body look so awfully sexual that I felt the tiniest bit of come start to leak out of the head of my penis.

He stood in the center of the room with a can of cheap beer in his hand, looking like he'd lost his friends. I considered going up to talk to him, but I couldn't think of what I would say. I was starting to get used to chatting with naked men at the Harley Hutt, but I wasn't sure if he'd be so at ease. Somebody called out, "Jose!" and he walked over to them. I knew I'd remember that name.

I thought I should think about leaving before I did something I regretted. I looked across the room and saw Isabella, surrounded by a group of staring guys. I couldn't tell what was going on, and I walked over unsteadily to investigate. I had become quite drunk.

I pushed a few people aside and saw Isabella turning around and screaming and lifting up her shirt. People cheered and one guy took pictures. Her dark brown hair flew around her and hit people behind her in the face. She was obviously drunk, her face bright red. Her husky, raucous voice called out, "Come and get it boys! If you dare!" Some guy said, "I dare!"

I walked through the calamity and grabbed her by the arm. "Isabella, what the hell are you doing?"

"Augie!" she cried and threw her arms around me. "I'm flashing my tits!"

"I see that. What for?"

She came up close to my face and said, "For fun. I haven't done this since Mardi Gras. Isn't it wonderful? Those guys turned me on so badly, I'm hot as a fuckin' rod right now. I need a guy, like soon, cause I wanna fuck somebody."

"I know what you mean, I'm like creamin' my pants."

"Augie, look at these fuckin' guys. Every stupid tradition they have is homosexual. They're all gonna be suckin each other's dicks tonight. Go get one of 'em!"

"I don't know, I don't think so."

"Don't limit yourself," she said. "You can find somebody here."

"Yeah, if I don't get my ass kicked first."

"Oh, nobody would do that." She patted me on the head. "That roommate of yours is amazing. I love soccer players. Is he single?" I shrugged. She looked around the room and then strode off in Tony's direction. I honestly wondered if Isabella thought I could find a man at a party like this or if she was just trying to make me feel better. The raw testosterone in the room was intimidating enough, but the homophobia had about quashed my sex drive, and I was mostly concerned about finishing my conversation with the allegedly bisexual Tony Valentine.

I looked toward Tony and Isabella, chatting next to the far wall. I began to walk over, but Tony waved me away when he saw me. Slightly hurt, I went to get another beer. The two naked guys from the bathroom had become the bartenders. They stood there looking cocky and mean, serving drinks at an insolently slow pace. I contemplated going up there and ordering a beer, but after just getting called a fag by one of them, the idea turned me off. I stood against the wall feeling dumb for a minute, but realized I should probably leave. I thought I could hang out with Victor when I got home.

Outside, the air hadn't cooled off at all. It had never rained, and the moon shone full. Stars sparkled across the night sky, and I knew I'd better appreciate them while I could. After graduation, in Chicago, I knew I'd never see them. I turned to cross the street, but heard some strange noises behind me. I looked back at the rugby house and saw four naked men standing on the porch. They were all holding something white: on further inspection I saw that it was toilet paper.

There was some hesitation and some unintelligible shouting, but eventually they all bent over, with their rear ends toward me, and carefully stuck the ends of the toilet paper up their assholes. They slowly rolled the paper down and then dropped the rolls to some people on the lawn. With the light from the streetlights, the long strips of paper shone brightly against the dark house, and did not break, as I thought they might. There was no wind. The guys on the ground held the toilet paper rolls with both hands, like they were flying kites. Then, one by one, the kite fliers lit the toilet paper rolls and flames shot up the white strips as fast as arrows. As the streaking fires neared the standing players' behinds, three of them jumped up and yelped and danced on their toes while a fourth remained still. The flames carried all the way up to his ass cheeks, but he remained immobile, his hands on his hips. When the flames were out and the toilet paper had disappeared, the one who hadn't jumped turned around, dusted the ashes off of himself, and threw his hands into the air in victory.

5.

Back at the Hutt, the heat was still in the house, and the lights on the stairway added to its insult. I could hear activity up there, on the third floor, in Victor's bedroom. Drunk, I was absolutely possessed with the need to join in with whatever was going on, to be accepted after that perverse environment at the party. I couldn't bear the length of each step, each breath, the crank of the cicadas coming from the outside bushes.

I bounded up the last set of stairs. I turned the corner on the third floor hallway and there they were in Victor's bedroom, my roommates, except for Tony, with their pants around their ankles and a porno on the TV. I didn't even see their faces at first, I only saw four pairs of legs, four pairs of underwear on top of scrunched down pants, four boners, four hands rubbing them.

Terrible fuzzy music sounded off from the television, where six nude women with wobbling double-sided dildos congregated in a doctor's office and were doing their best to simultaneously fuck each other and themselves. It was a sight I never thought I'd live to see. The shooting contest. The boys briefly looked at me. None seemed the least bit embarrassed, but I thought I saw Mark Israel turn slightly to the side, as if to hide his erection with his mammoth thigh. The faintest look of contempt was on his face.

"Get in here, Schoenberg," Paul called out. "And drop those drawers."

The sound of that got my dick hard, but what kept it hard was the sight of Victor's reddish-brown boner, the sheen so vibrant the shaft could have been cut from velvet. I sat down right next to him; his face was pained, his breath fast and shallow.

"What are you guys watching?" I pulled down my jeans, casually, as if this was a completely ordinary opportunity to undress.

"*Visit to the Doctor's*," Mark said, lazily moving his thumb over his dickhead. I shuddered to think of that penis inside me, it was fat as a bratwurst and twice as long, reaching just below the hair under his navel.

I couldn't look at the screen, the women were moaning in such a false, labored way that the whole affair struck me as obnoxious. The flexible, wobbling dildos went in one pussy and out another. One in an asshole, one in a mouth, one in a vagina and an asshole. And the whole thing taking place on an exam table. One of the women was clearly the doctor. Horn-rimmed glasses, hair pulled back in a bun. The stoic turned seductress.

Paul Veracruz stood up, overalls around his ankles and blue and green tattoos snaking downward from his shoulders to his tailbone. His dick was so thin and tiny that I could barely see it inside his hand, but with his ass hanging out and his few pubes standing straight up as if erect themselves, I got myself going and rubbed my dick with reckless abandon. It wouldn't take long for me to come, I knew that, just one glance at Jean-Claude Jolie, with his pink dickhead coming out of the brown stump, or Mark Israel with that scarred bratwurst in his hand, and even the soles of my feet felt like they might come to orgasm.

I imagined sliding my dick in between Paul Veracruz's golden cheeks, I pictured myself riding him like a horse. But Victor was closer. His hand covered only the very top part of his erection. His dick was definitely oversized and veering off to the right, away from me, but I still stared at it shamelessly: the mass of black hair above his dick, below it, along his thighs, his balls, the hint that there was more to come if only I could get a closer look, or at least a rear view. I held my dick by the base and waved it around a little, wanting to show it off. And why not? because Victor was watching me do it. I wanted to see if he'd come watching me or watching that porno.

"It's time for your pelvic exam, Ms. Jones," the doctor said to more moans. She stuck one end of the dildo inside herself and the other end inside Ms. Jones.

"But I just had one last week," Ms. Jones protested.

Jean-Claude Jolie guffawed.

"I always wondered what those were for," I said, watching the dildos.

And then, as all the boys furiously gripped and rubbed themselves seemingly for dear life, determined looks of concentration on their faces, Paul Veracruz let out a whoop and shot a load that went straight back to the top of the wall behind him. He didn't notice, but the last of it fell out of the air and landed in his spiky hair. "Ahhh!" he yelled, squeezing more come out of himself.

I envied Jean-Claude so hard, as he spastically rubbed that dick skin of his up and down—he had so much to work with, his fingers never even had to touch his dickhead, the foreskin did it for him. I imagined his pink glans must be fresh as an infant's, untouched and outrageously sensitive. A dildo in Ms. Jones's pussy, a dildo in the doctor's mouth. Jean-Claude said, "Bingo," and, as all the muscles in his body seemed to clench, three squirts of white juice poured from his dick and landed on the floor in front of him. His dick sprang back up when he released it, making it look as though he could come ten more times and be ready for more. Paul Veracruz ran a measuring tape from his dickhead to the wall. Mark Israel leaned forward as if trying to hear the TV better. He moved his hand up and down his dick slowly, then stopped, then rubbed really fast and the come fell out of him in a slow, drippy mess that landed on the ankle of his pants. He didn't make a sound.

I looked at Victor, so casual, such a mix of brains and rebelliousness, with a big brown dick that made me salivate like mad. I wanted that thing in my mouth more than anything. I tried to imagine the taste, the feel of his hands on me, and then I couldn't bear it anymore, things inside of me were contracting, something had been switched on. I leaned back and felt in sync for a moment with everything in the room: the nudity, the obscenity, the masculinity, the unbearable heat, Paul's ass, the flow of an almost piercing orgasm all throughout me, and Victor's climax right after mine. The feelings he must've had, I wanted to share those, I wanted to make him feel those things, because I was there, and I was human, and I was not some stupid video with tacky bleach blond chicks making fools of themselves for a buck. Spooge shot out my dick, flew across the length of the room, and landed directly on the face of Ms. Jones, who was on all fours on the exam table getting fucked by not one but two dildos.

"Whoa!" Paul exclaimed.

Victor was looking at me when he came, there was no doubt about it, because he was angled toward me, his dick was almost reaching for me, and the come sprayed out his penis with a horrible strength and flew to my face, landing directly underneath my right eye. Hot jizz ran down my cheek.

"I'm so sorry," Victor said, waddling with pants around ankles to rustle up a towel. Luckily, I was wearing contacts, and it was Victor, so I wasn't disgusted. I was actually kind of intrigued. Every time Victor looked at me he'd think, 'There's Augie Schoenberg. I came in his eye.'

Paul shut off the video, which seemed even more ridiculous now that everyone had come. I wiped Victor's sperm off of me with the towel and then Paul handed me the measuring tape. "Put this at the end of your dick and hold it there." He walked over to the TV and said, "Hmmm." Jean-Claude was squeezing his still-hard shaft, coaxing out the last of the come. Israel was half-way dressed, sporting that old white underwear. Paul's dick had shrunk back to its peanut size against walnut balls.

"And the winner is me, Paul Veracruz, with a distance of five feet, four inches."

"I demand a recount," I said, thinking I had made a fair showing.

"Sorry, only five feet one inch."

Victor put his now-gleaming dick in his boxers and pulled up his pants. "Augie, I am really sorry about that. It was totally rude."

I yanked up my jeans, now feeling for all the world like I was in a locker room. "I'm not disgusted, really. It was a first, at least in this kind of way."

"You'll remember it forever, Augie," Paul Veracruz said. "The first time Victor came in your eye."

"Don't you love how Augie adds this gay angle to everything we do?" Jean-Claude said, grinning from ear to ear.

Aghast, I said, "You know, this was not the most heterosexual event I ever witnessed," which was the wrong thing to say, because to save my pride I had implicated them and their faces got stiff and no one spoke.

"Really, though, Augie, I apologize," Victor said, wiping his hands on the towel.

"You don't have to. I enjoyed it." And then I left the room.

I slept so soundly that night that it felt like I hadn't moved the entire time. The circulation was cut off to my arms and in the morning I had to wrench them one by one out from under me. I dreamed of the Harley Hutt but in the dream I didn't live there. I stood outside on the lawn holding a suitcase and calling through the windows to Victor. He appeared with a baby in his arms and then stood at the window rocking and kissing the baby. He didn't say anything at all, even though I was yelling to him to let me in. He shook his head no and then pulled down the blinds. Tony and Paul came up the walk, talking to each other so rapidly I couldn't understand a word they were saying. I ran to them and asked them if they recognized me but they walked right past me as if I didn't exist. Jean-Claude Jolie drove by in a car. I felt the most sickening feeling in my stomach, like when you're lost as a child. Finally, Mark Israel appeared on the porch, wearing jeans and no shirt. I wanted to run to him and hug his hairy chest, but I stood where I was and waited to see what he would say. "Why don't you get the fuck out of here," he said and then spit. "You faggot."

6.

The boys of the Harley Hutt informed me that we were going to have a Back to School party. Ideas of who to invite raced through my mind: in addition to being the batboy for the lesbian softball team, I was also the former social coordinator for the campus Gay and Lesbian Alliance, and I thought I might be able to persuade those two groups and maybe some others to come and do something pretty wild. I spent the afternoon on the phone, in conspiratorial whispers with campus subversives, and then sailed down the stairs to attend our house meeting.

They sat in a circle in the living room. The group was in the middle of a heated argument about the bartender job they applied for. Apparently, Jean-Claude Jolie had gotten it and the others were not happy.

"That job was mine!" Paul Veracruz exclaimed.

"Dude, chill out," Jean-Claude Jolie said.

"It's because he's in a band," Mark Israel said. "They think chicks'll show up."

"So what?" Jean-Claude said. "It's a bar. That's what they want."

"Yeah, but you don't have any experience," Victor said.

"It's too fuckin' bad," Jean-Claude replied. "Get your own fuckin' job."

"Why don't you guys apply for jobs at a different bar?" I asked.

No one spoke. Then, Paul Veracruz said, "Yeah, but he got the job at the good bar."

The others let forth noises of agreement.

Tony Valentine said, "You guys are all dickheads. You don't show up to apply at the same time. You gotta do shit like that on your own."

"If there was only one job available, why did all of you apply for it? Three of you were obviously not gonna get it," I said.

Paul Veracruz said, "Yeah, but they should have given it to me."

"No, fuck you," Mark Israel said. "They should have given it to me."

"All right, all right. That's not what this meeting is about," Tony said. "Get to the party."

Mean-spirited looks flew across the room.

Finally, Paul Veracruz said, "OK, here's the thing." He patted the chair beside him and I sat down. His legs were spread so far that his overall-clad thigh pressed right up against mine. "Ted Demetropoulos used to do a lot of inviting people to the parties for us. And he's not here."

"He also used to DJ," Mark Israel said. "And I don't know who's gonna do that now."

"I could DJ," said Tony Valentine, and the others said, "Nah."

"You know what," I said. I had brought down a yellow legal pad and I looked down as though I were consulting important notes. "I just got off the phone with Jorge

35

el Jungle Boy. I threw the idea of the party out to him, to see what he would say, and he sounded very interested."

"Do you mean Jorge el Jungle Boy, DJ at the Dong Pipe in Chicago?" asked Paul.

"That's the one," I said.

The room erupted in surprised shouts. "He rocks!" "That's the best DJ in the country!" "How do you know him!"

"Ted introduced me. We got to be good friends, and I asked if he'd do us a favor."

"Augie Schoenberg," said Victor Radhakrishna. "You are a valuable friend."

I'd known for some time that the Dong Pipe was the favorite club of the Harley Hutt crowd. The bar was nothing to look at, but when Ted brought me there, I was fascinated to find that being introduced around by him opened up an entirely new world. I must've met a hundred people that night, and Jorge el Jungle Boy had taken a particular shine to me.

"The problem is," said Mark Israel, packing a bong with loose marijuana that'd been lying around on the table. "Ted used to invite a certain, um, how do you say? He used to bring over a very specific, uh...help me here, boys."

"You know," said Tony. "People who have a certain....*flair* about them."

"Flair?" I asked.

Victor jumped in. "Augie, it's a crowd who draws a sort of enthusiasm from the guests. They have a sort of," he paused, "*je ne sais quoi*."

I knew exactly what they meant, but I was having fun. "A what?"

Tony leaned toward me. "It's like, Augie, this. It's like, when you go to a party and you see all these people, but I mean there's not just like Joe Schmos and dickheads hanging around, there's like more interesting people. And it's like fun."

Jean-Claude Jolie cringed.

"But you guys always have lots of interesting people at your parties," I said.

"Yes," said Victor, "but we were wondering about..."

"Oh! You mean the fags and the nutcases," I said.

All at once they shouted, "Yes!"

"Well," I said, looking down at my notes. "The lesbian softball team is coming in bondage gear. The Gay and Lesbian Alliance is coming in reverse drag, the Feminist Alliance girls are coming dressed as Marilyn Monroe, and the Campus Communists are coming as Che Guevara."

Silence fell on the room. "What's reverse drag?" Mark Israel asked.

"Well, the gay guys are gonna dress up as men, and the lesbians are gonna dress like women."

Everyone laughed. "Dude," Paul Veracruz said. "You rock."

I sat there and beamed.

7.

Professor Arundhati Singh stood before us in a cosmopolitan silver wrap, looking like she may be more at home in Paris than in rural Illinois. The classroom's flourescent lights shone off of a jewel in her forehead, and her booming, British Indian voice flew around the room in such a noble, elegant way that I should have been rightly seduced by her.

But I wasn't. I was seduced by Jose Rubenstein. He'd come in late to the Indian literature class, all scattered notebooks and off-kilter glasses, in a Hawaiian shirt and a buzzcut, looking like a tropical baby chick. I knew I knew him, but I couldn't place him. Rubenstein. He looked Latino, but he had to be Jewish with that name. He sat next to me and I surveyed him peripherally.

He must've known me, anyway. He looked right at me when he sat down and gave me a, "What's up dude?" underneath the sound of Arundhati Singh's lecture. Rubenstein. Jose Rubenstein. I couldn't remember where I met him but I knew I liked him. The loudness of his shirt, screaming blue and white flowers, was practically comic, and it seemed intentional.

I should have been paying attention to the lecture. It was still summer outside, but school had started. I'd left the Harley Hutt with two sweet-smelling sterile notebooks, my clean slates ready to be muddled with scribblings, with doodles, with knowledge. Victor had laughed at me as I ran my hands over the covers of my new novels for the class, hesitant to put them in my dirty backpack. The fancy illustrations and the indication that the books were classics made them look ungodly important, and I wanted to get inside all of them at once, as if that were possible. Instead, I touched the outsides.

The smell of fresh paper was in my nose, overpowering the whiff of jasmine that came off of the professor. Arundhati Singh was catching on to me, I could tell by her gaze, she knew I was transfixed by something besides her and the syllabus for Indian Literature 348. She was finishing some diatribe or other about social politics, arranged marriages, wars....Jose took off his glasses and started cleaning them with his flowered shirt.

And then I knew. He was from the rugby party. At the end, the guy with the T shirt and no pants that was pouring beer over the players' assholes. I instantly remembered the leathery little dick, the paunch stomach, the affable grin. Jose Rubenstein. My own private Hispanic Jew. I'd get to sit next to him two days a week.

"August Schoenberg." A soaring voice broke my attention. Stunned, I didn't respond. "August Schoenberg," she called out again.

"Yes," I croaked, as though I were a five year old child embarrassed by my daydreaming. Someone behind me giggled.

"Mr. Schoenberg. Shall I call you August or do you go by a *nickname*?" She pronounced nickname with disdain, as if it was a newly-coined term that wasn't widely accepted.

"Uh, people call me Augie."

"Augie?" she sniffed. "I shall call you August and you will just have to suffer." More laughs from behind me.

"August Schoenberg. You have a beautiful name." Her movie star eyes sparkled at me. I couldn't help but blush. "August Schoenberg, I have a special assignment for you. Read the short story, *The Cowherd's Daughter's Story*, and then prepare a three page paper on the topic of arranged marriage. Thursday you will lead the class in discussion."

Terror took hold of me, but I didn't know if it was from the thought of leading the class in discussion or from the thought of an arranged marriage. I pictured a teenaged Indian girl sitting idly by in a hut while her parents negotiated for the dowry of a cow with a neighboring family. I couldn't imagine being wrapped up in such a mess. I thought I would rather commit suicide.

The thought of leading a class discussion, though, was bad enough. "Doesn't anyone else have to do anything?"

"Why, August, don't you have any faith in what I'm sure are your eminently great intellectual powers?" In another voice, that would've sounded like an insult.

I widened my eyes, unsure. The other students looked at me with sympathy, no doubt dreading the thought of being me. But it was just for show, I knew that inwardly, they rejoiced. Jose Rubenstein looked ahead at the blackboard, noncommittally.

"It's all up to you," she added.

Beleaguered, I wandered through the halls and found the room for my Emily Dickinson course. Because there was no film school at the university, I was an English major, which was the only department that had classes even remotely related to film. Three days a week I had the Dickinson class and the class in Indian literature. The other two days I had a Hitchcock film class and then a screenwriting class. I was very excited about the last two: though I'd committed myself to writing a screenplay about life at the Harley Hutt, the only thing I had on paper was part of a screenplay entitled *Last Boat to Manchuria*. I'd been working on it for six months and was sure it was going to be a runaway success. It was a tale of passion in pre-World War II Japan, involving an American smuggler and a Japanese opium addict. I thought it had the makings for a good story, but I wasn't very far into it, and my knowledge of film was a little dim. Embarrassingly, I'd never even seen a Hitchcock movie. I never told anyone this, but I'd never even seen *Psycho*.

During the poetry class, which had been led by a low-voiced man named 'Smith,' I actually managed to say a few coherent things about poetry. After staring at some Dickinson poems during the lecture, the language on the page had unscrewed itself, and I wasn't intimidated by it. I hoped the same would happen with *The Cowherd's Daughter's Story*.

Soothed by the hour-long sound of Smith's voice, I sauntered down the steps of the literature building and into the heat and sun. Jose Rubenstein was on the Quad playing frisbee with some friends. I walked past them and smiled, watching them run around and yell, acting like kids. The frisbee flew toward me and I snatched it out of the air. I threw it back to Jose Rubenstein in what was probably the most flawless, even frisbee toss of my life. "Thanks!" Jose called out. "That was perfect." I waved to him and then turned toward the Hutt.

    I sat down at my typewriter and clicked out *The Cowherd's Daughter's Story* paper in a couple of hours. Without the luxury of a word processor, I had to retype it several times, but when I was finished I lay down on my bed to read it, and a wave of satisfaction washed over me. The story was so old it had seemed fairly odd. The language was overly-formal but sort of sexual, and the fact that it'd been translated made it sound a little silly. It was full of lines like, "Oh, these charming and auspicious milkmaids with their ripe, ample breasts like the most abundantly pleasing of treasures, and just watch how they sway and giggle and dance by the riverbank," and "The lord was the most gracious of lords and that grace was benevolent to the charming milkmaid whose brief glance and gentle smile sent a glimmer of ecstasy through the impatient lord."

    It was difficult at first to tell what the plot was, what with all the general references to Lord Krishna and the other deities, but in the end I gathered it was about a milkmaid who was arranged to be married to this guy she didn't know, but had seen a few times by the riverbank. According to the story, all the milkmaids were in awe of this guy because he was the bravest and the most exalted and the most intelligent, but the cowherd's daughter was unsure of whether or not he was a rogue. Her parents made her marry this guy and then after the marriage, she realized that she's truly in love and gives a big speech about minding your husband, sort of like at the end of *The Taming of the Shrew*.

    I honestly thought the women in the story had been portrayed as complete airheads while the men were depicted as wise, respectable deities. I figured I'd take a feminist slant in the paper and argue valiantly against the oppression of women by chauvinistic male writers. Almost every paper I'd ever written had been from that perspective, and I almost always got A's, so I figured it was a safe bet. This time, though, I had the added ammunition of my outrage at the thought of an arranged marriage. I imagined what it'd be like to be the cowherd's daughter, and the words poured from my brain.

    Every time I glanced into the book for an illustrative quote, my eyes would land on a juicy one. Sitting at my typewriter, I giggled wickedly to myself as I inserted these trite little lines into the middle of my scathing sentences, hoping the quotes would be on target enough that just their mere appearance would turn *The Cowherd's Daughter's Story* against itself.

    As I quietly cackled on the bed, Victor appeared in the doorway. His hair hung down to just the top of his shoulders, framing his bronzed face, his bulbous nose, his dark pink lips. He wore black shorts, a bright blue T-shirt, and skateboarding shoes. I was lying down, but I could still feel my knees get weak.

    "Hey. Jean-Claude's band is playing at the bar tonight, if you wanna go."

    "Yeah, I do. I just finished my paper." I got up from the bed and tossed the pages onto the table. "I could use a stress reliever."

"Remember, the Back to School party is Friday night."

"Yeah, I can't wait." I had confirmed the date with Jorge el Jungle Boy, and had invited almost every person I could think of. I had high hopes for the party, but I was mainly hoping that Victor would get sauced enough to do something wild. The memory of the Truth or Dare kiss was still hot in my mind, and I wanted another one.

"What's the paper about?" he asked, hanging onto the door frame with his fingertips.

"Nothing!" I said, a little too quickly. "Just, uh, a milkmaid and stuff. You know." I could fathom bringing the paper to class and having the teacher read it, but if Victor read it, it'd be worse than being seen naked. It'd be as though he were looking into my soul.

"Lemme read it," he said, walking over to the table with a heavy, arrogant stride. I raced in front of him and snatched the papers and held them to my chest.

"Come on," he said, grabbing at my arms and poking me in the sides. He tore the paper from my hands and read it. I paced around the room, hot in the face. I was horrified to think Victor might find my grandiose statements about Indians to be patronizing. It took him an eternity to finish. He looked up at me and sniffed.

"Well, did you love it or did you hate it?"

"It was OK," he said, and dropped the paper on the bed. He looked off toward the hallway. "You have some strong opinions."

"I do," I said, emboldened. "I'm smashing outdated cultural conventions to pieces." I grinned at him, but he shrugged and walked toward the door.

8.

Jean-Claude Jolie's band came out for their encore. A small crowd of groupies were clustered around the stage, but the Harley Hutt boys and I sat at a table along the side. It was a new band for Jean-Claude; a re-working of the old one, The Turnip Truck, and the new singer had added some life to the music. This new incarnation, The Geeks, sounded considerably more professional. Watching Jean-Claude meticulously work his bass guitar in perfect rhythm with the other musicians gave off the impression this was serious business. There were no awkward beginnings with embarrassing start-overs. There were no missed notes.

The encore ended. We roared along with the crowd, dead set in our mission to see one of our own succeed. Jean-Claude, sweaty and clearly exhilarated, stood on the stage breathing hard. The self-deprecating name notwithstanding, I imagined The Geeks may become his life's work.

Victor walked over to me and said, "Do you wanna go home with me? These guys are gonna stay and drink more."

Three full pints of beer sat in front of Tony, Mark, and Paul, amber and unsipped. The prospect of having time alone with Victor was incentive enough to jump out of my chair. I couldn't help it, I had this crazy idea that he was a hot prospect and was pursuing me. I was lying to myself in thinking that we were on the verge of being a couple, but the thought of my empty bed made me want to ride this one out to the finish.

We walked out of the dark bar into the pitch-black night. Clouds had moved in and covered the moon and stars.

Victor and I came down a hill next to one of the dorms, the slope so steep the sidewalk had wooden railings. At the foot of the hill, trancey music from a garage party beckoned. Clear plastic strips were hung from the open door and as we walked past, the glowing space lit by blacklights shone purple against the night. I would've killed to go in, but Victor walked right past, as if he didn't notice the party at all.

The air grew progressively more humid with each step we took, but in an instant a cold breeze hit us and thunder roared in the distance. I shivered.

Victor looked over at me. "Do you want my jacket?"

I said no, but the wind was icy and I couldn't help but shiver again. "Here," he said, taking off his windbreaker. "You have to take this." He put the jacket around my shoulders and inwardly I glowed. The jacket smelled of Victor. The slightest aroma of incense drifted toward my nose, mixed with a tiny dash of cologne that smelled of leather. There was an underlying hint of cigarette smoke. The smell blew away with a gust of wind, but then returned when the wind died down. I inhaled deeply and felt so comfortable that I wanted to put my arm around him as we walked.

In between gusts of wind, there was a dead quiet that was almost eerie. Fog rolled in and gathered around the streetlights, and seemed to blanket the treacherous roar of the thunder. All the businesses were closed. No cars drove by.

"It's creepy," he said. "I hope we make it home before it rains. It sounds like it's going to be terrible."

"Do you wanna pull an all-nighter with me? I've got a case of beer in the fridge with our name on it."

He grinned a little, almost bashfully. "I would love to pull an all-nighter with you, but I've got class at eight."

"Yeah, I have class, too. Well, at noon anyway. Couldn't I lure you into being bad, though? We could hit that garage party. One last time before we have to get serious about things."

"You better be careful. I can get pretty bad." He immediately scoffed. He put an arm around my shoulder and said, this time in an utterly serious voice, "Augie, man, things have been kind of weird between us and I know we were usually drunk at the time..." He dropped off and stopped walking. He had a frown on his face that made me feel unabashedly helpless. My stomach sank. "I just—I don't want you to get the wrong idea."

Lightning flashed in front of us, so close that I jumped backwards and grabbed Victor's arm. Thunder sounded immediately afterwards in a deafening roar. In an instant, sheets of rain fell from the sky and landed on the pavement with the force of a spray of bullets. Victor and I huddled together in the doorway to a record store.

We were at least five blocks from home. "What do we do?" I asked.

"No choice. We'll have to go through it."

We counted to three and then on three we dashed out from the vestibule and ran down the street like we were being chased. We stopped at a red light, but saw no cars so we raced forward past the closed restaurants and the closed banks and the closed coffeehouse. Water soaked through my clothes so thoroughly that they stuck to my body and I felt like I was fifty pounds heavier. I pulled Victor's windbreaker over my head, but realized the effort was futile. The rain felt like it was coming down sideways. Puddles formed along the sidewalks and my gym shoes became sopped. We ran to the Quad and raced across it. The sprinkler system was on and it sprayed me in the face, adding a cruel insult to my already injured spirits. At the end of the Quad, I grabbed Victor by the shoulder and said, "It's no use. We might as well walk."

We tramped across the empty street, drenched and resigned to our fate. "Do you want your jacket back?" I asked. The windbreaker had become a cold, wet blanket around my torso.

"No, thanks," he said, looking at it skeptically through streams of water on his face.

I sloshed through the puddles. I was wet and cold, but grateful for it. I didn't want to hear the rest of that speech of his. We marched past the dim lights of Greek Row and down two more flooded blocks before we came to the Hutt.

Inside, Victor said, "I am going to the basement to put my clothes in the dryer."

"Good idea. I will, too."

We padded down the basement steps, my tennis shoes squeaking. I took off the windbreaker and held it up. Water flowed off of it in a fine stream. Victor took off his shirt. The rain had matted down his chest hair, making it look darker and more abundant around his nipples. He threw the shirt in the rickety old dryer and then I took off my shirt. His hair hung from his head in long black tentacles, clinging to his face.

"You look like a wet dog," I said.

"You look like a drowned rat." He unbuttoned his pants and struggled to take them off without falling over. I did the same, and once again we found ourselves standing in front of each other in boxers. When he bent down to put his pants in the dryer, his hair fell off the back of his neck and I saw a large, white, amoeba-shaped birthmark right below his hairline. I'd never seen anything like it before. There was absolutely no color to it at all, and it almost shone against the rest of his skin. I considered asking him about it, but figured I'd better not. Victor turned and looked at me, as if to assess the damage the storm had done. I put my pants and socks in the dryer and then Victor moved to close its door.

Daringly, I asked, "Aren't you gonna dry your underwear?" I pulled down mine and threw them in the dryer.

He thought about if for a second and then said, "Well, I guess I might as well." He moved to pull them down and then stopped, as if embarrassed. "Augie, look at you."

There I stood with a raging boner. "I can't help it," I said. "I'm going upstairs." I marched along the steps and through the dining room with Victor right behind me. In the darkness of the house, I forgot about being embarrassed and started to enjoy the stroll. Victor's feet pounded heavily on the stairs behind me, and when we got to the third floor I walked straight toward my room. Before I went inside, I glanced to the side and saw Victor walk the few steps to his room. When his left arm swung back, his genitals were revealed, and I saw his dick angling half a foot upwards in a full erection.

I went to bed and, soothed by the sound of the rain, fell into a semi-sleep state, wandering in and out of dreams and consciousness, not able to tell which was which. Some loud sounds on the steps woke me and I heard Victor and Tony talking quietly in the hallway. Tony was louder and out of breath and must have just come home. Victor, who I imagined had been serenely sitting cross-legged in his bedroom inhaling incense, spoke in a hushed tone I could barely hear. I felt like I was a child again and my parents had just come home from a night on the town. The faint smell of alcohol and cigarettes wafted into my room. My dream-touched mind mixed with the sound of rain pouring against my window and sent my spirit to a place of complete relaxation. "Where's Augie?" Tony asked in a loud whisper. I heard my door creak open. "No, don't," Victor said. "He's asleep." Tony said, "He's sleeping?" Another voice surfaced, I think it was Jean-Claude Jolie. He said, "Augie's asleep already?" and Victor whispered, "Yeah, don't wake him up." There were steps in the hallway and then the sound of Victor's door closing. Except for the gentle beating of the rain on the roof, the house became completely silent and sweet waves of adrenaline flowed through my veins. I thought I had never felt so safe.

9.

The next morning I ran into Mark Israel in the shower. I was washing my hair and wishing I could get used to the lack of privacy. I couldn't help that almost every day I was fighting off erections in the shower. Then Israel walked in wearing his old, holey underwear and pulled them right down almost as soon as he appeared. I turned around, hoping to avoid looking at him.

A shadow appeared on the wall. I glanced over my shoulder. Israel stood in front of my stall with a bar of soap in his hand, staring at me. The soap was brand-new and bright white; held against his hairy skin it looked incredibly pure. "Hey, Schoenberg, you're from Evanston, right? It's weird we never met each other. Where'd you live?"

I thought of my parents' 70's style duplex on the south end of town. I almost didn't want to tell him where it was. It was in a perfectly nice neighborhood, but I learned when I was in high school that other people considered it to be a ghetto.

"Oh, over on Mulford," I said. "How about you?" I kept to the wall, hoping he'd stop looking at me.

"Over by Northwestern. My parents are professors there."

I felt a small stab of jealousy. My parents were both junior high school foreign language teachers. They'd wanted to get their PhDs, but left school after I was born. I always wondered if they resented me; if they thought I had hindered their careers.

"Which grade school did you go to?" he asked. He turned on his shower nozzle, and I had to almost yell over the noise.

I told him I went to Harrison and he said, "Oh," in an almost surprised way, as if he couldn't believe I had gone to such a terrible place.

"It was nice," I said, which was the truth. It'd been a little hard by the time I got to high school, being around the rich kids from the lakefront, who I knew considered me to be from the poor side of town. "It was racially-diverse and religiously-diverse and the teachers were fantastic. I was very happy."

"Oh, yeah, that's great."

"Why didn't you go to Northwestern?" I asked, almost vindictively. If he'd been smart enough, he would have gone there.

"Oh, you know. Just wanted to get away from the folks for a while."

There was something vaguely dangerous about Mark Israel. Maybe it was jealousy: my envy of his body, of his parents' prestige, of his rampant masculinity, but for some reason I didn't trust him. He'd been giving me menacing looks around the house. I wondered what he was up to.

"It's not that I couldn't get in," he said, which sounded like a lie. "I just wanted to go away."

I turned off the shower and grabbed my towel. I quickly dried off and then wrapped it around myself. I stood in front of his shower stall like he had done to me.

I stared at his penis and felt another brutal stab of jealously. It was so thick it must have been five times the size of mine.

"Are you excited about going to Israel?" I asked, casually.

"Oh, yeah," he said, turning around. His ass was so entirely covered with hair that the water could barely reach his skin. "I think it's going to be the best time of my life."

"Good, good. I'm jealous."

When I walked into class Arundhati Singh was standing at the podium looking smart and intrigued. She held out her hand and said, "Your paper, Mr. Schoenberg." I pulled it out of my notebook and handed it to her, feeling like I had just delivered an urgent message. She read it through while I sat at my desk in a state of turmoil. I still didn't feel like I was competent to lead a class discussion. Jose Rubenstein ran in the room right before the bell and sat next to me. He was wearing another Hawaiian shirt, this one blue and green. He tried to catch my eye a few times and I didn't look back, but eventually he said, "Hey what's up, dude?" and I said, "Hey, what's up." A second passed, and then he said, "Hey, thanks for the frisbee toss the other day." I said, "No problem," and smiled. He looked around the room a little, and then up at Arundhati Singh, who was still reading, and said quietly, "I'm gonna light up a joint on the Quad after class. If you want to join me." I turned to him, curious. Strangers had never asked me to get stoned with them, let alone strangers I'd seen naked at parties. "Sure," I said. The slightest flicker of hope passed over me: the hope that he might not be just a friendly straight guy but a magically friendly gay guy that I'd never met before. I couldn't wait for class to end.

"This paper," Arundhati Singh pronounced, "is three pages long, and has no title. It was written by August Schoenberg." I forgot to put on a title. I thought I was ruined. "It is so well-written that I am going to read it to the entire class."

Joy sprang up in my head.

Professor Singh read the entire paper through. The way she accentuated each syllable and snared the ending of each word around her tongue made the paper sound like she had written it herself. I couldn't believe I had impressed a professor. When she finished, she asked the class for their reactions. There was a discussion about my paper and the story for the rest of the hour and then the class ended and I ended up not having to do a damn thing. I let out a sigh of catharsis, and the tensed muscles in my body relaxed.

I tried to steal out of the room unobserved but Arundhati Singh called after me and I walked over to her. "August, I'm giving you an A on the paper and it will count for extra credit."

Triumphant, I strode out of the classroom and went to find Jose Rubenstein. I felt that I deserved a healthy dose of free drugs. I searched outside of the literature building for a moment and then found him crouched against the wall behind a large bush. He looked terribly conspicuous, so I said, "Don't you think we should pretend we're not doing anything wrong?" He looked at me for a second, considering my idea. I couldn't nail him down. He wasn't grungy enough for the Harley Hutt and Trailer Trash crowd and he didn't look preppy enough for the Greeks. I thought maybe he was the kind that floated between groups, unsure of exactly where he fit in. I supposed he could've been a jock, after all, I'd seen him at the rugby party. But I didn't think he was on the team: the wiry frame inside the Hawaiian shirt wasn't an especially athletic look.

"You're right," he said, boldly. "I look like I'm up to no good. But we can't just walk around the Quad smoking dope pretending nothing's going on."

"Of course we can. No one would expect it."

"Yeah, you're totally right. I like this guy," he said, apparently informing the rest of campus.

We strolled along the Quad at two in the afternoon as if we were out on a sightseeing tour. We passed the joint back and forth and not one person even looked at us sideways. "You were right," he said. "Nobody cared." We walked along lazily, and then sat on the grass. "That was a great paper you wrote."

"Oh, I don't know. I was kind of embarrassed."

"Don't be. You got some brains in that head. So what are you, Schoenberg? South Sider? North?"

"Evanston," I said. From the way he said "south," like there was no "h," I could tell he was no North Sider.

"Ha! A lakefront liberal, huh? I hope you don't look down on me now. I'm one of those trashy Bridgeport types."

The pot was starting to kick in. The grass looked as elegant as the grass on a golf course green, and the air was laced with sweet, flowery smells. I longed for a pizza. Jose's eyes were getting puffy and his buzzcut stood on end. I wanted to focus on him instead of Victor. Trashy Bridgeport type or not, he seemed like a more realistic prospect. And he was so frustratingly adorable I ended up laughing for no reason. "Jose, Bridgeport is my favorite neighborhood in the whole world. Especially when I'm in the mood to get my ass kicked."

He pinned me to the ground, his fist jokingly clenched into a fist. "So you think we're a little rough down there? Yeah, only to you snots from the suburbs."

"Jose, cut it out. Ow! Listen, I love the South Side. To death. Just the thought of it makes me so happy."

"You mean it?" he asked.

I nodded.

He sat back on the grass and got philosophical. "You know, Bridgeport is the birthplace of democracy."

I couldn't help it. I laughed so hard that the newly enraged Jose ended up nearly strangling me. I tried to think of a peace offering. "Jose! Jose! I live at the Harley Hutt. We're having a back to school party tomorrow night if you wanna come."

"The Harley Hutt," he said with a smile, releasing me. I sat up. "That's a pretty wild place. Yeah, I'd like to."

"Cool, bring some friends."

"Actually, tomorrow is my birthday. I was lookin' to have a good time. Will I be able to get in?"

I hadn't thought we'd have an exclusive door policy. I thought any freak who wanted to could walk through the door. To play it safe I said, "Oh, don't worry. I'm working the door."

"Cool. I'll see you there." He sprang to his feet and patted me on the head. "Later."

I walked home high and free, savoring the green on the trees, and the look of some rabbits that darted around on the grass. I was sweating beneath my shirt and my jeans, but suddenly a cool breeze came in, and the air began to dry my soaked skin.

10.

I had a boyfriend once. His name was Mikey, and I met him when I was 18 and living in the dorms. My friend Roberta and I were talking one day and she mentioned this friend Mikey of hers who was so funny and so cute and she couldn't believe he was gay. I was curious and wanted to meet him, but at that point I had never even known another gay guy so I was nervous and asked her if I could see a picture of him. She took me to her room and I sat on the bed while she rifled through her desk looking for the pictures.

Roberta was my first friend at college, a tall, black, and theatrical woman who wore all sorts of strange fashion creations that were colorful and interesting—odd robes, pants with mirrors, huge scarves—but didn't subscribe to any particular style at all. It looked like she made them herself. Roberta and I met in the cafeteria: I was sitting alone one day at lunch eating a bowl of cereal and she walked right up to my table and sat down.

"Listen," she said. "I like this place, but the people in my dorm; those bitches have to go."

Interested, I asked, "Why, what's wrong with them?"

"I'm sorry, but all they do is sit around and talk about their hair and their nails and the guys they like and the sororities they wanna join. Is anyone on this campus even remotely sophisticated? I'm in the theater, and I need inspiration. I can't be hanging with these preppy chicks."

By chance, I had heard of a party at Trailer Trash, and thought she might like it. Anyway, I'd only been at school a month and I wanted to make as many friends as possible. "You know, there's a party tonight at Trailer Trash. You should come with me."

She looked skeptical. "Trailer Trash? Sweetie, I can't be partying with rednecks. Is that like a party of Klan members?"

I laughed. "No! It's like anti-white trash people. They look the part, but they're actually really cool. Also, it's right next to the Harley Hutt, and they have the best parties on campus."

"I've heard about the Harley Hutt," she said. "Isn't that where they do the Hokey Pokey naked?"

"I think so. But I haven't been there yet."

"Does this Trailer Trash party have any gay guys? All my friends are gay."

"Well, I'll be there," I said, glad to have an easy way to come out.

Her face brightened. "I love you. What's your phone number?"

I scribbled it down on a napkin and she put it in her bag, an enormous purple sack that was so jam packed it must've weighed fifty pounds. "I'll call you later. I wanna have the time of my life!"

She strode off with a waft of heavy perfume following her and I laughed to myself, thinking this must be the only place on earth where complete strangers walk up to you over a bowl of cereal and you both end up going to a party later that night.

Roberta forgot to ask me my name, and when she called that night she said, "Excuse me, but is this the gay guy who sits in the cafeteria alone eating bowls of Lucky Charms?"

I told her it was and she said, "Good, I thought I dialed wrong. Are you gonna be there in an hour? I'm comin' by."

At the party, Roberta went up to almost every single person there and introduced herself. She had a beautiful peal of a laugh that made people look over at her and grin. She walked over to me occasionally to say, "God, cutie, these people are too sweet. I'm lovin' it!" She carried around a bottle of apple wine and drank it straight from the bottle. By the end of the evening Roberta was dancing on a table in the living room, throwing her head back in delight.

"Here he is," Roberta said, handing me a couple of pictures. I leafed through them and liked what I saw. Mikey had short brown hair that was brushed up on top of his head in a mini-duck tail. He looked like he was a little shorter than me, and he had small brown eyes that made him look like he was constantly squinting. In one of the pictures he had on a surfing T-shirt and huge boxer shorts with turtles on them, and in another he wore an old bowling shirt with a nametag that read "Ned." I thought he was perfect.

"Are you sure he's gay?" I asked.

"Oh, honey. It doesn't get any gayer than him. He doesn't really seem like it at first, but trust me. Anyway, he listens to Madonna and watches soap operas at the same time. I mean, come on."

Roberta decided that Mikey and I would meet in the cafeteria for dinner. I was hoping there'd be some edible food that night, since the offerings were usually pretty nasty, so I consulted the meal schedule. They were having shrimp scampi, which was my favorite.

I was very nervous beforehand and called Roberta for reassurance. "Augie, he's so interested in you. I've taken care of the whole thing. I've talked you up so much he thinks you're Don Quixote, or Don Juan, or whatever his name was."

I walked into the cafeteria feeling like I was about to go on stage. I was sure Mikey was going to hate me. In the pictures, Mikey looked cool and together, like he already had his own style worked out. I still had braces and acne and shitty clothes from high school. I'd never dated anyone before. I'd never even kissed anyone.

Roberta and Mikey sat at a table, looking over their shoulders. Roberta saw me and waved, yelling, "Augie, we're over here!" He looked different than in the pictures; there was no duck's ass in his hair. He must've been nervous, because he almost had a scowl on his face. He also looked like he'd dressed up for the occasion: he was wearing a black turtleneck and jeans.

I sat at the table and Roberta introduced us. "Now you two chat," she said, and walked off.

"We got some food for you," Mikey said. I looked down and saw a plate with meatloaf and mashed potatoes. There is nothing more that I hate in this world than meatloaf. Horrific memories of torturous mealtimes with meatloaf in my childhood surfaced, and I said, "I'm sorry, but I think they're having shrimp scampi. I think I might go get some."

Mikey looked genuinely hurt, and said, "Oh, I'm sorry! I just don't like seafood, so I got this instead."

I hadn't realized Mikey might've picked it out. I thought Roberta would have. Realizing I'd hurt his feelings, I considered eating the meatloaf, but I really didn't want to. At risk of causing trouble, I said, "Look, I'll be right back. It's just I really look forward to shrimp scampi night."

He looked disturbed. "Oh, OK."

"I'll be right back." I ran to the line and found about fifty people ahead of me. I patiently waited till I moved up to the service counter, but it probably took about ten minutes and when I got back to the table Mikey was gone.

I thought he must've thought I was the ugliest guy who ever walked.

My appetite, small as it'd been, left me and I dropped the plate down on the table. I walked out of the cafeteria in a state of utter despair. I admitted to myself that I was destined to be alone for the rest of my life, and it was because I was so ugly and such a dork and nobody wanted to be around me.

I wanted to go to my room and play my Stevie Nicks tapes and close the curtains and never leave. I saw Roberta on the other side of the parking lot, made a sharp turn, and went in the back door of my dorm and pressed the elevator button. In my peripheral vision, I saw Roberta come streaking up the walk. The first three doors she tried were locked and she yanked on each one like it would give if she pulled harder. Finally, she tore into the lobby and yelled, "Augie, what the hell happened?"

I was on the verge of tears, and muttered, "Well, I guess he doesn't like me. He left."

Roberta let forth a scream that was so loud the girl behind the reception desk came out into the lobby. "NO, NO, NO!" she yelled. "He thought *you* left because *you* thought *he* was ugly!"

"What? But he's the one who left!"

"No!" Roberta said. "He thought you were the one who left!"

"But I didn't leave!"

"Yes you did! You both left! Oh my god, the things I do for you people. I mean could either of you possibly be any more sensitive?"

"But all I wanted was shrimp scampi," I said. "I can't stand meatloaf."

"Well, there was your mistake. Mikey loves meatloaf. He looks forward to meatloaf night!"

"But I look forward to shrimp scampi night!"

Roberta hung her head. "Oh, you children. You act like you've never been on a date before."

"Well, I haven't been on a date before," I said.

"Well, neither has he. All right, I know what to do. Just hold on. And don't go anywhere."

Roberta went to the house phone and talked into it for several minutes. I couldn't hear what she was saying, but she was arguing fervently with Mikey and it looked like she was repeating the same thing over and over.

Finally, Roberta walked back to me and shook her head quickly, as though she were trying to shake off the stress we'd caused her. "All right. He actually thought you ditched him, so you're going to go back in and try again."

"I can't! I'm too embarrassed."

"He likes you, and you like him, right?"

I nodded.

"Then go!"

I marched off solemnly and found Mikey standing at the entrance to the cafeteria, looking equally ill at ease. Luckily, he decided to handle things with humor. "Augie, where'd ya go? I figured you must've made an emergency trip to the bathroom after you saw me."

"No," I said, laughing. "I just wanted the shrimp."

"Oh, I'm sorry, Augie. I was just nervous."

Relief poured over me, and since no one was around, I hugged him. "I just don't usually do this." The feel of his body against mine, both strong and soft, was exhilarating, especially because there was a chance that I might be able to get intimate with him. I'd never felt that before, that chance, that possibility.

"Yeah, I don't either. I don't feel like eating anymore. Do you wanna go to the bar for a drink?"

I wanted nothing more in the world. "How would we get in?"

He smiled. "Oh, I've got a wallet full of fake ID's. Want one?"

We walked across campus while he pulled out ID after ID and we tried to find a match. It seemed like nothing on campus had ever looked so alive. I felt like I finally had a purpose. I felt like I was finally participating in life.

After bonding at the bar, with me sitting at the table amazed and feeling quite adult, we headed back to his dorm room, where his roommate was conveniently out of town. It didn't take much: just a few minutes of making out before we were both overwhelmed. Laying on top of Mikey, I inhaled deeply, smelling the smell of a man for the first time when it counted, when I could say that it was an experience I could own. He wrapped his hand around my dick and I sighed. "Stay like that," he said. "Don't move." I pressed my head as far as it would go into his chest and the smell on him, like ether, put me to sleep. I woke briefly and he said, "Did you ever do anything like that with a boy before?" "No," I said. "You?" He said no and then I fell into a deep sleep, the deepest I could remember since I was a baby.

Mikey and I went out for six months. I loved walking around campus in my brown corduroy coat with a guy by my side who loved me. I had always hated fall, with the way everything dies and the cold air comes in like a wave of depression. But being in love changed my mind. I loved autumn then, with its dark colors and deep smell of burning leaves, and for the first time I saw that season as a time of possibility. We had friends who were couples, and we could relax on weekends, instead of succumbing to that urgent need to go out searching and hoping for a partner.

But something happened. Being in love was harder than I had expected. I wanted to be with Mikey every waking second, and when that didn't happen and we had to be apart for even a few hours I'd get terribly depressed. I had nothing but highs and lows. When I was with him I felt like I was the only person in the world and when we were apart I felt despair so harshly that I became almost despondent. Sensing my imbalanced feelings, Mikey pulled away, and I had nights where I lay on my bed and cried for hours.

By the spring, it had begun to seem we were dating just for the sake of it. We weren't having fun anymore. I thought, Well I'm 18 and there's a ton of other guys in the world, so why don't I move on? Mikey apparently felt the same way and he told me one night that he thought I was interested in other guys and that I should probably pursue them. I said I probably should. I thought I was being mature.

I heard from friends that summer that Mikey had transferred to the University of Minnesota. I was secretly terrified that if I didn't find another boyfriend soon I may end up being single for years. I didn't tell anyone that I was deathly afraid of falling in love again. The roller coaster of emotions I'd had was tough, and I became self-destructive. I smoked till I got bronchitis every other month, I ate only once a day, I drank every night.

The next year came, and the next, and I never found anyone. Almost four years later, I woke some mornings and thought of Mikey for hours at a time. I thought I had blown the whole thing. I thought we should have been together for years. I never imagined that I would waste three and a half years of the best years of my life so desperately single that I was beginning to hate the world.

11.

Lesbians were crawling through the front door on all fours, pulled on chains by dominatrixes. I stood above them, dressed as Marilyn Monroe. It wasn't a dream; it was the Back to School party, and the first guests had just arrived.

"All right, ladies," I called. "Single file. No pushing, no shoving, nobody gets hurt."

"We'll see about that," one of the dominatrixes replied.

"Save it for the softball field, honey, we're all here to have fun."

I saw the lesbians in and then went to the porch to await more guests. So far, we had gay guys in Army fatigues, lesbians in bondage gear, and then the communists dressed as Che Guevara. Isabella and Roberta and the rest of the Feminist Alliance had asked me if I wanted to join them in their Marilyn Monroe costume idea, and though I was unsure if I could pull it off, I was glad I'd done it. Roberta had found a billowing white dress with little shoulder straps that looked just like the dress from *The Seven Year Itch*. Luckily, Roberta was an expert makeup artist, and had plastered so much makeup on me that with my platinum blond wig, I really did look like a woman.

I lit a cigarette and smoked it dramatically on the porch. The wild animal sounds of Jorge el Jungle Boy's music started to get louder. I'd never heard that style before and was told by Paul that it was called, fittingly, 'jungle.' I wondered if Jose Rubenstein was going to show. I was anxious to see if he'd recognize me. For their part, the Harley Hutt boys had been impressed with my costume. Victor said that he wasn't liable for what he might do to me. I held that as a promise.

Three guys in jeans and T-shirts walked by, staring at me like I was a zoo animal. One of them called out, "Is this the Harley Hutt?"

I said it was. They looked surprised after hearing my voice, and then the same guy asked, "Do you have to be a faggot to get into this party?"

"Yeah, you do," I said, which wasn't true, but I couldn't think of a better response.

They walked off laughing, and when they were a block away, started yelling, "Faggot!" at the top of their lungs. I figured that even at the Harley Hutt I wasn't safe from low lifes like that, but I knew I'd have to rise above it, so I rose above it.

I thought of the reason that I was no longer the Gay and Lesbian Alliance's social coordinator. The different groups that had showed up so far were fun individually, but I had a sneaking suspicion that I'd go in and find them all standing around separately in their own private groups, glaring at each other.

I decided I'd give the porch another few minutes before I went in. Luckily, I waited just long enough because Jose Rubenstein and pals showed up, wearing tight blue jeans with their shirts tucked in. I thought they were dressed like geeks, but I still got a sharp shot of anticipation in my gut. Jose had buzzclipped his hair to about a half an inch long, making him look even more like a baby chick.

They walked up the steps nervously, as if they thought they were in the wrong place. They stood in front of me silently and then one of them hit Jose in the arm. "Oh, uh, is this the Hutt?" Jose asked. "I mean, the Harley Hutt?"

"It is," I said, and they looked visibly relieved. "Happy Birthday," I said to Jose, as he walked past. He gave me a strange look and disappeared into the party. I turned to follow, nervously unsure of what I'd find.

I got a beer from the fridge. Paul Veracruz had stocked it with hundreds of cans of the cheapest beer imaginable, so that it looked like we had absolutely no food and all we ever did was drink beer. I considered the fact that walking around a party drinking cheap beer out of a can while dressed as Marilyn Monroe might look sort of unseemly, but I figured that since I had hairy legs and a man's voice it was just as well.

I was right about the groups of people. Almost the whole party was made up of the costumed people I had invited, and they weren't mingling at all. They stood in their uniformed groups in opposite corners of the living room, except for the gay guys, who had formed a small dance floor in front of the DJ booth. I saw my friend Harry dancing up a storm, so skinny the fatigues hung off of him, but my heart sank a little. I was hoping they'd bring someone new, but it didn't look like they had.

Paul and Jean-Claude were self-appointed audio-visual artists, and they'd strung up a half-dozen video screens from the ceiling. Animated hallucinogenic movies played on them, with rolling, colorful shapes and odd kaleidoscopes racing past and spinning around in mind-bending patterns that I guessed would look cool if you were on drugs.

I wandered around the party acting as the common denominator, trying to get people to talk to each other. Victor was behind the DJ booth with Jorge el Jungle Boy. Jorge had headphones on and was clearly busy, but Victor kept talking to him, almost desperately, as if he were trying to impress him.

There was a tap on my shoulder. I turned and saw Jose Rubenstein smiling at me. Without his trademark Hawaiian shirt, he looked considerably more bland, but when his beady little black eyes squinted at me, I felt a wave of affection.

"Is that you, Augie? The guy from the Indian class?"

"It is me," I said, and I drew close to him. "But tonight I'm sort of...different."

He laughed. "I see that. You really had me fooled. I thought you were a fuckin' girl. What's with the costumes? It's not Halloween."

"Oh, we're just having fun. You know, we gotta make our own fun out here in the cornfields."

"Oh, right," he said. "I can't imagine a party like this at my fraternity house. For a minute there, I thought you were all queer."

I hadn't known he was in a frat house. But rumor had it that gay sex goes on all the time in some of those houses, so I threw caution to the cornfields and said, "Well, some of us are queer."

"Like who?" he asked, perking up.

I pointed to the gay guys in army fatigues and said, "Them."

Jose looked over and said, "All of them?"

"Well, yeah. And the dominatrixes are all lesbians."

"Wait," Jose said. "What about that guy?" He pointed to Michael Farinelli, a guy with movie star good looks who I'd been in love with freshman year. Even three years later, I felt like an 18 year old nerd when I saw him, especially since—unlike me—he was always on the arm of some fantastic new boyfriend. The sight of his bad boy face and his rippled bod in camouflage pants, a green T shirt, and dog tags, was undeniably sexy.

"Oh, yeah! He's totally gay."

"Really?" Jose said, staring at Farinelli. He was too interested. "Are you gay?"

"Yeah!" I said, a little too joyously.

"Wow, I didn't know that. That's cool. I always wondered about gay guys—" He paused to look and see if anyone was within earshot. "I mean, how do you *find* a boyfriend?"

From the way he asked it, it sounded like he was asking for himself rather than out of general curiosity. "Don't ask me. I've been single for years."

He looked disappointed, and persisted. "What about these other guys? I don't understand how people *find* boyfriends."

"I don't know. Parties, through friends. The same way anybody does, I guess."

Jose looked wholly unsatisfied. "I was just wondering. I'm not gay or anything."

It was my experience that if a guy informs you he isn't gay when no one has asked, he is probably gay. I made a mental note to keep an eye on him.

"You know, Jose, it's a special night tonight. People have told me it's your birthday, and I thought I'd give you a present."

He looked interested. "What is it?"

I stood close to him, so that I could almost smell him, and slowly sang *Happy Birthday* in my best Marilyn Monroe voice. At the end, I sang, "Happy birthday, Mr. Rubenstein," as seductively as Marilyn Monroe did when she sang to Kennedy.

When I finished, he bore a sheepish grin. He grabbed me around the shoulders as if to hug me, but one of his hands moved down too low and lightly touched my ass. I pressed up against him. "That was cool," he said. I could just feel his dick against my leg, and it was hard.

"I can do a lot of cool things," I said.

"Can you?" he asked, and then looked around again, sipping his beer. "I hope I can find out what they are."

I smiled at him and walked away. I had gotten farther with him that I thought I would, and the fact that his dick was hard made everything suddenly seem possible. I thought I might finally get lucky. But it was early in the night and I didn't want to spoil anything by rushing.

The party was filling up. The dance floor had grown to take up most of the living room, and with the lights down and the video screens churning, it seemed we'd created the hottest spot in town. Victor stood next to the DJ booth surrounded by three beautiful Indian girls. They gazed at him admiringly while he shuffled his feet, looking altogether flattered. I wondered if any of them was the hot prospect he'd talked about. It would have been depressing in any of the three instances: all of them were absolutely gorgeous. Looking at Victor's beaming face, I couldn't help but feel jealous.

Roberta and I danced on the living room table with beer cans in our hands and the crowd below us moving so furiously they were almost running in place. Strobe lights were turned on. Roberta stuck her butt in my groin and we started dirty dancing in the worst way, so that it looked like we were practically having sex. Hoots and hollers filled the room, and it seemed like we'd thrown the best party at the Hutt in years. People packed the living room and the dining room and the kitchen and the only place the runoff could go was the stairway. There, a girl with dreadlocks down to her knees was dancing, and two girls in jeans and bras were making out. I surveyed the house for signs of Jose Rubenstein and caught a glimpse of him in the dining room. He looked pretty drunk, and I was planning to stop dancing soon so I could go talk to him.

"This is a dance floor, babe. Move it or lose it." Roberta nudged me.

I realized I'd been standing totally still. The strobe lights were turned off, and the music crawled out of its subterranean, meaty zone. I needed to cool off, so I climbed down from the table.

I gently made my way through the crowd, but already saw no sign of Jose. A dull ache of despair expanded in my stomach. Automatically, I went to the fridge to got a beer. Paul Veracruz rushed into the kitchen and grabbed me by the arm. Studded skeleton rings pressed into my skin. "Augie, get out to the dance floor. It's time."

"For what?"

"The Hokey Pokey."

We raced into the living room, where everyone was standing still. Jorge el Jungle Boy picked up a microphone. "Now, I've heard this is a tradition around here, so I want everyone to give it all they've got. Form a circle, everybody, OK no pushing, and you people on the stairs have to do it, too." The crowd did what it could to form a circle, but there were too many people. Marilyn Monroes elbowed their way past Che Guevaras and the recruits became interspersed with the dominatrixes. A girl with a purple mohawk stood next to gay dreamboat Michael Farinelli, and next to him was Victor and the three girls.

The scratchy record began with a little jingle that sounded almost like it came from a commercial. "I love this song!" I said to Paul.

"You put your right foot in, you put your right foot out..."
We all dutifully followed the instructions.
"You put your right foot in and you shake it all about..."
I shook my high heeled foot like my life depended on it.
"You do the Hokey Pokey and you turn yourself around..."

As we turned around clapping to the rhythm, I watched Paul Veracruz, with his tattoos and his piercings and his weird hair, and the Marilyn Monroes, and the dominatrixes, and loved to think how this inane and boring song seemed so incredibly subversive when danced to by this odd assortment of misfits. *That's what it's all about...*

By the time we got to *You put your rear end in...* everyone was openly laughing and shaking their butts in such an obnoxious way that I wanted the song to never end. But it did, and everyone applauded, and the gay guys looked impatient for the real music to start up again.

I pushed through the door and went on the front porch. The breeze outside was warm and humid but it still dried the sweat beneath my dress. Tony Valentine sat on the railing by himself, looking glum. He'd dressed down for the party, in an old beer T shirt and grimy jeans, but still managed to look like a cherubic suburban prom king. I sat down next to him.

He put a reassuring hand against my back. "Hey, dynamite, what's happening?"

"I'm getting too old for this," I said, feeling a little weary. "It'll take me two days to recover."

"Oh, you're a baby still. I'm twenty-four," Tony said.

"Are you?"

"Yeah, this is my sixth year of school."

"Well, you're making the good times last as long as possible," I said, knowingly.

"I guess. I'm afraid of going back to Chicago," he said. "I don't wanna deal with the real world."

I knew what he meant. After years of strutting around the countryside slow as molasses, the thought of rushing off to a Loop office every day at eight in the morning made my mind go blank. I didn't know if I could do it.

"Well, I'm sure everything'll work out for you. You have a lot going for you."

"Thanks, Aug," he said, and then leaned against the post and sighed. A forlorn expression hung on his face. "Schoenberg, sometimes you just gotta stop and think, ya know? I'm worried. I'm worried about the future. I think I'm gonna go up after graduation and all I'll ever be is some stupid high school soccer coach that everyone makes fun of. I feel like I've already wasted my life."

"Oh, for God's sake. If you don't wanna be a soccer coach then don't do it."

"I'm no good at anything else. I'm not smart like a lot of these people. I'm faking it in college. I don't belong here."

"That is the most ridiculous thing. You're young, you are smart, you're terribly good-looking and girls are lining up to go out with you. Quit feeling sorry for yourself."

"You think I'm good looking?"

"Well, yeah," I said.

"Thanks," he said. "I guess gay guys think so, but not chicks. They think I'm retarded."

"Oh, no!" I said, forcefully. "They don't!"

"Auige, I never told anyone this, but I have problems with women."

"Yikes," I said. "What's wrong?"

He took a long sip of beer. "I never told anyone, cause it's really embarrassing. It's like, when I'm with a chick, everything's totally fine, and I'm totally into it, but then, right before we have sex, I lose my boner."

I wasn't expecting that. My eyes were open as wide as could be.

"I'm not gay or anything, but I just can't do it. Right before it goes in, it just goes completely soft."

"Well, you're fine during the shooting contests, right? And that's while watching women on video."

"Yeah, I can beat off and I can get blow jobs and everything's great, but I can't fuck. Augie, I've never even had my dick inside a woman."

I didn't know what to say. I couldn't think of a shred of advice to give him. He seemed to be the picture of athletic youth and suburban good living. "So it's a psychological block. Have you thought about what might be the cause?"

"I don't fuckin' know, fear of something. Fear of I don't know what. You know, there's only so long that a girl will put up with it. Has it ever happened to you?"

"Oh, yeah," I said, which was sort of a lie. It had happened once when I was nervous on a one night stand, but I had eventually gotten it up.

"What did you do?"

"Well, the thing is, if you get stressed out about it, that makes it worse. Then it becomes a vicious cycle."

His face brightened. "That's totally it! It's a vicious cycle. And then it just gets worse and worse."

"Yeah, you just have to find someone you're just totally comfortable with, and relax as much as possible, and then once you do it once, you won't be afraid anymore." It sounded pretty thin to me, but Tony was overjoyed.

"Oh, my God. You're exactly right. All I have to do is do it once, and then I'm cured!"

"Right!"

"Thank you so much!" he exclaimed and hugged me. "You totally cheered me up."

I wanted to ask him about his earlier statement that he wasn't one hundred percent heterosexual, but I didn't think his ego could handle it. Anyway, people were streaming out the door at a constant pace, and it looked like the party might be breaking up.

"You've totally helped me. By the way, what happened with Isabella at the rugby party?"

"You know what? She told me to call her but I was afraid. But now I'm gonna. Can you believe I didn't even talk to her tonight over this?"

I nodded and then guzzled the rest of my beer and went inside.

The music was still going and there were still people dancing, but the crowd had thinned. I saw Isabella and Roberta sitting on the sofa and I plopped down between them, two glittering Marilyn Monroes joined by a hairy third. "What's up, beautiful?" Isabella asked in her throaty voice.

"God, Augie," Roberta said. "This place is nuts. I can't tell who's gay and who's straight. I love it."

"I don't love it," Isabella said. "How can I tell who I'm supposed to fuck? This nineties diversity is getting on my nerves."

"Well, you could fuck yourself," Roberta said.

"Hey! So, Augie," Isabella said. "Who are you interested in?"

"I was interested in this guy Jose Rubenstein. But I think he left."

"Jose Rubenstein? That's great. Is he Hispanic or Jewish? Or both?"

"I don't know yet. But he looks Latino to me. I don't see the Jewish part. Anyway,

I found out that he's a frat boy, but I sang *Happy Birthday* to him and pressed up real close and he had a boner."

"Wow. See, you can have any guy you want," Isabella said.

"I don't know, he left. Anyway, look at my options. Victor asked me to get naked with him right after we moved in and things have been pretty flirtatious ever since, but that's all they've been. Tony's all weird and said he's not totally heterosexual. The thought of dragging Jose Rubenstein out of the closet is exhausting. I don't know what to do. The gay guys in this town all think I'm a dork."

Isabella sat up straight. "Tony might like guys? Is he bisexual?"

I realized instantly I shouldn't have told her. "No, don't say anything to anyone. He didn't say he liked guys, he said he's not one hundred percent straight. Anyway, at the rugby party he had a boner. I could tell."

"Hmmm. Do you think he'd go for me?"

I couldn't believe she asked that. Information like that usually sends women running in the other direction. "Perhaps. Anything's possible."

"It certainly is," she said, with a self-satisfied look on her face.

I couldn't decide who'd be playing the other more in that situation. Inside, I grimaced. Roberta leaned over. "Augie, what's up with your roommate? Does he have a girlfriend?"

"Which one?" I hoped she didn't mean Victor.

"The black one," she said, pronouncing black as if it had two syllables.

"I don't know. I think he's single." I knew Paul Veracruz had a girlfriend, but I was pretty sure the rest of them didn't.

"Well, hook me up," she said, rubbing her hands together. She looked like she was waiting for something.

"You mean right now?"

"Yeah, man! Time's a wastin.'"

I got up from the sofa and found Jean-Claude amidst a crowd in the kitchen. I leaned in close. "What do you think of the black Marilyn Monroe?"

He rubbed his chin. "Oh, the chick you were dancing with?" I nodded. "Well, I could see some possibilities there."

"Good!" I said, thinking how was easy that was. "Go talk to her. She wants you."

"She does?" he asked, looking almost nervous.

"Oh, yeah! She's been talking about you all night!"

"Dude, that's wild." He wandered off toward the living room.

I had hoped to spend the evening worrying about my own love life, but it was becoming clear that others were in need. I got another beer from the fridge and pressed on.

Victor stood at the DJ booth, this time alone. Jorge el Jungle Boy was still spinning records. The lights had been dimmed again.

"Victor, have you moved from that one spot all night?"

He put a barely-controlled arm around my shoulder. His eyes were so glassy and wet that through the darkness I thought I could see my reflection in them. He didn't say anything, but swayed back and forth unsteadily to the music. I thought he might fall over.

"Hello," I said softly. "Earth to Victor."

He looked at me quizzically, as if I were a complete stranger. "Augie, you are totally rad. Have I told you tonight that you're just rad."

"Well, I think you're rad, too."

"Where's you boyfriend?" he asked.

"Ah, I don't have a boyfriend."

He exhaled sharply. "Dude, get a fuckin' clue." He waved an arm around toward the dance floor. "There are so many fuckin' guys out there. And you're such a beautiful lady." He hung his head. "Get a fuckin' clue."

I looked to the dance floor to witness the supposed crowd of guys, but all I saw was my friend Harry dancing by himself, and Michael Farinelli, who was kissing his boyfriend Vince on the couch. Roberta and Jean-Claude danced together, and Tony was talking to a woman I didn't recognize. I glanced toward the kitchen and saw Paul Veracruz and his girlfriend, Sheila, sitting at the table laughing. Mark Israel was in the hallway talking to Isabella.

Victor fell against me. I did my best to pull him up to a standing position, but he was bending down to get a bottle of schnapps that was on the floor.

"Are you sure you should have any more?" I asked.

He frowned and said, "Dude," in an irritated tone. He held the bottle up in the air, as if showing it off to an audience, and then opened it and started guzzling it. Half of it ran down his shirt.

"All, right, that's it. You're going to bed."

"Fuck you," he replied, and went to drink more. He missed his mouth, and the alcohol poured onto the floor.

Jorge el Jungle Boy turned around and said, "Watch out for my fuckin' records, man." I moved Victor away from the DJ booth and tried to steer him up the stairs, but he wanted to mingle. The Indian girls walked up to him, apparently to say goodbye. All of a sudden, Victor regained his composure and started to act halfway sober. He chatted with the girls for a few minutes, and then saw them to the door.

"Was that your fan club?" I asked.

"No. Those are some friends of my cousin."

Jorge el Jungle Boy's voice came on. "All right, people, it's about that time. I hope you had a wonderful evening here at the Harley Hutt. Let's give it up for our hosts."

The small crowd that was left lethargically applauded. Victor and I stood there and smiled.

"This is it folks, the last song, so grab the one you love and hold on tight. It's a slow one."

I wanted to turn invisible. The entire crowd instantly fell into couples, with the exception of the chick with the purple mohawk, who looked around hopefully. I was about to turn around and go upstairs, but Victor held out his arms to me. Relieved, I walked into him. He reeked of liquor. I put one arm around his lower back and one around his shoulders. I let myself be led in a dance so slow and ungraceful that we inched around the floor like two intertwined, drunken sloths.

"Augie, I've got the best-looking date here."

"That's funny. So do I."

He laughed and then pressed his hands up to my boobs. "Dude, you do something to me. I don't know what it is, but it's really fucked up."

"What do I do?" I asked, pushing my thigh in between his legs, hot beneath my dress, hot outside the dress, hot beneath his hands on my back, wishing he'd look at me instead of my tits.

"Oh, I don't know. But it's freakin' me out." His hand ran down my back and then landed directly on my butt. "Dude, that is the nicest ass I've felt."

I leaned against him and closed my eyes. I wanted nothing more than to go upstairs and pull off the stupid wig and dress and take off the makeup and lay on top of his brown, hairy body with an arm around his head and a hand wrapped around his penis. I doubted the likelihood of that happening, and prayed that the song wouldn't end. With my head resting against his, I could feel the roundness of his ear, and the hot, thick blanket of his hair. My dick was swelling up. I thought it must have been showing through my dress.

The song ended and we stayed locked in our embrace. People walked past us to the door, but no one seemed to pay any attention to us. It felt like we were completely alone. "Augie," Victor said quietly. "Come upstairs with me."

I wondered then if this was it, if this was the moment when everything would cease to be complicated and sharp and full of frustration, and life would become so incredibly easy that every rotten choice I'd ever made and every shitty thing anyone had ever done to me would painlessly float away and leave my mind strong and youthful and instantly at peace.

We marched slowly up the stairs. To people in the living room, it must have looked like we were going upstairs to fuck. I wasn't so sure. On the third floor, I walked to my bedroom so I could get out of the dress, but Victor took my hand. "No, come in my room."

I let him put an arm around me and steer me toward the doorway and then he leaned in close and put his lips to my ear. His breath flew hot against my skin and he moved his hand across my ass. My toes tingled and my heart raced and just as I turned to him, desperate for him, he blurted, "If you were a girl, I'd fuck you *so* hard."

I wrenched myself away from him and walked to my bedroom. I locked the door and then ripped off the wig and the dress and the fake eyelashes and the stupid high-heeled shoes. I tried to wipe the makeup off me with the socks from inside the bra. In the mirror, my reflection was smeared and bruised. Different colors swirled around, making me look like an accident victim. Red and blue and gold and silver came together on my forehead and under my eyes. Black ran down toward my cheekbones.

Victor was in the hallway calling my name, but he had no idea what he'd just said or how cheap it made me feel. He probably thought he'd just complimented me. It wasn't me he wanted. It was the idea that someone wanted him.

12.

My friend Harry and I walked out of the meeting of the campus Gay and Lesbian Alliance. It was a gorgeous, cool night in the last week of September. I wore my old corduroy coat, which reminded me of Mikey, and had my bookbag draped across my shoulder. The weather had cooled, but the lush vegetation around the Union remained. We walked in between enormous, almost furry bushes, and past an endless garden of flowers. The meeting had been a little depressing: there was talk of a chain restaurant that had been firing people for being gay, and then there was the constant, inexplicable rift between the gay guys and the lesbians. For the time being, we had worked things out, but I wondered how long that would last.

"So are those Harley Hutt guys gay or straight?" Harry asked. Harry had looked pretty good in fatigues at the party, but for the meeting he'd retreated back to his usual awkward self: brown hair that looked solidified from too much gel, oval glasses, and overpriced designer clothes that hung off his pointy frame. "They seem straight, but they're sort of different."

"I don't know. I think they're all straight, but there's been some weird shit happening." I told him about Victor and the boxers exchange, and the shooting contest, and the slow dance. "He told me if I was a girl, he'd fuck me."

Harry looked outraged. "He said that?"

"Well, no," I replied. "He said if I was a girl, he'd fuck me *so* hard."

"Oh, God," Harry said. "That's serious."

We passed by a trickling fountain with a copper statue of a nymph in the center and walked out onto the Quad. All around, there was the smell of cut grass. The sprinklers had been turned on, and a fine mist drizzled on us.

"Augie, watch out for that kind of thing. I've had drunk straight guys hit on me and they didn't even realize they were doing it. It can really fuck you up in the head."

"What should I do?" I asked.

"Stay away from him. And whatever you do, don't fall in love with him. He's gonna flirt with you until he's convinced you want him, and then he's gonna treat you like such shit that you're gonna get hurt."

"I don't know," I said, naively. "He seems like such a nice guy."

"It's yo-yo bullshit. He'll pull you in and push you away and you're gonna end up more bitter than you are now. Consider yourself warned."

"But if there's two people who like each other, can't they, at some level, have a relationship that's mutual even if they're not the gender or sexual orientation you'd think they'd be?"

"No straight guy is gonna fuck you," Harry said. "And if he was gay, you two would've done it already."

I knew he was right. But looking around the meeting that night had made the

Harley Hutt guys seem even more attractive than they already were. Michael Farinelli was in a relationship, Harry and I were just friends, and the others were either disgusted by the mere sight of me or so meanspirited I couldn't stand to be around them. I was at a party once and I overheard a guy from the group say to someone else, "That Augie thinks he's so great." Another one responded, "I know. And did you get a load of those clothes? Hello, Salvation Army." I couldn't fathom how I was supposed to have any confidence in meeting new people at the group after hearing something like that.

Harry and I came to campustown and fought through the crowd getting out of the movie theater. We came to a small Chinese restaurant where I was meeting Victor for dinner. We hadn't talked seriously since the party and he said there was some things he had to say to me. I was apprehensive: the prospects seemed dim.

"Well," I said, motioning toward the restaurant's door.

"Have fun, sweetie," Harry said, kissing me on the cheek. He looked in through the window. Victor sat at a table by himself, reading the newspaper. He wore a pair of wire-rimmed glasses and had on a gray wool sweater. "Is that him?" he asked.

"Yeah, it is." We stood and stared at him.

"I see the problem. He's gorgeous."

"I know."

"Remember what I said. Save yourself some grief." We hugged and I pulled open the door. As I walked inside, a guy on the street said, "Those two guys were gay."

"I turned in my screenplay," I told Victor. "For my screenwriting class. It's just the first part, but the teacher's gonna let me know if it's any good or not."

"That's terrific. Will you let me read it?"

"Maybe," I said, coyly. I was actually terribly nervous about it. *Last Boat to Manchuria* had been exciting for me to write, but if the teacher told me it was awful, I thought that I'd be ruined. If I had no talent at screenwriting, I didn't know what I'd do with the rest of my life. "We'll see how it goes."

The food arrived on big steaming plates. I ordered beef with broccoli, which was the only Chinese dish I had ever eaten. I couldn't think of why I'd order anything else, when I was always so satisfied with beef with broccoli.

"How's your literature class going?" Victor asked.

"It's fantastic. I'm in love with Professor Singh. She gave me an A on the first paper, and we're going to be discussing our thesis topics for the next paper soon. I actually can't wait to write it."

"What's it gonna be about?"

"Well, we've just finished reading Kipling's *Kim*. You can never tell in that book if the kid is British or Indian or both, so I think I'm gonna write about India, and whether or not it can be defined. There's a big duality in that character, and the construction of that character relates to the problem of defining India itself."

"Cool," Victor said. "You're deep, Schoenberg." He sighed. "Yeah, India's a weird place. Very crazy."

"Have you been there?"

"Oh, yeah. Every summer, to visit relatives."

"Wow. That must have been great!"

"Well, yeah, if you like it hot and crowded and in total chaos. There's some terrible things that happen there."

"Oh, it must've been cool in some ways."

"It was. When I was a kid, I used to run around with my shirt off and get fed by so many relatives I'd get fat. And it was nice to be in a place where everyone was Indian, and I wasn't the only one."

"I'd love to go there someday," I said.

"You should," he said, and there was a glint in his eye. "Maybe you can go with me."

The thought left me dazzled. I thought a trip like that would be more romantic than a trip to Paris. 'Where's Augie Schoenberg?' people would say. 'Oh, he's in Bombay with Victor Radhakrishna.'

"So, what happened at the meeting of homosexuals?" he asked, picking at his food with chopsticks.

"Ugh. The homosexuals have been in-fighting. But I think I took care of it. Also, there's some trashy restaurant that's been firing people for being gay."

Victor looked somewhat alarmed. "That doesn't sound right. What are they firing gays for?"

"They said they don't want AIDS in the food."

Victor looked at me with narrowed eyes, as if wondering whether he'd heard me right. "Are they going to sue?"

"They can't. There's no gay rights law," I said.

"Oh, but if they were fired for no reason, I'm sure they could sue."

"No," I said. "They don't have any recourse. They just have to swallow it."

"Augie. You can't get fired for something like that. There's employment laws. There's the court system."

"Yes, but if you were fired in this town for being gay you can't take advantage of any employment law or anti-discrimination law. We're not covered. And you can't sue. You have no legal grounds. That's why there's a gay rights movement."

"Well, I realize that," he said.

"We're having a day of action in a couple weeks. We're going to surround the restaurant with a human chain. You should bring your little friends from Amnesty International."

"Oh, definitely."

We ate in silence. I wondered if Victor was mulling over gay rights or if he was preparing to tell me that regardless of what happened at the party, he only likes girls. I watched him while he expertly manipulated his chopsticks over kung pao chicken.

"Augie, there's something I've been meaning to say." He sounded serious. I raised an eyebrow. "About the party." He looked over his shoulder to see if anyone else was around. There were only two other people in the place, and they were deep in conversation. "I realize I probably offended you badly and I feel absolutely terrible about it."

"You didn't offend me."

"Yeah, I did. I said some things I regret and it definitely wasn't fair to you."

"Really, it's OK." I had been hurt by the 'If you were a girl, I'd fuck you,' line, but I didn't want him to take back the things he said. I wanted to hear him say that I was the best-looking there, and that I had the nicest ass.

"It's not OK. I mean it, Augie. I know alcohol was involved, but it's no excuse. The way things went: it wasn't right."

I said nothing. I wanted his affection so badly, but the only way I knew how to get it was through drunken flirtation, flirtation he'd regret in the morning.

"Augie, I think you're the greatest guy, and I was horrified to think I might've hurt you."

That line endeared him to me even more. I couldn't stand to think I'd be forced to give up my insane hope that he wanted me. The weather was getting colder and I didn't think I'd be able to bear another fall alone. Ignoring my better judgement and Harry's advice, I laid my cards down on the table. "Victor, look. I like you. A lot. I don't care if you're not gay, I don't care if I am, but I'm not going to sit here and pretend that what happened was all some big drunken accident. I wanted you that night." Victor looked over his shoulder again. "I wanted you so badly I almost jumped you. I think you are amazing. I think you're the most beautiful guy on the planet. I spend all day dreaming of laying on top of you. I can't think about anything else."

Victor stared at me with his big, glassy eyes. There was an endless pause.

"I only have myself to blame," he said. "I led you on."

"No, you didn't. It's a two-way street. We both wanted to do the things we did."

He looked terribly frightened. He drank some water. "Wow. Augie, you're too intense for me. I don't know what to say. I don't know what I'm supposed to say."

"Say that you like me," I said, forcefully. "Because I think you do."

"Augie, I can't..."

"Tell me you didn't want to see me naked the first time you laid eyes on me. Tell me you didn't get a boner the night of the thunderstorm. Tell me you didn't like running your hand across my ass. Tell me you haven't thought of me naked when you beat off."

"Augie, will you shut up," he said, nervously looking around. The waitress came up and put down the bill and two fortune cookies. She slowly padded away. "There's something I have to tell you."

"Tell me that you like me, Victor," I pleaded. "Cause I like you so much."

He looked at me for a long minute, almost angrily. He pulled out his wallet and put twenty dollars on the table.

"If two people like each other, then why does anything else matter?" I said, leaning forward. "Who gives a fuck about categories and identities and all that other bullshit? You told me at the party that I do something to you. What's that something if it's not attraction?"

He sniffed. "I don't know what it is. Fuck, Schoenberg. I've never been through anything like this."

"Say it."

"Look, we've all been conscripted. We're all playing roles. None of us are free agents." His eyes surveyed me up and down. He threw his hands in his lap. "All right," he said, as if giving up. "I like you."

Relief surged through my veins. I smiled so hard I had to tell myself to stop. We stood up and as we walked out, Victor pushed me along by the shoulder, as if I was an unruly child. "Let's get the fuck out of here. I need a drink. And you're buying me one."

I drank four blue margaritas at the bar, and with the taste of salt still on my lips, I said to Victor, "When was your first wet dream?"

He looked at me with appropriately sleepy eyes: the bar was sort of sleepy that night—low jazz music, few people, blue neon lights.

"I don't think I ever had one. I've had sex dreams, but I always woke up dry."

I lazily imagined Victor's dry penis in a pair of underwear. "Who was your last sex dream about?"

He didn't smile, but pursed his lips trying not to, and wouldn't look at me.

"Come on, who?"

"Who was yours about?" he asked.

"No fair. I asked first."

He sighed and said, "It doesn't mean anything, but I did have a dream about you a week or so ago. After the party."

"And what transpired in this dream?"

He still looked awfully embarrassed. I looked straight at him, trying to force his eyes on mine.

"We were having sex!"

"Was it great?"

He took my margarita and drank the rest of it in one swallow. "Augie, man, you have no idea."

Arundhati Singh was lecturing about images of light and dark, about multiple constructions of characters, and how instability is reinforced by other instabilities. The sun poured in the side window of the room and we were drenched in brightness. I had so many papers in front of me and so much scribbling in my notebook and so many books open on my desk that it seemed like I should have been confused. But I was transfixed. We had handed in our ideas for our second paper and she made a list of the thesis statements and then spent the period adding on to them, expanding them, taking them to a higher level. The level of thought that was flying around the room had me enraptured, and for a few brief moments all the ideas came together so clearly, so naturally, that I thought I finally saw how ideas are formed, or at least how they form us.

"Explore the importance of the construction of identity," she said. "Why is that important? How does the setting reinforce this as a source of strength?"

I furiously jotted down every word she said. I wrote in between lines of text, blue scribbling against black type. I wrote in the margins. I wrote inside books.

"How do the characters define the place? Problematize the relationships to intervene so that knowing and representation are questioned."

Arundhati Singh had started out small, but the lecture had grown from a series of suggestions for paper topics into a soaring intellectual virtuoso performance, where she breathlessly worked her way into a certain zone that took flight and danced on top of insights so lofty they left my mind reeling. I never felt so inspired.

I'd been fed by the events of the previous night in Victor's bedroom.

"The darkness of the room undermines the light which contains the opposite...the need to establish stable standards...participating in a system that orders the world."

The subject matter can't be separated from the way you think about it. Augie, Victor said. I don't know what you're asking me to do. *How the events construct the character.* Just be yourself, I said. You don't have to do anything. *Significance of the ambivalence in the power play.* I don't know what to do, he said. I don't know what I'm supposed to do. *Paraxis—side by side juxtaposition. The first war of resistance.* Follow me, I said. Follow me and we'll end up in the right place. *The narrator vs. different voices vs. what he should be saying.* I've never done anything like this, he said, his lips shaking. Shhh, I said, my lips just released from the tip of his nipple. *The body becomes a site of negotiation.* My cheek against his cheek, my lips around his earlobe.

Two kinds of time/parallel, simultaneously in the past and in the present. Heavy breathing, shedding clothes, lips on lips. *Forming a link, hospitality.* Man against man, pectoral against pectoral, penis against penis. You are beautiful, I said. *Not seeing things clearly. The ideological burdens of the time.* I've dreamed about you, he said. More than I told you. *The collapse of the opposition. Standards of masculinity. Destroying the hierarchy.* Hold on to me, I said, grasping him, hold on to me harder. *Free will vs. determination.* I've got you, he said.

Yearning toward oneness. I'm scared, he said. I'm scared of what this means. *Crisis of belief.* Don't talk, I said. Mouth on mouth, hands around genitals, movement, fantasies, pictures floating through heads. *The capacity to connect.* The strength of the hard sex in my mouth, the taste of it, the arrogant potential of it. Down my throat, the hardness, the softness. *Providing resources for others. Accumulation of meaning.* Moans and thrusts and grasping, the hotness of the room, the sweat-soaked hair, the smell of night. *The body as a place for a type of ownership.* Enough, he said. I wanna see you. Face to face, side by side, the same but different, and reaching down deeply, so far down, to bring up the unbearable moment, the moment of no reality. *Humans have evolved. People become texts.* Faster, he said. Touch my balls. *The yearning for form and union can result in symmetry.* The feeling of being touched inside on the outside, the rough palm wrapped around the arcing penis, the rhythm, the friction, the culmination of desire. Oh yeah, he said. I'm coming, I'm coming. *Everything exists, nothing has value. The description is like a dream.* Are you coming, Augie? Are you? I said I'm coming, don't wait for me. I'm coming. *Reciprocity, the act of acting and being acted on.* Oh, God, Jesus Christ. *Purity vs. interconnectedness.* The warm fluid on top of my body. The way he lays in it on top of me. *No effort to save myself.* The raw intimacy, the closeness.

Victor sat on the windowsill naked, dark patches interspersed with light sections, staring at the moon. There's an eclipse tonight, he said. I rose, white as a phantom. I kneeled down before him and rested my chin against his thigh. *Where does he have the power and what does he do.* I don't see it, I said. Come here, he said. I stood and he sat me down on top of his legs. I leaned far back against his chest, he wrapped his arms around me and I placed my arms over his. *No linear break between them.* There, he said. The moon is disappearing. The bluish light in the room slowly crept sideways, inching along toward Victor and me, expiring, dividing the room in half, becoming doused.

It's amazing, I said. The night will be totally black. We won't be able to see each other. The crescent moon shrunk at a slow, practically unnoticeable pace. Only a sliver remained. I can see you, he said. Even in the dark. *The lightness in the room undermines the darkness in the heart.* I don't want to move, I said. I wanna stay like this. Will you go away with me, Augie? he asked. To where, I said. Anywhere, he said. A far away place. If we were sixteen, I said. Not twenty-two. *The binaries are not fixed.* There's things you don't know, he said. About me. *The temple, the Hindus, the rainy season.* You can tell me anything, I said. *Western time is linear, Eastern time is circular.* Only a tiny slip of white hung from the sky. I watched carefully, I was afraid to miss it, and in an instant the entire sky turned black. The stars intensified almost at once, filling in the blackness with a mad array of technicolor. My eyes reacted to the absence of light and the infusion of color with a quick contraction of the pupil. Did you see it, I said. Did you see it disappear? I didn't notice, he said. I was watching you watch it.

13.

I walked to the shower with the vague, uneasy feeling that I had done something wrong. Victor and I hadn't spoken in two days. When we woke up the morning after the eclipse, he pretended to go back to sleep and I got up and left. I didn't know what to say to him. The night in his bedroom seemed like a hallucination, but with my lips chapped, my face raw, and the musk of him still on me the next morning, I knew it'd been real. There was conflict about it in my head: for all the dreamy, geo-political orgasms I'd had, lost in the receding light from the moon, Victor had been at times ambivalent with his body language, lying back with his eyes closed while I stared at him, hoping for a clearer signal that this drunken mishmash of love was more than an experiment. I wanted a reality check that morning, or some sort of reassurance, and I hadn't gotten it.

I padded into the bathroom and found Tony and Mark standing around nude, talking to each other. Mark had his back to me and was stretching: his arms reached up and almost touched the ceiling, his huge back arched way in, and his hairy butt and legs effortlessly held the rest of him up. I'd felt so masculine in bed with Victor, wrapped up in sweaty embraces with the lights out and my dick hard, but the sight of Mark Israel's body put mine to shame.

Tony stood in the background, and at the sight of me he wrapped a towel around himself. Israel pulled his arms down and turned around and shot me a look of contempt. He moved to the side and fiddled around with his clothes on the bench, with an angry, disgusted look on his face. I'd seen that look before. In the locker room in high school I'd been looking at a guy who'd been standing around naked talking to people. He caught me peeking, and then put on his underwear. On the way out, when I walked past him toward the exit, he turned his head sideways and I saw that look. It said, "Don't look at me, you fuckin' faggot, or I'll kick your fuckin' ass."

I never thought I'd see that at the Harley Hutt.

I got in the shower, feeling meek and unwanted. I considered saying, "What's up?" but thought it was fairly clear that wasn't called for. Tony passed by on his way out and said, "Later," to Mark and they touched fists.

"So, Schoenberg," Mark said. "You're not religious, are you." It wasn't a question.

Startled, I said, "No, not really."

"Yeah, I noticed you didn't do anything for Yom Kippur. What do your parents think about that?"

"Not much," I said. "They're not religious either."

He said something I didn't catch, but I thought it sounded like, "Figures."

"We even had a Christmas Tree," I said, which usually got a laugh out of people. I always said to people, 'Well, what did you expect me to have, a Hanukkah bush?'"

Israel didn't find it funny.

"Are you religious?" I asked.

"Apparently more than you are," he said, in a snotty voice. He got dressed and then turned to face me. I didn't like it; the way he glared at me.

"So what do your parents think about having a faggot in the family?" he asked, but it wasn't like we usually used 'faggot,' it wasn't like Paul Veracruz saying, 'Dude, we like faggots." It was cruel, and he knew I'd be caught off-guard.

"They're happy about it. They said they love me no matter what flavor I come in." My parents had said no such thing, but I needed to salvage my pride in some way.

He sniffed and walked away.

I got dressed and then got ready to go to class. On the way downstairs, I stopped on the second floor landing, and heard Tony and Mark talking in their bedroom. I stood as still as I could and leaned against the wall, so that none of the floorboards would creak. I held my breath. "Fuckin' Schoenberg," Mark said. "What a flake."

"I can't believe that fucking homo," Tony said. "That's the last time I ever talk to him. Can you believe that shit?"

"It's simple: all that faggots like him wanna do is fuck us. That's their only goal. You should see that fuckin' fruitcake staring at me in the shower. I don't even wanna go in there anymore."

"I can't believe what he did," Tony said. "It's like he's a nine year old girl."

"That's what you get," Mark said. "You can't trust them. They don't know how to act. Fucking Schoenberg."

"That guy has to go," Tony said, with finality.

They talked in loud voices and had their door open. They knew I was home, and they didn't care if I heard. I had no idea what I'd done.

I went to my film class. I sat alone in the auditorium, eating a bag a fried potato skins and drinking a can of orange pop. I didn't want to be alone, but I didn't know anyone else in the class. We watched *Rear Window*. It was the first time I'd seen it, and I thought it was great. I tried to get lost in the film and conjure up the dreamy feelings I'd had the night with Victor, but it wasn't working. I wanted to imagine that the movie could take place in the Harley Hutt, and I could sit in my bedroom with binoculars, looking out at the dorms and the frat houses and witness all sorts of scandalous incidents behind the distant windows. But I knew that wasn't possible. All we had a view of was trees. I didn't even know if Victor would want to talk to me again. I thought he might tell me it was all a mistake and that I should fuck off.

After the film, I walked out into the sunlight. I was feeling progressively more low, but I felt I should be happy. I got what I wanted. But it was a foolhardy move. It was stupid. I couldn't trust Victor. He may very well tell me that the night was an interesting experiment, but a failed one. He may very well tell me he still wished I was a girl.

I wanted to go home, but the thought of running into Tony or Mark filled me with dread. I couldn't fathom why Mark Israel would be upset with me. I barely knew him. And I really couldn't understand Tony. After all, I had listened to his story about his penis and had given him supportive advice. Was this how he showed he appreciated it? Fear ripped through my head. I thought Tony might have thought that I told people he was bisexual, thereby ruining his chances with women. But there was no chance of that. I hadn't told anyone.

Except Isabella. She wouldn't have. There was no way that she could have. It goes without saying that you don't repeat that sort of thing, at least to the person it's about. But she must have.

I trudged along, feeling like I had no place to go. I needed to talk to a friend. I couldn't call Harry. He told me not to get involved with Victor in the first place. Isabella was out; it was anybody's guess what had happened at the party after Victor and I went upstairs. I supposed I could go over and see what the lesbian softball team was up to, but they weren't usually so interested in handing out advice about complicated relationships with men.

That left Roberta. I knew I could trust her. I headed to the theater building.

Roberta stood in the hallway dressed in a black and white maid's uniform. It looked as demeaning as it possibly could have, and when she saw me, she looked for an instant like she hoped there was a chance I hadn't seen her, so she could get out of sight.

"Augie!" she called, "you never come around here. What gives?"

"I wanted to talk to you," I said, kissing her. "What the hell are you wearing?"

"I know," she said, looking down at her costume. "They keep casting me as the maid."

"I don't understand. You've played lead roles for years."

"Well, that was when I was doing the studio shit and the workshop stuff. I graduated to the mainstage productions, and this is what happened. I'm just paying my dues," she said, and then assumed a boisterous, assertive attitude. "If they keep doing this, I'm filing a lawsuit, *and* I'm calling the NAACP, and they can kiss my black ass."

I laughed. "Call Jesse Jackson," I said.

"OK?!"

"Call Oprah Winfrey."

"OK?!"

A man in a pink blazer and a yellow bow-tie came out of a door holding a clipboard. "Excuse me maid number three. Let's go."

"Oh, I gotta run," she said, and kissed me on the cheek. "Call me later."

"Wait, what happened with Jean-Claude Jolie?"

Her face brightened, and a saw a glimpse of the Roberta I knew. "Oh, Augie, all I have to say is, have you seen the shape of his head?"

"Which one?" I asked. She threw her head back and laughed.

"I know, I know, both of his heads are amazing. But I'll tell you a secret."

I leaned in close. She whispered, "I think he's marriage material."

"Oh my God! Can you tell already?"

"Fuck yeah," she said. "I'm a woman."

Isabella opened the chipped door to Trailer Trash. She looked surprised to see me. "You never stop by," she said, her husky voice even more gravely than usual. "To what do I owe the pleasure?"

"Let's sit," I said. I'd decided that I needed to talk to her after all. I wasn't good at surreptitious visits to friends, but I wanted to feel her out.

The living room looked like it'd been ransacked. The coffee table held countless empty beer bottles and the ashtrays were overflowing with white and gray cigarette butts. Newspapers and clothes were strewn around the floor. The place had a terrible, moldy smell. Isabella lived with three other girls, and from what I'd been hearing, they were having people over every single night and drinking till dawn.

We sat on the couch. Isabella looked nervous, but I didn't think it was because of me. She pulled at strands of her hair and shook her leg. I figured she was horribly hung-over.

"I was just wondering if you had a good time at the Harley Hutt party."

"Oh, yeah," she said. Her voice held not a hint of weakness. "It was a good time, mainly. The DJ was amazing. Where'd you find him?"

"At the Dong Pipe. He's friends with Ted."

"How is Ted?" she asked. "I miss him so much."

"I know, me too. I haven't talked to him since forever. Jean-Claude told me he doesn't have a phone yet. It's anybody's guess, but he's probably having the time of his life."

"Oh, I'm sure," she said.

"So, is anything new? Any hot hook-ups?"

"No," she said, defensively. "Why would you ask?"

"Isabella! I'm just making conversation!"

"Well, apparently everyone on campus thinks I'm the world's biggest drunken whore," she said. "I suppose there's been rumors flying around."

"You can fuck whoever you want. I don't care. And I haven't heard any rumors."

"Well, it's not that simple. Guys can fuck around. But not girls."

Isabella was famous for her sexual exploits and her defensiveness was a little surprising. "Spare me the third-grade level feminism," I said. "Sexual aggressiveness is something you've always been proud of. You've always said that you'll do whatever or whoever you want."

She lit a cigarette. She was eyeing the empty beer bottles. I wondered whether she wanted to clean them up or drink the remains. "My past has caught up with me. I'm a laughingstock at parties. Fun, huh?"

"What happened?"

"I don't really wanna talk about it." She rose and went to the kitchen. She pulled two cans of beer from the fridge and sat back down. She gave one to me. "Breakfast of champions," she said, with a weak smile.

I held the can but didn't open it. "Are you gonna tell me what happened or not? I know you want to."

"Oh, Augie Schoenberg, knows all, sees all, and definitely tells all. There's no mysteries surrounding you, boy."

"Fuck you. What's up your ass?"

She drank a long swig of beer. "All right, all right. I'm sorry. I'm just pissed off. And I'm hung-over again and I'm mad at myself. I'm also flunking out of school. But enough about me. Look, I'm not really happy with the way things went down at your little party. I'm sure you had a fabulous time drooling over that Indian guy all night, but the festivities weren't so fun for everyone."

"What are you talking about?" I racked my brain to see if I could remember anything shitty happening to her, but I came up with nothing.

"Well, I was talking to your lovely roommate Mark Israel, perfect gentleman that he is, and, he told me that he, and I quote, 'wouldn't stick my dick in you if you were the last bitch at this party.' I said, 'What the fuck are you talking about?' And he said, 'Schoenberg told me. You fuck everybody.'"

I tried to remember myself saying something like that, but I didn't remember it. I pictured myself as Marilyn Monroe saying it. I still didn't remember anything like that.

"I've never said that. Not even when I was drunk."

"Well, whatever. Look, what's done is done. I can't blame you. I'd probably say that about me, too."

"Honestly, though," I said. "I really never said that."

"I don't give a shit. Mark Israel isn't the only guy on campus who thinks it. My reputation precedes me, I guess."

"He made it up. He has something against me, and I don't know what it is right now, but I'm going to find out."

"Whatever," she said, sounding more tired than mean.

I got up to leave. "By the way, did you say anything else to Mark?"

"Like what?"

"I don't know. Did you guys get into a fight or anything?"

"Well, after he called me a whore, he asked me if I wanted to fuck Tony so he could watch."

"What?"

"That's what he said. Where'd you guys find this guy? He's a winner." She stubbed out her cigarette with three harsh stabs to the ashtray.

"But Isabella," I said. "What did you say back?"

She sat silent, apparently thinking. "I don't know. Something bitchy. Oh, wait. I told him I wouldn't fuck a bisexual pig like Valentine if he paid me."

"You couldn't have. How could you say that?"

"Augie, he had just insulted me. What was I supposed to say? Anyway, I didn't say it to Tony."

"But they share a room. They're like best friends. Tony told me that in complete confidence."

"Then maybe his friend shouldn't act like such an asshole."

I was right. I knew she had said something. Tony should have never told me about his supposed bisexuality, or his faulty penis. I couldn't keep a secret to save my life. But it was unfair; it was unfair of Tony to burden me with some bullshit secret like that. It meant I'd have to lie if I was asked about it. It was unfair of Isabella to repeat it, even after being insulted.

I was about to leave without saying goodbye and Isabella said, "So, Augie, any hot hook-ups lately?"

I glared at her.

"I was just making conversation."

I walked past the bar and peeked in the window. Jean-Claude was working and Paul Veracruz sat at the bar. I pushed open the door, glad to find them there. I thought they could tell me how to contact Ted Demetropoulos. After hearing Tony and Mark, I needed some advice. Ted was gay and he'd lived with all of them and as far as I knew, there'd never been any problems.

"Well, look what the cat dragged in," Jean-Claude said, tossing around a white rag. Paul, in his ever-present overalls, patted the barstool next to him. No one else was in the place. "Get over here, Schoenberg. What do you want to drink?"

I plopped down on the stool and said, "Barkeep, I'll have a gin and tonic, please. Forget the tonic."

"Ooh, rough day, Schoenberg?" Paul asked, a shiny steel stud in the center of his tongue.

Jean-Claude poured the glass of gin and put it down in front of me. "It's on the house," he said.

"No, not really," I said to Paul. "I'm just stressed out."

He shook my shoulder a little. "Augie, it's your last year here. Enjoy yourself. You're almost done."

"Yeah, yeah. I know."

Jean-Claude leaned on the bar and smiled at me, his Asian eyes curling upward. "So, you were out late the other night with Victor. What'd you guys do?"

Paul let out a sly little cackle.

"Dinner, dancing?" Jean-Claude asked. "Back seat of the convertible?"

"We had dinner, yes, at Madame Chow's, and then we came here for drinks and then we went home."

Paul said, "Jean-Claude, was it me, or was there a strange rocking and bumping noise coming from Victor's bedroom all night long?"

"You know, Paul, I seem to recall that, too. It was an odd noise, something like the squeaking of a large mouse."

"No," Paul said. "It was more like the creaking of a door."

"Wait, I've got it. It was like the thumping of a bed on top of which two people were fucking!"

"You guys, stop it. Nobody fucked anybody last night." I wasn't technically lying. There had been no penetration.

"You could've fooled us," Jean-Claude said. "I didn't think Victor was into guys, but I guess you changed him."

Paul laughed. "I think it's adorable." He held up his hands as if pitching a newspaper headline to an editor. "'Straight guy abandons lifestyle in favor of tryst with gay coed.'"

"Stop it. You guys, nothing happened. I like him, but he wouldn't go for it." I might've been dumb enough to let Tony's secret slip out when I was drunk at the party, but I was smart enough to know that if people found out about Victor and me, Victor would blame me for it.

"We're just teasing you, Augie," Jean-Claude said. "Don't get upset."

"Really. Nothing happened at all. The only action was in my dreams."

Paul leaned back, conciliatory. "Ah, we're just trying to get your goat. We've noticed that Victor gets a little starry-eyed when you're around." He looked at Jean-Claude and they smiled at each other.

"Oh, only a little bit," Jean-Claude added. "You know, Augie, I saw this morning that Victor has a lifesized poster of you up in his bedroom."

"And the way he talks about you," Paul said, sitting straight up on the stool. "'Oh, Paul, that Augie is so intelligent, I just love talking to him. He really stimulates me.'"

"Shut up," I whined, punching Paul in the arm.

Jean-Claude imitated Victor further: "'And he has the coolest friends. I have never had such a great party before. Isn't he the coolest?'"

"Come on. Enough bullshit." Inwardly, though, I was eating it up. I very much hoped Victor had said those things. "Victor and I are good friends. I like him, too."

"Yeah, I like him three," Paul said. "If I was a gay guy, I'd fuck him."

"Stop, please."

"Oh, OK. Bartender, bring this young man another drink. I'm buying."

Jean-Claude went to get the bottle. "You know, Paul," I said. "Do you have any idea how to get ahold of Ted? I really need to talk to him."

Paul played with his eyebrow ring. "I don't know, man, that's a tough one. Ted doesn't have a phone up there yet."

"Do you know his address?"

He shook his head. "Hey, Jean, do you know how to contact Teddy? Augie needs to know."

Jean-Claude walked over to us with the gin and poured me a glass. He thought for a minute and then said, "You definitely can't call him. I know he lives in Edgewater, but I don't remember exactly where. God. I think you can find him at the Dong Pipe on Saturdays. Jorge el Jungle Boy said he was gonna start DJing there."

I thought I'd go up the next weekend. I really hoped Ted could shed some light on the situation in the house. He knew them all so much better than I did.

The little bit of gin got me thinking. "Isn't it weird? That you can know someone so well, but you're really only one step away from losing track of them?"

"Yeah, that's fucked up," Paul said. "But you'll find him. You might ask Victor. I think Ted is roommates with Victor's cousin."

"Also, do you guys wanna go to the day of action at the restaurant? We're gonna make a human chain."

"Oh, the anti-gay place. Yeah, I'll go," Paul said.

"Will the lesbian softball team be there?" Jean-Claude asked. "Those chicks were intense."

Paul agreed. "They were. At the party, one of them asked if she could string me up by my toes naked and beat me with a cane. I said hell yeah, but then she said, 'Oh well I don't think my girlfriend would approve,' and then walked away."

"They were good-lookin', too," Jean-Claude said. "In an athletic sort of way."

"Yeah, I'm sure they'll be there, unless there's a game, that is. But remember, this is for civil rights, not for ogling lesbians. You've got *Visit to the Doctor's* for that."

"Oh, we know," Jean-Claude said.

I went back to the Hutt and found the first floor empty. A pang of nervousness quivered in my stomach. I was petrified of running into Mark Israel or Tony. I was frightened to see Victor, and face the consequences of our night together. I glumly walked up the steps to the second floor and saw that Tony and Mark's bedroom door was closed. Behind it, I could hear the tinny blare of a TV. I went to the third floor. Victor had his door closed. I knew what that meant: don't come in. No one had ever had their doors closed if they weren't sleeping.

I went to my bed and lay down. I wanted to ask Victor if he could tell me how to get in touch with Ted. But I also wanted him to come into my room and tell me that he meant every word he had said that night: that he liked me, that he wanted me badly, that he wanted to run away with me. I was horrified to think he only said those things because he'd been drinking.

I went to the kitchen and heated up a frozen dinner. The sight of the lone plastic tray with the meager meal for one got me terribly depressed, and I didn't have the heart to eat much. The Hutt felt so eerily quiet that I felt like I was home alone. There were always people in the living room, and here it was, not two months after I moved in, and everything seemed divided and ruined.

14.

The night was cold and full of gusts of brutal wind. October was rolling in. An empty lot on campus had been turned into a makeshift pumpkin patch, the orange globes lighted by lights strung up from ropes around the fence. I walked as quickly as I could, my hands stuffed in my pockets, and when I got to the Hutt I surveyed it from the outside. No lights were on, not even the porch light.

Another day had passed with Victor's door closed and a forlorn, helpless feeling weighing down my stomach and my spirits. It was sad to say, but my self-esteem was so fragile that the closed bedroom door seemed as brutal as a physical attack. I thought he may as well have punched me in the face.

To save myself, I'd spent the afternoon and the night at the library, poring over the Emily Dickinson book. I couldn't bear to read anything from Arundhati Singh's class: the stories about Indians and their relationships left me with a constant, cinematic vision of Victor that torturously hung in front of my eyes as if projected on a moving screen.

I made my way to the third floor and crept across the dark hallway in the shadows, covertly and noiselessly. When I came to Victor's door, it was open. I peered inside the room. It was dark and completely empty. I inched across the hall and went into my room. I put my bag on the floor and heard the soft sound of a snore. I looked through the darkness and saw Victor sleeping on my bed in boxer shorts. He was curled up in the fetal position and his mouth hung wide open. It was an adorable sight, but I didn't know what it meant.

I thought maybe I should strip off my clothes and lay down next to him. I thought maybe I should wake him up so we could talk.

I took off my jacket and stood looking over the bed. I finally decided to take off my clothes and lie down. The thought of sleeping with his warm buns against my crotch was inviting enough, and I imagined I could put my arm around him and bury my nose in his hair.

It didn't work out that way.

I took off all my clothes and then sat down on the edge of the bed. Victor was taking up more room than I thought he would. I tried to lie down, but I could barely fit on the edge before he would groan and roll over and push me so close to the side I had to put my hand on the floor for balance. I attempted to push him over, but it was harder than pushing a car, there were no wheels on him, he was all dead weight. I crawled over to the other side of him, but he shot his leg out and kicked me and I fell off the bed.

I thought there must be some way to do this.

I tried to get on the bed again, but it was no use. He had completely overtaken it. His limbs flailed out in every direction I tried to go. His snore sounded self-satisfied and arrogant. The heat he gave off was oppressive. I decided to beat him at his own game and I strode into the hallway and then into his bedroom and lay down in his bed.

The wind shook the windows. It took forever for me to fall asleep, but eventually I drifted off, I don't know when.

Victor's arm was around my back. He was almost on top of me. I could smell his breath. It was still dark out, and the wind sounded like it had gotten stronger. Piercing whistles came through the panes of glass. I turned over onto my back and looked at him. He breathed in so slowly that it was almost impossible to tell when he was inhaling and when he was exhaling. He'd taken off the boxers. For the second time, we lay against each other completely naked. A wave of relief washed over me. He still liked me.

He grunted a little and began to talk in his sleep, in unintelligible rambling sentences. He exclaimed what I thought was the word No! over and over again, and I shook him a little. He looked at me with black, barely opened eyes. You were having a bad dream, I said. It was just a nightmare. He rested his head against my chest and exhaled loudly. Augie, he said. You weren't in your bed. You weren't in yours, I said. He kissed me on the nipple, gently, like you'd kiss a newborn baby. I missed you today, he said. Where'd you go? Why was your door closed, I said. I wanted to talk to you so bad. I know you did, he said, I just had to think for a while. I'm not very good at it, not like you. I ran my fingers through his hair, it was heavy and almost damp against my skin, I pulled some of it back and looked at his birthmark, white and practically glowing in the darkness. I love your birthmark, I said, running my finger over it. It's not like anything I've ever seen. It's so incredibly white. I touched it again, and he flinched. What, I said. What happened? That's not a birthmark, he said. That's not what it is at all.

I sat up, alertly. What is it? Is something wrong? Augie, he said, I'm scared of the future. I don't know what's gonna happen, but it isn't good. No, I know what's gonna happen. I know exactly what. I put my hands around his head and said What on earth is it? and he said Augie I'm losing my pigmentation. It's disappearing from my skin.

I knew what that meant. Vitiligo. I'd seen someone with it once, half the face brown, half the face white, in a cruel trick of nature. I held him close to me. There isn't anything they can do? I asked him. No, he said, there isn't. I don't know when it'll happen, but eventually everyone will look away when they see me. It's gonna be ugly and I'm scared to death. I'll never think you're ugly, Victor, I said, stretching out as long as I could to feel every inch of him next to me. I'll think you're as beautiful as ever. That's sweet, he said. But I know you'll find me disgusting, like everyone else with eyes. I'll go blind for you, I said, I'll cut out my eyes. I'd cut off my skin for you Augie, he said, but I'm afraid you wouldn't like what's inside.

It's a brutal night, I said. Tomorrow the wind'll die down and everything won't seem so bad. I wish that was true, he said. I wish tomorrow wouldn't be another step closer toward the inevitable. You're gonna hate me. You're gonna hate my guts next year. Why would I hate you, I asked. You will, he said. You're gonna wish I was never born.

Not knowing what to do or say, I took his genitals in my hand and before I could move any closer to him he was hard, and in an instant I straddled him, and while the wind beat the windows with a furious rancor, I watched him ease a condom over his dick, and when I leaned back against his raised thighs, he was inside of me.

The next morning, things did seem better. Victor was in higher spirits and I decided to try to forget about Israel and Valentine. I had a better deal going with Victor anyhow, and the two of them seemed, for the moment, insignificant. Even so, when Victor left the room to take a shower, I followed him as though I needed a protector.

Later, I was about to leave for class and I stopped in his bedroom. He was gathering books from around the floor and putting them in his backpack. I sat on his bed. I watched him for a moment with tremendous interest. Every strand of hair on his head intrigued me. Every slight facial expression sent my mind wondering what was happening in his mind.

"What are you up to? You have a devilish look on you face," he said.

"Nothing, nothing. I'm just here."

"Well, then, you're exactly where you're supposed to be," he said, in a sage tone of voice. There was a wise feeling in the room, maybe from the books, or from him, the look on his face.

"You're not gay, are you," I said, not as a question, but as a passing observation.

He looked at me like he was disappointed. "No," he said, quietly. "I am not. Can you tell?"

I wasn't quite as sure as I would've liked: the sex the night before had been slow and hesitating, but that could have been tiredness or it could have been ambivalence or it could have been ineptitude. "Sort of. I have paranoid visions that while we're having sex, you're dreaming of girls, hoping you'll stay hard."

Victor shrugged and said, "Maybe so."

"I was just wondering. It's sort of important for me to know. Can I ask why we're doing this, then?"

Victor sighed and looked around at things on the floor, as if they'd give him guidance. Rectangles of sunlight decorated the carpet. "I don't know what we're doing, Augie. You asked if I liked you, or rather, you ordered me to tell you that I liked you, which I did. I thought that was what was important."

"Oh, it is, I guess. I'm just going with the flow."

He stood up and said, "Come here." He held out his arms to me and I walked over to him. The weather was getting colder, and our clothes were getting thicker. He was wrapped up inside of wooly layers, and I pressed against him with my torso, trying to feel him inside of them. "You," he said, and then stopped. I imagined he was looking out his door to see if anyone was around. "You made me feel like the most attractive guy in town. No, not that. The planet. And that's a new one for me."

I kissed him and then pulled away. "Listen, do you have any idea how to get a hold of Ted? I'm going to Chicago this weekend and I need to talk to him."

Victor picked up his bag. "Do you need to ask him for insights about me? I probably know him least well of anyone in the house."

"No, no, but there's something else going on that I'm concerned about. It's not you. I can go to the Dong Pipe, but I'd rather get in touch with him before I go up there. Jean-Claude said he might live with your cousin?"

Victor started rifling through his desk. "He does, my cousin Jay. They have a place on Kenmore, and they finally got a phone. I have the number somewhere." He pulled out a scrap of blue paper and then wrote the number on a post-it note and handed it to me. "No gossiping about me."

"I won't, I just need a break from this town for a few days."

He squinted at me, as if wondering whether that was a backhanded form of rejection. "It just dawned on me, though, I will miss you this weekend. I think I'm getting used to sleeping with you next to me."

"That's terribly sweet. Next week, though, we have to talk. There's something bad going on in the house, but I don't want to get into it right now."

Victor looked away and glanced out the window. "That doesn't sound good. Whatever it is, I wanna know about it. Also, there's something I have to tell you, and it's really very important."

"That doesn't sound good either." I didn't want to be nervous all weekend. I dreaded to think what the mystery revelation might be. Victor's garbage can was right in my line of vision and it reminded me of the conversation we had in August, where he'd crushed a can of beer and thrown it in the garbage right after I asked him if he had any hot prospects. He'd said that he did, and at the time I hoped that this prospect was someone unattainable and really only a fantasy of his, but I was getting the feeling that there were going to be some harsh realities setting in soon. Seeing him at his desk in his wool sweater, though, I knew that I wanted him all to myself, and I was willing to fight for the privilege.

"On the bright side," Victor said. "I forgot to tell you: PJ Harvey is playing in Chicago in December. Do you wanna go with me?"

"Jesus Christ, of course I do! Do you have tickets?"

"I'll buy them this weekend. Just for the two of us. Have fun on your trip."

I walked over and kissed him on the cheek. He hugged me again, and he told me to be careful and watch out for muggers. I walked out of the room, grinning stupidly, and floated down the stairs. The thought of PJ Harvey live with Victor at my side was a stupefying prospect. I'd never seen a PJ Harvey concert, and I'd never been to a concert with anyone I loved before. I realized a second too late that I'd admitted to myself that I loved him. I was jumping into murky waters, but for some reason, I wasn't scared.

Book Two

And then a Plank in reason, broke,
And I dropped down, and down—
And hit a World, at every plunge,
And finished knowing—then—

       -Emily Dickinson

15.

We stood in the living room of the duplex in Evanston. "Look at that coat!" my mother said. "How much did that cost?"

I looked down at my beloved thrift-store find and said, "Four dollars."

"Four dollars!" My mother stood in sunglasses holding a Bloomingdale's shopping bag. Twenty-five years in Chicago and she was still a New Yorker. "Four dollars! I don't even have lipstick that cost four dollars. And that shirt. How much did you pay for that shirt?"

My arms shifted around inside the polyester. "A dollar."

"What is it made out of, plastic? What decade are you living in?"

My father looked at us sternly, a pipe hanging out of his mouth, resting on his beard. "He's expressing his individuality. If the boy wants to wear thrift store clothes, then he will."

"But I don't understand," my mother said. "Why don't you let me take you to Bloomingdale's? They have nice clothes there, by good designers. I mean, we're not rich, but we're not paupers either."

"August does not care for Bloomingdale's," my father said. "He's a Chicagoan. He likes Marshall Field's."

My mother scoffed. "Marshall Field's doesn't have old clothes. They have nice, quality clothes. What's happening at your college? Are all of the students on pot? Is that why you dress that way? We never raised you to take pot!"

"He is not on drugs, Marcy. He is an individualist and an artist."

"I have a charge plate, I'm willing to use it. Judy Weisenstein's son wears clothes from Burberry's. There's a shop on the Gold Coast. What will the Weisensteins think? They'll think we're bankrupt."

"Mom, I don't even know the Weisensteins. This is how everyone dresses on campus."

"Well, maybe at the Harley Place, but not in reality. No one dresses like that. You're living in the seventies!"

"It's the Harley Hutt," I said.

"What kind of name is that? Rich people in England name their houses Howard's End and Windy Corner. The Harley Hutt? It's not even pretty."

"August has found a group of young men who share similar values," my father said. "They're in the prime of their lives, and live by different rules than you or me."

"Than you or *I*," my mother corrected him.

"It's *me*."

"*I*. Everyone knows that. Augie, have I done something wrong? Are you rebelling against me?"

"Oh, mom. Quit being a Jewish mother. You're not even religious."

"I am a woman of faith!" my mother exclaimed. "Are they teaching you to be anti-Semitic at the Harley Hutt? Is that what higher learning is these days?"

"Look, it was nice to see you guys, but I'm going out. Dad, can I have some money?" I felt like an embarrassed child asking for it, but I didn't have any.

"You live on the brink of starvation!" my mother exclaimed. "It's not healthy to be so thin. I'm taking you to Dr. Silverstein for a physical."

The thought filled me with dread. Dr. Silverstein had seen my genitals more than any man in the world. As a teenager, he'd have me stand up in my underwear and then he'd sit on the stool and yank my underwear down with no warning, so that I'd flinch in terror. Then I'd have to stand in front of him, my underwear around my thighs, while he painstakingly ran his fingers around my testicles and glared at my newly-hairy penis with his big bearded face as though he were reading it. He took his sweet time with it, prodding me with fingers and having me cough and then doing it again, and again, and then I'd have to walk around the office nude so he could see my posture, while I prayed I wouldn't get a boner. It was absolute humiliation.

"That man's a pervert. I won't go near him."

My mother looked at me with shock in her eyes.

My father pulled out thirty dollars from his wallet and gave it to me.

"What are you going to use that for?" my mother asked.

"I'm going to a club to meet an old friend."

"A gay nightclub, is that where you're going? I know what goes on at those clubs. I went to Studio 54 in Manhattan when Andy Warhol was there. I was visiting a girlfriend in the Village and she took me there. There was drugs and promiscuous sex and insane people. You can't go to clubs."

"He's not going to a drug den," my father said. Then he looked at me carefully. "Are you?"

"No! I'm just meeting a friend for dinner and then I'm gonna watch him DJ. I gotta go."

"Is it a man you're meeting? You never tell us about your man friends. Is he your lover? Fran Finkel has a son who has a male lover. They live in Israel now. They're Israelis."

"I'm single. I keep telling you. I have to go. Thanks for the money." I kissed my mother on her cheek. She was still wearing sunglasses.

"There's Jewish boys you could meet. They have a club for gay Jews that has dinner socials. You could find a man of your faith."

"Let him go," my father said. "He has an engagement."

"Two men can get engaged in Holland," my mother said. "They have gay marriage there. It's legal there, there's no conservatives. You don't have to be single and go to nightclubs!"

"Goodbye," I said, and walked out the door.

I got off the L at Bryn Mawr and strode east toward the lake. With all the cement and asphalt and chain link fences around me, I breathed in and realized the slow stench of the country was off of me. There was nothing to be allergic to; the air that blew off the lake tasted terribly pure, and empty, and free of pollen. Even in the darkness, you could tell that there was a point where the buildings ended and the water began, cutting off all civilization with an endless streak across the horizon. I could hear the lake: there was a gentle rushing sound, and when I got further east, I could smell the dead fish. I put my hands in my pockets and tried to look mean. I was on guard: Small town boy that I had become, I wasn't used to seeing so many people on the streets I didn't know, or seeing so much traffic.

Kenmore was dark and imposing and weirdly quiet. There were enormous evergreen bushes along the sidewalks and stoic brown apartment buildings that must have been full of people but were completely silent. Silence in the city scared me: I thought someone must be lurking behind every corner.

I pushed open the door to Ted's building and a cool, musty mass of air hit my nose. The ceiling of the lobby must have been fifty feet high, and was covered in small, washed-out tiles. There was a bank of old elevators that had gates over the doors. The building must have previously been a hotel.

Ted opened his door and smiled. I realized how much of my confidence had been missing since he left town. There was a reason he was my idol: two years older than me and about ten times more masculine, he was exactly who I wanted to be. Anyway, he was the one who was responsible for getting me into the Harley Hutt in the first place, and I needed someone who'd understand my recent troubles. I exclaimed hello and he said, "Augie, it's only been a few months, but I've missed the sound of your voice."

Dressed in a ratty T shirt and old jeans, Ted still managed to look chiseled while playing the role of the casual, urban twentysomething. He had a crop of black wavy hair that he'd cut short, and it sat on his head in intersecting waves. His face was permanently covered in a stubbly shadow. There was masculine shape to his face, his features defined by sharp angles. His cheeks were almost hollowed out but he didn't look ill, he looked determined.

We hugged and I came in and sat on the couch. The apartment was enormous. I couldn't tell how many rooms there were, but the living room had about five hallways sprouting off of it. Perennial DJ and all around master of coolness, Ted had electronic music playing so softly you could barely hear it, and all the lamps had funky tapestries thrown over them. I wondered if Victor had stolen the idea from him.

"Did you find it OK? I'm glad you called, I didn't have a phone forever," Ted said, handing me a beer.

"Oh, yeah, yeah. It's a great place. Ted, you have no idea how nice it is to get out of that town and come to a place where there's actual real-live strangers."

"I know what you mean," he said, sitting down. "And, my place is right by the gay beach."

"There's a gay beach in Chicago?"

"Yeah, it's awesome. I went there every day this summer. This is your last year of school, right? My roommate is moving out next spring, so if you want to, maybe we could be roommates when you get up here."

It seemed almost too good to be true. "I'll hold you to that."

"Great. So, where do you wanna eat?"

I thought for a minute, of Victor's slow hands around my back, and of his deep, gentle voice, and of his large, arcing erection, pressed up against me. "I wanna go somewhere I can't downstate. How about Indian food?"

"Great," Ted said. "We're not far from the Indian neighborhood."

The restaurant was dead quiet, but full of large groups at enormous tables. Outside, the streets were in disarray: countless cars swerved and honked through the monstrous traffic on Devon, and scores of people strolled back and forth, dressed to go out. Some of the ladies wore elaborate saris, and the restaurant was across the street from the Sari Emporium, a double decker affair full of sari-clad mannequins. Small groceries with giant bags of rice stacked up inside and video stores with open-air fronts lined the block, their intense flourescent lights giving off harsh whitish-blue glares.

"So what the hell is going on at the Hutt?" Ted asked, pushing around a plate of chicken masala. "I miss it."

I was quickly devouring curried chickpeas and drinking a beer. I ate so fast that I was forgetting to chew the food. Ted had inspired me. I felt dumb thinking it, but after three years of friendship I was still excited just to sit at the same table as him. "First of all, what's with the shower there?" I said, my mouth full. "Why is it like a locker room?"

"I don't know. But it's really embarrassing. Every day I'd go in and see one of them nude and then I'd stand in the shower going, 'Oh, fuck, now what do I do? I'm *so* hard.'"

I laughed uproariously. "You did not get hard in the shower!"

"I totally did," he said. "I couldn't help it. Those guys are fuckin' babes."

All my anxiety about being in the shower with the boys faded, and seemed absurd. "What would you do?"

"Oh, I just turned to the wall and hoped nobody would notice. I didn't give a shit. So, have you done the shooting contests? Who's your favorite?"

"I like Paul Veracruz. His dick is tiny, but it turns me on for some reason."

Ted looked encouraged. "Yeah, he's a good choice. I used to fantasize about taking off those overalls of his. He also has a terrific ass."

I nodded. I was so glad I could level with him about peeping at guys and it was acceptable. Ted was considered to be way cooler than me around campus, and I was overjoyed to learn he'd been through the same anxieties. "I really wish you were there. Something's wrong in the house, though. Mark Israel and Tony are really mad at me, and I don't know exactly why. Israel basically called me a faggot, in a mean way, and

I overheard Tony and him talking about me. They said they couldn't believe what I had done and what I had said, and that I was a fuckin' homo, blah blah blah. I'm almost scared to go back to the house."

Ted chewed some of his chicken masala and said with his mouth full, "Oh, those two suck each other's dicks."

I was so shocked I threw my head back and laughed so hard the people at the next table shot me dirty looks. "What are you talking about?"

"Those two fuckers lay around in their underwear and watch TV and then at the end of the night, Mark pulls down Tony's undies and sucks his big wiener."

"No he does not!" I exclaimed, grinning stupidly. "You're lying!"

"He totally does! How do I know? They asked me to join in one night." He took a sip of his beer and raised a furry eyebrow at me.

"They didn't! I can't believe you. You are a liar!" My face got hot and I felt joy roll around inside of me. "What faggots!"

"Oh my god, I'd go walking past their room at night and I'd get a glimpse of Israel on his knees with his fat hairy ass hanging out and Tony leaning back moaning, 'Oh! Ah! Oh my God!'"

A pair of obviously gay guys with bleach blond hair, talking on cell phones, looked over at us disapprovingly. A large Indian family was beyond them, staring at Ted as he faked an orgasm.

"I can't believe it. I don't understand what their beef is with me."

Ted looked thoughtful. "Has Valentine told you that he's not, and I quote, 'one hundred percent heterosexual'?"

"Yes!"

"Did you tell anyone?"

"Yes!"

"Good," Ted said. "Tell everyone you know. He deserves it. He only says that to see if you'll suck his dick. He can't get it up for chicks for some reason, so he goes after us. He asked me to do it more times than I can count."

"Did you?"

"Hell, yeah! Have you seen that thing. It's huge!"

I laughed again. "I love you. You've made me feel so much better."

"Don't sweat those two retards. They're not worth the time."

I shoveled my food into my mouth, savoring the spicy flavor so much that I moaned. The food and Ted were setting off endorphins inside me that left me ecstatically happy.

"Also," I said. "I have more news."

Ted chewed and grinned. "All right, lay it on me."

"Victor and I have developed a sort of relationship. He's been flirting with me since I moved in and I've been pursuing him pretty aggressively, and we ended up hooking up. We've made out and sucked dick, and we've even had sex once. So far, it's been the best thing that's ever happened to me. I think I'm falling in love with him."

I was so proud, but Ted looked concerned. "Augie, Victor isn't gay," he said slowly. "He only goes out with chicks."

"I know, but he made an exception for me. It's weird, but I like it. I don't know what the future is gonna bring, but I'm jumping into this blind and happy. I've been single for so long. He likes me."

Ted glanced down at the table and said, "Augie, what do you mean you're falling in love with him? You know, he can't love you back."

"He can! He's doing a really good job of it so far." I said that too vehemently, like I was trying to convince myself and not Ted.

"Augie, do you know anything about him? I mean, I live with his cousin Jay, and I've heard some things."

"Well, what. Does he have a disease?"

"Augie, I wouldn't say anything if you hadn't said you were falling in love with him, but there's something you should know. I can't believe he hasn't told you."

"What is it?" Fear spread across my head and into the pit of my stomach.

"Augie, Victor is engaged to be married."

It didn't make sense. "What do you mean? He doesn't even have a girlfriend!"

"No, Augie. You don't understand. He's Indian. He's in an arranged marriage."

"What? He's from Downers Grove, not India! He's not from some village!"

"It doesn't matter. I guess that's how they do it. His cousin has already made plans to go to the wedding. He's marrying the daughter of some family friend of theirs who lives in London. She's a newscaster on TV. It's all been set up."

"I don't believe it. People don't do that anymore, that's archaic. He never said anything about that. He never said one word!" The restaurant seemed to fall quiet and the exhilaration I'd been riding on took a sharp turn downwards and spiraled into sadness and then anger and then insecure feelings of betrayal. It did make sense after all. He'd said he had a hot prospect. He said there was something he had to tell me. He said I shouldn't get the wrong idea, but I did anyway.

Ted looked at me with what I thought was fear. "Augie, how wrapped up are you in this guy?"

"Oh, only all my hopes and dreams of the last four years balled into one. I only rested every ounce of my hope for happiness on him. I didn't even admit to myself how much I liked him."

My throat swelled shut. My eyes were globby.

"I'm so incredibly stupid," I said. "I should've known. I've traveled. I always got A's in World Cultures class. He never told me!"

Ted shook his head slowly.

"I'm the stupidest retard on the planet. I'll be alone forever, and I deserve it!" Tears streamed down my face.

"All right, get ahold of yourself," Ted said, wiping my face with his napkin. I was sure the entire restaurant was staring at us. "You knew you'd get into trouble fucking around with a straight guy. You know that's a bad move."

I'd sunk to depths so low I could barely speak. A gravelly, elderly voice came out of my mouth. "He told me he wanted to run away with me. He told me he had dreamed of me. Well, he wasn't so straight when he had my dick in his mouth, was he?" I stared at the floor.

"Augie, Jesus, when did all this happen? You just moved in a few months ago."

Look, he's just another guy. Yeah, he's nice, but he fucked with you big time. You should be mad at him, not at yourself. If he couldn't make a commitment to you, he shouldn't have let you believe he would."

"That fucker, I'll kick his fuckin' ass. I need a drink. Waitress, a drink!"

"Augie, just wait till you move to Chicago. All the guys will adore you. You're so cute, and everybody likes you."

"Yeah, well the gay guys in Chicago can kiss my ass!" I screamed, crazed. Except for the sound of my voice, the restaurant was eminently quiet. Ted held his head in his hand.

A man came up to the table who was not a waiter. He stood in front of the table for a moment and then said, "Is everything all right, gentleman?"

I guzzled the last of my beer and said, "Hi, are you in an arranged marriage? I've heard that's popular."

"Augie…"

"Perhaps if you've finished your meal I can bring you the check," he said, motioning for us to get up. "You can settle the bill at the hostess counter."

"Yeah, well I'm gonna settle something else when I get home," I growled, rage spewing out of my mouth.

"All right," Ted said. "Let's get out of here. I'll buy you a drink. Or twelve."

Ted and I maneuvered our way through the darkness around large groups of families that were casually strolling down the street. The store windows had colorful posters of Indian movie stars and singers, but I didn't know who any of them were. Ted said he had to make a call and went into a small grocery store. It was too cold for it, but I sat down on the sidewalk and leaned against the building. Across the street loud, tinny music blasted from a record store from such poor speakers that it was impossible to tell what the melody was. In front of me, all I could see were legs and occasional small children, happily running in front of their parents.

I looked back into the store, and saw Ted on the pay phone, surrounded by humongous bags of rice. I wanted to be everywhere and to be nowhere. I wanted to go out and meet someone new and go back to the Hutt with a phone number and the potential for a new relationship. I wanted to go home and get drunk and pass out. I thought if Ted had told me that Victor was about to undergo a sex change operation I would have been less surprised. Cars honked, the song at the record store changed. Grandmothers in saris walked by with small children. A group of young people who could have been students at my college passed by and one of the girls looked down at me and said, "Tough times?" Her friend laughed and said, in a British accent, "Stop taking the piss." The guys in the group were dressed in quasi-formal clothes and wore expensive-looking glasses. They were a step away from being yuppies. Were they all in arranged marriages?

Ted came outside and sat down next to me. "Look, Augie, let's get outta here and go to the Dong Pipe. I gotta start DJing in an hour."

The thought of standing next to the DJ booth all night silently watching Ted play records had seemed exciting to me even an hour before, but at that point the prospect left me feeling woefully unenthusiastic. "I think I'm just gonna go home. I wouldn't be much fun."

"I can't believe you got so wrapped up in this guy. Just come out and have a few drinks. You'll feel better. And I can probably introduce you to some people."

"I don't understand it," I said, wrapping my hands around my knees. The cement was so cold against my ass that I shivered. "Is she moving from London to marry him?"

Ted looked unsure. "The wedding's in London, though. I think he's moving there. I don't think she'd give up a job as an anchorwoman."

"Well, Jesus, do women in arranged marriages even work? I mean, who knows! Maybe she won't be allowed to drive!"

"Augie, let's get up from the ground. Come out, just for a while."

In a sense, going to the Dong Pipe would help me get my mind off of Victor, but I didn't have the heart for it. I stood up. "Just let me have tonight. Tomorrow, I'll be rarin' to go."

"All right. Let me put you in a taxi, young man. I'll pay."

"No, no, my dad gave me money. I'll call you tomorrow. Tomorrow night, I wanna meet someone, and Victor Radhakrishna can kiss my hairy ass." Ted and I hugged.

"That's the spirit," Ted said. "He's just a man."

I tried to ride back to Evanston on the L, but I didn't make it. I got as far as Granville, where the thought of going any further was so horrible it was almost like terror.

I didn't want to see my parents.

I never told anyone this, but my mother said something to me once that I'll never forgive her for. When I was 18, on a weekend trip home from school, during the proverbial post-coming out aftermath of shocked, indignant relatives, I was in the kitchen about to open a package of imitation crab meat. My mother was in one of her bimonthly two day long depressive rages and stood at the sink banging dishes. Her hair fell down in sloppy clumps, her clothes were fifteen years out of style. She wore those old clothes almost aggressively during these rages, as if to say to my father, "Look at this crap I have to wear, you failure." As if she didn't have the same job as him, which she did. I don't know, maybe it was just that she was trying to confirm her own negative opinion of herself.

My father was of course hiding in his study, as he did during these times, and I resented him for that in an enormous way. I couldn't fathom how anyone could cower under such clearly planned outrageous behavior. My father would try to warn me of her moods, using sign language and mouthing words I couldn't interpret, and I'd breeze past him and call out, "I can't understand you. What?" and go deliberately into the same room as my mother and pretend like nothing was out of the ordinary, because I knew she couldn't stand it.

So there I was, holding a steak knife over my crabmeat, waiting to slice open the plastic, trying to ignore the fear in the pit of my stomach from the vindictive premenopausal nightmare standing at the sink, but still salivating at the sight of the red and white flakes below me.

As I slid the knife into the plastic wrapper, the banging of the dishes got louder, until it was so clearly a temper tantrum that I looked over and saw her banging a saucepan into the sink with both hands over and over, as if she was some retarded urchin who was also blind and deaf.

"Knock it off!" I yelled. "What the fuck are you doing?"

She turned off the water, set down the pot, and looked at me with eyes that were almost blackened they were so withdrawn. In the silence, she appraised me up and down and said, "You. You ruined the family. I just wanted you to know that."

I still had the knife in my hand and I figured I could march over and stab her to death, or at least slap her and call her a cunt, but I decided to rise above it. I left for school that afternoon, and after a day and a half she called, as I thought she would, and left a message on my machine as herself; she was back to normal and pretending nothing had happened, which is how it always happened.

I didn't return any of her messages for two months, but eventually she got ahold of me. It was a typical conversation—gossip about the ladies she knew, madcap stories about the strange goings-on at Nieman Marcus the weekend before, ribbing me about being single. She even tried to make me laugh a few times. At the end, in an almost murderous manipulation, she said, "Are you all right? You seemed so angry the last time you were home."

So the resentment lasted, and lasted, and when I did go home I was so tense that every word anyone spoke put me on edge. I scanned the room with unnecessarily peeled eyes. I had ruined the family.

"Do you know that you're talking to yourself?"

I looked up and saw a queer little Indian guy about my age sitting next to me at the bar. I'd been at the bar, lord knows which one, for more than a few hours, and had last count of how many drinks I'd had.

"I'm not embarrassed. I don't think I'll see these people again. Anyway, what's this place called? I didn't think to look when I came in."

The guy looked somewhat amused, not with me, but at what he was about to say. He grinned a little to himself and leaned toward me. "Who knows? They're all the same after a while. The Hormone. The Thrust 'n Bump. The Rawhide. Buns 'R Us."

I nodded instead of laughing. There was something off about this guy. He looked too young to be out drinking. His body was so skinny that it didn't match his face. His eyes were full of amusement, but the skin surrounding them was inordinately heavy, and serious. His jawbone was the widest part of his head. I imagined underneath the geeky plaid shirt he was wearing, he had the chest of a boy.

"Am I bothering you? It looks like you had a rough night."

"No, you're not bothering me. I had some fairly unfortunate news tonight, but nothing I can't survive."

"Oh," he said, staring ahead at the mirror behind the bar. "Unfortunate news. I'm sorry about your loss."

This time I laughed. "No, no one died. What was your name again?"

"Well, I never told you what it was originally. It's Ramesh. Ramesh Singh."

We shook hands while I told him my name. Drunk, I was about to ask him if he was related to Arundhati Singh but instantly thought that would be stupid. In India, Singh must be as common as Smith.

"Yeah, no one's dead, it was just your average 'fall in love with a straight guy who's in an arranged marriage' kind of thing. Only slightly devastating, and really quite expected."

He eyed me carefully. "Oh, yeah. Happens all the time."

There was the sound of ice being poured from buckets further down the bar, a rush of hard rocks against metal. I really had no idea where I was. I knew I was in Rogers Park somewhere between the Indian section and the Russian Jew section, but that could be anywhere. The outside of the bar had struck me as vaguely familiar when I saw it, or at least vaguely gay.

"Do you live in the neighborhood?" I asked, hoping to be centered.

"No, I live in Hyde Park. I go to the University of Chicago."

"Hmm. Wonderful. Didn't Einstein teach there?"

"Oh, I've no idea. Probably. It's funny, though. It's not a very well-known school. So many people in Chicago couldn't tell it from the University of Illinois. And all these students who've spent their entire lives embroiled in accelerated education are looking for validation. Do you know that we lead the nation in suicides?"

"You're also known for having the worst social life."

"Which explains why I'm up here."

"So what do you want to do with your life, Ramesh Singh?"

He stared at the mirror for a moment, and then said, "I suppose once I graduate I'll go on to graduate school and then after that I'll get a job that I'll hate and then be miserable for the rest of my life."

"Well, that sounds like a good plan."

"It might be a short life. Or at least a lot shorter than the average life. Of course, I could just shorten it right now and go jump in the lake."

I had an urge to roll my eyes, but instead I looked past him. I hadn't realized it before, because I hadn't looked, but all the lights at the far end of the bar were red. The few people gathered around the pool table and the dart boards had a sinister, reddish glow to their faces. The alcohol had never brought me up that night, at least not since the restaurant, but had done the opposite. Looking at my largely cretinous companion in front of all this, the music so terrible it may as well have been static, I thought we may all be trapped in some unpublicized section of purgatory, where nobody burns, but is eternally surrounded by depression and stink and weird little characters who say the most debasing things.

"Do you know anything about arranged marriages, Ramesh?"

"Let me tell you something, Mr. Schoenberg. The world is a very nice place, if you're straight."

16.

I pulled up to the curb on a dark side street in East Lakeview, scraping the hubcaps against the pavement, bumping the car in front of me and then the car behind me as I tried to park my parents' oversized car. I'd spent the day moping around the house while my mother tried to figure out what was wrong with me, but then decided to pull myself up by the bootstraps and go out. Ted had been summoned by some friend or another in need and couldn't make it, but it was just as well. I wanted to go out alone and meet someone. With Ted, I knew I'd be overshadowed.

I grabbed a squeeze bottle from the underneath the seat that I'd filled with gin and tonic. In the darkness, I sat motionless and gazed out at the buildings along Melrose Street, sipping the alcohol so fast that I felt drunk almost immediately. I was mainly a beer drinker, but this night I wanted to be buzzed when I walked into the club; I was so inexplicably anxious that my mouth was dry, my heart was beating fast, and I was having trouble thinking clearly. But almost as soon as I began to get nervous about how nervous I was, the gin kicked in and the anxiety started to ease out of me like piss from a bladder.

I tossed aside the empty squeeze bottle and pulled out a magazine I'd brought with me. It had a discount coupon for the club inside, which I tore out, and I peered at the adjoining advertisement. There was a list of events for the week but for this night all that was shown was the nude torso of a muscular guy with his arms in the air. I figured that meant business as usual.

Down the street, a group of people walked out of a three-flat smiling and laughing. A guy that could've been me stood in the doorway waving goodbye to the group. Through the car windows the sound of their talking and laughing was unintelligible and warped, but it sounded, for just a second, like pure happiness. Watching them walk along the street, I felt jealousy so strongly I wanted to cry out. It seemed almost unreal to me that people my age could have a nice apartment on Melrose Street, on the cusp of the lake, in the gay ghetto no less, and could walk to almost anything that was worth doing in the city.

I thought they must be the luckiest people in the world.

Halsted Street was teeming with gay guys. They scurried along as if late for work, dressed in dark, fine clothes and black Oxford shoes. A few dressed more informally, in jeans and baseball caps, but even they looked like they'd had their jeans professionally pressed. I walked in between the other guys on the street, and since I was so excited to see so many other gay guys, I felt like a part of the crowd, but I knew I didn't look like it. I was wearing a twenty-year old parka I'd pinched from my dad, and underneath I wore a geeky sweater that had a dickey attached. On campus, I thought people may think of the sweater as unique, but I had a feeling in Chicago people may wonder if I was homeless. On the bright side, I had cut my hair in the bathroom earlier that night. I'd lopped off my curls with the scissors in a haphazard way, hoping to make myself look like an ancient Roman soldier. I wasn't sure if I'd succeeded, but I felt like I looked like a different person.

When I walked into the club I was charged the discount price without having to give the coupon, which I was glad for, because I felt like kind of a nerd bringing a coupon to a dance club. I looked around and knew I wouldn't know a soul. The thought made me hopeful.

The club was loud and smoky and hot as hell. Instantly, there was sweat on my face. I could feel the vibration of the music in my lungs and even in my esophagus. I checked my coat and got a beer. It was so smoky it was hard to see, but the club was so full of people and so huge that it seemed like the club went on endlessly, as if there were no back wall.

I was under the impression this was the coolest gay club in Chicago, after all, they had the largest advertisements in the newspapers, but the crowd was a little too preppy for me. I wandered to the back of the dance floor looking for a crowd against which I wouldn't seem so different. Anyway, I was looking for an adventure. I danced around in a large circle, trying to maneuver my way toward a corner where I spotted a group of people in more adventurous clothing.

There was a short girl with copper-colored hair and a silver dress dancing on a step and a guy dressed all in white with a backpack, holding a Polaroid camera. Another guy near them was wearing a big fur hat and another had a football jersey and a pierced eyebrow and lip. Intrigued, I moved closer. The guy with the pierced face wasn't cute, but he was sexy in a sort of menacing way. I danced closer to him and was shocked when he came right up to me. I tried to dance in as cool a way as I knew how, but this crowd was on something: they were jumping up and down and waving their hands in the air. A siren went off. Two bodybuilder type guys wearing nothing but leather g-strings came in between me and the pierced face guy. I tried to move around them but one of them grabbed me by the hips and all of a sudden I was trapped between these two, which wasn't sexy, it was weird and rough and they smelled. Another siren went off but it wasn't a fire alarm it was the DJ, and then two platforms slowly rose up from the dance floor and three guys appeared in tiny leather shorts. They jumped up on the platforms and began to strip. I tried to pry myself away from the rigid forms of the g-string guys but they were both twice the size of me and I couldn't move or even breathe. Gathering all my strength together, I pushed with both hands against the pectoral muscle of the guy opposite me and he relented; I sped away and sat on the edge of the dance floor trying to get my breath back.

For confidence, I got another beer, which would have to be my last, since I was nearly out of money. I made my way back to the corner and found the group of club kids huddled together on the step posing for Polaroids. Then, the girl in the silver dress handed out baby pacifiers and they took a picture with those in their mouths. I smiled and turned around and started to dance. A hand grabbed at me and I resisted, thinking it was the leather guys, but I looked around and it was the pierced face guy pulling me over to the group. I huddled next to them and posed for more Polaroids. I thought it was amazing I hadn't been in the club for ten minutes and was already taking pictures with people.

Newly optimistic, I danced some more, but the pierced face guy was talking to a guy in camouflage pants that had been leaning against a post. Even so, the club seemed to have opened up and I felt like I could have my pick of whoever I wanted. I looked around the dance floor critically instead of sheepishly and decided who I thought was sexy. I didn't look far, though, because there was a guy dancing right near me that I hadn't noticed before. He was tall and thin with a mop of brown hair on his head, and he wore a cute T shirt that had a picture of Grover from Sesame Street. The shirt was so adorably regressive that I felt comfortable enough to approach him.

I danced over to him and, realizing that my whole interaction with the Polaroid crowd had been silent, introduced myself.

"I'm Augie," I yelled.

"What?"

"I'm Augie!"

"Oh! I'm Dave!"

We both smiled. The thought of talking more seemed hopeless because of the noise, so we kept dancing, eventually close enough that my arms were around him and our legs were intertwined. Even so, we managed to keep the beat, sliding against each other, rubbing our hands against each other's backs. And because it was late and I was drunk and because I was so incredibly mad at Victor and because Dave's dick was hard and I could feel it, I leaned forward and kissed him. Our tongues met and slid around and our lips glided off of each other's with such ease that my mind unwound and I felt strong and incredibly confident. The kiss felt better than any had since my first kiss. It felt so shamelessly easy. We held each other in a tight embrace, grinding away and french kissing in the middle of the dance floor, losing track of the beat. Our dicks were rock hard and pressed up against each other through our pants and it felt like the most natural thing in the world—the same but different sizes, different shapes.

I pulled away for a second and leaned my head against his chest. After a second, I looked up at him: his hair hung down in his eyes as though he were a human sheepdog.

"Are you too drunk?" he said.

I walked to the edge of the dance floor and sat down. The alcohol was still hitting me hard and I was feeling strange. Dave sat down next to me and put his arm around me. It was a feeling I rarely felt in public, and I savored it. I couldn't believe how easily I had met him.

"You're pretty cute," he said. "I've never seen you around before. Where are you from?"

"Well, I go to school downstate but I'm staying with my parents in Evanston. Where do you live?"

"In Bolingbrook," he said. That was a small suburb, I thought, at least an hour from the city, practically rural.

"With your parents?"

He nodded. "I'm getting ready to move to California, though. I'm leaving on Tuesday."

I looked past him toward the dance floor, as if he didn't exist at all. I thought about asking him to do something after the club closed, but couldn't see what the point would be. He sat next to me looking content, and he was sticking to me like glue. But I didn't know where we would go and anyway we were both staying with our parents.

"What's wrong?" he asked.

"Nothing. It's just my luck."

"You know, I went to school downstate for a while, but I moved up here about four years ago. Where do you live down there?"

"On Cherry Street. At the Harley Hutt."

"Oh, shit," he said. "I've heard of that. I used to live two blocks from it. Has that place gone gay?"

I was glad he'd heard of it. "Oh, no, no. I'm pretty much the only gay guy there. I think. It's funny; you must've left town right before I got there."

"It is funny. I wish you would've been there. I was always single."

"One of life's cruel coincidences, I guess. What are you gonna do in California?"

He looked away. "Oh, I don't know. I'll do anything, really. Just so long as it's different than this."

"Looking for adventure?"

"It's strange, though. I might have found it right here."

We kissed again, softly, and slowly.

He pulled away and said, "Why don't you come to California with me? What do you have to do here?"

"Nothing," I said. "Well, it is my last year of college. I sort of have to graduate. I don't know. What would I do in California?"

"Date me," he said and then he kissed me again. I would've liked nothing more in the world than to date him. He was telling me exactly what I needed to hear. I wasn't hard to please, either: he was young, cute, and seemingly sane. That's all I asked for. Even so, I couldn't imagine packing up and leaving town seven months before graduation.

The music stopped and the house lights came up. A barback in a black T-shirt, carrying a flashlight, walked by and said, "All right lovebirds, time to go."

Dave grabbed my hand. "Come with me. I don't want to go there alone."

"You shouldn't have left downstate. We could've dated then."

"I know, the timing's wrong. But who gives a fuck? Aren't you sick of Illinois?"

I thought about it. I didn't know anybody in California, and I'd be two thousand miles away from anyone I did know. "No, actually, I'm OK with it. You should stay here."

The bouncer came by and told us to leave. Grudgingly, we stood. Dave said to wait while he found his friends. I had a pang of insecurity. I considered leaving; I didn't know if he was going to come back. I'd been blown off by nicer guys than him.

I decided to get my coat. While I was putting it on, Dave walked over with some friends.

"There's a party," he said. "If you want to go."

Fantastic ideas of a sweltering after hours party full of flashy and exciting Chicagoans raced through my mind. I said I'd love to go.

We walked outside and the air hit us like a brick. It must've been fifty degrees cooler than in the club. The sweat on my face and my hair felt like it might freeze. Dave grabbed my hand and we walked down Halsted swinging our arms not caring if anyone saw. His friends were obnoxious and so energetic they were jumping around ahead of us hysterically.

"I'm glad I met you," he said. "I haven't met anyone in ages. Right when I saw you, I knew I wanted to meet you."

"But you're moving," I said, conversationally. "That's a mistake." I squeezed his hand.

"Yeah, well, I've been in this town for too long. It's so full of assholes and the winters suck. I want to be where the action is."

"A place could be whatever you make it. Chicago's not so bad. I'm sorry, I'm not trying to make you feel guilty. It's just I live in a smaller town, so the city seems so amazing to me."

"It can be. If you're with the right people."

We came to the building where the party was supposed to be. Dave's friend rang the bell, but no one answered. We stood outside for a few minutes looking hopeful, but it became apparent there was no party. I looked at Dave. I thought about asking him for his number, but it seemed pointless. I lived two hours away, and he was moving away.

"Well, it was nice to meet you," I said, inadequately.

"Yeah, well, when do you go back to school?"

"Monday."

"Well, maybe I'll see you." He looked at me wistfully.

"I'll see you," I said, confidently, and kissed him again. His friends continued to ring the doorbell. It felt nice to be on the participating end of a public display of affection for once, rather than being on the irritated observing end.

"OK, I gotta go," I said. "I gotta return daddy-o's car."

"The offer still stands," Dave said. I looked at him briefly and then I ran across the street to Melrose.

The next night was Sunday, and I should've gone back to school, but instead I went to the Dong Pipe with Ted. I wanted some more time to think about what I was going to say to Victor. I needed to have a plan of action, otherwise I'd end up acting like a snotty bitch toward him, making snide little comments with my hands on my hips, and end up feeling miserable. I needed to meet another boy. This time one that lived in Chicago.

The Dong Pipe was empty and noisy, a bad combination at a bar. Ted and I stared at each other not speaking. "Can we get out of here?" I asked. "There must be a club or something."

"There is. The Revolver Hammer is gay tonight. And I can get us in free."

We rode in a taxi going northwest and ended up on a dead end street along the river. The street was ancient and had old trolley tracks down the middle. No cars were parked on the streets and the buildings all looked deserted. When the taxi stopped, I asked Ted where the club was, and he said, "Don't worry, I'll show you."

We walked along the sidewalk and came to an imposing black building that had absolutely no sign or visible door. "How do you know it's the Revolver Hammer?" I asked.

"Well, you just have to know," Ted said. "And all the cool people know."

I figured I couldn't top that. We showed our IDs to a man who came out of a door that had miraculously appeared along the outside wall. As soon as we walked in, I stood in front of the dance floor in awe. The club was as enormous as an airplane hangar. Stairways and catwalks hung from the club's walls in countless different spots, making it look like there were scores of different rooms and levels. I glanced upwards, like I was downtown staring stupidly at the Sears Tower, and saw Dave's friends dancing on a catwalk that went across the dance floor. I almost yelped. I was wearing the exact same sweater as I had been the night before. I never thought once I'd see Dave again, and if he was there, I'd be too embarrassed to talk to him. Anyone would remember that ridiculous sweater. He'd think I wore it every day. I ushered Ted toward the back of the bar, telling him there was someone I didn't want to see.

It wasn't true. I did want to see Dave. I didn't know what to do.

Ted and I walked up some metal steps that led to a small room with couches and a bar. We got drinks and sat down. "What if he's here?" I demanded of Ted. "I'm so embarrassed!"

"Just take off your sweater. God."

"My T-shirt has really bad armpit stains, though. It must be six years old." I took off the sweater and showed him. The T-shirt really was bad. There was a faded commemoration of Taste of Chicago from years past, and there were holes in the back, and dark yellow pit stains.

"You look fine," Ted lied. "Go find your new boyfriend."

I wanted to stay in the little room all night. Ted and I had a couple of beers, but he ended up talking to a friend for a long time, and then they went outside to get high, so I decided I may as well go dance. Leaving my sweater balled up in the corner, I courageously marched downstairs and plowed my way through the crowd to the center of the dance floor. As soon as I threw out my first move, Dave was in front of me, smiling.

We kissed, and then we hugged. I was mortified. I thought I looked like the biggest slob on the planet.

"I'm excited you came. I never thought I'd see you again," he said.

"Yeah," I replied, halfheartedly. We danced for a few songs, but I didn't want to move my arms much, for fear of revealing my putrid armpit stains, and I ended up looking and feeling stiff and unmotivated. I kept turning around so I wasn't facing him, which I'm sure looked like the biggest sign of disinterest ever, but I couldn't help it. Dave looked fantastic in a tight black shirt and baggy, foreign-looking jeans. He had obviously put some thought into his appearance, unlike me.

Dave kissed me on the cheek. "We're going," he said. And then he left.

17.

The Hutt was dark and quiet when I got home. The only noise came from the sound of creaking floorboards on the stairway, which popped and moaned even though no one was walking on them. I crept up to the third floor, hoping I wouldn't wake anyone up. I didn't want to talk to anybody. The smell of my room hit me when I walked into it: the faint odor of old wood and cigarette smoke, and an overwhelming smell of what I assumed was myself. In the darkness I took off my coat and dropped my bag on a chair.

I heard the sound of breathing and when my eyes adjusted to the absence of light I saw Victor on my bed, snugly encapsulated beneath the blanket. It was the last sight I wanted to see. After what I'd learned, I hardly wanted our first interaction with each other to be silent, or for that matter, intimate.

I took off my clothes and put on some pajamas and proudly marched myself down to the living room to sleep on the couch. I only owned one blanket, and Victor was using it, so I tried to fall asleep without one. It wasn't easy. My mind wouldn't relax, knowing it was supposed to fall asleep in a different room than usual. The couch had a moldy smell, it reeked of old beer, and the cushions were so old and overused they had absolutely no buoyancy to them at all.

I stared at the graffiti art on the dining room walls. In the darkness, the intersecting shapes looked like varying shades of the same, bland hue of gray, like colors on a black and white TV. The empty DJ booth looked forlorn. Moonlight poured in the front windows, casting a blue light around the couch. I tried to think of nothing, and then I think I succeeded. I thought of nothing and nothing came.

I was being carried by something strong and I didn't know who it was or when I was picked up or why. We traveled upwards in bumpy lurches. I forced myself totally awake and saw Victor's hand around my side. It was still night. He smelled of incense and of garlic wafting from his pores. I leaned my head against his bare chest. I wanted to tell him to put me down.

"You're going to be so happy with me," he said, quietly. "I got the PJ Harvey tickets, and tomorrow I'm going to make you dinner. I didn't know you'd stay up there an extra day."

Those were statements, they weren't questions. I was too groggy to think up a reply.

We came to my room and he set me on the bed. He crawled in next to me and pulled the blanket over us. I didn't want to be there. It was foreign, it wasn't right, I looked at Victor and thought, 'he doesn't belong to me.'

"I missed you this weekend, I really did. I moped around not knowing what to do with myself, and Jean-Claude and Paul made fun of me so bad."

"Not Tony and Mark?" My voice was deep and muffled, as if I had a head cold.

"Hmm? Oh, no. They've been sort of missing in action. I don't know where they are."

"I can't imagine," I said.

"Did you miss me?" Victor asked, and then pressed his forehead to my temple. His breath smelled rancid, moldy garlic. The heat from his body felt repulsive against my skin. Things weren't going like I wanted. I was caught unconscious and unprepared.

I sat up. "Not exactly. I was really busy and I went out every night with Ted. You know how it goes. New clubs, new people."

Victor hesitated for a moment and then pulled me over to him with both hands. "But come on. You didn't miss me? Augie, you've been my life lately." He kissed me on the mouth, badly, and I struggled against him, pushing my palms against his chest, but I had no power over him. Using every muscle god had given me, especially those in my ass, I wrenched my torso away from him.

"Look, I'm tired and I'm in a really shitty mood and I'm not up for any fuckin' around, so just lay off of me. All right?"

Victor released me, forcefully, and glared at me with eyes that I couldn't see in the darkness. "Do you wanna tell me what the hell your problem is?"

"No," I said, defiantly. "I don't. You don't have much longer to worry about it, though. Because, Victor, once you're married, we can't keep sleeping together."

He sat in silence next to me.

Emboldened, I added, "I don't think your wife would approve."

That isn't how I wanted to handle it. I didn't want to be an icy bitch and make a snide, sassy comment to him that expressed how pissed off I was. But I did it anyway. I was an icy bitch.

Victor shook his head. "Who told you that; I haven't told anyone that. That's personal. Was it my cousin? He knew I didn't want anyone to know."

"I should say it is personal information. But don't change the subject. Who gives a fuck who told me? How could you not tell me? I don't understand. It's just common courtesy, I think, I don't know. I mean, don't you think you should've told me?" My icy exterior melted away and my vulnerable interior rose to the surface. I was on the verge of crying. "How come you didn't tell me?"

"Augie, I tried to tell you three times." He held three fingers in the air and shook them at me. "You always managed to change the subject. I tried, I really did."

"I don't understand. You're from the suburbs. You're at a big university. How could you be in an arranged marriage? That's for village people."

"Oh, Augie, I'm from a different culture than you. That's how it's done. I don't have to do it, I guess, but everything's been planned already."

"You're not from a different culture, you're as American as me. You grew up in station wagons and minivans. You ate at McDonald's. Don't you think this is a violation of your civil liberties?"

"No, but there's parents and another family. It's not just me; there's expectations of me. You weren't supposed to find out this way. I was going to tell you three times. I know, it's my fault."

"It is your fault. I had no idea arranged marriages went on in Downers Grove, for God's sake. You should've told me. Then, I wouldn't be laying here like a fool with some guy who's fuckin' around on a lark before his real life starts."

"It's a cultural thing. I thought you knew. Didn't Arundhati what's her name ever mention it?"

"Well, yeah, in *The Cowherd's Daughter's Story*, but that's three thousand years old!" He sighed and looked away. Venom filled my head. "Who is she?" I demanded. "What's her name, and what does she want with you?"

"Christ, will you relax? I can't change what's going to happen. She's a family friend, that's all you need to know. She doesn't want anything from me."

"Oh, is that all I need to know? Is it? Well, have a nice life with some chick you don't even know yet. You better have enjoyed those blow jobs, cause those were probably the last you'll get for the rest of your life."

He got out of the bed. I didn't want him to. My insides were calling out to him, but my insides couldn't speak.

"There are things, Augie, that are beyond my control. Not everyone has the world at their feet like you do. You're in control of your destiny. Mine has been planned for me."

I turned my head away and dropped it on the pillow like a recalcitrant child. Victor walked from the room and went downstairs. I heard the kitchen door open and close, and then the sound of the microwave, and then a ding. I stared at the wall, grimacing, and did not sleep.

18.

It was a Tuesday afternoon, a cold, sunny October day. Looking outside, everything looked like it had died. The trees stood bare, the grass had lost its brilliant green luster, no insects tried to get in the windows. It was before the late autumn decorations of Halloween, with its glowing pumpkins and piles of burning leaves, and it felt like the world had taken a brief respite from its imagination. The campus looked sterile, and lacking in charm. Even the birds looked lonely.

Nobody was home. I moped through the Hutt, feeling sorry for myself. I couldn't just sit around and watch TV, or read a book, or call friends. I was possessed by a need to wander from room to room and look to see if there was anything interesting lying around. I wanted so badly to give up on Victor and become inundated with thoughts of spectacular new people and fascinating new diversions.

I couldn't think of any interesting new people and my only hobby was collecting baseball cards. Baseball season had ended.

I thought I should have moved to California with Dave.

I peered into Mark and Tony's room, curious as to what I'd see. I tiptoed in, quiet as an insect, and breathed in deeply and slowly. There were two beds, on opposite sides of the room, two desks, and an enormous entertainment center that had a giant TV and a VCR and a stereo and something else, but I didn't know what it was. The colors around the room were uniform: deep blue and maroon comforters, brown desks, light brown bulletin boards decorated with snapshots and scraps of paper with girls' phone numbers scribbled on them. Jen, Angie, Hillary. There was a cordless phone, an electric razor, an electric toothbrush.

I knew there must be some part of the room that showed more insight into their characters. As it was, all I saw was the average male dorm room. If they sucked each other's dicks every night, I wanted to see evidence of it.

I peeked under the beds: dust balls, an empty pizza box, stray socks. In the garbage can: crumpled papers, chewing gum, cigarette butts, a used rubber. On my hands and knees, I scanned the floor. Long, black pubic hairs, most likely Mark Israel's. A brown, curly head hair, Tony Valentine's.

I realized I was in danger of being discovered in what was really a pretty awkward position. I had a slight bit of apprehension, but only enough to excite me, not enough to scare me.

I went to the closet. Tennis rackets and suitcases and plastic crates full of magazines sat on the floor, stacked in a disjointed fashion on top of themselves. In the background, golf clubs, in the foreground, hanging casual clothes. To the right, a small bookcase jammed against the wall. Old books from classes and occasional pop fiction novels lined the shelves.

I had no idea whose stuff was whose, since there was only one closet. I tried to guess. The golf clubs had to be Israel's, the tennis rackets must have been Tony's. The Stephen King books were Tony's, the John Grisham books, Mark's.

I wondered where their pornography was.

I left the closet and went to a old wooden dresser on the far wall. I pulled open the drawer second from the top and found a fluffy heap of old white underwear. I gingerly removed a pair and looked at the label. Size 36. It was five sizes bigger than mine. The fabric was so thin it was transparent. I could see my fingers through the hazy cotton. I rooted around underneath all the underwear but found nothing else.

I pulled open the top drawer: lambskin condoms, Vaseline, old photographs, souvenir keychains. The third drawer from the bottom: socks and pajamas and four white jockstraps. A Hawaiian print swimsuit with no liner inside. I slid open the bottom drawer and found a neat stack of Hustler magazines. I picked one up and flipped through it. A woman lay on her back squeezing her vagina lips together with her fingers. On the next page, she held them open. It was hardly the first time I'd seen a photograph like that, but I realized my mouth was open in astonishment. It was so typical to see female breasts and pubic hair and butts, but as I witnessed the full gynecological views, I was as shocked as the average prude. Perhaps as surprising as the vaginas were the women's facial expressions, which were molded into looks of absolute surprise and absolute relief.

I flipped to the back of the magazine. A platinum blond, Nordic-looking secretary was in the process of disrobing for a nearby man who was dressed, as far as I could tell, like a German soldier. The woman took off her skirt and the man dropped his pants and the two fucked against the desks with ridiculous, determined looks on their faces. His dick was oversized with a large vein through the shaft and his pubic hair was dark blond and fuzzy, while her pussy hair was black as night and thin as a mustache.

I wondered why Mark Israel would beat off to pictures of thinly-disguised Nazis fucking Aryan secretaries. I wondered if he planned to bring the magazine to Israel.

I returned the magazine to the drawer and found that all the rest of them were Hustlers, except one. It was called Leg Show, and for some reason it seemed vaguely familiar. The copy was dated 1989 and was dog-eared and filthy. It must have been one of his first girlie mags; I bet he'd never throw it away.

Inside, the women were reclined on couches and floors with their legs in the air. They were bent over windowsills with their assholes and pussies exposed, they wore high-heeled shoes, they stuck their fingers up themselves. Something stirred in my head, my heart palpitated, and I lost my balance for a second. I knew why.

Flashback, 1984, Evanston, Illinois. Augie Schoenberg sits in the basement with best friend Scottie Rozenofsky on opposite aqua-colored loveseats. Around them lay giant stacks of obscure girlie magazines, found in the alley garbage can of a bachelor neighbor, by the hundreds. Scottie and Augie carry the magazines back to the Schoenberg basement and slowly leaf through them. Augie wonders why they all contain women and none contain men.

"This one," says Scottie, "this Chinese chick can stuff a peeled banana up her cunt and then shoot it across the room in five equal pieces."

It's the first time Augie hears the word cunt in casual conversation. Under the circumstances, it seems appropriate. "Do they show it?"

"Well, they have a banana sticking out of her. The caption says, 'Peel and eat!'"

"What's that magazine called?" Augie asks, incidentally.

"Leg Show," Scottie responds, and tosses it aside. "Did you even notice, all girls look the same naked? It's just tits and pubic hair and ass cheeks."

Augie Schoenberg agrees. "If you've seen one, you've seen them all."

"Not like I care or anything, but did you ever notice that chicks are always nude in movies and shit, but not guys? Not like I care."

"Not like I care," Augie responds. "But it's always naked girls and never the guys. Maybe a guy's butt in a locker room, but never dicks. Not like I care."

"It's totally like that."

"Yeah!"

Scottie Rozenofsky responds, "Not like I care or anything."

Mrs. Schoenberg descends basement stairs and Augie and Scottie make anxious move to cover up magazines, to no avail, and Mrs. Schoenberg freaks out and calls Mrs. Rozenofsky. Scottie is sent home, confiding to Augie, "My bitch mother is gonna freak. And my fuckin' dad is gonna skin me alive."

Augie wonders if it's a figure of speech and then watches out upstairs bedroom window after Mr. Rozenofsky gets home. There's the labored, maniacal sound of parents fighting, the sound of people losing their heads amid unbearable frustration. Augie crouches down near windowsill and picks up a convenient pair of binoculars. Through the double lenses, he witnesses Scottie Rozenofsky hung over a wooden chair, his pants off but his tight white underwear on. Mr. Rozenofsky, tall, intimidating, fat, in white shirt and tie, removes enormous black belt and whips Scottie's white cotton ass cheeks with vigorous gusto innumerable times. The view is oblong and myopic, but the sound is in stereo, carrying out the window and across the side yard, through the window and into Augie's ears.

Scottie Rozenofsky struggles and kicks and screams and eventually falls limp over the chair, as if broken. Mr. Rozenofsky throws out lashes with the force of a man splitting wood with an axe. Augie Schoenberg gets enormous, painful boner and almost comes in pants. Augie Schoenberg masturbates nightly to image of helpless Scottie Rozenofsky in white underwear hung over chair with brute clothed father brandishing leather belt, administering humiliating ass whipping.

The yanks on the penis don't work well. Semen doesn't come out yet. Orgasms are weak and difficult to conjure up. Penis is too small. Technique is bad. Copy of Playboy with nude Madonna pictures is not exciting enough. Balls don't rise up or down. Hair has barely grown in. Desire is flat and hard to locate. The back page: an assortment of photos, a new band, the Red Hot Chili Peppers, men, naked on stage at rock show, wearing argyle socks over genitals, their white asses bare. Augie Schoenberg yanks and rubs and white fluid sprays onto furry pink carpet in bathroom with no preceding orgasm.

Flashback: the suburbs, Evanston, Illinois, small brick houses, small green lawns, a collection of Oldsmobiles parked on street. 1985, a hot summer, a late afternoon. Augie Schoenberg knocks on door of distant neighbor Paul Cirrincione. No answer.

A bold Augie Schoenberg enters unlocked house and is greeted with cool air, the faint smell of the sea. Green shag carpeting, the sighing sound of an air conditioner newly at rest.

The house has a college-aged daughter who dates men much older than her. Augie Schoenberg walks up steps under the pretext of seeking out Paul, but is determined to rifle through sister's bedroom and find Playgirl magazines. The upstairs, a long curving hallway. Step by slow step. Sounds of yelling in the background. The neighborhood children causing a ruckus, a father berating a boy in the back bedroom. The noise is comforting, father and son are occupied, mother and daughter are out, and Augie Schoenberg enters sister's bedroom and goes to nightstand full of notebooks and fashion magazines and yearbooks. He is not supposed to be here: he knows it's a gross violation of protocol so serious he can't imagine the consequences. Yelling of Mr. Cirrincione, "Hah? What did I tell you? Hah?" Cries of a pre-teen boy who is still a boy.

Augie quickly lifts up Cosmo and Seventeen and purple notebooks with stickers of unicorns and unbelievably finds Playgirl magazine. The naked man is tan and thirtyish, photographed from the upper thighs up, the perspective is skewed, he can't tell how big the penis is, there are no hands for reference, no feet. He considers taking out penis and comparing sizes.

More photographs. Firemen holding firehoses naked, a dark Hispanic man, large ass cheeks, so prominent and hairless Augie smiles. Black man, hairy chest, small light brown penis rests atop coarse pubic hair trimmed into perfect triangle. Blond man fishing nude with bulbous white penis, the head the size of ping pong ball. Another Playgirl. Dangerous yelling in background. Augie knows he could be discovered at any moment. No idea of consequences.

Nude man on motorcycle from behind. Hairy, Italian guy, hairy ass on motorcycle seat, he could be Mr. Cirrincione. Two-toned penis, light brown leathery shaft, beige head. College guys. Nude with footballs. Nude in running shoes. Nude on the Quad. All college guys together from behind, ten asses, ten legs, ten backs, ten masculine heads. Ten lily-white, sideways looks, smiles.

Enough. Augie can't bear the delicious anxiety, the nudity, the apprehension, the threat of discipline in the background, the potential for abuse. He could leave, he could walk down the shag carpeting steps and pretend it never happened. He could keep it all to himself and be content. But there's a drive in him, a relentless urge to see, to experience, to be invisible and find out what happens when you're not supposed to be there.

Augie Schoenberg creeps toward back bedroom, following the voices, the cries. "Hah? What are you stupid? Hah?" "No!" "Hah?"

Augie comes six feet from bedroom doorway and stands still. Father looks down at crying pre-teen boy on bed, browbeating, yelling, neither notice Augie.

"I'd a mind to take the wooden paddle to you, you stupid fucker. I'd a mind to teach you a lesson you'll never forget. Hah?"

"No!"

"What did you say to me? Hah?" Mr. Cirrincione in dress pants and polo shirt, hair busting out the arms, no beer belly, trimmed, athletic, younger, hard line face, wears sunglasses around the block, drives a convertible, fills out the ass of dress pants. Brown shiny shoes. "You stupid motherfucker!" Crack on head with hand. Wedding ring against head. "What the fuck did you say to me?" Smack on face, then three more, fast, open palm on head. "You're lucky you don't get it as bad as me. My ass was bruised for eighteen years from your grandfather. I'd a mind to call him up and have him take a whip to your bare ass. Hah?"

"No!"

"What the fuck did you say? Did you smart-mouth me?" Crack on head. With one hand, turns son over onto bed, rips down pants and beats white ass with hand in rapid, successive spanks that are as loud as cracks of belt. Father spanks son faster to the point of absurdity. Bicep muscles visible, veins in neck visible, dickhead pushing through dress pants visible.

Paul writhes around on bed yelling incomprehensibly. Father spanks harder and faster, holding son by the back of the shirt. "And you don't fuck with me! You don't ever fuck with me!"

Father stops spanking and stands over son, glaring down at him. Admires son's red ass. Pulls back leg, kicks son in ass with brown shiny dress shoe. Stops to think. Takes off dress shoe and beats son in ass with it. Animal wails from son, the heel against his ripped flesh. Grunts from father, animal in department store clothes.

Augie Schoenberg stands paralyzed with fear, now imagining the consequences. Dick in weird state between erection and shrinkage. Admires father's ass through pants. Daydreams of glimpses in locker room of Cirrincione's penis.

Flashback: the swimming pool. Augie alone with Mr. Cirrincione in locker room showers, Sunday morning. Mr. Cirrincione in blue square bathing suit, tied at waist with white strings. Augie on clandestine mission to see the sexiest father on the block naked. Water over half-nude flesh, the face of a guy from Miami Vice, a suave drug dealer, Roman, curved, previously broken nose, hairy pectorals the size of Augie's head, long, bulging legs. Take it off, Augie thinks, you sissy. Take it off, now. Idle chat. Banter. Other fathers enter, all unattractive, fat, pasty. Sons come in, some get nude, daringly. Small, childish dicks, no pubic hair. Augie looks away. Paul Cirrincione enters, takes shower near father, father pulls open bathing suit to let water run over dick. Take it off, you fucker. Pulls down bathing suit and leaves it on floor. Augie stands immobile, entranced. A dick half as long as Augie's arm hangs down past low hanging golf ball sized balls. The almost-bruised, dark-peach sight of male genitals. The almost purple dickhead. The sagging, crinkled nut sack. No pubic hair. The bald white sign of a shaved area. He turns, Augie's dick is hard beneath bathing suit, but he doesn't care. Ass is overlarge and hairy, the buns powerful and meaty as hams, the legs supporting them as if under strain, as if out in the wild, half-man-like, half-mythical, muscle bursting beneath leather flesh: a faun, a centaur.

The walk out of shower room. The legs moving the ass in a slow gait. The perfection of the design, the unbearable beauty of the form. The thoughts of the unattainable. The future.

Consequences arose. In the doorway, Mark Israel with a mean look on his face.

Leg Show open in front of me, Israel's drawers open, the closet door hanging open. My mouth open, but no sound. "What the fuck are you doing, Schoenberg?"

The first reaction I had was to say, 'I was just looking for a pen.'

"I found this in the bathroom." I picked up Leg Show and threw it on his bed. "Is it yours?"

Look of consternation on Israel's face. Not sure whether to be mad at me or not. Upset I was trying to seize control of the situation.

"What? What the fuck is it? What are you doing in here?"

"I was just returning the magazine. I thought it must be yours."

He snorted. "Get the fuck outta here," he hissed. Half-man, half-pussy.

"Sorry." I strode out of the room. I figured it could have been worse. I looked behind me and saw Mark looking around but not moving, as if checking the room for signs of contamination.

19.

Because there was so much tension between Mark, Tony, and I, it was remarkably easier to think of them as sex objects. After all, how could I feel guilty fantasizing about doing unspeakable things to them when I hated them? And view them as sex objects was exactly what I planned to do that night as I stacked up some old crates next to the Harley Hutt's garage and crawled onto its roof with a pair of binoculars hanging off my neck. It was a warm Indian Summer night and I figured I could stay up there for hours if I felt like it.

I knew that the best view into Tony and Mark's bedroom was from that roof, and I planned to watch those two until I saw some real evidence of homosexuality, or as Ted put it, dick sucking. I wasn't mad at them because they were assholes, so much as I was concerned that they were secretly being faggots but openly criticizing me for being the same. I knew I'd never swallow that hypocrisy.

After some struggling and a nasty cut on my arm, I made it up onto the roof shingles and slid across them on all fours like a cat. In the darkness, with the knowledge that I was a spy, I felt inordinately slinky and unabashedly naughty. I couldn't help but giggle to myself.

I lay on my stomach facing their room. The level was right, but the window was farther away than I thought it'd be, and there was a telephone pole partially obstructing my view. Even so, they had the curtains open and there weren't any blinds. Yellow light shone from the room.

I put the binoculars to my face. My eyes flinched from the light, two circular blasts of yellowy-white, and then I looked again. I had a close-up view of a wall. I crawled to the left a few feet and put the binoculars to my face again. This time I saw the top of a TV—my eye holes swaying unsteadily from my unsteady grip—the side of a desk and what I thought was part of Mark Israel's head.

I stared and stared until my arms got tired but nothing moved. It was going on midnight. I wondered how long I should wait. For variety, I gave a look over to Trailer Trash, but saw nothing except a girl I didn't recognize smoking a cigarette on the couch.

And then, without the binoculars I saw Mark Israel stand up and walk across the room toward the window. For the first time, I realized that if he was looking, he'd be able to see me. I lay against the shingles as closely as I could. Mark wasn't looking out the window, though, but stood in a white T shirt sifting through some stuff beneath the windowsill. He turned his back. I put the binoculars back to my face.

Tony popped up and the two chatted momentarily, smiling, and clearly happy with themselves. Mark playfully punched Tony on the arm, and Tony feigned injury. I couldn't follow their movement very easily, the view was too close up, and they kept falling out of range, but when I located them again Mark stood looking down at something, and when I found Tony he wasn't wearing pants.

That penis of his shot upwards so obnoxiously far that it was hard to believe I wasn't looking at pornography. Against the background of his grey T shirt it was immaculately defined, curved, oversized, almost prehensile. Apparently, he had no problem getting it up under the right circumstances.

Mark lightly grabbed it with one hand; I looked up at his face, which was smirking. Soon enough, Tony Valentine turned around, put one foot on the bed, exposing the gap between his ass cheeks, and rested his arms on a shelf. Mark Israel lowered his jeans and underwear, took them off, spit into his palm, and then got right behind Tony.

I could see nothing more than the hulking figure of Mark, in a shirt and no pants, grasping Tony's sides, the hairy ass barely moving, but I could guess the rest.

I made my way down from the garage and trotted back to the house. I got my information. I thought of a thousand ways I could have fun with it, but I figured it was best to play it cool. If I got anymore crap from them, they were in for it. Barebacking in the bedroom. How like a couple of wannabe heteros to risk it—to think they were above risk. I went upstairs and walked loudly past their door.

The next night, all six roommates of the Harley Hutt planned to sit around together drinking beer. We hadn't hung out together in a while, and it was almost necessary that we did, because otherwise it would have really seemed that there were problems in the house, that Tony and Mark were teamed up against me, that there was an unspoken cold war between Victor and me, that Jean-Claude and Paul knew something was wrong but no one would tell them what. I decided not to be nervous around Mark and Tony, but to be brash and bold, and pretend I wasn't harboring any resentment toward anyone.

Tony, Jean-Claude and I watched TV while Victor, Mark and Paul made popcorn and talked in the kitchen. The mood of the evening thus far was hardly festive. Jean-Claude held the remote and was fixed on watching a documentary that showed a circumcision being performed. A newborn was in a baby seat in an operating room. A doctor stood before him, tying the baby up in restraints. The baby began to cry.

I groaned but Jean-Claude said, "Let's see what happens."

After the baby's arms and legs were tied up, the doctor pulled out a stainless steel object and did a little maneuvering in between the baby's legs. Thankfully, the image was not close enough for us to be able to see what was going on in detail, but the sight of the doctor tying up the baby and the knowledge of what he was going to do to the helpless kid was sinister enough.

The narrator said the doctor had put a ring around the baby's penis and then an attached razor would slide back and slice off the foreskin. I was amazed that anyone with a conscience could do something like that to a baby and be able to live with themselves.

The doctor stood peering down at the crying baby with a look of intense concentration on his face and then forced one of his arms forward. The baby let out a wicked scream that made my stomach turn. The scream turned into a howl and then a shocked silence and then another scream and then silence and then screaming. The baby breathed in, vomited on himself, and then his head slumped to the side.

"In shock from the procedure," the narrator said, "the baby has vomited and passed out."

I thought of the scar on my penis. As I'd grown older, it had gotten deeper and more jagged, with ridges and valleys and outstretched little points that looked like a collection of thorns, as if my dick had worn Jesus's fateful crown. That was supposedly my Jewish covenant with God. I thought I may have a few words to say to God if given the chance at a later date.

Jean-Claude's face was crinkled into a look of bewilderment. "That was the most disgusting thing I ever saw."

Tony had his legs crossed. "I'm glad it wasn't me. Did you hear him scream?"

"You assholes are lucky," I said. "You got to keep your entire penis."

They both nodded. Victor came into the room, followed by Mark and Paul. "What was with the screaming?"

"Dude," said Jean-Claude. "You just missed the most foul operation. They showed a baby getting circumcised."

"Cool," said Mark Israel, munching on popcorn. "Lop that thing off."

"You didn't have to listen to him scream," I said.

"Oh, I'm surprised Schoenberg would say that," Israel sneered. "The Jew who isn't a Jew."

"It's not just Jews who do it," Paul Veracruz said. "I'm circumcised and I'm proud of it. Who wants a smelly thing on there?" That disappointed me. Paul was so gregarious about being anti-establishment that he seemed almost smug when he spoke out in support of it.

"Didn't you ever take a shower?" Tony said. "It's not hard to wash."

"It is smelly," Victor said. "When I was in India, I was walking down the street past a gang of schoolchildren. They walked right past me, almost surrounding me, and I smelled the most disgusting smell I ever smelled. I asked my friend what it was and he said, 'That's the smell of smegma.'"

I sat forward and said, "Then they should take a bath, not undergo a surgical procedure after birth. Don't you think it's morally wrong to tie a baby up in restraints and then slice something off of his penis? It's painful trauma."

"They don't remember it," Mark Israel said, with disdain.

"You could also cut off their arm and they wouldn't remember it. What kind of reasoning is that, Israel?" I was getting hot. Nothing made me angrier than people who were glad about their own mistreatment.

"Who wants dick cheese?" Paul Veracruz said. "Besides, uncircumcised dicks are ugly, and chicks don't like it."

Jean-Claude Jolie threw his arms into the air. "Hold on, hold on. My dick is *not* ugly. And chicks; chicks love it."

"They don't do it in Italy," Tony said. "I've been there."

"What were you doing in Italy looking at guys' dicks?" Paul said.

"Fuck you! I have relatives there!"

"What were you doing in Italy looking at your relatives' dicks?"

"Fuck you!"

Victor spoke above them. "They don't do it in India, except if you're Muslim. But I'm glad my parents had it done for me. It's clean and it's neat and I don't have to worry about diseases and things."

"You are such a hypocrite," I said. He looked at me, frozen. "You do all that bullshit work for Amnesty International, fighting for imprisoned people overseas, while a widespread human rights violation is happening right here, and you speak out in favor of it."

"Oh, come on!" Israel yelled. "You're desecrating your heritage!"

Victor sat speechless. I continued. "People have lost their penises. There are botched circumcisions."

All the boys had a vaguely sickened look on their faces. The conversation changed, but the night was not as fun as it probably would have been otherwise. The only strange incident was that Tony Valentine was warming up to me. I was nice to him, but cautiously. Anyway, talking to him made me feel less like I was intentionally not talking to Victor, who I was intentionally not talking to.

Tony and I walked down Cherry Street on the way to the gas station to buy cigarettes. It was one in the morning and we had the campus almost to ourselves. The bars should've been getting out by then, but I saw no signs of it, or maybe no one had gone out that night.

"Can you believe that Israel?" Tony said. "I'm glad my parents left my dick alone. They probably wouldn't have if they weren't from Italy."

I imagined Tony's parents at the hospital after his birth, resolutely refusing to have a circumcision performed. It seemed to me like that was a real act of love of a baby.

"Well, I guess I can't complain," I said. "My penis works fine, and I have no major problems with it." I realized a second too late that even in saying something so neutral, I'd inadvertently brought up the fact that Tony's penis wasn't working fine.

"You're lucky then. To not have to worry about it must be nice."

"Tony, God, I didn't mean that as an insult."

"No, it's fine, really." He paused but I saw a look of consternation on his face. Trouble was brewing. I'd been awaiting the moment he'd confront me for days.

"I don't get it, Schoenberg. I thought you were my friend. I totally trusted you. I told you really personal information. I thought it went without saying that you don't repeat it."

I thought it was best to ask what he meant exactly. I had no idea what his version of events was. "Repeat what? I haven't said anything to anyone."

"Oh, right. All right, that's cool, dude. Nothing happened."

"Tony, what the hell are you talking about?"

"You told her, dude. You told Isabella about my penis. How could you do that? It's the worst thing anyone has ever done to me. What are chicks gonna think of me now?"

I thought for a split second. "I didn't tell Isabella that! Not at all."

"Right. Don't lie, Schoenberg. I mean, you're like a little girl, babbling gossip to everyone just because you've heard it. I mean, grow up."

"I never told her that! Not even close. Who told you that I told her?" If it was

Israel, he had lied.

"Dude, what does it matter. Don't you get it? People aren't gonna wanna hang out with you if you act like that. I liked you, Schoenberg. I thought we were gonna be good friends."

"Fuck you," I said. "Who told you that I told her, and what did I supposedly say, because this is news to me."

"Mark told me, who do you think? He said Isabella came up to him drunk and said she wouldn't fuck an impotent pig like me if she was paid to do it."

So she said impotent instead of bisexual. I wondered which scenario was worse. I couldn't figure out if Isabella had got it wrong or if Mark had, or both of them.

"Tony, she said that because Mark told her she was a whore. He also tried to get her into a three-way with you two, which she didn't want to do. She probably just said that as an insult. I never mentioned your penis thing to anyone. And I have no reason to lie. It seems like you already hate me."

He looked at the sky and didn't answer. The moon shone full, but with the cold weather moving in to stay, it hardly seemed as romantic as it had even a month before. We crossed the street and came to the store. The only noise was from the buzzing of the fluorescent lights above the gas pumps. We walked across the tarmac and I went in and bought the cigarettes. When I walked back outside I looked at Tony in his leather jacket and oversized sweater and almost couldn't believe how confident and mature he appeared to be. I was surprised to realize I knew that the outside was only a facade.

I rejoined him, packing my cigarettes with gusto, and we started to walk back home. "So you really never said that?"

"No. We talked on the porch and then Roberta asked me to set her up with Jean-Claude. After that, I was hanging out with Victor."

"Yeah, I saw that. But, before Roberta and Jean-Claude were dancing together, I saw you on the couch with Isabella. You were telling her something."

He had really put some thought into this. I didn't remember the sequence of events in that kind of detail. "We were talking about the rugby party. She'd been flashing her tits and going nuts. That's all we talked about."

He got out a piece of gum and put it in his mouth. I opened the cigarettes, took one out and lit it. "The rugby party. Well, then did you tell people I told you I wasn't a hundred percent straight?"

"Jesus, Tony, could you be any more insecure? I didn't violate your confidence. Give me a fuckin' break."

"Well, I was worried about you, Schoenberg. I mean, I trusted you with big secrets. You can't tell people that shit."

I could've been nice and said that I understood, but I resented the implication that I was immature and loud-mouthed and a flake. "Then don't tell big secrets to people you don't know very well. It can be a burden on them."

"It's my fault? I thought friends told each other stuff." He choked on his words and threw his hands out in front of him. "You turn things around and try to make other people feel bad about shit you did. It isn't right."

I had no idea what the fuck he was talking about. "I have no idea what the fuck you're talking about."

"I'm sposed to feel bad cause I asked you for advice? I had problems and I didn't know what to do!"

"You wanted someone else to shoulder the burden for your problems, because you're not big enough to deal with them. You transferred the weight of your insecurities onto me, and now you're punishing me for it, because you're too afraid of your own problems to figure out solutions. You wanted someone else to blame so you wouldn't have to blame yourself."

He chewed his gum for a moment and then said, "Wow. Can you repeat that?"

We looked at each other and then we both laughed, nervously at first, and then assuredly.

"Look, Schoenberg, I really was let down. But I trust you. If you said you didn't say it, then I believe you."

"I didn't say anything, you fucker!"

"All right, all right! To be honest, though, Mark and I have been a little weirded out by the situation with you and Victor. Are you guys shackin' up?"

I thought of the scene I'd witnessed through my binoculars and I put my guard up against hypocrisy. "You know, I like him a lot. But I've found out that he's engaged to be married. So, no. I wish we were."

"Married? No, he isn't. He isn't even dating anyone."

"It's arranged."

"Really?"

"Yep. That's what he said. Maybe no one's supposed to know, but I don't give a shit. It's going to happen right after he graduates. She's a newsreader for the BBC."

"He never told me that. So how come you two were in each other's bedrooms all night? You can't tell me there's nothing going on."

"Look, I hoped something could happen, but we're two different people. He isn't even gay, I don't think. Anyway, I wouldn't want to burden you with one of my problems." I gave a sly little grin.

He pushed me. "Aw, Schoenberg, you're a fuck-up."

I stood in the shower. Paul Veracruz was in the first stall soaping up his tattoos, Tony was in the second washing his ass, and I was in the third, the closest to the exit. I felt so much better after talking to Tony that I wasn't anxious walking around the house anymore. Water ran over my head and my eyes and I unabashedly ogled Tony's body. From behind, he conjured up Mr. Cirrincione, the bottom half of his body was so meaty and animal-like. It seemed that his torso sprouted up from his ass as an afterthought, as a separate species. Water, soap, hands running over himself. I wanted so badly to forget Victor, as if that was possible living in the same house as him. I wanted the past two months to disappear like the proverbial dead goldfish disappears, flushed down the toilet. Paul walked by and grinned at me. Then he came back for a second, pointed at me and laughed. I made a face at him, not knowing what was going on. I returned to staring at Tony's butt. I felt warm and fresh, and newly vigorous. Mark came in, bending down in front of me, pulling off the underwear, maybe the very pair I'd fingered. Tony looked over and flinched. "Jesus, Schoenberg." "What?" I asked. He said, "What are you doing?" I looked around, and then I looked down, and I saw that my dick was totally erect.

20.

The building looked the same as any chain restaurant, but it was decorated on the outside with a white picket fence and a porch swing. Marsha Wallenberg, an athletic blond woman who was the captain of the lesbian softball team, stood on the grass in front of the restaurant with a collection of picket signs. She wore sunglasses and held a bullhorn.

"The Harley Hutt boys!" she called out as Jean-Claude, Paul and I approached. "Take a sign." I looked skeptically at Mountain Folks restaurant. Its attempt at recreating down home scenery was tempered by the knowledge that there were five hundred other restaurants exactly like this one. It'd become clear at the Harley Hutt who supported old-time family values and who didn't. Mark told Jean-Claude that Tony and him eat breakfast at Mountain Folks all the time. Paul made an attempt to remind Mark that he wasn't in favor of anti-gay discrimination, but Mark Israel laughed and said, "I don't give a fuck what they do to gays. They don't have to work there." There was a minor argument after that, with Jean-Claude asking Mark if he'd be in favor of discrimination against Jews, and then Mark got mad and said, "That's not the same thing."

Victor had been nowhere to be found. I hoped he was out rounding up the Amnesty International people to go to the protest, but I had a feeling he might not show at all.

Paul and Jean-Claude leafed through the picket signs. One said, "Equal rights for lesbos now! White trash food get out of town!" Another read, "God is gay!"

"I want that one!" Paul said, and proudly hoisted it over his shoulder. The sight was hilarious: heterosexual, tattooed punk rocker proclaims to the world that God is gay. I picked up the white trash get out of town sign and handed it to Jean-Claude.

People were steadily streaming up. Harry arrived with some friends and an older woman I'd met at the meeting who'd been fired. She looked to be in good spirits, and was proudly smiling. The rest of the lesbian softball team was there, dressed in their team jackets, sporting identical ponytails.

The Campus Communists showed up in an old VW van—a collection of lithe, almost albino-like people, who appeared to be frightened. The Feminist Alliance girls arrived last, although I didn't see Isabella or Roberta. I knew Roberta had rehearsal for her play, and I figured Isabella was hung over.

The group assembled into a cluster. Marsha Wallenberg took over. "All right gang, this is the plan. We're going to surround the restaurant and everyone hold hands. Once we've done that, I'll lead the chanting with my bullhorn. If the police bother us, just stand still and don't resist, and whatever you do, don't hit them. Harry is passing out cards for everyone with a number to call if you get arrested. It has the number for the student legal service on it, which has offered to help anyone in case they have trouble with the police."

Harry walked around the group diligently handing out cards. On the far end of the parking lot, a small group with picket signs of their own appeared, but I didn't recognize any of them.

"Who are they?" I asked.

Marsha looked over and said, "Uh oh. It's Reverend Timmons."

The group had signs which read, "Got AIDS yet?" and "God hates fags." One of them read, "AIDS kills faggots dead."

"Who's Reverend Timmons?" I asked, sickened by the messages.

"Oh, some psycho Christian. He's started to show up at all the protests."

"Is that Christianity?" Paul said. "It doesn't seem very Christian to me."

The reverend and his flock stood still across the parking lot. They stared at us with gaping eyes, as if we were aliens, as if we were not even human.

"All right gang," Marsha said. "Let's show this restaurant what we think of them!"

The group cheered and we slowly moved into a circle around the perimeter. I was planning to stand in between Paul and Jean-Claude, but then I thought it'd be fun to see those two holding hands, so I stood on Jean-Claude's right side and Paul grabbed his other hand. A few customers stood in the parking lot, unsure of what to do. They stared at us with narrowed eyes. Harry stood on my other side, and I grabbed his hand.

"Where's Michael Farinelli?" I asked.

"Oh, he wouldn't come," Harry said. "He's afraid someone from his work will see him."

Under the circumstances, I understood, but it still seemed like a wimpy move. A man and two little boys walked out of the restaurant. They looked like your average suburban people, in tacky discount department store clothing. They pushed past the circle in between Jean-Claude and Marsha and the father said, "Now look, boys, these are a bunch of homosexuals. Look at the black one. I can spot a pansy a mile a way." He laughed. "Isn't that something? A black faggot boy. I wonder what his people think of that!"

The little boys looked at us, crinkling their noses.

Jean-Claude said, "Hold me back, dude. Please, hold me back." I squeezed his hand.

When the circle looked to be complete, Marsha Wallenberg came on the bullhorn and shouted, "*Two, four, six, eight. Mountain Folks discriminates!*" We all repeated it in a muscular roar that was a lot louder than I thought it'd be. We chanted it again and again, and the crowd of customers in the parking lot got larger. They stood paralyzed a few yards from us, their eyes wide. The slogan changed: "*We're here, we're queer, get used to it!*" That one was my favorite, and I loved hearing so many people say it at once. Paul Veracruz seemed to take particular pride in it, moving his head along with the rhythm.

"*We're here, we're queer, get used to it!*" The police arrived. At least a dozen squad cars pulled into the lot at an insolently slow pace. "Uh, oh," I said. The cars rolled up to the front of the lot in a single file line in the morbidly accurate formation of a funeral procession. "*We're here, we're queer, get used to it!*" Uniformed cops started to get out of the cars. They all bent down and pulled some things from a cardboard box on the ground. They stood near their car doors, but something was off, the cops looked funny. They were putting on latex gloves.

"What the fuck are those for?" Jean-Claude shouted.

"I told you," I said. "They think we all have AIDS."

The police began to tie surgical masks over their faces. "Jesus Christ," Jean-Claude said. To top it off, the police one by one put on plastic face shields that came down from their hats. "That is unnecessary," Jean-Claude said.

Two police vans pulled up. Police in riot gear piled out the back, some holding German Shepherds on leashes. "*Two, four, six, eight, Mountain Folks discriminates!*"

"Bring it on!" Paul yelled.

"Oh, my God," Harry said. "We're going to be attacked by dogs! If any of those cops fuck with me I'll kick 'em in the nuts."

"*Equal rights are human rights!*"

I grabbed Jean-Claude and Harry's hands tighter. It looked like we were all about to get creamed. My heart raced. My mouth had gone dry. The only thing that kept me from panicking was the feel of the two hands I grasped.

"Disperse." A police bullhorn sounded out, monotone and robotic. "Disperse or you will be charged with mob action."

"We are peaceful protesters!" Marsha Wallenberg called through the bullhorn. "We are law-abiding citizens!"

Jean-Claude Jolie raised his head and began to sing. A deep, booming baritone arose from the circle in the direction of the police. He slowly began to belt out "We Shall Overcome." The crowd joined him after a few notes and we sang so loudly and so beautifully that the police, who had lined up in front of us, looking for all the world like uniformed dentists, stared at each other, wondering what to do. *We shall overcome someday.*

The circle swayed from side to side in time with the song. The perfect mix of men and women in the group made the singing into a beautiful harmony. Jean-Claude sang loudest of all, nodding his head slowly toward the police. The song somehow made even the smallest voice in the circle audible. The smallest voices joined together and rose up and by some unknown force, lifted themselves to a place that seemed to float just above our heads. All the voices joined together with Jean-Claude's, whose voice was not only the loudest, but the lowest, and drowned out the next warning from the police. The dogs barked. The staff of the restaurant had gathered at the windows.

"Oh, shit," Harry said.

"Disperse!" the police called.

"We are peaceful!" Marsha countered.

There was the sound of a rocket being fired. There was a clunk and then a bomb went off. The dogs barked and growled. A white cloud overcame us and Harry shouted, "Tear gas!" He let go of my hand and pulled his shirt over his eyes. I looked at Jean-Claude, who'd closed his eyes and continued to sing. Paul was coughing and struggling to breathe. There was a stinging in my eyes so strong I thought I'd vomit. Fear and panic swept over me, but I didn't let go of Jean-Claude's hand. *Someday.* People ran in front of us, mere illusions in the cloud. Hazy whiteness was everywhere and pain and nausea. I closed my eyes and held Jean-Claude's hand for dear life. *We shall over...*

We sang and sang, two solitary figures, black and white, among the darkness behind my shut eyes, and the horror of the poisonous white cloud outside of them. Dogs growled, people screamed. A second bomb went off. Paul was hurt, I heard him yell, "What the fuck! Get these fuckin' dogs off of me, you motherfuckers!" He let out a cry, and it was serious, a wounded child. I looked over and couldn't see anything. My eyes were covered in a film of pain, it hurt to try to look at anything. There were rough sounds of cops yelling, "Get that fuckin' faggot!" Jean-Claude continued to sing. I heard Marsha Wallenberg let out a terrifying wail. "We are peaceful," she screamed. "Peaceful. You motherfuckers."

"They're biting me, they're biting me!" Paul yelled. Then his voiced was snuffed out, there was a low groan, they must've been kneeling on his back.

Jean-Claude held my hand tight and sang. "*We shall overcome.*" I couldn't join in. Tears streamed down my face, and my stomach churned and moved. I thought I was going to have diarrhea. I thought I was dying.

"Get the faggot who's singing," a cop yelled. "And let the dogs at him first."

"Better they bite him before he bites us, the AIDS faggot."

"Come on!" I yelled at Jean-Claude. "Let's get outta here!"

He kept singing. I pulled at him with all my might. "Are you crazy? Let's go while we have the chance." I tugged and tugged, and finally he relented. The dogs sounded like they were right in front of us. Blind, I figured we had a seventy-five percent chance of running into a cornfield. There, we would be safe. We ran across the grass and stumbled into a rock garden. We must've been on the side of the restaurant. I pictured the back of the place, with its mock outhouse, and knew there was a field beyond it with endless rows of corn. I pulled Jean-Claude, who was coughing and breathing hard, at what seemed like a rapid stride, but was probably a clumsy, slow romp.

I opened my eyes again; we were out of the gas. The wind came toward us off the plains. Stalks hit my face and scratched my arms. I thought we were almost to freedom. We stumbled through the field, the smell of manure and pesticide burning my nose and lungs. We collapsed in the dirt.

We took turns vomiting, and then I staggered to my feet and walked farther back. I dropped my pants and shitted out what felt like the entire contents of my colon in a runny, violent torrent of hot brown crap. It got all over my shoes. I collapsed backwards with my pants around my ankles and tried to catch my breath. My entire head was full of jagged pain. I thought a vessel inside my brain might explode.

After a number of minutes of hyperventilating, my head cleared to the point I thought I could regain my composure. I took off my pants and underwear and then wiped my ass with the shorts. I threw them aside and then put my pants back on. Using a leaf from a cornstalk, I tried to get as much diarrhea off of my shoes as I could.

I crawled up a few feet and found Jean-Claude collapsed face down. I huddled up next to him and shook him. "Are you alive?" I asked.

"I'm dying," he croaked.

"I don't think you are," I said. "Give it a few minutes. This shit will wear off."

He struggled to sit up. "Jesus," he said. "What the fuck happened?"

"I'm worried about Paul," I said. "I think he got attacked by dogs, and I'm sure he got arrested."

"So did Marsha."

We crawled back toward the edge of the fields and peered out at the parking lot. Most of the cop cars had gone, and most of the people. I had no idea where the rest of the protestors were.

"Isn't it different now," I said. "It looks like nothing happened."

"Look there," Jean-Claude said.

In front of one the police cars, Paul and Marsha lay face down on the pavement, their arms in handcuffs. Their heads were pressed to the ground. Paul's shirt was almost ripped off. The two bodies didn't move. They looked like corpses.

"Those motherfuckers. I don't know how those pigs live with themselves."

"They have small, ignorant minds," Jean-Claude said. "They do anything they're told."

We walked back into the maze of corn and tried to find a safe way to get home.

Paul said, "They had us lay in the parking lot forever. The dogs had totally eaten me up. My clothes were almost completely torn off, and when we got to the station they took Marsha and me to a holding cell and made us take off all our clothes. Then, we had to stand there naked for like an hour while all these cops came in and made fun of us. They told Marsha she was so fat and ugly and so like a man it was no wonder she couldn't get a guy to have sex with her.

"They thought I was gay." He spoke in a tired, low voice that was so unlike his usual enthusiasm it killed me to hear it. "One told me my dick was the smallest he'd ever seen, and that it must be good for fucking guys up the ass. They made us bend over and then they stuck their fingers up our assholes. They did it when we came in and before we left. It was the most humiliating thing I ever experienced. They told us we must have drugs stuffed up our assholes."

"Write down everything that happened. You can use it in court," Jean-Claude said. He passed me a bottle of whiskey. The three of us had been killing it on my bed for most of the night, while Tony, Mark and Victor watched movies in the living room. "My mom's a big-time lawyer. She can help you."

Paul said, "They told me I must've liked having their fingers up my ass. They said, 'Isn't that what you faggots get off on?' That Marsha, you should've seen her. She was standing there nude, and she kept trying not to cry. They wouldn't stop insulting her. I've never heard anyone speak to a woman that way."

"Oh, if I'd been there, I would've kicked their ass," Jean-Claude said.

"No," Paul said. "It doesn't work that way. They said they were going to charge us with attempted murder because we supposedly bit them. They said, 'You AIDS faggots are gonna die sooner than you would've anyway.'"

"I don't get it," Jean-Claude said. "You're not even gay."

"It doesn't matter," I said. "It's what they think you are."

I lay in bed staring at the ceiling. I'd missed classes, I'd been gassed, I'd run from attack dogs, and predictably I couldn't sleep. Sometime in the middle of the night, my door slowly opened and a dark, silent figure approached the bed. Victor sat down on the edge and said, "Hey crusader for justice. What happened today?"

"I don't wanna talk about it."

"Augie, I wanted to go, but I couldn't get out of class. I couldn't miss it today."

"Yeah, well, you have your priorities."

He put his hand on my shoulder. "Come on, don't be like that. I bet it was fun, running from the cops."

"It wasn't fun," I cried. "It was terrible. Why weren't you there? They had dogs on us, and tear gas and Paul almost got killed. Jean-Claude and I escaped through the cornfields, but just narrowly. If it wasn't for the student legal service, Paul and Marsha would still be in jail. I can understand why Tony and Mark wouldn't be there, cause they're dumb fucks, but I was sure you'd go. You said you would be there."

"Augie, I didn't have time. I'm sorry."

I rolled over and faced the wall. "I bet you had time to plan your stupid wedding. Now get the fuck out of here."

"It doesn't have to be like this," he said. "We could enjoy the time we have."

"Oh, I'm enjoying myself. I'm having the time of my life. You're a hypocrite, Victor. You only care about yourself. You call yourself a political activist?"

Victor sighed and got up and left. I didn't want him to leave, though. I wanted him to stay with me all night.

21.

I sat on the top of the steps alone, gazing down at the living room. We'd come from a Halloween party at Trailer Trash on a mission to smoke opium. Had it been a few days earlier, I would've gladly tried it to gather information for the plot of *Last Boat to Manchuria*, but by then it seemed pointless. My screenwriting instructor had just returned my screenplay. He called it trite and derivative and overly-melodramatic, with wooden characters. He suggested I scratch the whole thing and start over with something more worthwhile. I read his words, standing on the grass outside the literature building, as if they weren't real, like they might change if I rewound the day and started it over again. I'd no idea what I would write in its place, but the scene below me looked like a good start.

Isabella, dressed as Wonder Woman, suggested the group get naked and wrap themselves in plastic wrap. Most seemed unsure, but Paul Veracruz dropped the canvas hat and whip of his Indiana Jones costume and became the first to disrobe and wrap himself up as snugly as leftovers. Tony, the soccer player, and Mark, the cop, followed, mercifully. Mark had swaggered around the party flashing a badge and shining a flashlight in everyone's eyes, which gave me the chills. I was on edge after the day of action fiasco and I was on edge around Mark Israel anyway, so the combination was unfortunate.

Roberta and Jean-Claude relinquished their roles as Billy Dee Williams and Diana Ross from the Billie Holiday movie in favor of playing the roles of Roberta and Jean-Claude in plastic wrap, and Victor, formerly dressed as Batman, modestly removed his costume in the corner.

It was just as well: the Batman mask had made him look alarmingly mysterious, and nearly sent me into despair. In his bed, I had felt that for just a moment I was finally back to living life like everyone else does. But that passing contentedness had been robbed from me just as soon as I grasped it, and now I sat above the room watching a perfectly even number of guys and girls smoke opium in my living room, nude, wrapped in plastic wrap: Paul Veracruz and his girlfriend, Sheila, Roberta and Jean-Claude, Victor, Isabella, Mark and Tony, and two blond girls I didn't recognize. Perfectly even except for me—the odd man out—Augie Schoenberg, a.k.a. Armando Aguilar, the right fielder for the Chicago White Sox, imagining I'd be so happy in this costume, as if it'd make me feel like I was a star, or at least a different person for a while.

To my horror, Isabella loosened her Saran Wrap till it floated off of her like so much dead skin. She stood before Victor naked, her brown pussy hair as thick and coarse as a badger. Soon, Paul and Sheila removed their plastic coating and Paul's little arrow-shaped dick sprung upwards into an erection. The couple eased themselves to the floor and began making out.

Roberta and Jean-Claude did the same and before I could gasp, they were openly having sex in front of everyone. It didn't look sexy; it wasn't like in the movies. Roberta lay back motionless, as though she were infirm, and Jean-Claude mounted her, balanced on his hands. The only thing touching her was his dick.

Paul and Sheila looked no better. The view of Paul's ass was nice, but Sheila lay on the ground, staring at the ceiling, looking almost catatonic. Paul removed his dick from inside her folds and then walked himself forward on his hands. He thrust his crotch toward her mouth and she opened her lips to take his penis in, the flesh of it shining from the juice from her pussy. Her head lifted off the floor, reaching up with her neck to swallow more of his dick.

Isabella crawled over to them on her hands and knees, still wearing her Wonder Woman tiara, and quickly rubbed Sheila's clitoris.

Mark Israel sat against the wall, a giant blob of hairy flesh, with one of the blond girls balanced in his lap. He easily held her up with his hands planted under her tiny ass cheeks, and then he lowered her down over his boner. The difference in size between them was remarkable: the girl looked for all the world like a chihuahua straddling a grizzly bear.

Tony and the other blond chick exchanged shy glances. Paul Veracruz was still fucking Sheila but now Sheila was rubbing Isabella's cunt. Victor sat in a chair motionless.

The blond girl approached Tony. I could only imagine the horror going through his mind. I wondered if he'd be able to get it up. The girl, nymph-like and alabaster white, planted little kisses over Tony's face. He sat back and didn't touch her.

Isabella crawled toward Victor and then sat on his lap. I almost cried out. Victor put a hand on her hip and looked up at her expectantly. Meanwhile, Roberta bounced on top of Jean-Claude, who was on his back. Israel fucked the blond chick from behind. The nymph girl worked Tony's oversized, wobbly penis with her tiny little hand, coaxing it gently up and down with a determined look on her face.

I'd had enough. I went up to my room, almost nauseous. If Isabella and Victor were going to do it, then I didn't want to watch. The sex in the room looked so mechanical and robotic that it was practically obscene. I understood why sex should take place in private, where reality can't be seen by anyone except willing participants. I understood why sex is so unrealistic-looking in movies.

For a second, I thought maybe I'd join in, but knew there was no one who'd have sex with me, especially in front of other people. After a while, Roberta came up and asked what was wrong. I wanted to tell her that I was disturbed that no one had even mentioned using condoms, let alone actually used one. But I didn't say that. I just told her I was tired. I'd heard them talk: they were only concerned with whether or not the girl was on the pill. If they didn't think they were at risk for anything besides pregnancy, then I decided to let them be fools. I lay in bed and stressed out about the house, about lung cancer, about ridiculous neurotic things. I figured I would die young, a failure at screenwriting, and practically a virgin.

The door to Arundhati Singh's office was closed. I knocked once, softly, hoping she was there. I'd decided to ask her for information about arranged marriages in

India. I wanted to pretend I was going to use the information for a paper, but we'd already covered that topic and had moved on to religious conflicts. I knew I'd have to tell her the truth.

A quiet voice said, "Come in."

I pushed open the door and peered inside. A string of beads hung from the ceiling. I divided them in two and walked through the opening. She sat at the desk looking interested but tired. An almost green pallor hung on her face. Above her was a poster of the Taj Mahal.

"Hi," I said. "I hope I'm not bothering you."

"No! In fact, I'm more than happy to see you." Her usual brightness returned once she spoke, but I had some reservations about disturbing her with my problems. It seemed like she had something serious on her mind.

I sat down. "Well, I had a few questions for you, but they don't necessarily relate to the class."

She gave me a quizzical look, but said, "Oh, August, I'd be more than happy to help you with whatever you need. What is it?"

I struggled to think how to put it. "Well, there's someone I know who's Indian, but I found out a little too late that this person is in an arranged marriage. I had kind of been interested in dating this person, but it seems that the prospects of that are pretty slim. I don't know, I just thought that an arranged marriage is something that doesn't happen in the United States. Or even really in India. The stories we read about arranged marriages were so old, and we've read contemporary stories about people who seem to date and then marry like anyone else."

Arundhati Singh sat up a little and looked me right in the eye. "Oh, arranged marriages are alive and well in India, and also among Indian Americans. It's not a tradition that seems to be in much danger of dying out. But yes, there are those who choose not to go the traditional route. There is a degree of personal choice involved."

"But how much personal choice? Is it something that's required or can you just make up your mind to marry whoever you want?"

"Among Indian Americans there's more freedom to do as you wish, but then the parents and the extended family are quite concerned about keeping the culture intact once they're in the United States. It can be a source of some contention. Now, is this person you're talking about Hindu or Muslim?"

"Hindu," I said.

She nodded. "Among Muslims, the tradition is more strict, but the woman still has the opportunity to say no. The idea in arranged marriages is that the financial circumstances of the couple will be worked out in advance so the couple won't have money problems. Also, the two are encouraged to get to know each other so that they'll know if they like each other, but the idea Westerners have of romantic love is much different in India. Marriage comes first, love comes later."

I thought that over. I supposed our idea of falling in love was influenced by the fairy tale idea of falling in love with Prince Charming and riding off into the sunset. I had never thought of romantic love as a cultural convention.

"But isn't it viewed as a violation of your personal liberties? I mean, what if you're not ready to get married, or you don't want to get married at all?"

Her face brightened a little. "In Western culture, the idea is that love will conquer all. In India, it's thought that good planning will help the couple deal with problems. It's just reversed. Traditionally, though, Indian culture doesn't have the same ideas of falling in love and living happily ever after. Also, it's not considered desirable for a woman to not be married at all. There's always a lot of pressure from the parents."

"But I don't understand why this would happen in the United States. Wouldn't someone who was born and raised here want to do it the American way?"

She leaned back in her chair and looked up for a second. "Well, that all depends on the situation. You refer to your problem as having to do with a mysterious, 'this person.' Is it an Indian woman you have fallen in love with?"

"No, it's an Indian man." I was so glad to say that. I wanted to be able to tell her the whole story, since she was the only person I knew who could give me advice that would shed some light on Victor's actions.

"Oh," she said, looking at me delicately. "I see. Well, that can be very complicated. Same-sex relationships are very rare among Indians, even in America."

"It's not that simple, anyway. I don't even think he's gay. I have no idea what's going on. But I couldn't have been more surprised to hear about the marriage. He was born and raised here, and grew up in the suburbs like I did."

"Do you know anything about the marriage? Do you know who the wife is?"

"She's a family friend, I think."

"It's probably an arrangement that the families worked out long ago. The parents were planning for their children's well-being. I suppose it's possible that he could opt out of an arrangement, but if the wedding has been planned already that would be very difficult."

I really had no idea how much pressure Victor was under to go through with this. I'd been prone to thinking of him as being a wimp for marrying this girl, but there wasn't much sense in that, since I had no confidence that Victor would want much of a relationship with me anyhow.

"But if he really wanted to, could he say that he didn't want to marry her?"

"Well," she said. "It's hard to say without knowing them, but I suspect he probably could. His parents might be a little upset, but I'm sure they'd start suggesting other women to him after a time."

"All right. Thanks for the information."

"Oh, I hope it helped."

"It did, it did."

Her face hung low. I wondered if she always looked like that close up but I had never noticed, or if there really was something wrong. "By the way, is everything all right?"

She looked startled. "Oh, yes," she said and gave a small laugh. "I'm fine, I suppose. But my son has been ill and I've been under some stress."

"Oh my god, I'm sorry!" I exclaimed. "I shouldn't have bothered you with my stupid problems!" I felt like the world's biggest asshole, interrogating her like a selfish nincompoop while her son could very well be dying.

"No, really, it's fine. I enjoy talking to you." Her voice sunk to a soothing, reassuring place. "You have a sharp mind, you know."

I felt foolish even entertaining the thought of a compliment when she was dealing with problems so much more serious than mine.

"I really feel awful. I shouldn't have intruded. But I hope your son will be OK."

She looked at the wall. "Well, at this point I don't know, but I'm hoping for the best."

I didn't want to press anymore. I could imagine a lot of things, and didn't need to force the details from her.

"I'm sure he'll be fine," I said.

She looked at me hopefully. I thought my generic consolation would have absolutely no impact on her, but her pleading face gave me the sign that she had really needed to hear it.

22.

The cold weather arrived in full force and I had to abandon my beloved corduroy coat for a ski jacket. The wind blew across campus in fierce, cruel gusts and even the ski jacket offered limited protection. I dreaded to think of January and February and the blizzard-like conditions that would bring.

On a particularly cold and gray Tuesday I sat in Arundhati Singh's class long after it had gotten out. We'd been reading a Salman Rushdie book and I was commiserating about how much better of a writer he was than me. The entire class had left, but I sat in the empty room, not wanting to go to the Dickinson class and not wanting to go home.

Jose Rubenstein walked in, clad as always in a Hawaiian shirt. He wore his silver glasses and had a thoughtful look on his face. I wondered if he had another class in that room, but I also hoped he was coming in just to talk to me.

"Hey, Schonenberger, what are you doing?"

I didn't bother to correct him, the mistake was so cute. "Oh, I was just thinking, I guess."

He sat down next to me and looked straight ahead, just like I was. "Yeah. Sometimes you just gotta stop and watch the grass grow."

I was glad he didn't ask what was wrong.

"Do you graduate this year?" I asked.

"Oh, yeah. Finally. It's a big deal for the folks. I'm the first to go to college."

"Really. What do you think of this class?"

He sighed and shifted a little in his seat. "I don't know. I wanna like it, but I don't think this chick likes me."

I figured everyone must like Arundhati Singh as much as I did. "Why not?"

"You should see what she wrote on my paper. She said I had some vaguely interesting points but that I had failed to convince her of anything."

I felt almost embarrassed that she had liked my papers so much. "Uh oh."

"I guess I'm not a brain like you, Schonenberg."

"I could help you with the next one, if you want." I had no idea how, but I wanted to do something nice.

"Really? That's awesome." He looked around the room as if there were other people there. "I like this guy," he said to the invisible others.

I giggled. He scribbled something on a piece of paper and handed it to me. "Call me anytime you want, Schonenberger. We'll get together and drink some beers. Oh, yeah, and work on the paper."

"Well, first things first," I said.

He patted me on the head. "Cheer up, buddy boy, the sky ain't fallin.'"

I hoped he was right.

The turkey sat on the dining room table of the duplex in Evanston. It was three-fourths intact, but the meal was done. The only people at the table were my parents and me. Everyone else in our family was either dead or living thousands of miles away, and I didn't have any brothers or sisters. We'd eaten the entire meal, but had barely made a dent in the food. Seeing the turkey sitting there with only one side cut away made the meal seem like a terrible waste, as if the bird didn't deserve to die just to feed our measly family on Thanksgiving.

To compensate, my parents decided to dissect my life. "Are you in a relationship?" my mother asked. "With a man?"

I wanted to disappear, or at least crawl under the table. "No!" I said. "I'm single."

"He's a bachelor," my father said.

"A bachelor? What's a gay bachelor? August, I don't think this gay lifestyle is working out for you. Shouldn't you settle down with someone?"

"Mom, I'm only twenty-two!"

"You're almost twenty-three," she said. "You're not getting any younger."

"He's younger than we were when we got married," my father said.

"They have gay marriage in Denmark," my mother said, ignoring him. "You could do it there. And in Holland. Why don't you get married?"

"I don't have anyone to get married to. Besides, you have to be Dutch. You can't just show up as an American and get married."

"Maybe you should dress nicer. Who wants to marry someone in thrift store clothes? Tomorrow, we'll go shopping."

"People should get married because they love each other, not because they have nice clothes," my father said. "That's frivolous."

"It's frivolous to look nice?" my mother said. "Is that a crime?"

"I can't get married until I meet someone. I live in a small town. It isn't easy."

My father said, "Things will pick up when you're in Chicago."

"You can go to the social group for gay Jews," my mother said. "Barbie Liebman's son went to those meetings. He met a nice guy and now they have a townhome in Lakeview. It's right by Wrigley Field. I shudder to think of the property taxes they're paying, but oh no, they had to live where the gay neighborhood is. I don't know why; they're married. They don't go to gay nightclubs anymore, like some people."

"Mom, I can go out to clubs if I want to."

"He's young," my father said. "He likes to go dancing."

"Dancing," my mother said. "He barely danced at his own Bar Mitzvah."

Memories of a banquet hall full of family friends I barely knew raced through my mind. I wore a blue suit and a yarmulke and was told I could dance with whatever girl I wanted, which was supposed to be an honor, but I didn't want to dance with any of them, at least not for the slow dances. I wanted to dance with David Gold, a guy from my junior high school. Of course, that had never happened, at least outside of my dreams. Despair fell heavily on my head.

"You could move to Israel, and work on a kibbutz," my mother said. "Sandra Bernhard did that. You like that woman. She goes on Letterman."

"It'd be like a dream to live in Israel. I would jump at the chance," my father said.

"Why did you have me circumcised?" I blurted, almost crazed.

"What!" my mother screamed. "Have you lost your mind?"

"It's a tradition," my father said. "It's a covenant with God."

"It's a brutal mutilation, and you did it to me willingly. I have a scar now, an ugly scar. And I'll never forgive you for it!"

My mother burst into tears. "You deride your own religion. We raised you better than that!"

"It's a mainstay of our faith. It's not to be misrepresented," my father said.

"It's an act of ignorance. It's blind adherence to authority, from the days when people were illiterate and stupid. And you both bought into it like lame-brained sheep. You can't even think for yourselves!"

"What have I done?" my mother cried.

"August, I think you need to go lay down for a while."

"I do! Because I'm too hot-headed to deal with any of this bullshit. Thanks a lot for the turkey!" I bounded out of the room and went upstairs. My heart was racing and I felt an incredible amount of fear. I had no idea why I said what I did, but it took away for a moment the longing I felt for Victor and the aching loneliness that plagued every thought I had. For a few fleeting seconds at the table, I felt like I had other things in my life to worry about. But minutes later, I knew that I didn't.

23.

I walked into the Hutt with an enormous travel bag over my shoulder. I hadn't wanted to stay in Evanston all weekend, but the thought of coming back to campus didn't sit right in my head either. I felt like I didn't belong at home and I didn't belong at school. The thought of either place weighed on my head like a hefty blow.

Jean-Claude sat in the living room alone, drinking a cup of coffee. He had a book open on his lap. The room was lit by one small lamp.

"It's amazing," I said, bringing in the wind with me. "All by yourself, you've managed to make this room look like a nineteenth century library."

He gave a dry little laugh. "Well, I am the house intellectual."

"You might be right. Where's your girlfriend?"

"She's still in St. Louis for Thanksgiving. I think they were having a family reunion. So, Augie, you missed all the action around here."

I sat down and unzipped my jacket. "What action? Another evening of opium and Saran Wrap?"

He shook his head slowly. "I came back on Saturday and things were out of control. Your friend Isabella went into heat."

That didn't sound good. I prayed she hadn't slept with Tony, or anyone else.

"On Friday, she slept with Mark Israel. And then on Saturday, we had a little party, and she spent the evening with Victor."

"What do you mean 'spent the evening with?'"

"Like, Victor gave her the hot beef injection."

I rested my forehead in my palm. She knew how depressed I was over him. It couldn't have been more arrogant of her. "Oh, well," I said. "I don't own Victor. And Isabella certainly will do whatever she wants. Still, it's pretty sleazy."

Jean-Claude nodded. "Yeah it is. I mean, she's like a joke around here now. Tony was going, 'I'm next!' But he said it to her, and she was like 'OK!'"

"Oh, my God. I wish she would flunk out already. Or die of cirrhosis of the liver."

"And what about Mark and Victor? Would you wanna fuck somebody that one of those two just fucked?"

I was astounded by how unsexy accounts of sex could seem. Secondhand stories of who slept with who made sex sound greedy and self-important. "What idiots. They just wanna fuck somebody for the sake of it so they can feel like they had a wild and crazy youth. Not too many girls wanna sleep with those two."

"No, they don't."

I stood up and yawned, but the yawn turned into a groan. "I don't get it. This house hasn't been half as fun lately as I thought it would be. Weren't there more parties in other years?"

"There totally was. Nobody's getting along. I don't care, though, I'm spending most of my time at Roberta's. I wanted to tell you, thank you for setting me up with her. I've never met anyone quite like her."

"Oh, it was my pleasure. So, is Isabella here tonight, perhaps in someone's bedroom?" I honestly thought there may be a chance she would be.

"I don't think so, dude, but I haven't been upstairs tonight. Your boyfriend Victor has been asking about you, though. I think he missed you this weekend. He didn't go home for Thanksgiving. I don't know why."

"Ha! I hardly think he missed me at all. My absence doesn't usually drive men to fuck the nearest available woman."

He looked at me intently, his eyes droopy and white as milk. "I don't know what's happening between you two. But you should talk to him. I know that you want to. The silent treatment is not your specialty."

He was right. I was terrible at trying to avoid people. I went up to my bedroom and sat on the windowsill. I pulled a bottle of brandy from the floor and poured it into a plastic cup. I'd seen Tippi Hedren and Suzanne Pleshette drinking brandy in *The Birds*, and I thought I'd give it a try. It seemed like an incredibly mature drink to me, and I wanted nothing more than to grow up and be rid of campustown bullshit. When I sat in the auditorium watching *The Birds*, I felt the strongest envy of Tippi Hedren. She drove around San Francisco in her convertible, with no need of a job or worries about income to stifle her, pursuing the man she wanted on a whim. But it was her arrival in Bodega Bay that made the birds start attacking everyone. For some reason, she upset the balance in the small town, and then the environment turned against the people, leaving them all beaten and bruised.

During the discussion, I told the instructor that I had tried to come up with a reason that her presence in town would cause the birds to start attacking everyone, but I couldn't think of anything. He said that it had to do with sadistic voyeurism and fetishistic scopophilia. I asked what those were, and another student said they were tools used by the filmmaker to satisfy the supposed level of castration anxiety in the intended audience.

I was still a little hazy on the concepts, but the idea was that the female character is portrayed as a flawless image of beauty and that reassures the male spectators that she is not a threat, but her lack of a penis reminds the audience of their castration anxiety, which presents a need for the woman to be punished.

I actually found myself admiring Tippi Hedren; she didn't threaten my penis. But I read later in the class essays that my admiration for her was narcissistic visual pleasure, which when combined with voyeuristic visual pleasure produces the desire to see. I guessed it was Freudian.

I wondered if my experiences in the shower at the Harley Hutt were voyeuristic or narcissistic or both. I certainly had the desire to see, but it was when I wanted to participate that problems arose.

The brandy seeped down my esophagus in a slow, burning wave. Almost immediately it rebounded from my stomach and came back in my mouth in a gush of acid. I swallowed it again and my stomach burned and roared. I'd been in pain for the past few weeks. I thought I was developing an ulcer.

Nevertheless, I took another swig of brandy and felt the tension ooze out of my neck and shoulder muscles. If Tippi Hedren could handle it, then so could I. I was exhausted from the weekend and the train ride back to school, and I sat in silence, wondering what to do. I was too high-strung to sleep, I knew that, but I couldn't imagine what else I could do late on a Sunday night.

I wished I had a TV in my bedroom so I could at least turn on some music videos and drown out the noise in my head. Because there was noise, but then I heard something different.

It was far away and it was tinny, but I could tell that it was laughter, a woman's, too euphoric to be sober, coming from Victor's room. Then I heard talking, muffled but still intelligible, and I knew who it was. Isabella was over.

I walked over to the wall and crouched down by the radiator. The heat came on for a minute and I couldn't hear much but when I did, it was Isabella, and she said, "I mean, what are you gonna do, spend the rest of your life with some gay guy?"

And then I heard Victor and he was laughing.

I woke in my bed wearing my clothes. It was still night. The room was freezing. I kicked off my shoes and pulled the blanket over me. The only sound was the hiss of the radiator. I wrapped the blanket around me as tightly as I could, trying to trap all the heat. I dozed off momentarily, my mind still fuzzy from the brandy, and then my door squeaked open. My first thought was that Victor was coming in. My stomach burned anew. I hadn't really spoken to him in weeks, and after what I'd heard earlier, I didn't think I wanted to speak to him ever again. Footsteps came toward me, bearing a figure in white athletic shorts. It wasn't Victor.

He sat on the bed and put his arm around me. Tony Valentine. "Augie, man, how was your weekend?"

"Fine," I croaked, my voice scratchy from sleep.

"I missed you, dude," he said. "It seemed like this weekend went on forever."

A sense of anticipation came over me. I wondered just how much he missed me.

"Why are you sleeping in your clothes?" I shrugged. "Get out of those," he said softly, pulling at the sleeve of my shirt. I went limp and let him pull the shirt off. After it was over my head, my hair stood on end from static electricity. Tony smirked and patted my hair down. "Are you gonna sleep in your jeans?" I shrugged my shoulders again. "You can't sleep in those, Augie. Take those off." He unbuttoned my pants, and I flinched from ticklishness. I felt like I was at the doctor, getting felt up. I wasn't an actor, I was the subject.

The jeans came down and my dick stood hard inside my underwear. Tony peeled off my socks and then noticed my erection. "Oh, ho," he whispered. "Look at you." He rolled onto the bed and pressed himself against me. The feel of his warm, hairy torso against my boner was better than the feeling from the brandy. It was a feeling of replenishment.

He put his face down into my neck, but he didn't kiss me. Our bodies were dry, our genitals encased in cotton. The radiator gave a slow, burning warmth that slowly wafted over to the bed. I reached down and slipped my hand into his pants. I grabbed the top of his dick and wrapped my hand around it. The skin was elegantly soft above the hardness beneath it and I expertly moved my wrist up and down till he moaned. You're amazing, he said. Keep doing that. He pulled down his underwear by the ass and his entire shaft was revealed, big as my forearm. I grasped his penis like my life depended on it, rubbing it so softly and quickly that Tony closed his eyes and said I don't know what you're doing but don't think of stopping. My fingers never touched the head of his penis, but simply moved the skin from the shaft up till it reached just over the tip of his dick and then I pulled it down. I was fascinated by the ease of the motion, by the speed of it, by the amazing feeling he got from having a dickhead that's been protected from wear and tear. I wanted it in my mouth.

Stop, he said. I'm gonna come. I released him, and he pulled off my underwear. My dick slapped against my stomach and Tony put a hand around it. He was cold, and his palm was hard. It felt like my dick was being rubbed by a glove. I pushed him on his back and grabbed the base of his dick and then fed the top of it into my mouth. I had never sucked one so large and had to open as wide as I could. I slid my tongue around its head, slowly and muscularly, and then closed my lips around it and fed it down my throat till I almost gagged. Jesus, Tony said. The head tasted of salt and sour food, but it felt warm inside me and I wanted it down as far as it would go.

Tony lay back with his eyes closed. I let the dick out of my mouth and it dropped against his abdomen in a wet splat. I grabbed it again and jiggled my wrist. Tony reached out and took my penis in his hand and ground his fingers around it slowly. The feeling was almost unbearable, he was touching me in infinitesimal spots that I could never find on my own. Pinpoints of ecstasy started to engage themselves inside me. I wanted more. I wanted my mouth on his, I wanted my dick in his asshole. I ached to reach out and place a finger or two over in between his buns. I couldn't reach, though. There were levels we would not go to.

Eyes closed, he breathed harder and faster. The muscles in his chest tensed, he rolled his head around, and then for a second was completely still, he shouted quickly and a stream of hot goo landed on my arm. Oh, he cried. Oh, shit. He caught his breath and then pulled me on top of him. You're fuckin' amazing, he said.

My dick was still rock hard, and I could feel a dabble of pre come moving upwards. Tony rolled me onto my side and his head went downwards. I held his head with both hands and he took me inside his mouth. There was an awful scraping feeling. Don't use your teeth, I told him. He came back up and wrapped his hand around me again. I lay my head against his chest and shut my eyes, dreaming of him naked, fantasizing about running my hands over his ass. I wanted to slide myself into him so well that he would beg for more.

I dreamed of Victor's hand around my penis, and the feeling of Tony's dick in my mouth and the thought of Mark Israel's ass getting spanked with a belt. I dreamed of Mr. Cirrincione nude, twirling around under the spigot, his bathing suit on the floor, and of the woman in Leg Show with a banana up her cunt. I dreamed of thick, veiny foreskins and hairy, mule-like dicks that hung off of disgusting men from dirty gay porno mags. I dreamed of the Kama Sutra for men, three Indian guys with dicks up their asses and in their mouths. And when the pictures in my head came together as one, and the feeling of Tony's hand in different places started to feel like it was all over the place at the same time, I burned inside my ass and on the outside of my dick and the two feelings merged and then I yelped and felt a brief moment of weightlessness, and then squirted juice onto Tony's stomach and fell back on the bed.

Tony held me close to him. Good, he whispered. That was awesome. He kissed me on the forehead. We lay silent for a few minutes and then Tony sat up. I don't have to tell you Augie, this can go no further than this room. If I find out you told anyone, I'll be very upset with you.

Oh, fuck you, I said. I'll tell the entire campus if I want. Kiss my ass.

I'm warning you, Schoenberg, he said. I talked to Isabella this weekend, and I know now that you did tell her the shit I told you. I'm really pissed off about it. Just remember, don't tell anyone.

He got up from the bed and looked for his underwear. You're a fucking pussy, I said. You're fuckin' with the wrong person. Now get the fuck out of my room.

Listen to me, he said. Not one word to anyone. I'm not a big proud homo like you, that marches in parades. I have a reputation. So keep your mouth shut.

I'm going to tell every single person I know, I said. And you can learn to deal with it.

He made a fist. Remember. Not one word.

What was wrong with Mark Israel tonight? I asked. Does he have a headache?

He glared at me, naked, athletic shorts dripping out of his hand. He glanced quickly toward the door. I turned and looked and saw Victor standing in the doorway in boxer shorts. He stared at us silently, eyes wide and alarmed.

Remember what I said, Tony said, pointing at me. He walked past Victor without saying a word and left the room.

Victor was motionless. On Tony's way out, his ass looked wobbly and dimpled.

He's a fat pig, I said to Victor. Don't you think?

24.

I didn't learn. I didn't learn the first time, and I did it again. I went into Tony and Mark's room when they weren't home. I wasn't looking for porn this time, although I did find some, but I watched their TV so I could see Victor's fiancee. Tony and Mark were the only ones with cable and I found out from the TV guide that there was a British station that had news from the BBC. I was quiet and I was careful, but it was a dangerous operation. I'd no idea what Mark Israel would do if he found me in there again, especially now that I'd moved in on his blow job territory.

Anyhow, I was mad at all of them, not just Tony and Mark. They'd had another shooting contest that afternoon, but this time I wasn't invited, I don't know why. I came home from class around four and while I walked past Victor's bedroom the door was pushed closed by somebody's hand, but I couldn't tell whose. When I got into my room I heard the unmistakable soundtrack to *Visit to the Doctor's*. I'd have thought that at least Jean-Claude or Paul would have felt guilty over excluding me, but neither of them had said anything about it to me at all, even later on when Paul invited me to go to a party with all of them. I'd said no, which was the only way I could think of to salvage my self-esteem.

The guide said the news came on at midnight, so at the designated hour I stole through the empty house and into Tony and Mark's bedroom on tiptoes, sat down on the floor, and with my face almost pressed against the TV screen, pushed the on button. After a minute of searching, I found what I was looking for. Channel 47. The News From London. And there she was in front of me: a young, gorgeous woman in a black suit and a flaming red blouse. She had big, almond-shaped eyes surrounded by fake eyelashes and eyeshadow that had the slightest bit of glitter in it. She had a long, thin nose. Her long, black hair was tied up in the back with what looked like a gold butterfly. Her skin was the color of honey and it almost glowed. The caption labeled her Sarita Gupta.

I sat back and raised an eyebrow at her. I knew she was my age, but I was having trouble putting that into perspective. There she was in London, reading the news on TV in an expensive black suit, thoughts of her upcoming marriage dancing around her mind, while I sat in rural Illinois wearing thrift store clothes and worrying about how I would pay for groceries.

I thought I must've made some rotten choices in my life.

I tried to find faults with her, but I couldn't. She had perfect hair and a perfect, energetic little face, and a cute little body, and a cute hairdo, and some sharp clothes, and a light and airy accent that almost made Arundhati Singh sound like a bellowing savage. I wanted to find something wrong with her so badly, but realized it was no use. As if that would change the way my relationship with Victor stood, or the way her relationship stood with him. As if it mattered if she was ugly. As if Victor had chosen her for her beauty.

I watched her read a few stories about the Clinton administration and the environment and the war in Bosnia. She smiled just the slightest bit and she unintentionally winked once. I smiled and winked back.

I turned off the TV, depressed. I had no plans after graduation. I would probably have to move in with my parents. I imagined Victor and Sarita in the back of a black London taxi, swirling around the curving streets in between double decker buses, on their way to some fantastic fashion event or other, or perhaps on the way home from a tennis match at Wimbledon.

It was odd, but all of a sudden, arranged marriages didn't seem strange to me anymore. After graduation, their lives would instantly take off into a secure and mapped out future, while my life would regress back to childhood in my childhood bedroom with my parents treating me like a child. The prospect of finding true love didn't hold much promise for me. I thought I may as well get married to a woman I didn't know, rather than spend my life getting played by confused guys carrying weighty emotional baggage.

I stretched back on the floor and pressed my cheek against the cold floor, as comfortable as if it were my own room. I stared underneath Tony's bed and saw a short stack of books. I reached out and grabbed the one on top. It was old and musty, and had a picture on the front of a teenaged guy sitting naked on top of a hill, looking down on a town below. The picture was black and white and looked old. The guy's hair was cut in an odd, incongruous style, and he had a peasant's face.

I opened up the book and saw a caption behind the front page. It said, "Sicily, 1907." I flipped through the book and found that all the pictures were of young, naked Italian men from around the turn of the century. Some posed on terraces, others posed indoors, but all the models shared the same, post-pubescent look: their genitals were completely developed, but their faces were not fully the faces of men. Their dicks stuck out from their bodies with an exaggerated boldness, plump as the dicks of donkeys, and hairy as those of men, but were connected to bodies that had flat, unmuscled chests, and boyish faces.

I leafed through the pages. It was so different to see old pictures where the people weren't stifled inside of old, boring clothes, but in poses where their sexuality was unmasked. In one picture, a guy had a flowered garland around his head and was standing on a stone terrace. It looked like he could've been in ancient Rome. Another had a guy reclining on a slate bench, and the photo was awash in a fuzzy gold color. The next page showed three teenagers from behind, gazing out at the sea. The photo wasn't color, but was tinted in delicate blues and browns. Their butts were oblong and hairy, and filled me with mad sexual cravings, although the uncanny thought that they all were probably dead was slightly disturbing.

Two black and white boys lay around a garden, grape vines descending from the roof. Their uncircumcised dicks rested lazily against their stomachs. A guy at least in his twenties stood naked in a doorway with his arms outstretched to meet the morning. A series of pictures at the end of the book showed a teenager sitting alone on a stool, a footlong dick descending to his thighs. Beneath a fountain, three guys lay in each other's arms. Two guys wrestled naked, standing up. I ran my fingers over the pages slowly, as if I could make them real by touching them.

I thought if I could do nothing in life but look at pictures like these I'd be happy.

I wanted to go through the rest of Tony's collection of books, but that thought was instantly driven from my mind.

There was a pounding on the stairs and then Mark Israel strode into the room with an animal look of either drunkenness or fury on his face. He bent down and ripped the book from my hands and yelled, "What the fuck are you doing in here?"

I remained on the ground. I was too scared to stand. "I was just watching your cable."

"You don't have the right to do anything in here, you fuckin' pansy. I oughta kick the shit out of you right now." His face was red, he breathed hard, saliva dripped from one corner of his mouth.

"What is wrong with you? Jesus."

"Who the fuck do you think you are, Schoenberg? Are you trying to turn everyone in this house into a faggot?"

I couldn't figure out if he was mad about Tony and me sleeping together, or just mad about me being in the room, or getting a boner in the shower. "Yeah, I am. But that shouldn't be hard. You guys are pretty close to it as it is."

"You watch your fuckin' mouth, you fuckin' faggot. You've got a lot of nerve trying to seduce Victor, and then when that failed, trying to get into Tony's pants too. He just told me what happened. You're a disgusting faggot who needs to be taught a lesson." He stood with an arrogantly aggressive stance, his legs were still but he was throwing his chest out as if he might lunge at me at any moment.

"For your information," I said. "Tony came into my room trying to seduce me. And Victor's wanted me since day one."

"You're a fucking liar. You've been trying to convert everyone, like all the faggots do. Tony likes girls. And so does Victor. And so do I."

"Then why do you have Tony's dick in your mouth every night? I've seen you on your knees with your big, fat, hairy ass hanging out and Tony's cock down your throat. You're a bigger faggot then me."

He glared at me with a glare of absolute rage, but didn't say anything.

"Anyway," I said. "If you guys had better luck getting girls, you wouldn't need to be sucking each other's dicks. Girls think you're a fuckin' pig. Don't you think they've told me?"

"I do not suck Tony's dick. I'm not a faggot like you. I'm warning you, Schoenberg, you'd better shut the fuck up."

I would've, but he called me a faggot, and I wasn't gonna stop till I got him back. "Your little boyfriend got tired of you and needed someone else to shine his pole. I guess you don't have it anymore Israel. Your dick suckin days have passed, and now you're just a washed up, fat old Jew who couldn't find a girl to fuck if you paid her. The whole campus knows about you and Tony, because I told them. I've made sure every girl on campus thinks you're a faggot."

The veins in his neck throbbed and the tendons became visible. He came toward me with his arm back. I screamed and tried to get up and run out the door. He got me by the shirt and dragged me to a standing position. There was commotion on the stairs, people coming home. I heard Paul Veracruz at the door saying, "What the fuck is going on?" Mark Israel threw me down on the bed, pulled his arm back and cracked me in the head with his fist. I sat silently, in shock. I looked up and saw Paul push Mark and then Mark push him back. Jean-Claude came in the room and yelled, "What the fuck is this?" and got in between the two of them. The three shoved each other and yelled and then Jean-Claude pushed Mark Israel against the wall and finally, they were all still. Just past the doorframe, I saw Victor race past the bedroom, so quickly I wasn't sure if I had actually seen him at all.

"What the fuck is this about?" Paul yelled, in a booming, frightening holler.

Tony appeared in the doorway. "Ask him," I said, pointing to Tony. "He's dragged me in to some unspoken braintrust of cocksuckers that plays by its own rules. You all can go fuck yourselves."

"You just had to make trouble, Schoenberg," Tony said. "You couldn't just be cool about things."

"I didn't make any motherfuckin' trouble!" I screamed. "You did, with your late-night blow jobs. Fuck you and burn in hell!"

Jean-Claude said, "Augie, get out of here."

"No, I won't!" I yelled, defiantly. "How dare you assholes treat me like I'm some cheap whore that you can go to any time you want your dicks sucked. This might be fun and games for you for four years, but this is real life for me. I'm not playing." I glared at Tony.

"It's no wonder you're always single, Schoenberg," Tony said, twisting my last name into a jeer, as if it were itself an insult. "You're a fuckin' bitch. Even faggots wouldn't want to be around a bitch like you."

I sailed toward him, my gym shoes squeaking against the floor, and with the precision of a vindictive eleven year old girl, kicked him squarely in the nuts so hard he fell to the ground, yelping. I stepped over him and into the hallway.

Mark Israel said, "Look at that! He's crazy. He's completely out of control."

I marched upstairs to my room and saw Victor peering out from behind his door. When I walked by, he closed it.

25.

The next morning, I sat on a stone bench facing the Quad, encased in my ski jacket. The bench was as cold as if it were layered with snow, but the feeling against my ass was calming me down. My whole body felt red, and hot, and like it was moving too fast. I held my head facing the freezing wind as it batted me from side to side.

Roberta stole up the west end of the Quad, wrapped in a long, wool shawl. She wore an enormous, fuzzy beige hat. The sight of an old friend almost made me well up in tears, but it was really the sight of a woman that comforted me. I'd spent almost six months surrounded by nothing but men, and was exhausted by the thought of deep voices, and wounded egos, and the constant smell of sweat.

"Why are you outside? It's December." She sat next to me, breathing hard. Streams of white breath flew from her mouth. The bulky shawl spread over onto one of my arms.

"Thanks for coming. I know you're busy with the new play."

"It's fine," she said. "I have a small part, but at least this time I'm not the maid."

"What are you?"

"Oh, I'm an alien or something. I'm this queen of outer space that comes on at the end and lectures some guy. I think they wanted somebody sassy, so they got me."

"Next semester you'll be doing lead roles again. Listen, there's been some problems at the Hutt, and I have to move out. Do you know anyone who's got an extra bedroom? Either for now, or for next semester."

"What do you mean you have to move out? What happened?"

I told her about Tony and our night together, and about Mark Israel and how he hit me in the head.

"He hit you!" she shouted. "What did the other guys do?"

"Oh, there was a big brawl, but Paul and Jean-Claude broke it up. But I just can't stay there anymore. It's nothing but stress and complicated relationships. I'm always on edge, I'm always afraid something horrible is gonna happen."

"I had no idea. I thought everything was going OK now."

"It was, sort of. I wanted to live there for four years, but once I moved in I upset the balance somehow, and now everything's ruined. Ten years of Harley Hutt traditions, destroyed by Augie Schoenberg."

"You didn't ruin anything," Roberta said, grabbing my arm. "Tony and Victor and Mark are awfully confused. They're afraid of you, Augie. You're self-assured enough to be straightforward and honest all the time, and that scares them. They want you to be as lost as they are so that they don't feel so mixed up."

"It's because they think I'm a fuckin' bitch," I blurted. "Tony told me."

Roberta was not sympathetic, but was stern. "You have a lot of power, Augie Schoenberg. And it's genuine. You underestimate how big of an effect you have on people. You influence everyone you're around. You should be mad at them, not

136

criticizing yourself."

"I really felt something, though," I told her. "With Victor, I had feelings I hadn't had in four years."

"In a different world, Augie, you'd be together. This is real life. It ain't fair."

"I thought things had finally worked out for me. This August, I was on top of the world. Now, everything has spiraled into shit."

"Spare me the dramatics," Roberta said. "I get enough of it in the theater department. Listen, my friends Paloma and Pilar have a couple of extra bedrooms. I'm sure you can stay there. If not, maybe Trailer Trash can put you up."

"I don't know. Ask your friends. I'd like to leave tonight."

Roberta looked concerned. "I'll call the girls tonight and I'll make sure Jean-Claude helps you move your stuff. He can drive you."

A group of students walking by stared at us. I kissed Roberta on the cheek. "Thank you so much." In another story, or from a different perspective, Roberta and I could've been lovers, braving the winter winds of the prairie to nestle next to each other and whisper words of comfort into each other's ears. From the back, we must've looked like a picture out of another century, in old clothes with nothing but stone and grass around us. From the front, we looked like an interracial couple in modern times. But the reality of the situation existed only in our minds. We weren't even in control of our own image: it was as if we existed only on film and were spinning frame by frame in front of the campus, being surveyed by a seedy collection of voyeurs.

"I'll call you at the Hutt. Sorry you have to move out. Israel is the one who should."

"My days of sadistic voyeurism are over," I said. Roberta gave me a puzzled look. "Let them have the place," I continued. "It'll be a graveyard there without me."

"OK?" Roberta stood up and sailed away, her shawl flapping in the wind. She passed the literature building and the foreign language building, and then blended into a crowd and disappeared.

I lugged my enormous suitcases out of the closet and threw one on top of the bed. I opened it and found it half-full of old things from one of my desk drawers when I was in the dorms. I fished around and found some old pictures of Roberta and Mikey and me. It was only four years earlier, but we were smaller by degrees, our frames almost wispy and our faces smiling in crazy, obnoxious smiles that we'd never make in the present.

I found an old love letter Mikey had written me. A small lump formed in my throat at the sight of the tight, masculine handwriting. At the end of the page he had written, "I don't care what happens in the future, or what happens right now, or about anything, really. All I think is that you're wonderful." The feelings from those days poured back; the feelings of innocence that at the time I didn't know were innocence, the optimism, the bold eagerness. I remembered how fascinating it was to know the note was a love letter and that it was signed by a man. I never considered at the time that I wouldn't have felt that again so many years later. I threw the photos back into the suitcase, disgusted with myself.

I hastily took shirts and sweaters from the closet and dumped them into the suitcase. I opened another suitcase on the floor and dropped in stacks of papers from my desk drawers. I didn't want to go through anything. I wanted to pack in ten minutes and be out of the house. I kneeled on the floor, gathering together big piles of notebooks and books.

Victor came in, as usual without making a sound. I pretended not to notice him. He looked at me for a moment and then pushed the suitcase on the bed to make some room for himself, and sat down.

"That was some bad shit that went down yesterday," he said.

"It was. Luckily I had some roommates who came to my aid."

He ignored the implication and said, "So what is this?" pointing to the suitcases.

"What does it look like. I'm moving out."

He appeared to mull it over in his head. "I wish you wouldn't. Can't you work something out?"

"No. I've had enough. I need to get back to some semblance of reality. I want to enjoy my last semester here, not have to worry about clandestine late-night encounters with morally unscrupulous asshole roommates."

"I'm not an asshole," Victor said. "This place won't be the same without you. Why don't you just stay until the end of the semester?"

"It's practically over. Finals are next week. Don't worry, though. If you're lucky, maybe I'll see you sometime next semester. We can reminisce." My tone was sarcastic, but I actually hoped we could.

"Augie, you don't understand. I'm graduating in two weeks. I'm going to London in January."

I stared at him, dumbfounded. "You're graduating? You never told me. Jesus, Victor, do you tell anyone anything, or is everything a secret?"

"There are no secrets," he said. "Only life. I just take it as it comes."

I threw down a pile of paperback books. "Jesus Christ, who the fuck are you, the Dali Lama? Give me a fuckin' break."

"Don't fight with me, Augie. That's not how I want to remember you." I looked into his eyes, the doe eyes I loved, the sweet, sad drooping eyes that made me love him. "And I'm gonna remember you," he continued. "Always."

My shoulders dropped and I stared at the floor.

"Listen to me," he said. "This may be the last time I see you. I'll write you from London. I want you to come to the wedding."

I wanted to go more than anything in the world. "I don't think that's a good idea. Anyway, I'm afraid of flying."

He got down on the floor and sat as near me as he could. His thigh touched mine through jeans. "I don't want this to be goodbye. I want it to be see you soon."

"You know, I've seen your wife on TV. Or your fiancee, or whatever she is. She's absolutely gorgeous."

Victor raised an eyebrow at me. "She is. I like her."

"Oh, you like her?" I exclaimed, like the fucking bitch I supposed I was. "Well I'm glad you like her, Victor. That should make for a wonderful life. God, married at twenty-two to a girl you like. You've got it made, motherfucker."

"All right, I'm not gonna do this." He stood up and dusted off his pants. "You know, Augie, you can act hurt and you can act like you were wronged, and maybe you were, but I'll tell you something. Of all the people I met in four years, you were the only one who came anywhere near to being close to me. Maybe we didn't have much together, but it was more than I had in all of college. I never had a serious girlfriend. No girls ever hit on me. You made me feel like I was attractive, and maybe that's a feeling that's normal for you, since you're so goddamn confident, but I've never felt that before." He paused and frowned at me. "My heart is cold," he said. "I don't know who I am, and all I ever feel is nothing. I used to pray that someone could come along and make me feel something, just for a moment, make me feel anything. Something instead of emptiness, and blankness, and stolid monotony. And you were the only one who came."

I couldn't look at him. I looked at the open suitcase holding remnants of previous years. Scribbled notes, old magazines, empty picture frames. The smell of pencils.

"Meet me in London," he said. "Get over your foolish pride and come to my wedding. I'll even send you plane tickets."

"What about the PJ Harvey concert? Do you still want to go with me?"

"I totally forgot. Of course I want to go with you. I'll give you the tickets and I'll meet you in front of the theater. It's at the Aragon Ballroom, right?"

"No," I said. "It's at the Cabaret Metro. It's the week in between Christmas and New Year's."

"I'll be there. I wouldn't miss it for the world." I was frowning so hard he looked back at me with a look of consternation, as though he knew I needed a pep talk but didn't really want to give me one. "Look, nothing has ended. Come to London in August. I'll show you the city. Have you ever been to Europe?"

I shook my head.

"Aw, you've gotta see it. It's fantastic. We can go out clubbing every night."

"We'll see," I said. I walked over to him and put my arms around him. "We'll see if you remember me."

"I will," he said, in a low voice. "I will."

I carried my suitcases down the stairs in a haggard, slow process that made me feel like I was eighty years old and struggling to walk. When I approached the first floor Jean-Claude and Paul jumped up and came up the steps. They took my suitcases from me and easily whisked them down.

"Augie, man, you don't have to go," Jean-Claude said.

"It sucks. I don't want you to leave," Paul said. He put down the suitcases and hugged me. "None of this is your fault."

"And Israel is going to Israel," Jean-Claude said.

"I know, I know. It's just that there's too many bad memories here. I'd be miserable. But I'll miss you guys."

"We'll miss you too, dude," Paul said, releasing me. "But we still live in the same town. We'll see you."

I grabbed a suitcase and walked toward the door. Paul opened it and Jean-Claude followed close behind me. I walked onto the porch and when I got to the sidewalk, I wanted to look back at the Hutt, but I didn't.

Book Three

It was not Death, for I stood up,
And all the Dead, lie down—

>   -Emily Dickinson

26.

"Are you sexually active?"
  I didn't know how to answer. I supposed I was, but only sort of.
Her fat hands were kneading my stomach, pressing far into my lower abdomen, so that it felt like she was going to grab hold of one of my kidneys and yank it out.
  She looked at me and cocked her head, waiting for an answer.
  "Yes, I guess so."
  "Are you heterosexual?"
  "No."
  "Are you homosexual?"
  "Yes."
  "Have you had an HIV test?"
  Rage burned in my head as hotly as the acid in my stomach. "No," I said, defiantly.
  "Why not?" she asked placidly, as if it was common knowledge that I should be diseased, as if I must automatically be at hazardous risk for disease. As if gays are the only ones who get it.
    "I don't have any reason to." What did she know? For all she knew, I could've never been fucked up the ass at all. This lady, though, was not a doctor, but was a nurse practitioner. I figured she must have just taken a class on AIDS and was anxious to use her newfound expertise, so much so that the HIV question was the first one I got after the homosexual one.
  She kneaded and kneaded. "When was the last time you were anally penetrated?"
  I almost gasped. Even me, Augie Schoenberg, former resident of the most notorious den of iniquity on campus, was shocked by the nakedness of the question.
  "I don't see how that relates."
  She kneaded some more and then told me I could sit up.
  "Well, it's important to know. There are things, you know, that can be spread."
  "Such as what?"
  "August, I know you're being defensive about this, but with your kind of problem

I need to know. When was the last time you were anally penetrated?"

"Madam, that is none of your business."

She said, "Hold on a minute," and left the room.

I told myself I'd be damned if I was gonna reveal the details of my sex life to some pervert of a nurse practitioner who was looking to treat me like an AIDS patient. I might not have been an angel, but I was no whore, either, and even I knew that my problem had nothing to do with sex.

Hazy visions of the bottle of brandy in my old bedroom came into my mind. I remembered staring out the Harley Hutt window, drinking the bitter stuff down while my stomach was in the midst of an acidic war. I'd taken antacids, but they did nothing. Then, the day after I moved out of the Harley Hutt, a sharp, bone-grinding pain surfaced in the lower left corner of my abdomen, and no matter how I twisted or turned, and no matter what I ate or drank, it could not be relieved. I even stopped going out drinking for a while, and spent most of winter break watching old movies in the duplex in Evanston.

There was one night, though, where I went for broke. I couldn't stand sitting around in the house, knowing there were a million men in Chicago looking for love, so I took a long swig of Pepto Bismol, wiped the pink residue off my lips with the front of my hand, and headed down to Lakeview. Once there, I stood alone at a dark, crowded club and not two minutes later a guy who looked like a Marine came over and introduced himself.

He must have been fifteen years older than me, but as his bulky hand lightly gripped mine, and the leather from his jacket touched my wrist, that seemed like a good thing. "I'm Danny," he said, refusing to let go of my hand.

"Augie," I croaked. I took a swig of beer for confidence. This wasn't some campustown overgrown teenager, this was a man.

He bought me a beer, which I was glad for, since I was almost completely broke. I stared at him in amazement while he made conversation. I never in my life dreamed I'd run into a gay guy like him. His face was the slightest bit weather-beaten, and with the leather jacket he looked like a reckless L.A. cop from the movies. My stomach began to burn.

Later, at his apartment, we stood in his bedroom and I realized to my horror that I'd made a terrible mistake. While this guy seemed like an absolute stud at the bar, with his short dark hair and muscular frame and smooth pick up lines, at home he seemed like a borderline mental case. The apartment was all white and immaculately clean. I sat down on the couch, which seemed to make him uncomfortable, so I stood up and he walked over and readjusted the cushions. In the bedroom he had no pictures on the walls, no photographs on the dresser, no loose change on the floor. In fact, the only personal items in the room were condoms, arranged in a pyramid on the nightstand.

There must have been a few dozen of them and I wanted to ask, "How often do you do this?"

I retreated to the bathroom feeling nervous and tired. I tried to pee but nothing came out, and my penis had shrunk to such a sad, small size that I was confident I would not attain an erection that evening. I hoped for a rope ladder to fall out of the sky so I could crawl out the bathroom window.

Like a fool, I gave myself a pep talk, went back out into the bedroom and went through with it. It wasn't bad at first: I actually did get a boner and it was sex, after all, not like the dark, intrepid, almost chaste, fumblings of Victor and I, but real sex, as in I was sliding my aqua-blue colored, latex-coated penis up the Marine's hairy behind. But he started talking while we were doing it and that bothered me. "Yeah, you like it," he said. "Why don't you fuck me harder. Yeah." I started to laugh, which didn't go over well, and I ended up not having an orgasm. He stroked his own dick until he came, and after that lay on the bed with a frightening scowl on his face. I got dressed feeling really stupid, wishing I'd just stayed home.

Two weeks into the spring semester I sat in my Shakespeare class dreaming about a paper I was going to write. We'd read *Henry the IV* and I was going to write about the tavern scenes in the play, where Falstaff and Hal wiled away the hours at the Boar's Head Tavern, getting drunk out of their minds and, as the book put it, waking up on benches afternoons. Out of nowhere, an intolerable, searing pressure surged inside my intestine. I knew I'd have to get to a bathroom quickly, but I always hated public restrooms, and thought maybe I could hold it till the end of class. The pain returned stronger and I grabbed my jacket and ran from the room and down the hall. In the bathroom, all six stalls were unbelievably occupied, and I raced out of the building and across the Quad toward my new apartment. It was January, but sweat gathered on my face. I could feel it as it froze against the sharp winds. I didn't think I'd make it home. I thought I'd end up with a gush of sloppy diarrhea in my pants.

I took my key out of my jeans and threw open the door. I charged across the kitchen. "I have to go to the bathroom!" I screamed, even though no one was home.

Once inside I yanked down my pants so hard I cut my hip on my fingernail, and when I sat down a piece of shit flew out of my asshole at five hundred miles an hour and landed in the toilet with the sound of a cannonball landing in a swimming pool. A spray of water rebounded against my rear end. A torrent of semi-formed shit followed, falling out of me so drastically that I was frightened I might lose my colon in the toilet. Lastly, a tiny squirt of diarrhea leaked out and landed on the surface of the water with a barely audible splat.

"Oh!" I bellowed.

After I came out of the bathroom, I took baby steps through the kitchen, as though I were elderly and my joints were so creaky that I could barely walk.

I had to go back to the literature building to get my Shakespeare book. When I got there, the empty, sun-drenched classroom calmed me a little. I grabbed the enormous anthology with both hands and prayed I wasn't dying.

It'd been happening every day. When I wasn't sitting on the toilet, it felt like I should have been. I couldn't explain it: it didn't matter what I ate, it didn't matter what I drank, I always felt like I had to take a shit.

Beleaguered, and convinced I had colon cancer, I marched myself to the health service, and all the nurse wanted to know about was my sex life.

We argued, she pressed for information, I became more stubborn. Truth be told,

I'd never been fucked up the butt without a condom. If I had AIDS, it was through osmosis.

"Have you been losing weight?" she asked.

"No," I lied. I was teetering pretty close to 120 pounds.

"Oh, your clothes always fit you so baggy?"

"Not only are you a nurse, but you're a fashion critic. You're good."

She sighed. "Well, perhaps we can have a doctor arrange for you to have a lower GI..."

"Oh, God, isn't that a little extreme?" I wanted her to tell me that I had the stomach flu, and that I could cure it in seven easy days on antibiotics.

"You know, HIV testing is free at the health service."

I almost smacked her. "Maybe you should take the test."

She laughed. "August, I've been married for seventeen years!"

I left the room. It was so antiseptic. That must be the smell of mercury, or insulin. Clear blood on the floor.

I got a prescription for something called Belladonna. At the pharmacy window, the pharmacist was a bright woman about my mother's age who had the voice of an easy-listening DJ. "Belladonna," she raved. "The Egyptian drug. Cleopatra used to take it, to make herself more beautiful." She leaned on the counter and blinked at me. "It dilated their pupils—it made them look like cats." I certainly could have used some help being more beautiful. I thought it over and figured I might like it.

The nurse confronted me in the hallway. "August, have you ever checked out the resource center? They have some wonderful cookbooks for vegetarians..."

"Oh, I'm not a vegetarian. I'm a beef lover myself."

"Yes, well, your diet, you're so thin. I really think they could help you there. People like you...all that information is great. I really think you could find some things that could help your diet."

Her skirt was so large, it was circling around her in billowing waves, trying to encompass me. White lab coats in the background, uniforms, hushed discussions.

"And when you come back next week, make sure to tell them you need an appointment with an MD."

"Not a nurse practitioner."

"No."

27.

I sat on a cement step on a staircase behind the library. I held a cigarette in one hand and smoked it intermittently, but with each drag the smoke seemed to descend straight down through my lungs and into my colon. I cringed and shifted around, but knew that the problem was not the way I was sitting, but the cigarette. I couldn't make myself put it out.

There was snow around, packed hard under layers of ice, but there was runoff from the mounds. It was what my mother called the January thaw: the temperature had surged to around forty and the sun shone brightly. There was a patch of ice under my jeans, but I sat there intentionally. I wanted to feel cold, and clear, and be rid of any germs I might've contracted at the health center. There were pathogens in that building: there was meningitis, there was tuberculosis, there was rampant flu. I wasn't being paranoid either: I overheard people in the waiting room. I figured no germ could grow in this temperature. Nothing was growing behind the library, anyhow, the landscape consisted only of snow and mud.

I wished it were weeks earlier. I hadn't felt any better then, but the look of campus since the day of action disturbed me. All the young, smiling people mixed with the old, regal buildings used to make me exhilarated, but it had all begun to seem like an illusion, and a trap. I longed for Chicago, and to be anonymous, and so lost in the chaos of the city that I could forget my own problems.

Not like that had happened the last time I was in Chicago. In between Christmas and New Year's, in that weird limbo where nothing is happening and everything and everyone seems blanketed and muted, I stood outside the Cabaret Metro, clutching the PJ Harvey tickets in my pocket. I felt like an ass: I cursed myself for being so naive as to think Victor would actually show up. He must've given me the tickets to hold as a nice way of getting rid of me. Even so, he had said he wanted to go, but I didn't have his home number and there was no way of confirming.

The most overwhelmingly forlorn feeling passed over me, along with exhaust from the PJ Harvey tour bus, and the smell of Camel cigarettes from the people in line at the will call window. Everyone else was in groups, and there I stood, on what was supposed to be the headiest night of my life, alone, staring down Clark Street to Addison, desperately imagining Victor rounding the corner outside Wrigley Field and racing toward me with voluminous apologies.

It was bitter cold, but I stayed outside until almost nine o'clock. I'd heard the opening band play, a loud, bassy, surreal sort of hip hop, and watched what I imagined were the Chicago equivalents of the Harley Hutt crowd file into the theater. I wanted so badly to waltz into the theater with Victor by my side, present two tickets for the usher, and then look around slyly at the crowd, as they all doubtlessly wondered who on earth two such unimaginably cool dudes could be. Instead, one of the bouncers called over to me, "Hey, tough guy, the show's startin.'"

I debated for a minute, not wanting to give up on my pathetic vigil, but eventually turned to the bouncer, drunk with misery, and opened my jacket. He put his hands inside, looking for guns or bottles of whiskey or knives, or any other implement that I could possibly commit suicide with. He smiled. "I don't think your lady friend's showing tonight, big guy."

I studied him. He had a shaved head, a black leather jacket, combat boots, and jeans that looked like they'd been to Beirut and back in the early eighties. Black, flame-like tattoos climbed up his neck.

"He isn't a lady, he's a man," I commiserated.

"Oh, that's the worst kind," he said, roughly patting my inner thighs. "Low down dirty dog." He felt my back and, just for an instant, my back pocket. "Want me to kick his ass for you?"

"I'd love you forever," I said, not caring how it sounded.

He looked to the side and breathed in. "You can do better than him. Have fun tonight."

I walked past him and he patted me on the shoulder, and then on the ass.

I got a beer. The bouncer hadn't fazed me. I'd been hanging out at the Cabaret Metro since I was 16 and knew that that scene, still clinging to its late-80s personality of the dressed in black with mohawks crowd, was so full of faggots it was alternatingly reassuring and nauseating.

The theater was decrepit, but it was perfect. Every wall, every surface, every person, was coated in black and grime, with marijuana smoke perfuming the air like a dead skunk. I pushed my way to the front of the crowd. My stomach was churning but I angrily defied it, or at least told myself that I did, until the concert began. The crowd surged forward and pushed me to the barricade.

The music was a slow grumble, a love song full of vindictive potential and the anticipation of a massive catharsis. Victor. Victor. I couldn't remember what his hair felt like, I knew I had run my fingers through it. I couldn't remember what it felt like. I remembered my hand wrapped around his penis, and mine in his, and the pubic hair against my wrist. The slow, dark rush of feelings, the merger of intellect and sexuality, the defiance of categories, the autumn night, my lips running over his balls. His dark lips around my erection, pulsing, and sucking, trying so hard to coax me to orgasm, to be in control, to give a master performance. I drank the last of my beer and threw it to the ground, where the bottle smashed into pieces.

Groans, groans, guitars, an organ. The mix of punk and spinsterism, the effort to be abnormal. I don't know what you're asking me to do, Augie. I don't know what to do. I was starting to sweat, it poured down my face and left me feeling clean, and empty, and eminently pure. I sang along with the lyrics at the top of my lungs, inaudible below the blasts of the guitars, a wild holler to a different place, a darker, bodybag-strewn hell that few knew of. Not to London, and that newscaster, and those black, black taxis.

I was getting to that place, that numb, beautiful place where everything was quiet and I felt absorbed and wet and full of bulk. The moon, the darkness, the silence, his thighs underneath me. Will you go away with me, Augie? As if there was anywhere to go but backwards, which no one can do. Deafening roar of guitar cuts, shouting, drum blasts.

The crowd shot their fists into the air on all sides of me, I was yelling but I couldn't hear myself. I was shouting for dear life. Bodies pressed up against me, warm ones, and I couldn't tell if they were male or female, but I was hungry for that heat, that nourishment. I screamed to the stage like a maniac. PJ Harvey looked down at the crowd, a pair of fake gold eyelashes at least three inches long sprouting from her eyelids. Her guitar, twice the size of her, hung off her shoulder still vibrating.

I wanted no alcohol, or cigarettes, but just to stay in that place for eternity, encased in noise and hot bodies, singing desperately toward the stage. I wanted to never leave, like I ended up doing, to spend the night drunk and alone at a gay strip joint.

28.

I sat at my desk in my bedroom. It was smaller than my room at the Harley Hutt but it was a million times cleaner and a million times more modern. I was comfortable in the new apartment: there were no drafts, there was no filth, there was a semblance of sanity. My new roommates Paloma and Pilar were both calm, rational intellectuals with elegant glasses and thin quantities of brown hair, and they were always up for doing new and interesting things. Since I'd lived there, we'd gone to poetry slams, foreign films, and had once gone ice skating. I couldn't imagine all the Harley Hutt boys together for a night of wholesome fun at the ice rink, although I imagined they all might go if they were drunk enough.

I exhaled till there was no trace of breath left in my lungs. I was doing what I could to relax, and shake off the constant hint of anxiety that was lodged in my brain. It'd been tough: every time I sat down to eat, I almost panicked, hoping there'd be no consequences afterwards.

Paloma and Pilar had gone out on a double date with their boyfriends, and Pilar had left a tray of brownies for me in the kitchen. The smell had overtaken me and I was salivating like a dog, but I knew that if I ate one it would go right through me. I didn't want to think that way, but I figured now that the roommates were gone I could eat one and if I had to go to the bathroom a lot, I'd have the place to myself. My mind fought off a small wave of depression at that thought, and I turned to my desk drawer and pulled out my new screenplay. Since *Last Boat to Manchuria* had been assailed as being trite with wooden characters, I figured I'd write a story based on real life and see how unwooden that would be. I was taking no prisoners. Everyone from Victor Radhakrishna to Mark Israel to the nurse practitioner was in the story, and I was shamelessly distorting them all to make them seem worse than they were in real life.

The experience with the nurse had been bad enough, but it was her assumption that I had AIDS that really got me. I started neurotically going through all the possible situations that could have given me AIDS. None of the scenarios seemed very likely. Once, an HIV-positive guy at the campus gay group was talking to me and a tiny speck of saliva flew out of his mouth and landed directly in my eye. I had read that saliva doesn't have enough HIV to infect you, and I knew it couldn't live outside the body. I wasn't sure if it would live for the half-second it took to fly into my eye, though. Other than that, I'd always had sex wearing condoms, except for oral sex, but I didn't think anyone had ever come in my mouth.

Over and over in my head, the memories of past sexual interludes played back, and I tried to piece together who had had an AIDS test and when and if they told me the results. The whole thought process was dumb, I know, I should've just had the fucking test, but I couldn't imagine what I would do during the days you had to wait for the results. I thought the wait might drive me to a nervous breakdown. I shuddered to think I would graduate, move to Chicago, and begin my life in the real world with a chronic untreatable medical condition, whether it was some digestive problem or AIDS. I told myself to stop this. Think of Victor. Get your mind off your stupid body.

The *Henry IV* paper I was writing for Shakespeare class was keeping my mind on Victor. Prince Hal, heir to the throne of England, made merry with the common folk at bars until the time came when he was to grow up and become king. Then, amidst all his promises to bring them into the royal wold, he left everyone behind.

I sighed and looked at the floor. My report card lay on top of a copy of the Chicago Sun-Times. I'd gotten straight A's the semester before, except in screenwriting, in which I got a C. To me, a C in a workshop class like that was a personal insult. It was like failing. I considered that the problem may have been the instructor and not *Last Boat to Manchuria*, after all, three other professors seemed to like what I had to say. But I knew I was responsible for the content of my work, so I tirelessly plugged away at the new screenplay, hoping by some odd miracle that this bitter, almost sickening story would win me some much-needed creative success.

The newspaper had been on the floor of my bedroom for a week, but I couldn't throw it away. I'd bought the paper so that I could at least for a moment feel like I was in Chicago and not stuck in the cornfields, but there was an article in there that had shocked me so horribly that I'd been plagued with nightmares ever since. The dreams seemed to last all night, and I could never wake up from them, at least until my alarm went off. Almost masochistically, I picked up the paper and read the article again.

Body ID'd as influential professors' missing son

The body of a young man that washed up on the 63rd Street Beach yesterday was identified as Ramesh Singh, 22, son of noted University of Chicago professor Deepak Singh and Illinois State University professor Arundhati Singh.

The coroner listed the cause of death as drowning. Ramesh was reported missing over the weekend, after a roommate said he failed to return home from a trip to a downtown nightclub. A call was placed to 911 from Navy Pier Saturday night, where witnesses claim to have seen a young man jump off the pier into the lake and then disappear. The Coast Guard declined to send out a search and rescue party, saying there wasn't substantial evidence that anyone was in the lake, and that the chance of anyone surviving for any length of time with the water temperature at 36 degrees was slim.

The Singh family launched a desperate search effort for the young man last week, plastering the city with fliers and holding daily news conferences. Arundhati Singh said that her son was ill, and had left his medication at home.

Funeral services will be held tomorrow in Hyde Park. In lieu of flowers, the family asks that a donation be made to the American Foundation for AIDS Research.

There was a picture of him in the newspaper, and the image was stuck to my brain throughout every day and throughout every night. While I slept, Ramesh would come alive in my dreams, and the small, square mugshot from the newspaper grew a torso and arms and legs. The memory of that weird night I met him was nightmarish enough—in that strange Rogers Park bar the night I found out Victor was getting married—and now Ramesh, that odd, gawking little guy, was starring in my nightmares. I'd never in a million years have guessed he was really Arundhati's son. The world couldn't be that small. He'd said he was going to jump in the lake. A joke, really. How else could I have taken it?

I was desperately trying to piece everything together. Arundhati had told me in her office that he'd been ill, but she hadn't said with what. I could imagine that perhaps he had cancer or something, but the obituary suggested making donations to an AIDS group, which basically implied that he had AIDS. I had no clue that Arundhati's husband and son lived two and a half hours away from her. It was no wonder she'd seemed so stressed out that day. I'd gone by her office a few times, but the door was always shut tight with the lights out. I didn't know what I would say to her anyway.

I crawled into my bed and closed my eyes. It was only eight o'clock, but I'd been so drained from stress that I knew I'd fall asleep quickly. Almost as soon as my head hit the pillow, Ramesh Singh appeared in my mind, standing outside a restaurant on Navy Pier, shivering, obviously freezing. The jeering, multicolored-lights from the ferris wheel in the background looked alarmingly sinister. In the water, a replica of an old regatta creaked against its ropes. A ticket booth, plastic-coated chains strung from posts, a gangplank. The lake, black, big as an ocean, carried wind across it that hit Ramesh's face in cruel, battering gusts. His face refused to react to it, but stared straight ahead at nothing. Slowly, he walked toward the edge of the pier, near the cotton candy booth. He stepped behind the booth, as if that would provide protection from the wind, and when he reappeared, he was naked. What surprised me most was the look of his hair. It billowed in the air, straight up, black as the asphalt. Black, brown, hair, skin, white teeth, pink lips, softness turned to harshness, and the unbearably vulnerable look of a naked person in winter. He turned to face the restaurant and then fell backwards into the lake, cheeks puffed out as if he was trying to hold his breath. A second or two later three people ran out of the restaurant bellowing something hard to understand, they weren't wearing jackets, and they also were whipped by the wind. "Call 911," they yelled. "Somebody call 911!"

The initial blast of cold water on bare skin must've knocked the air out of him. For a few seconds he backfloated, his face just peeking out above the surface and then he went under, head first. A small turret of foam appeared, created by his body and especially his feet as he sank backwards and was pulled out to sea by an undertow or a current or whatever kills so many people in that lake every year.

There was a moment of panic in his head. *I don't want to do this.* And then a steadfast urge to be quiet, and alone, and rid of the illness that was clogging his brain, and his body, and his entire sense of reality. He must have had AIDS. He must have been sentenced to death at 22. He was ashamed of being gay. He didn't want to tell his parents, even though they were intellectuals. They were parents first.

I jerked myself awake, sweating even though I thought for a second I really was facing the wind on Navy Pier. I told myself to relax, reassured myself I wasn't dying, and somehow I fell asleep.

29.

I pushed the red start button to the movie projector and confidently waited the second it took for the film to catch and the plates to start spinning the reels. When the familiar, airy whirl of the machine began, I leaned forward and peered out the projectionist's window till I saw the screen light up and the previews begin. I stepped back and surveyed the scene: two giant Teflon-like plates spun around furiously, one heavily, underneath the weight of the entire film, and the other quick and maniacally, waiting to absorb the feed. The film ran past the flickering bulb in the projector, making the noise of crinkling paper. The booth was sultry, two stories above the theater's seats, absorbing all the hot air from the auditorium, and the heat from the droning projector. I padded backwards in my black Hush Puppy shoes, and grabbed my keys from my pocket. There were four more projectors to thread up.

Harry had told me about the job opening. He knew the manager, and I was hired as soon as I applied. I'd become so sick of being poor, and bored, and satisfied to sit around the apartment feeling sorry for myself, that I knew it was long overdue that I started working. Anyway, the theater was only five blocks from my apartment.

I raced to the next theater to do all by myself the minimum wage duty of being projectionist and usher for five theaters at once. I'd read that in the 80s, union projectionists made twenty bucks an hour, but there was no union in town, so I got $4.35 an hour to do the work of about ten people.

But I didn't care, really, because I loved the job. Each night, I dressed all in black, put on my argyle socks and my black shoes, and strode toward the theater practically grinning. I started to feel important again, directing people through the sold-out crowds in the lobby, sending them in the right direction. I loved tackling a big line at the concession stand, making up Cokes and popcorn bags so fast people's eyes spun. I loved the late show, when everything quieted down, and I was the only person left, except for the manager in the office counting out the cash.

After work, I'd go to the bar and get a drink from Jean-Claude and a teriyaki chicken sandwich, and I was content. I didn't even miss partying that much. Paloma and Pilar didn't seem to need it, and I was following their example.

Mercifully, a new drug from a new doctor had worked. I'd gone into the health service on the verge of all out paranoia, thinking my case was hopeless, and that I'd get in another argument and leave the exam room feeling worse. But Dr. Rimaldi had strode into the room on a caffeine buzz that was both authoritative and generous.

"You, sir, have got problems with the plumbing," she said rapidly, glancing at my chart.

She read through the rest of the chart, brown eyes beneath black plastic glasses, darting around, skimming, scanning. Her hair was blond and pulled back in a tight, blue clip. She couldn't have been over thirty.

"It sounds to me like you just have an irritable system."

"So what does that mean, exactly?" I asked, desperate to reassure myself I wasn't dying of cancer.

"The cause is unknown," she said, still looking at the chart. "It just means the muscles along your large intestines are doing too much. They say it can be caused by too much anxiety, too much smoking, too much drinking, but really it's a mystery. It's not considered a serious medical problem, but the symptoms are annoying."

"What do I do?"

She took out a prescription pad and scribbled something. "Take this pill. It'll stop the cramps you have."

I thought if the drug could take away that feeling, then I'd be a happy man. She handed me the prescription and left the room. I looked around the office, grinning to myself, and saw above her desk a small black decal with a pink triangle on it. Below it were the words "Ally." I thought if I wasn't gay I'd marry her.

It was a Thursday night, and the theaters were all almost empty. We only had one good movie, and it was a foreign film that not many people had showed up for. The manager's door was closed, a small beam of light shining out through the bottom of it, so I had the lobby to myself. There was a rap at the glass. I turned to the exit door and saw a slight, hooded figure standing with its hands in its pockets. I smiled to myself and ran over. When I opened the door a flash of brutally cold wind overtook me and I ushered the cloaked visitor inside. He ripped off his hood.

"Damn, Schoenberger, man, it's fucking cold outside. My nuts are like ice."

"I'll warm 'em up for you, Senor Rubenstein," I said, grasping his jacket and kissing his cheekbone.

He looked around nervously for people and then sculpted his face into an affable grin. "Hey. You can call me Jose."

I pulled away and walked toward the concession stand. "How are ya? I haven't heard from you in a couple days."

He unzipped his jacket to reveal a blue and white Hawaiian shirt. I would've laughed, but I was actually glad to see it. We'd been hit by a freak snowstorm every day for a week and a half and I and the rest of the town had become demoralized.

Jose leaned against the counter. "Ah, shit, Schoenberg, I've had a ton of crap to do. Tuesday night, I had four papers to write. Yeah. I wrote four. And then last night I had to go to this barndance shit for the fraternity."

"Sounds like fun," I said, thinking there was nothing less in the world I'd rather do.

"Oh, God," he said. "And they set me up with this chick from Delta Delta Delta. Yikes. What a fuckin' dog."

Jealous, I asked, "So, did you invite her back to the house for a nightcap?"

"Christ, I woulda puked. Eeek. Anyway, my house is on probation for alcohol violations."

I giggled. "You losers. I would've helped you with the papers, though."

He stepped over next to me and put a palm around the basket of my pants. "You can help me do something else, later..."

"Come with me," I said. I pulled out my keys and took him into the largest auditorium. My vision went totally black for a minute, until I could find the aisle lights that dotted the floor. It was a dark scene in the film, the French one, something was happening in a bedroom, silently, two people staring at each other. Only four people sat in the theater, all of them alone.

"Where are we going, Schoenberger?" Jose whispered.

I shushed him, and walked up to the front of the theater. A tiny stairway led to the stage in front of the screen. I walked up it and then quickly moved to the side of the screen and darted backstage. I turned around and realized I was alone.

I walked back out toward the stairway and saw Jose standing there looking lost. He raised his hands. "Come on!" I whispered, and waved my hand impatiently at him. He ran up the steps, tripped on the last one, and ended up sprawled out across the stage. Someone in the theater coughed, loudly. "Oh, for God's sake," I said, and pulled him by the arm. "Let's go!" He got up and I yanked him around the screen to the backstage.

They must've had stage shows there in the past. There was an enormous area behind the screen with all sorts of lighting equipment and ropes and pulleys laying around, the smell of sawdust. "What'd you bring me back here for?" he asked.

I took him by the hand and led him close to the screen. The movie was reflected on the back of the screen in reverse. Jose resisted upon seeing it, and tried to pull away. "They can't see you," I said, of the audience. "But they can hear you."

"They really can't see us at all?" he asked, and I shook my head. I gazed up at the enormous screen, in awe of its sheer size, and the realization that the apparent depth was more of an illusion than you might think looking at the screen from the front. Jose and I were so dwarfed by the image that there was the slightest feeling of vindictiveness in me; we weren't even as big as the coffee table on the screen, let alone the human beings, but stood insignificantly below the proceedings, nonexistent to the actors and even the audience.

I grabbed his other hand and leaned toward him. Heat spilled out of his open jacket and I got as close to him as I could. He put both arms around me and then looked to the side at the movie. A naked French guy was walking around the kitchen. "Whoa," Jose whispered. "Now that's explicitness."

"Shhh," I said, trying not to laugh.

The French guy went into the bathroom and started to wash his dick in the sink. "Dang, Schoenberg," Jose whispered, "what kind of filth are you assholes showing here?"

"Jose, shut up, the people can hear you."

"Hey, look! That guy ain't circumscribed!"

I laughed and pulled him closer to me. He wouldn't take his eyes off the screen. "Check it out, he has blond pubic hair. I've never seen that."

"Come on," I whispered. I wrenched his head around so he'd look at me, and kept a hand against the back of his buzzcut.

He kissed me lightly on the lips. "Are you circumscribed, Schoenberg?"

"Of course I am," I said, softly. "I'm Jewish. And you've seen it, remember?" For the past two weeks, he'd seen it almost every night. "You're a Jew, too," I said, trying not to break out in laughter. "You should know how it goes."

It was a joke. Jose wasn't Jewish at all, but Mexican and Catholic, with a Jewish name that ended up on his family tree for reasons he did not know.

"I'm the world's sexiest Mexican Jew," he said.

"Here, here." We kissed again, deeper and more aggressively. His lips felt like silk; they rolled off of mine with a gentle pressure that felt arrogantly expensive. I wondered if I was the first boy to taste them.

Jose's dick, compact and perpetually erect, jutted into my upper thigh. I ground myself against it. He moved a hand to one of my buns and felt it so lightly and gingerly that my dick swelled into a humongous boner that practically cried out for relief. I thought of Jose's light brown, hairless ass and craved to be inside of it; I hadn't been able to so far, but he had promised.

"Come back to my apartment tonight," I said. "I don't wanna go to another hotel." Jose had refused to be found out as gay, even by people who wouldn't care. Instead, he'd been renting rooms for us at the Motel 6. The first time it was romantic: Jose had brought champagne and a case of beer, and it was sort of a novelty to be in a hotel in the town I lived in. But by about the fifth time, it had become tedious and felt so wholly unnecessary that I was getting frustrated. As if Paloma and Pilar would care who I slept with, or would tell anyone. They didn't even know who Jose was.

He didn't answer, but looked back at the screen. The blond guy was in the shower with a similarly naked Italian-looking guy with a tiny dick.

"Now that dick," Jose whispered. "That thing's so small it's all foreskin. The foreskin's longer than the shaft!"

I looked at him and pulled him to me with both of my arms around his waist. "This is cool, Schoenberg, I like this." I waited for an answer about the hotel. "Come back to the frat house," he said. "My roommate's out of town."

"What are you, crazy? That place is full of assholes. We could be killed."

"Nah," he said, this time whispering. "They're good guys. I'll tell 'em you're my cousin."

"Who on earth would believe that?"

"Well, we're both Jews, right?"

"Yeah, but you have quesadillas at the Seder."

"I'm circumscribed," he said and grinned obnoxiously.

I playfully hit him on the forehead. "It's circumcised."

"I know, I'm just fuckin' with ya."

30.

"Augie, are you sure about this?" Roberta asked, running her hands through her hair. She'd been growing it out, and it rose from the top of her head in a never-ending circuit of wide, black links. Two gold hoop earrings dangled from her ears. We sat in the empty auditorium of the main stage in the theater building. The dark stage and the bare seats left the theater without mystery, but there was nonetheless potential in the air, the possibility of greatness.

"He's a nice guy. He makes me laugh, he's cute, he likes me, so what could be wrong?"

"For God's sake, he's a frat boy. You detest them. I once recall you saying, and I quote, 'That system stands for everything to which I am opposed: compulsory heterosexuality, sexism, homophobia, racism.' You were the one who told me that story about the black guys who got tied to trees naked and had crap thrown at them for hours on end. And then when they moved into the house, they got racist phone calls; calls placed from inside the house. And then you also said…"

"OK, OK, I think the system is shitty, but this is an individual. And he is gay, he just hasn't come out yet." It may not have sounded like it, but I did realize I was defending a relationship that I would have criticized had it involved someone besides me.

Roberta turned from me and sighed. "Been to the Motel 6 lately?"

"Come on, that's not fair. You don't even know him."

"Well, it sounds terribly romantic. You can take trips to the vending machines together, you can go get a bucket of ice, there's maid service…"

"That's not fair. I'm supportive of everyone else's relationships, but whenever I date someone, people have a problem with it. It's not as easy for me. I can't just go to a party and meet some completely together guy like Jean-Claude. I've tried for years. It doesn't work. I have to take what I can get, and Jose Rubenstein is the best thing I've got. Or, really, the only thing."

Roberta pulled her legs up and hugged her knees. "Is that what you're doing? Dating? It sounds to me it's more like risk-taking. Or self-sabotage."

"What am I supposed to do?" I cried. "I'm at my wits end. How long am I supposed to be single for? I was single when I was nineteen, I was single when I was twenty, I was single when I was twenty-one…"

"Yes, but you have to pursue relationships where you're going to be treated well, Augie…"

"…I'm twenty-two and I'm single, sort of. I don't fuckin' know. And I am being treated well. I'm ecstatically happy. I just wish my friends could find it in their hearts to share my happiness, instead of picking apart every little thing until it seems like I'm forever cursed and they're not. I deserve to have an active love life, too, you know."

Roberta threw her feet on the floor and picked up her bag. "Look, I have sympathy for you and your plight, August Schoenberg, but I'm not gonna sit here and listen while you tell me how wonderful it is to date frat boys." She stood and glared at me. "I'm sorry I wasn't there for you for the thing with Victor, but I didn't even know what was going on. Anyway, it's time you realized that you're still young, and stop weighing your life against whether or not you've been in a relationship. You're a creative person, you have a lot going for you, and I'd give you more credit than that.

"I have to go to rehearsal, but listen to this first. You might be willing to jump headlong into this relationship, but I don't like it at all. I know exactly what's gonna happen. He's going to be nice at first and then you're going to fall in love with him. Then, people are gonna start finding out about the two of you, he's gonna freak because he's in the closet, and he's gonna blame you for telling people even when you haven't. You'll resent him for it, but still try to make the relationship work. There'll be arguments, he'll insult you, you'll get depressed and start drinking too much.

"In the end, he'll stop returning your calls, the two of you will break up, and you've just had another reason to think you're destined to be alone for the rest of your life..."

"Well, yeah, maybe, but..."

"No, let me finish. After the two of you break up, he'll suddenly realize what a pain in the ass it is to be in the closet, move out of the frat house, go to the gay bar in Champaign, or Chicago, or wherever, meet a guy, and then the two of them will show up somewhere where you are, arm in arm, looking happy as clams, you'll get more depressed and have psychosomatic medical problems."

She exhaled and continued to glare at me. "You're the best friend I have in the world, and I'm sorry we haven't seen more of each other this year, but you're a genuine, honest person and I'll be damned if you're gonna get involved with people who are gonna play your ass like a deck of drugstore pinochle cards while I sit by congratulating you."

I stared at the ground. I was beaten.

"How do I know all of this?" she continued. "Because you've described these kinds of relationships to me, Augie. I learned it all from you." Her voice broke. "Start taking your own advice."

"I've seen you in here more often than not, drowning your sorrows, young man," Jean-Claude said, just starting his shift. "Four o'clock in the afternoon is early for you."

I lit a cigarette. I'd been at the bar so long, I'd gone through one pack, and had a new one lined up underneath. "Are my cheeks wet?" I asked.

He stared at me closely. "Dry as a bone, Schoenberg."

"They shouldn't be. Your girlfriend just told me a thing or two."

Jean-Claude tossed the rag aside and came around the bar. He pulled up the stool next to me. "Can I have one?" he asked, and took a cigarette. He blew out the smoke of the first drag and said, "Yeah, she's good at that. But you know her better than me. It's cause she worries about you. She doesn't want you to do self-destructive things."

"Oh, bullshit. She was just trying to portray me as a hypocrite, which is a favorite pastime around campus. Anyway, I think all my friends actually want me to be single.

It's easier for everyone if I remain de-sexed and non-threatening. I'm like an annoying relative that's always around, even though I wasn't invited."

Jean-Claude frowned. "You underestimate yourself. Who are you mixed up with now?"

"Oh, this frat boy. Nothing bad has happened. I just think I might be breaking some of my own rules."

"You could be," he said. "You know how that group treats people in our crowd. They ain't too nice."

I shrugged and guzzled some beer. "Your relationship isn't perfect, is it? I mean, there are problems, and abnormalities, right?"

"Abnormalities?"

"I just wonder if I should stop telling people everything. I have a feeling that the rest of the world is keeping their dirty little secrets to themselves, while I'm out blabbing everything, thereby making myself feel like I'm having weird experiences that no one else does."

He bobbed his head a little. "That's a possibility. Well, yeah. Of course. Everyone has weird shit happen behind closed doors."

"That's it! I'll pretend that nothing out of the ordinary is happening, and then everything will seem normal!" It sounded terrible, even to me, and I was the one who said it.

"Augie, man, you should just go home and chill out. You're politicizing every little thing. Everything you do carries with it this enormous sense of importance." He threw his hands in the air. "There's impending doom all around. You're gonna drive yourself fucking crazy."

I nodded. "I agree with that last part."

Jean-Claude went behind the bar and leaned over and looked at me. "One thing I wanted to tell you: you know, you're entitled to take the lead in these relationships you have. You don't have to wait until something happens and then react to it. Create your own reaction, man."

It was the best advice I'd had in years. Straight guys didn't sit around waiting for shit to happen, they went out and got what they wanted, and felt like they were entitled to it in the first place.

"You're right, you're right."

"Look. I don't know what's going on with that frat boy, but if you're not getting what you need, tell him to fuck off. I don't wanna see another repeat of that mess with Victor."

"Yeah, I know, I'll be careful. Nobody fucks with me and gets away with it!" I smiled, as if it were a joke, but Jean-Claude didn't smile back.

31.

"Have you heard from Victor?" Isabella asked. We walked along the main drag of campustown after running into each other at the record store. There was a fairly icy distance between us: when I caught her eye over a rack of CDs she waited for me to say hello first. Even so, we left the store together and made our way into the impossibly sunny day and walked past waist-high snowdrifts.

"I haven't, no. We were supposed to go to the PJ Harvey concert together, but he didn't show. I guess he's in London."

Isabella pulled a cigarette from a pack of menthols and stopped walking to light it. "Well, yeah. On to bigger and better things. Must be a nice change from this shit town."

I didn't say anything. I knew she had slept with Victor at least once, although if they had ended up sleeping together at the orgy, that would be twice. I couldn't help feeling jealous.

"Anyway," she said, coughing, "I've stopped drinking. Well, at least I haven't drank for like two weeks. It's been murder." She coughed again, dryly and deeply.

"Wow. Congratulations. So what have you been doing with yourself instead?"

She looked at me sideways, and it dawned on me too late that that could have been an insult.

"Well, just living, I guess. Trying to pass classes so I'll actually graduate in May. I don't really want to be on the six year plan. Anyway, other things have come up. I need to get out of school pretty fast."

She obviously wanted me to ask what those things might be, so I didn't ask. "Yeah, we've overstayed our welcome here," I said. "I work with someone who's nineteen, and she stared at me in awe when I told her I was twenty-two. She actually said, 'That's so old!'"

Isabella stopped to adjust her shoe. She grabbed my shoulder to balance herself. "No way," she said, in a false voice of surprise. "That's too unbelievable."

We walked past the campus bookstore and came to the Quad. Dirty remnants of the snowstorms from the week before lay piled up near the bushes in the form of grey, landlocked icebergs. The sidewalks had been snowplowed.

Isabella stopped underneath the gates to the Quad and turned to me. Her face was red: this time not from alcohol, but from the cold. "Augie, look, I have to ask you something."

Nervousness opened up inside my stomach. I couldn't figure out why, but I got so instantly scared that I became nauseous.

"Do you think you can loan me some money? I don't have a job and I'm kind of in a bind."

I was shocked she asked me. I was well-known to be continually broke. "Geez,

Isabella, you know I don't even have a bank account. I'm flat broke. How much do you need?"

"Even just a little bit. See..." She looked over her shoulder. Students walked past us en masse, completely uninterested in eavesdropping. "Augie, I'm pregnant."

I would've thought all the alcohol she drank would have killed off any invading sperm, but apparently that wasn't the way it worked. "God, by who?"

She hesitated for a moment and then threw her cigarette on the ground. She stamped it out with her shoe and said, "It's Victor's."

"But how do you know?" I croaked. My mouth went dry again. My heart skipped a beat, and then beat too hard. "Didn't you sleep with Mark and Tony and Victor and who knows who else?"

She looked disgusted. "Augie, no. Mark Israel couldn't get a boner that night. All he did was suck my pussy. And Tony can never get it up. Victor's the only one. I mean, I never told you this, but Victor and I were seeing each other for some time. At least for a month and a half."

"You're lying!" I barked. "You never dated him!"

"Augie," she said, quietly and hurriedly. "Fine, call it what you want. Fuck buddies. Lovers. Clandestine escapades, I don't give a shit. He fucked me at least a dozen and a half times."

"Well, did either of you assholes think to use condoms?"

"We did. It broke one time. It only takes one time."

"I know that!" I yelled. "And you want me to what, pay for the child's upbringing?"

"Will you shut up?" she said, looking around. "I'm not having the child; I'm having an abortion. Augie, I don't have any money and I don't know what to do. If my parents find out I'm pregnant they'll never speak to me again. They already think I'm a whore."

"Jesus. Jesus." She stood in front of me, pleadingly, in her drab olive coat that was ten years out of style. Her mouth was pinched into a look of disdain. "Why don't you ask Victor for the money? I hear his fiancee is rich."

"That's funny. Thanks. Look, I thought maybe you could help me, but I see that you're otherwise concerned. Thanks a lot."

"I wish things were different, Isabella. I wish you two would have had some consideration for me. I was in love with that guy, and neither of you cared. You even knew he was engaged and you still fucked him. Repeatedly! Were you trying to show me up?"

"Augie, I didn't give a fuck about Victor. I was drunk every time and I only fucked him because he was there. I don't know why you were so wrapped up in him. He's hairy and gross, he has a weird dick, he smells, and he's not good in bed. Can you imagine what this kid would look like?" She smiled, as if that comment was cute. "It'd be a monster."

"Oh, you're a cunt," I said. "To treat this so lightly, like it's all just a big accident. To fuck people for sport. To refer to your own unborn child as a monster. You are a cunt!"

She tried to slap me but I blocked her arm. She stepped backwards. "I'm sorry we were ever friends," she said, inching away. "You're just as narrow-minded as the rest of campus. You just think you're cool because you're gay. Well, let me tell you something, Schoenberg. You should hear what people say about you behind your back. You annoy everyone. All your friends complain about you, even Roberta. And Victor, do you know what Victor said? He said that after you two slept together, he threw up for two days. Just the thought of you naked sent him to the toilet vomiting. He was just being nice to you afterwards. You sickened him."

She was lying. He didn't throw up. *It was not death, it was not death...* I glared at her, the wind whipping my face and neck. She put her index finger in her mouth and gagged, and then pointed at me. She began walking away, then turned and held up two fingers. "Two days," she said, and then stuck her finger in her mouth again. I leaned against the gate and watched her walk away, trying to make my mind go blank. Everything in my brain was sinking, falling down to my toes, making my heart beat irregularly and my stomach cramp up. *It was not death, it was not death...* I imagined Victor hugging the toilet. I shook my head furiously. An image of Isabella with her legs spread and her cunt hooked up to the abortion machine, whatever that is. A scream, a whoosh, a thud. *It was not death, for I stood up, And all the dead, lie down.*

"I got you something," Jose said. He pulled a small, wrapped package from his desk drawer and handed it to me. We were at the frat house in his bedroom. I sat on the bed, glad the wall was behind me for support. I'd spent the rest of the day with a massive lump in my throat and my heart beating zigzags around my chest. I needed to be around Jose more than anything. I couldn't have stood to be alone.

Paloma and Pilar were out of town. I paced the apartment until it was time to leave, and then rode over to the frat house on an old bicycle that was laying around unlocked in the parking lot to my building. I grimaced the whole way, falling a couple of times on invisible patches of ice. Bruised, and slightly wet, I made my way up Greek Row to the frat house. From the street, the house looked like a mansion, but the exterior was only an illusion. Inside, the place was more like a barracks. Jose's bedroom certainly looked like a dorm room: two beds, two desks, small rug on the floor.

"You didn't have to do that," I said, inwardly glowing with happiness. "I've never had a valentine before."

"Really. A nice guy like you?"

"I forgot it was Valentine's Day. I didn't get you anything."

He waved a hand at me. "No problem."

I ripped open the paper and found a videotape, entitled "Intimate Massage for Men." The picture on the cover showed a naked guy lying on his stomach while another nude guy massaged his butt. "It's wonderful," I said, laughing. "I can't wait to use it."

He crawled toward me and sat next to me on the bed. "I can't wait, either."

I rubbed the fuzzy hair on the top of his head and then we kissed, slowly. I wanted to be taken away, dreamily and romantically, to a place where I could forget everyone and be at peace.

Jose pulled back. "Isn't it cool? We're just two guys, and it's not faggotty at all. All those other fags are like women, but we're more like men."

I groaned. I had little strength to defend myself. "Jose, saying something like that; don't you know it's insulting to me? I'm not considered to be a manly man, I'm considered to be a total fag. People have bothered me about it my whole life."

"You aren't a fag," he said. "You're a regular person."

"Ugh. Look, I haven't been treated that way. Gay guys are always trying to differentiate themselves from all the other gays. Just leave everyone else out of it. The only thing that matters is us."

He looked uneasy, and made a face. "I'm a regular guy. I'm masculine. It's 'cause I don't wear makeup and act like a fruitcake, like all the faggots do."

I didn't want him to ruin things, but he was ruining things. "Everybody's got different personalities."

He considered it for a second. "You're a reasonable person, Schoenberg. I like that."

"God, you're a nutcase. Come here." I pulled him near me and then got on top of him. We made out for what seemed like hours, fully clothed, waiting as long as we could to start disrobing each other, holding on to the anticipation as if that were better than sex itself. The dim light from his desk lamp cast a bluish, fluorescent haze around us and made the room seem silent, and fixed, and impossible to change.

"I love you, Schoenberg," he muttered. I looked instantly at his face. His eyes were half-closed. "I've been lookin' for you for a long time, but I didn't know it."

I didn't know what to say. He was being too premature.

Instead of speaking, I reached down and undid his belt buckle. I kneeled on the floor and slid off his pants and then slid off his boxers and relished the sight of his sprightly little boner and miniature balls. I rested my arms on his thighs and moved in close to his penis, which was quivering slightly in its attempt to reach for the sky. I closed my lips around the top of it and held it there, tasting it, smelling it, absorbing the warmth of it. "Eeek, gads, Schoenberg. Oh." There was an explosion. A blast of cold air overcame me, there was a bright white flash, something banged against the wall. People yelled, male voices, absurdly loud and agitated. Jose jerked upwards and reached in vain for his pants. I shot my eyes to the right and saw a gang of guys standing inside the swinging door. One of them had a camera.

"We got you now, Rubenstein," one of them said. "On film." The guy with the camera waved it around. The flash had gone off right when my lips were around Jose's dick, and there I'd been, kneeling on the floor with it hanging out of my mouth, like the biggest faggot cocksucker in the world.

"What the fuck!" Jose said, standing up. He made a half-hearted attempt to pull up his pants, but then waddled over to them with the trousers still around his ankles. "Gimme that motherfucking camera you assholes."

"No way, Jose," another one said, in a cocky voice. "We're publishing this one on the internet. It'll live forever." Jose grabbed for the camera, but the guy who was holding it jumped back a few feet, laughing, knowing Jose couldn't get far with his pants like that. Another guy stuck out his leg and Jose tripped over it and crashed to the ground. I sat watching the scene with my mouth open, not sure if this was a drunken prank or the culmination of a campaign to expose Jose's homosexuality, or both. There were five guys, all white with short brown hair, all in brown boots, all in blue jeans with brown belts, all with their button-down shirts tucked in.

Seeing Jose flail around on the ground was too much for me. I stood up and marched over to the ringleader. "Hand over the camera, asshole."

"Who the fuck are you? Some gay prostitute?"

If I was bigger I would've punched him. "I don't give a shit what your beef is with Rubenstein, but don't drag me into it. Hand it over."

They laughed and one of them yelled, "Fag!" in a mocking falsetto voice.

Jose regained his pants and stood. I realized then that he was about a foot shorter than any of them. "Everyone get the fuck out of this room, now," he said.

"Can you believe it? That was perfect timing, right as he's got a guy sucking his dick. And we got it!"

"I knew that fuckin' guy was a homo!"

"Remember," the guy with the camera said. "This picture will be on JoseSucksCock.com any day now." They all laughed and filed out of the room.

Jose shut the door and bent down on the floor, rubbing his leg.

"Jesus, are you OK?" I asked.

"Just buzz off, Schoenberg!"

"What?"

He put his hands up in front of him. "Just. Just get outta here, all right?"

"Don't get mad at me," I said. "Be mad at your fucking roommates. I told you it was a bad idea to come here."

"Schoenberg, I'm warning you. Scram. Now."

"Piece of shit. You're a fucking piece of shit."

"Now, Schoenberg!" he yelled, and raised his hand as if to hit me.

I snatched my ski jacket off the bed and strode out of the room with what dignity I could muster. Down the hall, I saw three of the guys milling around, laughing. Instinctively, I looked down at the floor, dreading the thought of making eye contact with them. Along the floor, where it met the baseboard, I saw a roll of film. Quickly, as if I were picking up money I saw on the floor at a bar, I snatched the film, put it in my pocket and sailed through the exit door to the stairs. I ran down the steps and outside as fast as I could and then walked back to my apartment, forgetting about the bike.

Safe inside the confines of the apartment, I made my way to the bathroom where I had a massive attack of diarrhea. I sat on the toilet feeling purged and anemic but I was still fuming mad. I was too angry to be sad. I knew my friends had warned me. I just wanted so badly for them not to be right.

32.

Augie Schoenberg
Shakespeare 351
March 8, 1996

Gentlemen of the Shade: A look at the tavern world in Shakespeare's <u>Henry IV</u> plays

    The first and second parts of Shakespeare's <u>King Henry IV</u> function as historical texts which document the playwright's account of Henry IV's troubled reign. To break up the political story, Shakespeare inserted a comic subplot throughout the plays, set in and around an Elizabethan tavern. Here, noble and common characters interact with each other under very specific circumstances. Far from being just a meeting ground for a bunch of drunks, the tavern world serves as an alternate world: It's a place with its own names, language, morals, and value systems. The tavern world has its own ideas of time, loyalty, honesty, justice, courage, and work. Each character spends much time debating these ideas with one another, anxious to validate their own opinions and justify their existences, which are often of questionable repute. In contrast to the reputable and stoic court world, the tavern world harbors people who need to escape. Prince Hal, a temporary tavern-goer, uses the Boar's Head tavern to escape the stuffy environment of the court world and strives to disintegrate his reputation for future gain. Falstaff—though he's ambitious—seeks to find an alternate view of courage and manhood and hopes that Hal will bring him into the royal world after Hal becomes king. The result is telling: though the tavern world functions as a comic plot device, it is a construction of an alternate world: a festive, though blurred, place where characters can escape the realities of everyday life. Under their own rules and conditions, the tavern-goers poison themselves with alcohol and try to bypass class divisions and manipulate conventional standards so they can succeed on their own terms.

Augie Schoenberg
Screenwriting II
March 15, 1996

SCENE 32: EXT. CAMPUSTOWN STREET. NIGHT.

Augie talks on pay telephone to Javier, the day after the incident at the fraternity house. Augie is on a brightly lit commercial street, but few people are around. It's still bitter cold outside, and he wears his ski jacket zipped up to his chin and a blue and green ski cap. Hard packed snow and ice line the sidewalk and street. Frost clouds up the store windows. Movie theater marquee lights shine in background.

> AUGIE
> Hey, Javier. It's me, Augie.

INT. BEDROOM AT FRATERNITY HOUSE.

Javier holds phone to his ear and hesitates.

> AUGIE
> (impatiently)
> Hello?

> JAVIER
> (barely audible)
> Oh, hey what's up, Augie.

EXT. CAMPUSTOWN STREET.

> AUGIE
> Hi, uh, what's going on?

> JAVIER
> What do you mean what's going on?

> AUGIE
> I mean, what happened last night? Are you all right?

> JAVIER
> (long pause, then a sharp exhalation)
> I'm all right now. Look, what do you want? I mean, why are you calling me?

> AUGIE
> Why do you think? None of this makes any sense to me. What

the hell was that last night? Why do you live there?

JAVIER
Look, don't call me anymore, all right? I almost got killed last night because of you, and you're not real high on my list right now.

AUGIE
(outraged)
Killed? Because of me? It wasn't my fault, though.

JAVIER
Look, Schoenberg, I told you to lock the door, but you wouldn't do it, would you? So this is what we get instead. Thanks a lot. All you had to do was listen to me, Augie. But no, you wanted to take chances.

AUGIE
You never said that! You never told me to lock the door!

JAVIER
Then get the wax outta your ears, Schoenberg. I asked you three times to lock the door, and you refused, eager as you were to get my dick in your mouth.

AUGIE
How can you say that to me? That never happened. I mean, God, you told me that you loved me last night!

JAVIER
You're on drugs, buddy boy. I don't fall in love with faggots. Especially faggots that get me in trouble with the boys.

AUGIE
(coldly, resolutely)
They broke down the door. It was locked, and even if it wasn't, they broke it down anyway. You're just afraid. You're saying all this because you're terrified of yourself, and who you are. You're supposed to be my friend, not my enemy. You're supposed to look out for me, not dump me using manipulation and lies.

JAVIER
Dump you? Schoenberg, we were never going out. You just

thought we were.

AUGIE
(closes eyes)
You know, it's funny, Javier. I was at the laundromat tonight, and there was a couple there doing laundry together. The guy was folding the towels, while the girl sat at a table reading a magazine. She was singing along to some stupid song on the muzak, and for a second I felt such incredible jealousy that it almost scared me. I never in my life thought I had the capacity to feel jealousy for people doing something I never want to do in a place I never want to be in. But I did feel it. And it scared the shit out of me.

JAVIER
I have no idea what the fuck you're talking about. I gotta go.

AUGIE
One thing that always surprised me is how some people take relationships for granted. It seems to just happen naturally for some people. I thought you understood it'd be harder for us. I thought you'd stick it out. (Laughs) I guess it's fine that gay marriage is illegal, cause I wouldn't have anyone to get married to anyway. I can't picture what he might look like. I don't even have a type. But, anyway, he's elusive, and far away, or maybe he's unborn. I never thought of that. He's not around yet, he hasn't been born.

JAVIER
Are you drunk? This is all such bullshit.

AUGIE
Have fun with the frat boys, Javier. I have the film of me sucking your dick, if you want copies of the pictures.

Augie hangs up phone and walks out of phone booth toward the movie theater. Javier slams down phone and then picks it up and throws it across the room at the wall.

33.

Mark Israel was killed. Jean-Claude, Tony, Paul and I silently drove up the interstate to Chicago for the funeral. When Jean-Claude called to tell me the news, I sat dumbfounded with the phone in my hand, staring at the wall. The first word that sprang up in my head was "terrorists." But it wasn't that. It was a car accident in Tel Aviv.

"Dude," said Jean-Claude. His voice had been fervent and possessed with an odd vigor. "He's only been gone for like three months. I feel like I just saw him yesterday."

"What the hell happened?"

"I don't know, man. I guess he was going out with some friends and then a truck ran a red light or something. And then..." I imagined a compact car smashed to smithereens by the side of a road. "It sucks, dude," Jean-Claude continued. "He just e-mailed me and told me what a great time he was having. I guess he loved it there."

I pictured Mark Israel walking around Tel Aviv in khaki shorts, a white T shirt, and sandals, with a grin on his face and some bronzed, Middle Eastern female by his side. It was a cruel twist of fate: a dream trip to the Holy Land ended in tragedy. I felt terrible about it, but wasn't exactly in a state of mourning, so much as I felt debased, and frightened. Paul Veracruz asked me if I even wanted to go to the funeral and I said, "Of course!" bitterly, as if I was offended by the question, but until I found out they were driving up for the service, I hadn't planned to go. In the end, though, thinking of the brutal finality of death and the almost breath-stealing shock of a young death made all the bullshit at the Harley Hutt seem utterly insignificant. As if it mattered now whether or not Mark and I liked each other.

The mood in the car was appropriately somber: all of us had terrible hangovers. There'd been a party at Trailer Trash the night before, the first outside party of the spring. It'd been freezing but we were determined. I showed up with Harry, hoping the sight of two attractive and young gay studs would drive the male party guests wild, but the only excitement was Tony Valentine—so incredibly drunk that he started bawling, crying out into the alley for his departed best friend. At that point, we moved on to the bar, where I had a time of it trying to avoid Isabella.

It was the end of March, but it hadn't warmed up at all, and the farms along the interstate were covered in gray and white. The sun shone but provided no heat. I gazed out at the fields, praying for spring. The winter had made me feel deaf and dumb, and on the verge of paranoid claustrophobia. I was still having nightmares, but now they weren't just about Ramesh Singh—Jose Rubenstein and Mark Israel were showing up, too. We hit the suburbs, and I rested my head against the back of the car seat, almost in disbelief that we had lost a friend so quickly. The mood in the car was depressing enough, but I was glad I was awake and not sleeping. In bed, I didn't feel safe anymore.

My mind wandered, turning from Victor to Isabella to Jose. It was awful to think that all those friendships that had started so well had ended so terribly. What was more terrible, though, was how many times I had privately wished Mark dead in the last semester. And now he was. Just as I got so depressed about my personal life that I thought I might finally snap and descend into the schizophrenia I feared I might have, Paul Veracruz shook my shoulder. "Snap out of it. We're there."

There, on the inner drive, the lake was east of us, so far across the park that it was impossible to see it. The temple stood to the west, modern, big as a museum. We walked up stiffly, wearing suits, none of us comfortable but it was a funeral. I looked at my watch. 2:03 p.m. My heart sank.

"You guys," I said. "Forget it. We can't go."

"What?" Tony said, irritated.

"It's three minutes after two. You can't go to a Jewish thing late. They won't let you in."

They all cursed and looked away from each other, and then up at the temple.

"Let's try it anyway," Tony said, and we walked up the stone steps, there must have been fifty of them, and then pulled on the doors. They were locked.

"Jesus fucking Christ," Tony said. "God damn it."

"This is a rotten deal," Jean-Claude said.

"I don't get it," Paul said. "You can go into church an hour late if you want to."

Tony pulled on the doors again. "Forget it. It's useless." He turned to me with rage in his eyes. "Maybe if you hadn't been so fucking late getting to the Hutt today we would've been on time, Schoenberg."

"Fuck you! I had to wait a half an hour at the Hutt before you were even ready."

"Enough," Jean-Claude said. "I don't want to hear it. There's nothing we can do about it now."

We sat on the steps and waited for the service to end. To see the Harley Hutt boys in suits, sitting out on the steps because we couldn't make it to the temple in time was the most depressing sight I'd seen in some time.

The doors opened, people strolled out, we stood up. When the last of the mourners had exited, we found Mark's parents and went over to them, Tony leading the way.

Mr. and Mrs. Israel were two tall, dark, drugged-looking people, who helplessly scanned the horizon, like they might see Mark strolling up the driveway at any moment.

Mrs. Israel grabbed Tony's hands and said to Mr. Israel, assuredly, "It's Mark's friends."

"Mark's friends," Mr. Israel said and shook Jean-Claude's hand. After we were all introduced, Mrs. Israel took one look at us standing next to each other in our suits and started crying and then hugged and kissed us all and said, "It means so much to me that you're here." I felt like an asshole for ever thinking I might not go.

"You didn't get to go inside!" Mr. Israel said, and I said, "No, we're really sorry," and Mr. Israel said, "Come in, come in. It wouldn't be right if you guys didn't get to pay your respects."

Humbly, we walked in the temple. It was vast and cavernous but filled with bright light from the skylights, and the white walls, and the shining edges of gold. A framed portrait of Mark sat on the casket; he was wearing a suit and tie and was younger than when I knew him, and smaller. It must have been his senior picture from high school.

And all at once my heart skipped around so roughly that it felt like I was being attacked from the inside, and then my large intestine cramped up so badly I almost cried out in pain. I was sure that I was suffering from a chronic, undiagnosed heart problem and would soon die. I tried to tell myself that it was just stress. There'd been too much death in my life: Mark Israel, Ramesh Singh, Victor and Isabella's unborn baby. When I saw her at the bar the night before she wore a half-shirt and a new belly button ring. She wasn't pregnant anymore. I looked at Mark's picture on the casket and for the first time it occurred to me that he was inside of it, mangled, lying down, decomposing. A wave of terror swept over me. It felt like the temple had no air. I grabbed out for support, but no one and nothing was there: I lost my balance and my breath and dropped down to the floor.

34.

I lay on my back with my shirt off and the suction cups of the EEG machine attached to my chest. There was a gentle whirring and then slowly, a paper strip ran out of the printer, filled with straight black lines and red mountains. I knew my fate lay in that paper, and at that thought, my heart beat faster than it should have. I weakly tried to calm down, but I was beyond the point of being able to talk myself out of it. Anxiety had become a constant.

"You know," the technician, a wispy blond woman, said. "We had one guy in here, and he was so hairy, we had to shave five different spots on his chest just to put the wires on him."

"Wow," I said, giving a small laugh, as if I was amused by that comment, instead of instantly thinking, 'She is trying to be nice by making conversation. Act like you think it's funny and then smile. You can worry about dying afterwards.'

My reactions were planned, and deliberate, and one hundred percent the result of acting.

We finished the test. I was unhooked, dewired, descutioned, and then met the doctor.

It was a comfortable office—not an exam room—with a desk like you'd find in a study, and leather chairs. Beyond the window, on the other side of the L tracks, was a canopy of gargantuan trees, the branches black with moisture. The L train passed, snaking around a curve. I squinted at the placard: Ravenswood Line. The thought filled me with what I thought was happiness but was really serenity. Quiet, tree-lined streets and oversized Victorian houses spread out in the foreground, but these were nice ones, not like the Harley Hutt. I hadn't thought to ask where I was when I was brought in. I just lay back in the bed and let them work on me, which didn't take long. For the emergency room, I wasn't serious.

"Well," the doctor said, staring down at the printout. The top of his head was bald, but the remaining hair was almost the same color as his scalp. "It's a consistent delay. Every third beat. Kind of like a jazz beat."

"What does it mean?" I asked, not wanting to be terrified again, but to be reassured, and at ease.

"Heart murmur, most likely. You didn't know you had one?"

I shook my head.

"It shouldn't be a problem. When I listened to your chest I could barely hear it. I would say just go on and have a normal life."

"But what about my irregular heartbeats? It palpitates and sometimes beats so hard it almost knocks me down on the ground. Well, today it did."

"It's stress," he said. "From the echo we found you have no valve problems, your heart's normal sized, you don't have any blockages."

I sat back and considered things. I was certain that I'd be the youngest person on campus ever to die of a heart attack. Apparently, that wasn't in the cards.

"What happened to me today? Did I just faint?"

He nodded. "You sure did. You knocked your head on the floor a little, but a bump on the head won't kill ya. What did you have to eat today?"

I thought about it, but couldn't remember anything. "Well, I think...well, nothing."

"And what did you have to drink last night?"

I hung my head, pretending I was trying to remember, when in fact I knew exactly what had transpired. "Eight beers."

He looked at me with mild curiosity, apparently waiting for me to go on.

"Two shots of tequila. No, three. A wine cooler. A 40 of Crazy Town."

The doctor's mouth opened and he said, "Anything else?"

I should have just shut up, but I said, "A gin and tonic."

The doctor regarded me silently, as though he were upset I'd been playing stupid all along.

When I walked out into the waiting room I saw my parents immediately. My mother sat in her chair looking for all the world like Jackie Kennedy in dark sunglasses with a scarf around her head. They stood and my mother ran over to me. "Oh my God, we thought you were dead! They called and said you were in the emergency room and we didn't know what happened, but could only think the worst." She put her arms around me and covered me with the familiar smell of perfume, and wool, and what I assumed was makeup. My father, towering over us, wrapped us in his eminently larger arms, and we stayed huddled in the waiting room for a minute or so, my mother quietly crying, while I repeated, "I'm not dead," over and over.

"Come back to Evanston," my father said, his arms folded. "Stay in your old room for a couple of days."

"We'll look after you," my mother said. "I can't bear this. Twenty-two with heart problems!"

"There's nothing serious, I've been checked out. I just fainted. Anyway, I have to work, and school's almost over. I have a lot of work to do."

"You'll kill yourself with stress!" my father said, for the first time sounding upset. "You work yourself to the bone, and for no thanks and no pay. Stay at our house, I beg you."

I looked through the glass walls and saw the Harley Hutt boys on the curb. Jean-Claude was popping wheelies in a wheelchair. "Nah, my friends are gonna drive me back. Anyway, Paloma and Pilar will watch out for me."

"Thank goodness you live with some nice girls," my mother said. Her voice turned to a whisper. "You had so many problems with the Harley boys." She glanced outside. "Do they take drugs?"

"No! Mom, look, I'm going back to school. Nothing's wrong with me, I was just hungry."

"He needs money!" my father cried, scrambling for his wallet. "He can't afford to buy food!"

"Oh my God! He's starving!"

"I'm not starving," I said, laughing. "I have plenty of food. I eat like a horse." Seeing me laugh, the guys came inside, Jean-Claude pushing the wheelchair.

"Hospital regulations, Mr. Schoenberg. You'll need to be taken out in this," Jean-Claude said.

My mother gave a cry of surprised laughter, and then Paul and Tony took me by the arms and forced me into the chair. "Don't make us get the straightjacket, sir," Paul said.

"Oh my God," my mother said. "Be careful with him. That's my only son. If he ever drops dead, I'll commit suicide."

My father stuffed some money in my shirt pocket and then I was whisked away. In the parking lot, I looked back inside and saw my parents wistfully gazing out at me through the waiting room glass. Tony Valentine rubbed my shoulders. "Are you all right, Schoenberg?" he asked. "I don't think I could stand to go to two funerals in one day."

"He's fine," Paul said. "Just a hangover and a funeral. Bad combo."

"We just need to shove a bacon double cheeseburger down his throat," Jean-Claude said.

"Yeah, we're gonna put some meat on that skinny little white butt of yours whether you like it or not, Schoenberg," Paul said.

"Oh, god, clog my arteries until I have a heart attack," I said, moving along at a brisk clip, getting stared at by everyone walking by. "At least I'll have a nice ass."

We came to the car. "We wouldn't kill you, Augie," Jean-Claude said, obnoxiously lifting me out of the chair and putting me in the back seat. "Nobody'd clean up the mess."

35.

April had come and brought some much needed warmth. I left my screenwriting class and when I got outside the literature building, I unzipped my ski jacket and inhaled the long-overdue smell of spring. I walked almost contentedly through a grove of trees next to the Quad. The sun broke through the still naked branches in sharp streaks of gold and illuminated the darkened underside of a small gazebo. I slowly crept over to it, hoping to find a place where I could be at peace for the few minutes I had before I had to be at the theater. When I walked up the steps, I saw a slight, absolutely still figure with her head down. It was Arundhati Singh, wrapped in a long beige overcoat.

"August Schoenberg. How nice to see you!"

"Hi!" I exclaimed. "How are you? I'm surprised to see you here, I haven't seen you in months."

"Yes," she said, her face looking warm and pleased. "Well, I've been away. Tell me, how are things going with you?"

"Great. Classes are fine, and I'm just about to graduate, so I'm really excited."

"Congratulations. What do you plan to do afterwards?"

"I'm not sure yet. I'm working on a screenplay now, and if it works out, maybe I can sell it to Hollywood and live happily ever after." I laughed, as if that were the least likely scenario.

"Perhaps you will. You're a fantastic writer. Have you taken the workshop classes for screenwriting?"

"Yeah. I just got back some pages from the instructor and he's been really encouraging. He says he thinks there might be something to it, the screenplay, I mean. So, I'm excited." Relieved was more like it. My whole outlook on my career changed when the instructor gave me back the first pages. He said they were, "terrifically exciting."

"Well, I look forward to seeing your pictures at the local cinema."

"We'll see," I said, unintentionally grinning. "So, how are you?" I didn't want to ask about her son, but I was wondering if she was still teaching.

She looked toward the cement below us and said, unconvincingly, "I'm fine. I really am. It's been an absolutely terrible few months. But I am holding myself up."

"Good," I said. "You know I dropped by your office a few times, but you weren't there. I imagined you were in Chicago."

"I was. Yes. You know, my husband lives there, and my son. And my daughter lives in France. So, I am all alone out here." She gave a weak smile.

"It's nice to have you back. This campus would be immeasurably bleaker without you."

"Well, that's nice of you, but I feel it might be even bleaker without you next year. I wonder if you know how much you have to offer the world, Mr. Schoenberg."

I blushed, eating it up.

"It's funny," she said, looking out toward a newly-budding flower bed next to the literature building. "You remind me of someone."

I raised an eyebrow and smiled.

"It's my son. My son Ramesh. He was just like you in so many ways. A gorgeous, almost violent writing style, cynical yet generous, ungodly thin, creative. The chaotic beginnings of early adulthood." She looked at me with heavy eyes. "You're exactly like him."

"That's a wonderful compliment. Thank you so much."

She scoffed and then looked embarrassed, as if thinking she'd just said too much.

"Well, I hope his spirit will live on anyway," she continued. "Losing a child is certainly a descent into the recesses of hell." This time she smiled, apparently to unnecessarily reassure me she wasn't insane.

I couldn't see what would be accomplished by telling her about meeting him. "I'd imagine his spirit would live on," I said. "In you."

She grabbed me and kissed me lightly on the cheek, the scent of jasmine floating off her wrists. "Somehow you know just the right things to say."

The telephone rang. I was in my bedroom by myself, studying for finals. I longed to be out at a party, or at the bar, or anywhere besides my room. I was bored, I was horny, and the thought that these would be the last tests I would take, perhaps for the rest of my life, did not console me.

I considered letting the machine get it. I had paranoid suspicions that Jose Rubenstein or Isabella or who knows who else might call and start to make trouble. Truthfully, though, I was longing for some excitement so much that I almost hoped it would be trouble on the line.

"Hello?"

"Schoenberg," a gruff, male voice said. It wasn't Victor, it wasn't Jose, I didn't think it was Paul, it wasn't Jean-Claude, it definitely wasn't Harry. I thought perhaps it was Mark Israel from beyond the grave.

"Hey, Tony," I said.

There was a pause. "How'd you know it was me?"

"Woman's intuition. So what's up with you, mysterious caller? It's almost midnight."

"Look, Schoenberg, what are you doing?"

"Oh, I'm having an orgy. Wanna stop by? Everybody's coming."

"Ha, ha, you're funny. Hey, meet me at McGregor Hall in fifteen minutes. I gotta ask you something."

"Oh, God, am I in trouble again? Listen, I didn't tell anybody anything, I don't know anything, I didn't hear anything..."

"No, you're not in trouble," he said, irritated. "Just meet me there, Schoenberg. Do it."

"Why don't you just come over here? I have an apartment, we don't have to talk in a well-lit public area. I haven't done anything unscrupulous, at least not lately."

"Just do it, Schoenberg. Please. Fifteen minutes."

"Oh, all right," I said, but I was actually curious to go. McGregor Hall was about the only building on campus I'd never been in, and I'd heard it had a little-known swimming pool on its second floor. Anyway, Tony's midnight phone call had such an air of nighttime soap opera to it that I couldn't resist. I was bored at Paloma and Pilar's, so much so that I was starting to feel like life was going on without me, and I privately missed the Harley Hutt so badly that I was hoping Tony would take me there afterwards so I could see it.

He stood near the bike racks in his bomber jacket. The curls on his head were getting longer, but as I got closer I could see that his hair was thinning in the corners of his forehead. I walked toward him stealthily, wishing I'd worn all black.

"Agent Schoenberg reporting for instructions. The eagle has landed. The chair is against the wall."

"Knock it off, you clown."

"So what are we doing here?" I ran my fingers around his temples. "Gettin' a little thin, huh?"

"Come on," he said, nudging his head toward the building. "I wanna show you something."

We walked toward the darkened building: old brown brick, oversized windows, barren green doors. Tony pulled out a key ring and, with some effort, opened one of the doors.

"How'd you have keys?"

He chewed on a piece of gum. "I'm a PE major. Sometimes I need to be here after hours."

"Oh," I said, unable to imagine what those reasons might be.

Inside, the building smelled of chlorine. We walked slowly through the halls, which were lit by only the faint bulbs from the emergency lights. "So there is a pool here."

Tony didn't answer. We came to an elevator shaft and he stuck a key in the call box. An overwhelmingly loud, grinding sound roared above us. When it stopped, we stared at the doors, and after a long minute, the doors opened. We stepped inside and Tony pressed the button for the second floor.

We slowly began to rise. Tony chewed his gum and then turned to me. His eyes looked fairly concerned. "Schoenberg, you scared me to death the other week. I thought you were gonna fuckin' die."

"All I did was faint. I wasn't dying."

"Schoenberg, I lost my best friend and then I thought I was gonna lose another one. It was the scariest fucking day of my whole entire life."

"Tony, you weren't scared. Anyway, I thought you hated me."

"Christ, Augie, I don't hate you. This has been the worst semester ever, and it should have been the best. I've been sick. I've been so sick that I was such a dick and I didn't do anything to stop Mark from freaking out on you. And then Mark died and I felt like everyone else left in the world despised me."

I didn't know what to say, but he seemed so awfully vulnerable that I put my arms around him and hugged him. The elevator stopped, but I knew we had a minute before it would open. He squeezed me back.

Eventually we untangled ourselves and I said, "You know, Valentine, you're hard to read. And you're inconsistent. If you were a character in my screenplay I'd get an F."

"Yeah, I ruin everything, don't I? Everything I touch turns to shit."

The doors creaked open. We stepped outside and walked through a winding, wood-paneled hallway. The smell of chlorine had become overpowering. Soon enough, we were in a locker room. The smell of old socks and mold reminded me of high school days when that smell made me want to puke. Even the possibility of seeing the quarterback for the football team nude didn't temper the nausea.

"I wanna show you the pool," Tony said. We walked through the showers, dry and empty, and then through another door till we came to a small staircase that led to some bleachers. The pool was in front of them, light blue, shimmering, swaying slightly in the near-darkness. We sat down and gazed out at the water for a minute as if it were the ocean. The small, lapping sound of the water against cement quietly echoed off the walls.

"It's funny," I said. "That's probably the largest body of water in Central Illinois."

"Yeah," Tony said, brightening up. "It's full Olympic size, and we have swim meets here. I taught a class here once, just grade school kids, but I wore a whistle around my neck and played the role of the coach pretty good..." His voice dropped off. He pulled a small bottle of whiskey from his jacket. He offered it to me and, against my better judgment, I took a swig. Like I'd thought, the liquor burned my entire stomach and attacked a certain spot in particular—the place where I thought I'd had an ulcer. I'd since learned from Dr. Rimaldi that that was the opening of my small intestine, and it was chronically inflamed.

"Jesus," Tony continued, somberly, this time. "I sound like a fuckin' stroke. Bragging about teaching kids how to swim. I'm a fucking failure."

"Lord, you have your whole life ahead of you. If you brought me here because you're feeling sorry for yourself again, I'm leaving."

"No, no." He put his arm around my shoulder. "I gotta tell you something." He drank some of the whiskey and then quietly burped. "Look, you know, I was pretty upset when Mark passed away, but it's not really what you think. We were best friends, definitely, but there was something more..." He drank more whiskey. "There was something more to it." He looked at me for help.

I waited for him to go on, pretending I had no idea what he might say.

"I mean," he continued. "Don't you think that everyone is basically bisexual?"

"No," I said.

That was the wrong answer. He drank again. "Christ. You're not making this easy. Schoenberg, look. Mark was like..." He turned slowly toward me. "Mark and I were, we were at times involved sexually with each other."

"Really?" I said, neutrally.

He studied me for a second to see if I was being sarcastic. I hadn't tried to be, I was trying to be tactful. I figured he was in some pain.

"Yeah," he said, staring straight ahead. "It's hard to say that. Well, I guess you'd know. I'm sorry, Schoenberg, but you're the only one I can tell."

I patted him on the stomach. "Aw, Tony, you could've told anyone. We don't hang out in an anti-gay crowd, you know."

"Well, I'm not gay per se," he said, nervously. "I mean, I'm not like all the way gay or anything. Not like that's a problem, but I'm just not."

"Oh," I said. "God, I never knew. That's a shock."

"Yeah, I figured it would be. It feels good to tell someone. I mean, besides his parents, I probably grieved the most. I mean, when we missed the funeral, I almost cried."

"Oh, I'm sorry, Tony. It's too bad you had to go through that alone."

"It is too bad!" he said. "I felt totally alone, and like nobody cared!"

"Well, Tony, nobody knew the real story. You guys kept it secret." I almost added 'sort of' to the end of that, but caught myself in time.

"Oh, I know. Listen, Augie, that night we spent together. I just wanna say that I'm so sorry about that. I basically took advantage of you."

"No, you didn't really."

"But Augie, Mark and I were fighting, and it was like an act of revenge. I used you. And that's why Mark was so mad at you. We got in a fight that night and I told him I was gonna go spend some time with somebody worthwhile. So you moving out of the Harley Hutt was my fault!"

"No, no," I said. "Mark hated me anyway. It was a Jewish thing."

"That's stupid, it wasn't a Jewish thing. Nobody even thinks you're Jewish. All anybody ever notices about you is that you're gay."

"Oh, thanks!"

"Well, I didn't mean that like it sounded. Anyway, if you hate me, I understand. Cause I totally used you and you have every right to wanna kick my ass."

"I would kick your ass, Valentine, except now you're a fucking widow."

He laughed. "You're all right, Schoenberg." He leaned back on the benches. "You sure you don't hate me?"

"It's water under the bridge. I wish things had gone more smoothly at the Hutt, but hey, nobody can change the past." I eyed the pool, and a volleyball that was laying around on the ground. "Anyway, I bet I could kick your ass at nude water polo."

He stared at me as if I were insane.

"First one in gets the first point."

Tony and I lay nude in the sauna, wet with boners, but across from each other, on separate benches. When does the janitor come in? I asked. At three, he mumbled. We should get outta here, I said, we should get dressed. I don't wanna, he said, his dick vibrating in the heat, far away from me, but to look at it was all I wanted, I didn't want to touch him. The sight of his ass and his thighs during the water polo match was like a dream, and practically filled me with sorrow. College was ending, no more fun and games. I wanna stay like this forever Schoenberg, he said, his ass bulbous beneath the weight of his torso, and not grow up. Face it, babe, I said, you're a man, now. There ain't no turning back. Tony lazily dripped some water from a cup onto the rocks, his erection looking like it was attached to his navel. The hiss from the stones was so comforting it was like a sneeze, or the last second of ejaculation. I wish I wasn't so afraid, Tony said. I wish I was like you. I'm scared, Augie. *Hiss.* Act like you aren't, I said. That's all there is to it. Beyond that, you have no control. My dick's hard, Augie, he said. But I can't even figure out who I wanna fuck. It just goes limp every time. I'm not equipped to do it. *Hiss.* Just find a person. It sounds to me like you could have whoever you want. He stared at the ceiling. I want you, Schoenberg, he said. You're lying to yourself, I said. You're just saying that because I'm here. He looked down at the boards. You're right. I'm fucked up. We gotta go, I said. We won't be alone for much longer. Lazily, he got to his feet and then held out his hand to me and pulled me up. He opened the door and when we stepped out the cold air hit us so hard that we ended up shouting.

36.

The doors to the movie theater were completely fogged up. A freak warm spell had moved in at about nine o'clock, and it became warmer outside than it was inside. I leaned against the cash register and stared out at the mist, daydreaming, as though it may be possible for me to open the door and be transported into another time and place.

The late shows had all just started. I was feeling low that night, and not low because I was depressed about Victor or my physical condition or my lack of plans after graduation or my nonexistent bank account, but because Jose Rubenstein had come in for the late show accompanied by gay dreamboat Michael Farinelli. Jose paid. Michael was smiling, as always, and in a terrific mood. He yelled out hello and how are you and shook my hand, while Jose stood next to him with a twenty dollar bill in his hand, his eyes unblinking, his lips pursed together.

"We'd like two for *The Last Planet III*, Augster," Michael said, almost breathlessly. "It's so cool that you work here. I bet you love it."

"Oh, I do," I said. "Together or separate?"

Michael turned to Jose.

"Oh, uh, separate. I mean together," Jose mumbled, and then put twenty dollars on the counter.

I picked it up with the tips of my fingers, as if it were poisoned, and then handed the change to Jose. "Theater Number One. To the left. Enjoy the show."

"Thanks, Augie!" Michael called out, and then leaned in close to me. "It's nice to know we've got family working here," he whispered, and then winked.

"Well, you know, we're everywhere," I said.

Michael and Jose walked back to the theater. I turned to watch. Michael opened the door for Jose. I wanted to laugh. *Last Planet III* was about the worst movie we'd ever had there, and I was sure they were going to have a terrible time. Even so, I was mortified by the thought that Roberta was right about Jose. It was a small town. Michael was bound to get to Jose at one time or another. And Jose was bound to have sex with guys.

I couldn't help it. I wanted to brush it off and say, "So what. I'm graduating in a few weeks. Fuck 'em." But all the insecurities I had freshman year when I was in love with Michael Farinelli came rushing back to me and I started to sink lower and lower, knowing they were in the theater on a gay date. "Cocksuckers!" I yelled out into the lobby, frightening a woman who had just come out of the bathroom.

I pulled out the cash register key and walked across the lobby to the staircase. I went up to the main theater's projection booth and peered out the window. Standing on my tiptoes, I gazed around the almost empty, cavernous theater looking for those two. I didn't see them at all. I went around the projector to the second window and then saw them, in the next to last row. Jose had his arm around the back of Michael's chair.

"Oh, how sweet," I said. I paced around the booth, making snide remarks to myself, angry more at myself than them. I couldn't believe how jealous I was. Jose had never taken me to the movies, and in fact had refused to be seen with me in public, except for in the parking lot of the Motel 6.

I couldn't resist taking a second look out the window. To my horror, Jose and Michael were kissing. I was shocked a couple of scaredy-cat faggots like them would suck face in a theater, but they were doing it.

"There's other people in there!" I said. "Someone will see them!"

I clumped down the stairs, banging into the walls, not caring if I got hurt. It wasn't that Jose was upset about being exposed at the house, he just didn't want to be with me. He wanted someone better-looking and more preppy and purportedly more discreet. I figured Michael Farinelli must be the best lover any man had ever had. None would say that about me.

I regained my post at the closed concession stand, staring into the fog, praying for my shift to end. And just when the clouds in my head turned to darkness, and I was almost scared to think that that's how my brain worked, that it took me down to levels that left me feeling like I had nothing underneath me at all, there was a clink on the glass doors, and four figures appeared, smiling and waving.

"Oh my God! I totally needed this!" I grabbed the keys and raced to the doors. Standing outside of them was Jean-Claude, Roberta, Paul Veracruz, and Sheila. I threw the doors open and fell into their arms, kissing and hugging all of them.

"You guys, I was so depressed! I can't believe you're here."

"We're taking you to a party, young man," Paul Veracruz said.

"You're taking me to a party?" I almost cried tears of joy. "That is so incredibly awesome. I love you guys!"

"We love you too, Augie," Roberta said. "Now get your shit and let's blow this joint."

I told them to hold on and ran to the manager's office. I begged to be let off early, and he finally said it was OK. I'd never asked to be let out early before, and I figured if he said no, I'd just quit. I was moving to Chicago in two weeks anyway.

I put on my coat and went toward the door, then remembered it was almost seventy-five degrees outside, and took it back off. Outside, Jean-Claude and Paul were passing a flask back and forth while Roberta and Sheila lit cigarettes. I grinned stupidly, thinking how much I'd missed hanging out with them. I'd spent almost the whole semester at either the theater or a doctor's office or at home, watching TV with Paloma and Pilar.

I opened the doors and relished the gentle air against my skin. "This feels so fantastic! No more ski jacket!"

Roberta laughed and grabbed me around the shoulders. Paul and Jean-Claude and Sheila surrounded me with their arms, too, and pretty soon we were all walking down the street in a big huddle, with everyone's arms protectively around me while I talked excitedly in the center.

"And then Jose Rubenstein came into the theater with Michael Farinelli that guy

I was in love with freshman year and now they're dating I guess well those faggots were in theater number one and they were kissing those fuckin' homos and let me tell you something if those two cocksuckers ever come into my theater again I'm gonna kick their fuckin' asses oh yes I will."

"Augie, you're a man possessed," Sheila said.

"Hey, Paul," said Jean-Claude. "Michael Farinelli. Isn't that the guy with the really tiny dick who hangs out in the locker room at the rec center cruising for guys?"

"Oh my god, yeah!" Paul said. "Everyone on campus has heard of that. Haven't you, Augie?"

I laughed and said, "Thanks for trying to make me feel better, you guys, but his dick's probably huge."

"No, seriously," Paul said. "I was in the locker room at the rec center and Michael Farinelli was in there cruising for guys. He kept staring at me, and all I could think was, what a fucking loser!"

"Oh, yeah!" Jean-Claude said. "I've seen him in there, too. What a dweeb. He must go there every single night, staring at naked guys like a total pervert."

"Oh, I've heard that, too," said Roberta. "Everyone says, 'Isn't that Michael Farinelli the one with the small dick who stands around in the locker room staring at guys?' And I always say, 'Yep, that's the one. Now me, I hang with gays like Augie Schoenberg, not them other faggots.'"

"I love you guys!" I said, walking faster and faster, relishing the feel of eight arms around me, the warm air around me, the thoughts of the past and the future slowly turning in the right direction.

Book Four

The mob within the heart
Police cannot suppress

      -Emily Dickinson

37.

"This is big."

Ted Demetropoulos and I sat shirtless on beach towels at Hollywood Beach, soaking up the extravagant rays from the sun. It was mid-July on the northern lakefront tip of Chicago, it was a hot and humid ninety degrees, and there were hundreds of gay guys red as lobsters wearing sunglasses and holding cell phones to their ears. Ted and I sat cross-legged, staring at each other as if we were the only people there.

"You have no idea how incredibly big this is, Augie. You are gonna freak."

"What's big!" I demanded. "Is it somebody's dick?"

He laughed but all I could see were his teeth. His eyes were hidden behind a pair of black sunglasses. "This is so big!" He giggled and then got to his feet and jumped around. He ran toward the lake and intercepted a football that a group of guys in Speedos were throwing around. After he caught it, he ran toward the volleyball nets, as if that were the end zone. Far from being annoyed, the group in Speedos were delighted Ted had caught the ball. Two of them waved their hands in the air, each trying to get him to throw it back to him. Ted hugged it to his chest and then unsuccessfully tried to shove it down his swimsuit. I looked toward the lake, a shimmering expanse of flat azure blue with white sailboats dotting the horizon. In the distance, I heard Ted yell, "Come and get it boys!"

An obnoxiously slim, overly-tan guy in a purple, skintight bathing suit walked past my towel. "Ecstasy," he said, under his breath. "Forty bucks."

I pretended I hadn't heard. I was curious to try it, after all, it was the new drug of choice among the faggots, and I'd been hearing about it for years. Mostly, though, I'd heard stories of coming down, and extreme bouts of depression, and thought maybe that was one drug I should avoid. Even regular old marijuana gave me anxiety attacks.

Sand sprayed in my face. Ted, still laughing, ran by and then collapsed on his towel, face down and breathing hard. I studied his backside through his floral print swimsuit and felt my dick begin to grow. Yeah, he was my role model and my idol, and at that point, my roommate, but I still carried a secret torch for him. I'd spent two months in our Edgewater apartment contemplating making a move on him, but our friendship was kind of brotherly, and I wondered whether or not that move would feel as incestuous as I worried it might.

"Augie," he said, rolling around. He dusted sand out of the hair on his pectorals. His nipples, flat and dark pink, were tiny as dimes. "Ask me if I love this place."

"Ted, do you love this place?"

"Oh my fuckin' god this is faggot heaven. I need a drink. Go ask those guys with the Bloody Marys if I can have one. Or ten."

"Yeah, right. So tell me! What's big?"

He sat up and kneeled down next to me. "Oh yeah. Sorry, it's just I've wanted that guy in the blue Speedo for like three years. Oh my god. You can see his dick through that thing."

"Anyway!"

"Oh, all right." He lowered his voice. "So, you know that lawyer guy that I met last week?"

I shrugged.

"You know, the yuppie guy who has a Vespa and lives in that mongo loft in Bucktown? You remember, I told you about him. We went to dinner at Arrondisement, that French place, and then he took me to the casino..."

"Wait, was this the guy who had the lizard and took it out on a leash for walks?"

"No, that was Joe. Yuck. No, this guy's name is Winston. I met him last Tuesday night; we were at the bar and I was talking to him at last call..."

"Oh, the blond guy!"

"No, that's Walter!"

"Ted, I can't keep track of all these guys. How many people are you dating right now, anyway?"

"None!" he said, defensively. Then, "Well, a few. Anyway, listen. Winston and I were talking about one of his friends, and I said to him, 'God that guy looks so familiar, who is he?' and he said, 'That's the reporter guy from the news, Johnny Lipinski,' and I said 'Is he gay?' and he said, 'Oh, yeah.' Can you believe it? I've seen that guy on TV for years. So then I said to Winston, 'Wouldn't it be funny if you could go to a place and see all the famous gay guys in Chicago that nobody knows is gay?' and Winston said, 'Ted, you can,' and I said, 'What!' and he said, 'You can!'"

"No you can not!"

"You can!" he said. He put an arm around me and spoke in a conspiratorial whisper. "I said to Winston, 'There is not some club of famous gays in Chicago,' and he said, 'Oh, yes there is. I was just there last week.'"

"Where is it?"

"I don't know. It's some private club in the Loop. He said it's on one of those streets that looks like an alley but it's really a street. Like Federal or Plymouth or something. He's gonna call me tonight with the address."

"You're going?"

He nodded. "And you're going with me. I heard one of the White Sox goes..."

"You are a liar." He grinned. "Is it Armando Aguilar? Please tell me it's Armando Aguilar!"

"I don't know; who's that?"

"The right fielder!" I screamed. "Is it him?"

"I don't think so, but I don't remember his name."

I dropped back onto the sand and gazed up at the sky, blue as the lake, the few white clouds as brilliant as the sailboats on the water. Anticipation took hold of me and my stomach started quivering. But it wasn't pain and it wasn't irritation. I felt light as the air, and exorbitantly hungry. I had a gnawing inside of me that left me breathless, a craving for something risky and mysterious and full of promise. I wanted to go to this private club and shine like the glare off the lake. I wanted to crack that place open and suck out the marrow.

We ate dinner at Saigon, a French-Vietnamese joint near our apartment, wearing our bathing suits and sandals and white T shirts. Ceiling fans spun lazily above us. Ted's face had become markedly darker throughout the afternoon, and my vision had become scorched from the sun, so that in the dim restaurant I couldn't make out anything unless it was directly underneath a light. My money, in the ass pocket of my swimsuit, was moist from a late-afternoon stroll into the lake. When the check came I peeled off a couple of dampened twenties.

"Dang, Schoenberg," Ted said. "How much cash are you carrying?"

I burped, sweet remnants of my coconut curried shrimp refluxing into my mouth. "A ton. I still haven't got a bank account, so I cash my weekly paycheck on Fridays and live like a king for four days, and then I starve for three." I'd taken a temp job at a bank and spent forty bone-grindingly long hours a week affixing labels to files. So long as it was enough money to fund my weekend exploits, though, then I figured the job was worth it.

"You won't need money tonight," Ted said, his eyes far away and black. "Everything at the club is free."

We stood and walked toward the exit. "Sounds like my kind of place. What should we wear?"

Ted pushed the door open. A warm blast of humidity overtook us, and filled me with glee. The sidewalk on Bryn Mawr was full of people eating at outdoor cafes, people cruising by on bicycles, cars streaming along with the windows rolled all the way down.

"I'm going like this. It's a formal club, but when younger people show up, or at least poor guests, they don't care what you wear. Anyway, we look like beach babes. Nobody'll be able to resist us."

"God, I think we look more like beach bums. Shouldn't we go home and change? I mean, I don't have a watch on, or regular shoes, or anything."

Ted lay an arm across my shoulders. "Augie, let me tell you something. On weekends, never wear a watch."

In the cab, Ted checked the messages on his cell phone. Behind the skyscrapers, the sun was moving down slowly, burning out, but it didn't seem to matter because the next day was Sunday and we could do the beach all over again.

"I got it," Ted said, clicking off his phone. He gave the address to the driver, and we snaked off Lake Shore Drive onto Michigan Avenue. We rode past the endless department stores, and over the river, and past the Art Institute till we turned on

Jackson. In the heart of the Loop, everything was dark from the blockade of skyscrapers, and when we pulled up to the building the sun had set.

Ted was right, it was in the south Loop, on a block-long side street that I'd seen many times before. To me, though, all the buildings, tall and imposing in their turn-of-the-century grandeur, looked deserted.

"Here it is," Ted said, and rubbed my shoulder. I paid the cab fare and after we got on the street, I looked up at the building. It was a massive, limestone skyscraper with a small green awning in front of the door.

"I think we should've dressed up," I said.

"Have confidence, young man," Ted said. "This place is gonna rock your world."

We squeaked through the lobby in our flip flops, bits of sand falling out my shorts. A reception desk was staffed by a young man in a ridiculous, carnival-esque blazer that had gold buttons and obnoxious shoulder pads.

"We're looking for The South End Club," Ted said.

The attendant looked at us with false skepticism. "You a member?"

"We're guests of Winston Vespucci."

He looked down at a book on the desk, and then ran a finger along one of the page's columns. "Ted and Aggie?" We nodded. "Fifteenth floor. Elevators to your left."

We walked through the lobby. Ted said in a hushed tone: "Winston's already there, so we'll know somebody."

"Good. Otherwise I think we might get thrown out."

The elevator was ancient and moved so slowly we had time to turn around and check ourselves out in the mirror. We did look pretty good: our faces were nicely tanned, and my hair had even lightened a little in the sun. The outlines of my cheekbones were roasted into a nice shade of pink. Ted suddenly pulled his bathing suit down to his knees and lifted up his shirt. "Do I have a tan line?" he asked, straining his neck around and standing on his toes so his white, hairy ass would show in the mirror. My dick got so hard I had to adjust it so I could contain it in the waistband and not have it stick straight out. In the facing mirror, I saw his genitals, alabaster white against monstrous black hair. The contrast against his brown legs sent me into a state of protracted weakness.

"Your back is burnt sienna," I said, feeling intelligent. "Your ass is like cream."

"What the hell is burnt sienna?"

"It's a color. It's one of the Crayola crayons. Pull up your pants, the door is opening."

There was a ding and we stepped out into a red, carpeted hallway, lined with Victorian, gold-patterned wallpaper. Two heavy, wooden doors stood closed in front of us. There wasn't a sound.

I pulled on the doors but they wouldn't open. "Is there a bell?"

Ted shrugged. I knocked on the doors but nothing happened. The hallway wasn't very long and there were no other doors in sight. "Maybe the party hasn't started yet."

"Let's sit." There were two chairs near the elevators, so we sat down and Ted pulled out some cigarettes. I looked at him as he lit his lighter and felt giddy with anticipation. I wanted so badly to be flirtatious and reckless and open up that old heap of a skyscraper and inject it with something virile. I told Ted he had a nice ass. "Do you think I should shave it?" he asked.

"No way. Keep it natural, it's very sexy."

He smirked. "What do you think of my pee-pee?"

"It reminds me of something." I knew I shouldn't tell him, but I wanted to keep things interesting. "When I was eight years old I went to the swimming pool with some friends. On the way out, I stopped in the locker room to unnecessarily rearrange everything in my bag. So two guys in their twenties come walking in and they were the biggest babes I ever saw. So I sat on the bench with the boner of my life growing inside my shorts and one of them sits down on the bench across from me and starts asking me if the water's cold and did I have fun today, blah blah blah. So before I know it he's pulled down his cutoffs and he's sitting bareballed on the bench talking to me. He's looking right at me and I'm looking right at his dick, which wasn't really long, but was the thickest one I'd ever seen. It was practically wider than the balls, and the head of it was so nice and bulbous and wonderful that it seemed like it had its own personality."

Ted smiled and crossed his legs. "Did you stay for a while and watch?"

"No, I had to get out of there. I practically almost fainted. I mean, at that point, that guy's dick was probably fifty times the size of mine, and I was so shocked by it that I was almost paralyzed. To this day, though, the smell of Coppertone suntan lotion gives me the biggest erection."

"Oh, I've got plenty of memories like that," Ted said, stubbing out his cigarette.

"Anyway," I said. "When I saw you pull down your bathing suit, that's instantly what I thought of. Your dick's just like his."

"Nah," Ted said. "You were a little kid. It just seemed big to you."

"Oh, no, I saw plenty of tiny ones. This was the real thing."

"Do you have a big dick?" Ted asked. "I can't believe I've never seen it."

"No," I said modestly, and then to prove I didn't have low self-esteem: "But it's very good-looking."

Ted laughed and got up from his chair. "Let me see it!" he said, yanking at my suit.

I curled up into a ball and screeched. "No! Please, please. Oh, god you're evil."

Luckily, I had tied my suit as tight as I could, and all Ted managed to do was yank me around the carpet by the tie strings. Behind us, someone cleared his throat.

A man a few years older than us in an olive suit stood before us. He wore black plastic glasses and his hair was short and spiked up with obvious amounts of gel. "Problems?" he asked.

We stood. "No," I said. "Just horsing around."

"My name's Julian. I'm the valet. Winston says you're his guests." We shook hands. He looked at Ted and said, "By the way, we enjoyed your show in the elevator."

"Thanks," Ted said, invitingly, not the least bit embarrassed.

"You know," he said, quietly. "Security cameras...Anyway, let me show you in. It's just through these doors."

It had become quite clear in the vast, wood-paneled room, with the sound of clinking glasses and quiet masculine laughter, that Ted and I were the evening's resident bimbos. Everyone else was at least in their thirties and they all were in shirts and ties. I sat on a brown leather sofa entertaining a group of five or six guys who laughed heartily at everything I said, and then caressed the sides of their beers with their fingers.

"How old are you?" the guy next to me asked. I recognized him from TV commercials: an awkward-looking personal injury attorney who solicited for clients in a monotone voice during late-night reruns.

"I'm old," I said, in my standard campustown response. "Twenty-two."

They all looked at each other and then laughed deep, throaty laughs that gradually increased in volume until the lawyer patted me on the back. "You're a fucking baby."

"But I'm almost twenty-three!" I cried, playing it for all it was worth, and was met with more laughter.

A bearded guy standing across from the couch said, "Yeah, but you look nineteen."

"Oh, right," I said, grinning sheepishly. I scanned the room, searching for any baseball players, or more specifically, Armando Aguilar. So far, I hadn't seen him, but I was keeping hope alive, and getting pretty drunk while I did it. There was an intense, anticipatory sense of ecstasy inside of me, that, with the help of the alcohol, was taking me to heights that were precariously steep. If Armando Aguilar didn't show up, I'd be horribly disappointed, but if he did, I thought I'd be the happiest guy on the planet. I needed to walk that extreme slope. I wanted to know if I could get to that place, that shining, elusive place where absurd, masturbatory dreams came true. I had to know if a place like that existed.

One of the guys plopped down on the couch next to me. He looked about forty, but dressed young, in sleek black pants and a blue, almost shiny, shirt. His hair was black and not curly, but thick enough that it stayed brushed back on its own. I turned and looked right at him. He had a stubbly face and eyes surrounded by the slightest of wrinkles.

"So, what is it you do?" he asked, in a slightly bored tone that suggested he realized it was a rote question but actually wanted to know.

"Well, I work in the fascinating world of temporary employment, but I'm really a filmmaker. I've written a screenplay and I'm gonna send it out to agents pretty soon."

He nodded a look of approval. "What's the screenplay about?"

I smirked. "Hot gay sex."

The group laughed again and the lawyer said, "I think I like this guy. Let me get you a drink."

The guy in black pants looked at me slowly, sizing me up. "Did you go to film school?"

"Nah, I was an English major. But I was still able to take some film classes and some screenwriting workshops."

He pulled out his wallet. "You know, I know some people who work in publishing. If you're looking for a gig, call me up. Maybe I can get you in as a copy editor or something, so you can pay the rent while you're writing your scripts."

I took the card and stared at it. "Thanks a lot! I could really use some help." The name on the card was Winston Vespucci. "Hey, I know you, you're Ted's friend."

"Just call me," he said, almost too quietly. The other guys in the group were talking amongst themselves and drifting away. "Also, did they tell you about the pool? There's a gym and a pool and a locker room in the back."

"Really?" I put the card down the crotch of my bathing suit. "I should go find Ted."

He leaned back against the couch. "Maybe we'll take a swim later. You're dressed for it."

I smiled and stood up. "Maybe we will. But I only swim naked."

His eyes lit up and I walked away.

Ted and I stood at the mirror in the ladies' room. "You can cut the testosterone in this place with a knife!" he exclaimed. "They're all so goddamn masculine. I want all of them."

"They're very fatherly, aren't they? I've never been around too many gay guys over the age of twenty-three."

"Oh, my god. I love it. My dick's been hard since I walked in. I'm hittin' on like five guys right now."

"Me too," I said, adjusting my hair and running my finger underneath my eyes. "So I just ran into Winston. I think he was trying to hit on me."

"Let him. He's been hitting on everyone in sight all night long. Can you believe that shit?"

"Faggots," I said. "There is just no accounting for them. I wouldn't mind taking a ride on that Vespa, though. So who are you gonna go after?"

"Do you know who I met out there? You'll never guess!" Ted looked over at me, almost panting.

"Who?"

"Augie, the guy from the movie we rented last week. Pete Delmonico."

"Wow, is he a fag? What's he doing in Chicago?"

"I don't know, maybe he's on Oprah or something. I've been trying to get him drunk. Do you think he'll come home with me?"

"If he does, Ted, let me know when you're fucking so I can videotape it and sell it for a million dollars."

"Augie this is the best night of my life." He put his feet together and looked forward. "Back to the trenches, young man. Gorgeous men with big dicks and fat bank accounts await."

"But who are you?" I pleaded, giggling. I had backed him into a corner and I wouldn't let him get away.

He looked down at me with a grin. "Don't worry about it. I'm nobody, who are you?"

"No way, mister. You're somebody, I'm sure of that. Out with it. Show me some ID."

He laughed and slid a massive hand around my back and down to my ass. "I'm somebody who's likin' what I feel."

188

"Uh uh, buster. I don't let strange men feel my bee-hind. Wait a minute. I've got it. You're a sportscaster on ESPN."

"Close," he said, his face glowing. "You're getting warm." He easily squeezed my entire ass cheek with one hand.

I couldn't place him. I knew I recognized his face: worn from the sun, vaguely Spanish, a black goatee, bright brown eyes, muscular neck with a thin gold chain descending down into a crop of black chest hair that peeked out of his shirt. Oddly, though, his face looked familiar but not his hair. There was nothing to it: short, severely dark brown on the verge of black, just cut with clippers. I told myself this had to be easier than I was making it. He was over six feet tall, his pecs were practically busting out of his dress shirt, he moved his mouth as though he were chewing gum even though he wasn't. He was too built for an actor, too gorgeous for a politician. I knew that I knew him.

"Maybe I'll recognize you from behind," I said, smiling slyly. "Turn around."

"Nah," he said. I yanked him by the arm and led him around. His shirt was tucked into his dress pants. His ass was disproportionately large and sculpted into two mounds that pushed the pants to their limit. I felt it lightly, pressing against the buns while he clenched them so they were hard as cement. I moved my hand down and felt not the edge of underwear but a half-inch wide elastic strip underneath each bun.

"Are you wearing a jockstrap?"

He grabbed my hand from behind and turned around. "Maybe. I want you to keep doing that but not with people watching."

And all at once it made sense to me. The jockstrap, the chewing gum, the pants stretched across the huge ass, the fact that I knew his face but not his hair. I had previously only seen him in a face mask. He was the catcher for the White Sox.

He put an arm around me and we stood stomach to stomach. I rested my head against his chest. It wasn't Armando Aguilar, the sleek, arrogant, budding star that had me enraptured since I'd first seen him three years earlier, but Johnny Martinez, the veteran catcher who drew little notice but was well-liked and seemed as if he could stay with the team as long as he wanted. He had a fatherly look to him, an affable look of strength and ease, that showed he wasn't like so many cocky, young athletes who were out for big contracts and fame, but was someone who just happened to have a job that he did well. Of anyone on the team, he'd be the last I'd pick as gay. "Are you drunk?" he asked, gently.

"No," I lied. "Stone sober." I slid my hand around his back and into his pocket. I pulled out his wallet. He didn't resist, like I thought he would. I ran my fingers over the sleek leather, as soft as silk, and opened it. There it was. An Illinois driver's license for Johnny Martinez. Birthdate: 1965. Sex: M. Eyes: Br. Hair: Br. Organ donor: Yes.

He took it away from me and put it back in his wallet. "I knew I knew you," I said. "You're a star."

"Yeah, in my dreams. I'm what the baseball card collectors call a common."

"Not in my book," I gushed. "I think you're fantastic."

He moved his mouth again like he was chewing. He looked to the side and then said, "Yeah, well, I think you're pretty cute. Come on, lemme get you a drink." I rested my hand on his forearm, the skin as smooth as the leather on the wallet, but warmer, and with a comforting potential. If I played my cards right, those meaty arms might melt under my touch. He put his hands gently on my sides, just above my pelvis, and said, "Do you want another drink? Or do you wanna get outta here and go somewhere else?"

The prospect left me reeling. I couldn't imagine even walking down the street with him. It would necessarily feel far away, and cinematic, as though it were happening to someone else and I was spying on them from behind.

"Say, Johnny, what do you think about taking a swim?"

"It's a possibility," he said. "But I haven't got a suit."

"That's kinda what I had in mind."

He grinned and walked toward the bar. I followed him, walking along in my sandals as though they were floating on a bed of air.

I stood in the locker room and stripped off my T shirt.

"Augie, let's turn this place into the Playboy mansion for faggots. What should we do?" Ted asked.

"God, get everybody naked and fuck, I guess. Jesus, Ted, I'm a ball of nerves. Johnny Martinez has been hitting on me for like an hour. Do you think he's gonna follow us in here?"

"I hope so. He's fuckin' hot, and I'm dying to see that ass."

"Oh!" I yelled out. "Someone's gonna have to hold me back." Ted untied his suit and pulled it down to the floor. He stepped out of it slowly, his dick in a full, swinging erection that veered off to the side, the shaft pulsing and the head almost purple. He could have been a Marine, with his hairy but still slightly-pubescent chest and muscles that looked hard as bone. My chest may have been flat but my dick was hard as a bone, and when I pulled down my suit the cold air hit my ass and I felt uncommonly naughty. Taking off a bathing suit has always made me feel horny, in the way that you go from clothed to damp and bare-assed in one split second.

"You still have sand in your pubes," I said. I naughtily reached over and started dusting them off.

"Get outta here," he said and then whipped me in the ass with his bathing suit.

The door creaked open and Ted and I fell silent. We sat down on the bench trying not to laugh, looking toward the entrance, our dicks hard and smiles on our faces.

Johnny Martinez appeared, followed by Winston Vespucci.

"Wow," Johnny said and stopped dead. "What do we got here?"

"Oh, we're just having drinks," I said.

"Yeah, it's a locker room, though, boys," Ted said. "No clothes allowed."

Johnny's eyes widened and he looked the least bit shy. "I guess that can be arranged," he said. He put down his beer and then started unbuttoning his shirt.

I would've killed for a shot of whiskey.

"It's just us boys, though, right?" Winston said, facetiously. "I don't want any girls to see my penis."

"Don't worry," Ted said. "It's just us guys. Nobody'll look at you."

Johnny laughed nervously, and took off his shirt. Big as he was, there didn't appear to be much fat on him. Just pectorals the size of my head and hair and light brown skin and a small gold chain with a tiny crucifix on the end. My dick was openly throbbing, and it was hard not to want to cover it up, or to feel out of place, but to just lean against the locker staring at Johnny Martinez as he slipped down his dress pants with his back toward me—the white straps from the jockstrap brightly framing the naked, imperfect ass that on TV was covered in white, polyester perfection, but in real life was decorated with stray hairs and the occasional mole, and separated by a vast, black crevice that was either made completely of hair or completely of shadows.

In the showers, an aqua blue and green tiled room that had a dozen or so spigots sprouting out of chromed poles, Ted and I turned around and around and made the motions of taking a shower, as if we were honestly there to clean up and not relieve our throbbing boners. Mine had shrunk slightly, from the inner voice I had telling me this was a locker room and erections were not acceptable, but I knew it was OK, and I knew it was necessary, and when I saw, in the distance, Johnny and Winston chatting with each other and hanging up their clothes in lockers I felt a feeling of luckiness that was hard to accept.

We could have very well been standing in the White Sox locker room.

"Let's go, boys," Ted called out, his black hair matted to his head, making him look younger, and cleaner, and strangely more innocent.

Through the slight trace of steam in front of me, I saw Johnny Martinez yards away—a naked vision that was so impossibly real and so agonizingly close—shut the blue locker and turn toward me, stripped and bare except for the almost invisible gold crucifix, a hulking man with a fierce, tan and red penis angling upwards and out of its foreskin with the strength of what must have been muscles instead of tendons, walking toward me as though through a lens, and then into the shower room, where my myopic vision projected him onto the virtual screen in front of my eyes.

He took the nozzle next to mine and let the water coast over him. He pushed a stream of water into his armpits, the hair underneath them long and sinewy, and said a few, talky things about nothing, as if we weren't both standing there with boners about to do something sordid, and premature, and undeniably wanton. In the background, Ted and Winston had fused into one being made of four arms and four legs and two heads that were completely indistinguishable.

"I've never taken a shower with a famous athlete," I said, inching toward him.

"It's no big deal, is it?" he said.

"It's hard to believe the rest of the team gets to every day," I said. "They probably don't know how lucky they are."

"They probably don't care," he said. "Except for maybe one other."

"Ooh," I said, "that's scandalous. But I think one's all I need." I gripped his penis, wet but still hot in my hand.

He wrapped a wide, confident hand around my aching erection and said, "One's all I need." His hand felt even bigger than my dick. Just one corner of his palm rubbed a haggard, purple-stained patch on the underside that I knew well. A couple of his fingers caressed the head with five times more width than I had myself, and sent a constant wave of almost insufferable, unbearable gratification all through me and down to my shaking feet.

He looked at me with his eyes unblinking and his mouth slightly ajar, as though he were shocked, and moved his hand up and down me with infinitesimally slow, effortless rubs, while my hand coasted up and down his dick shaft as alternatingly smooth and jerky as a violinist moving his bow. There were muffled cries in the background beneath the sound of rushing water. I turned my head to look and see Ted and Winston in their moment of ecstasy, but Johnny put a hand around the back of my neck, so massive it covered the bottom portion of my head and said, "Don't look at them, look at me."

I looked at the sad, staring eyes, the disbelieving mouth, the practically inaudible gasps coming from inside him, the contracting muscles beneath his skin. I felt the awesome control he had over my sex, holding on so securely to something so vulnerable and untrained, with such determined zeal and such utter concentration. And before I could have anticipated, it was too much for me. I shook beneath the water and my eyes rolled around and the floor seemed to grow hot underneath my feet, and the only thing still holding me up was Johnny's hand that refused to let go, or even move faster so that I could predict what might happen, but slowly snaked around and around with such exacting pressure that my mind went stupid and all that I felt was a mind-numbing fulfillment and the overwhelming sense that I might rise and break free from my bones and ascend to a greater place.

When I cried out he whispered, "I've got you, I've got you," and I shook like a dog, wet and self-absorbed, my head hung and my hand still cascading over the brute strength of Johnny's shaft, my come dissipating in the stream below me, my breath steamy, my eyes wet, the surge from an invisible place inside of him making him grow warmer by degrees, so that I felt the heat, and the force, and the essence of his longing that was squirting out of its muscle and through its dilated eye and onto the sweaty floor. I collapsed in his arms.

Mr. Sid K. Gupta and Mrs. Dimple V. Gupta

and

Mr. Sanjay Radhakrishna and Mrs. Sonia Radhakrishna

Request the honour of your presence at the

marriage of their beloved children

Sarita and Victor

On Saturday, the twenty-third of August, Nineteen ninety-six
at one o'clock in the afternoon

Osbourne Hall
43 King's Road
Chelsea
London SW3

Programme

On Saturday 23 August 1996
Wedding: 1:00 pm to 2:15 pm
Sumuhurtham: 1:28 pm
Lunch will be served from 11:30 am

Reception at Le Dome
Maiden Street, Covent Garden, London WC2
Cocktails and Refreshments 6:00 pm
Dinner 7:30 pm

RSVP to Gupta family, London, UK 020 8555 8763 or Radhakrishna
family, Chicago, US (708/555-9876

38.

I licked the envelope and sealed it. Inside was my finished screenplay and I was sending it to a script agent in L.A. I knew rejection was almost a certainty, but even so I was placing high hopes on it, on the off chance acceptance came my way. Anyway, I had a book that listed dozens of agents and I figured that each time I was rejected I'd just send it out to another one. Eventually, somebody had to bite.

"What did you end up calling it?" Ted asked. We were in the living room, me at the table, Ted in front of the stereo. It was a late afternoon, the first week of August. Ted and I were too poor to afford an air conditioner, so we were sitting around in our underwear, and still sweating.

"Well, Ted, I'll tell ya...." I said, confidently, as if I were addressing a talk-show host. "I was going to call it 'Descent into Hell,' but I thought that was too dramatic, so I struggled with it for a few months and eventually I had an idea. While I was sitting around at work, bored to death, I decided to jot down interesting little phrases that I noticed in documents, or in the newspaper, or wherever."

"Yes," Ted said, putting a CD in the stereo, his tan line peeking out of the waistband of his underwear. "And what sorts of interesting phrases did you find?"

"Well," I said, and looked down at some papers on the table as if they had information I needed to answer the question. "One that I liked was 'Eventual Exoneration.' I also found the phrase 'Fertile Octogenarians,' but I couldn't think how that related to my story. But my favorite in the end was 'The Unborn Spouse Situation.' I found it in an old legal document, so old it was typewritten. For days, I couldn't get it out of my head. I had no idea what it meant, and I still don't, but I couldn't think up a better way to sum up my experience with all the guys who have fucked me over."

Ted settled into a ratty, red armchair we'd picked up at the thrift store. He threw a leg over one of the arms and I was faced with the outline of his dick and balls through his briefs and the mass of black hair spilling out the sides. The apartment on Kenmore with Ted was turning out to be as bad as the Harley Hutt: I was constantly horny and faced with circumstances that made it worse. At that point, though, at least I had Johnny Martinez to satisfy my insatiable cravings for men.

"So you're calling it 'The Unborn Spouse Situation'?" he asked, dubiously.

"Yes. Do you love it or do you hate it?"

"I love it," Ted said, lighting a cigarette. "You're gonna be famous."

"I hope so," I said, but there was something else on my mind. "Ted, I've turned into a borderline whore."

"You? I thought I was the whore of the apartment."

"No such luck." I put my hands on my knees. "So, you know how I hate my job, and it's so boring it almost kills me, and I have to be there at eight a.m., and I'm late every day, and I'm so underemployed and underpaid that I'm about to have a nervous breakdown?"

Ted nodded and exhaled a line of smoke. "I had gathered as much."

"Well, I don't work there anymore."

"Oh. Uh, congratulations, I guess. Well, how are you gonna pay the rent?"

I turned toward the table and looked out the window. Our front view was of the front windows of the apartment across the courtyard. "I told Johnny that I was miserable at work and he said, 'So quit,' and I said, 'I can't. How would I pay the rent?' and he said, 'Augie, Jesus,' and he took out his wallet and he gave me a thousand dollars."

I looked back at Ted, embarrassed and feeling guilty. I didn't go to college so I could be supported by some guy who I happened to be dating at the time. I needed reassurance that I wasn't doing anything unscrupulous.

Ted's mouth hung open. "You *are* a whore!"

"Oh, Ted, please tell me I'm not! You'd do the same wouldn't you?"

He frowned slightly, in a snobbish fashion. "I just don't know, Augie. Gosh, money for sex. I for one am shocked."

"Fuck you, you are not. You would do the same, you little fucker."

"I know, Augie, I totally would. So no more temping, huh?"

"No," I said. "And if this screenplay works out, no more working ever. Thank God for that. Anyway," I added, still defensive. "It isn't money for sex. Johnny and I are dating."

"Sure," Ted said, sounding unconvinced. He got up and walked over to the kitchen. My eyes followed his exit, unable to get off of the sight of his ass through the underwear. Johnny Martinez notwithstanding, I thought I might always be attracted to Ted.

"MmmnUTollnswwwyrb."

"What?" I got up and went into the kitchen and found Ted naked with his head in the freezer. "What on earth are you doing?"

"Trying to cool off. Give me your underwear. I'll put it in here with mine."

"No thanks."

The air from the freezer spilled out around Ted's head in white, swirling gusts. Behind his shoulders was a mountain of snow and ice, topped by a box of popcorn shrimp. "So what's going on with this London thing? Are you going to Victor's wedding?"

"I'm not sure yet." I eyed the invitation on the kitchen table. "The whole thing sounds very fancy. Chelsea, Covent Garden. I don't know if I'd fit in. Who knows? Maybe Johnny will fly over with me and we'll have a romantic weekend."

"Maybe," Ted said into the freezer, "you can show up at the wedding and when they ask if anybody objects to the union you can stand up and say that Victor's your boyfriend."

"That's a fantastic idea." I rummaged around on the kitchen table, tossing aside junk advertisements and offers for easy-credit credit card ripoffs. "That'd teach him to mess with me. But, I don't know, Victor was one of those once in a lifetime people. He's engraved on my brain."

"Well, the wedding rings are gonna be engraved soon so you'd better get over it."

"What is this?" A long, tan envelope with Queen Elizabeth stamps lay underneath a mailing from the record club.

"It came yesterday," Ted said, glancing over. "I thought you saw it."

"No, I didn't." I knew who it was from. The handwriting, scrunched up and frustrated-looking, the address on Ladbroke Grove, Notting Hill. When I opened it up, carefully, savoring the feel of the light envelope paper, a blue folder fell out, which read 'British Airways.' Inside of it, a plane ticket from O'Hare to Heathrow on August 21 to return anytime within the next ninety days. A small, folded piece of notepaper was left inside the envelope.

"Well, well, well," I said, smartly, trying to cover the fact that a lump had developed in my throat.

"Is that from Victor?" Ted asked, moving toward me, and peering over my shoulder. Even the smell and feel of a naked man next to me couldn't get my eyes off the paper. The pheremones, the hormones, the ions, whatever else was in the air—all of them ceased to matter. I felt outside of myself, watching a poor, gay sap stand in his kitchen almost bawling over a letter he received from a guy he tells everyone he isn't still hung up on.

> Hey, Augie,
>
> Bet you wondered who this is. Well, it's me Victor your old friend, hah hah. What's up? Having a blast in Chicago I guess. Living with Ted must be a total trip. You guys are probably rockin out every night, huh? Hey, say hi to Jean-Claude and Paul and everybody. I totally miss you guys and the old days at school.
>
> All right, I know, you're probably all pissed off at me cause of the concert, where I didn't show up. I meant to, but I couldn't go cause I had to drive my brother to the hospital. He cut his leg open on the stoker next to the fireplace and my parents freaked out and then the whole family had to pile into the minivan to go to the hospital. We're Hindus so we have to do everything in groups of sixteen, hah hah.
>
> Anyway, to make up for it, I want you, young man, to get your sorry ass to London and come to my wedding. I even sent you a plane ticket (enclosed). We gotta hang out. You've no idea how much you'd like it here. I think you'd fit right in (Shakespeare, smart people, nightclubs, beer).
>
> Sarita (that's my fiancee) wants to meet you and have you over for dinner. That's up to you if you want to come. She's got a great place, a townhouse in Notting Hill and you'd love it. That's where we're going to live. After the wedding, I'm going to graduate school to get an MBA. I know, corporate world, here I come.
>
> Please use that plane ticket, Augie. The whole thing bothers me, too. I can't answer the why of what's happening, or even the

what at times, but in some strange way I look at my life now and wonder if what's changed is for the best, or if I've made a horrible mistake. I dream of the Harley Hutt and the hot weather, and the sunny sky, and the night we had on the windowsill staring at the moon. I don't know what I'm saying anymore, I'm just rambling, but come to London in a few weeks, Augie, cause I don't want to have a wedding without you there.

 Victor

"Wow," Ted said, reading over my shoulder. "That's intense. Are you gonna go?"
 I couldn't speak. Snot was dripping out of my nose and onto my lips and my vocal chords felt like they were paralyzed. Ted handed me a paper towel and I blew my nose.
 "No," I said, finally. "Of course I'm not going. I'm dating one of the White Sox. Why would I wanna go and relive all that other bullshit?"
 "Aw, Augie," Ted said, putting a hand on my shoulder. "You're still in love with him. Why don't you just go? Maybe it'll be closure."
 "Yeah, right. It'll be more like 'kick me and I'll come running back to you.' Anyway, I can't stand here sniveling, I have to go to Comiskey tonight. Johnny gave me a ticket." I managed a smile. "I'm sitting in the wives' section. How's that for irony?"
 "It isn't irony, it's all working out for you. You've got your spouse. He isn't unborn after all."
 I laughed a dry, mirthless laugh. "We'll see how long he sticks around. I don't make a very good kept bitch." I threw the letter down on the table.

A cloud of depression and anxiety hung over my head throughout the game. The seat was great, but I couldn't pay attention. I ordered myself beer after beer, and since I didn't have a job anymore I didn't care if I got wasted. There didn't seem to be any possibility of me screwing things up anymore, but that gave me no satisfaction. The only thing that kept me from sinking down to frightening depths was the sight of Johnny on the field, dressed in his grey and black uniform, the mask around his face, the awesome throw he made in the fifth inning that killed a base stealing attempt. I wanted to tell myself that I had made it. The screenplay was in the mail, I had a man who liked me, I was living where I wanted to live, but I felt like the unluckiest loser on the planet. I ached to go to London and see Victor. I was almost starting to forget what he looked like, the intricacies of his face, the timbre of his voice, the smell on him, but I didn't see how I could go. It would be torture, and I'd spend the whole time wracked by jealous rage. I had Johnny Martinez in my life. That should have been enough.

For some strange reason, Johnny decided to take me to dinner after the game, but it was a dinner where all the other players were going to be. Apparently, I had more experience in these matters than Johnny did, and knew that there'd be no way they'd all believe that I was just some friend that he had brought with.

"Why not?" he said. We were in the car, a hulking black SUV, on the way to the restaurant. "All you gotta do is just not act like a faggot for an hour. Is that so tough?"

"But that's not the point. It doesn't matter what I act like. People are going to be suspicious anyway. I might think I'm acting like a truck driver but some asshole is gonna suspect me of being gay, and that's fine with me, but it isn't fine with you. They're all gonna wonder why you have some gay guy with you."

"You're making too big of a deal of it. Nobody's gonna pay attention to you at all. Just act normal and there'll be no problem."

"I'm warning you, this is going to lead to massive unhappiness on your part. You're gonna have to lie and make excuses and then I'm gonna have to do the same. I'd love to meet the team but you're putting yourself at risk of exposure with me. You should know that."

Johnny laid on the gas and swerved around a truck. We blew up the expressway at ninety miles an hour, the Sears Tower, black with spotted dots of lights, was directly ahead of us. "All right, Schoenberg, fine, just sit out in the car then. Is that what you want? Don't go."

"Look, you wanna stay in the closet, fine, but you can't have it both ways. Some of us went through the grief of coming out when we were young, so we wouldn't have to deal with this bullshit at your age. Don't try to drag me back in."

He accelerated even more and raised his voice, the first time he'd ever done so. "You have no fuckin' idea what I've been through! You think it's easy being me? I can't take you out for a nice dinner without you acting like a fuckin..."

"Bitch!" I screamed. "Say it! I'm a fucking bitch!"

He slammed on the brakes and pulled off onto the shoulder. Restrained by my seatbelt with rushing cars firing by outside the door, I entertained the possibility he may beat me to a pulp.

"Augie," he said, quietly. "I am not going to fight with you. I'm Cuban and I have a bad temper. Just go to dinner, order some food, whatever you want, and don't hang on me, or kiss me, or tell me you love me. Is that acceptable to you?"

"Fine," I said, with a fake smile. "One hundred percent acceptable."

After I was introduced around, I looked for a seat. The White Sox sat around a table made for about twelve, but there were no two seats together. It was just as well; I didn't want to talk to Johnny anyway. I recognized everyone, but what amazed me was how much larger they looked in real life. Usually, people from TV look smaller in reality, but not the Chicago White Sox. They were all at least six foot three and were busting out of their clothes. From the look of the platters of steaks that the waitresses were carrying around, they'd be busting out of them more before the evening was out. On the far side of the table, I spotted Armando Aguilar staring into space with an empty chair next to him.

Sensing a golden opportunity to enjoy myself, I sailed around the table and plopped down next to him. Since Johnny was convinced I could act straight for an hour, I figured I'd have a go of it and do my best Jose Rubenstein straight guy imitation. Armando looked over at me for a moment and I looked down at the menu. I looked over at him, admiring the curve of his almost oriental eyes, and the deep, warm brown tone of his skin. Sensing my stare, he looked back.

"What was your name again?" I asked.

"Armando," he said, in a clipped, heavily-accented ejaculation. Relief poured over me. Foreign people are always terrible at guessing who's gay because everyone seems foreign and kind of strange to them anyhow.

"Augie," I replied and we shook hands. His grip was so powerful I almost winced.

"You are friends with Yonny?" he asked in a thick, painful blurt.

"Oh, yeah," I said, my Bridgeport accent blaring and nasal. "We've been friends for years. I love that guy. Have you been out on that boat of his?"

Armando looked skeptical. "The boat?" Then, he smiled. "Oh, yeah. That's a great boat. Very big."

"I'll tell ya, Armando, I've been on some boats before, but that must be the biggest. Now some people have little sailboats, but oh, no, not Johnny, that motherfucker's gotta go out and buy himself the biggest goddamn boat to ever grace Lake Michigan."

At the sound of my voice, Johnny looked over from the other end of the table. His piercing gaze was all too clear: watch yourself. For his part, Armando was watching me intently, too, trying to keep up with how quickly I was talking.

"We took that thing out the other day and oh, man, was that gorgeous. There were so many people out sailing it just about took my breath away. Now me, I'm a landlubber myself, so I get sorta nauseous out there, but so what, that's what I say. No pain, no gain. Or something like that. Do they have a liquor license at this establishment?"

I could see that Armando had no idea what I was talking about. "That boat," he ventured. "That's great for to take out girls."

"Oh, you're telling me! Now if I had my way, I'd be out there every day, but whatta ya gonna do, a guy's gotta work, am I right or am I right?"

Armando nodded. "Where do you work?"

"I'm a screenwriter myself," I said. "You know, I write movies."

"You write movies?" Armando asked, looking interested. "That's fucking cool."

"Well, the White Sox organization ain't too shabby." I noticed a slim black box attached to his belt. "Say, Armando, can I borrow your cell phone?"

Fighting off a glare from Johnny, I took the phone and went into the bar. Aside from an old guy at the end who was reading the newspaper and a couple on the other side of me, the bar was pretty much empty. I dialed Roberta's number.

"Sweetheart, you're never gonna guess where I am."

"Hi, Augie, I'm fine, how are you. Or, OK, where are you?"

"Some steakhouse downtown. I'm with the White Sox. Have I told you? I'm dating the catcher. Anyway, we're having a fight, so I'm sitting next to Armando Aguilar and I'm talking his ear off."

A peal of deep laughter came over the phone. "Christ, Augie, you're dating a baseball player? That is too sweet. How do you get yourself into these messes?"

"Good luck I guess. Listen, so I've been in love with Armando Aguilar for like three years, and now I'm having dinner with him and my boyfriend is on the other side of the table glaring at me. Isn't that funny?"

"Schoenberg, you deserve every rotten thing that ever happens to you. You are so nasty!"

"Isn't it great! Hey, I gotta go, but we should meet for drinks this weekend. I miss you guys."

"Yeah, no kidding. Hey, Jean-Claude's band is playing on Friday and I have a performance on Saturday, at Steppenwolf, baby, I'm moving on up. How about Sunday? Come down to Ukrainian Village, you've never seen our place."

"I will. Alright, I gotta get back to the team. Hot beef awaits. From the steaks, I mean, not the team."

"I know exactly what you mean, Schoenberg. Goodbye. And be nice to those guys!"

The fireplace was burning in Johnny's bedroom, casting an orange glow over his face as he spoke to me. Except for his quiet talking, the room was eminently quiet, and peaceful. Not a sound came in from the outside: his neighborhood was as silent as I'd experienced in the city. His house stood in the middle of an unassuming tree-lined street in Roscoe Village. No sirens wailed, no car tires screeched.

"I realized as soon as we sat down at the restaurant that you were right. There's no reason you should have to hang with those guys and not be able to be yourself. I don't want you to have to compromise your ideals, or your beliefs, especially for some stupid old lug like me."

I could've simmered with happiness and nestled myself further into his arms, but I wasn't as concerned with my own ideals as he might've thought, and anyhow I was more concerned that he'd blame me for exposing him as gay rather than that I was nervous about some stupid dinner with a baseball team. Anyway, after the way he stared me down at the restaurant, I didn't believe for a second that he was sorry.

"Johnny, I wasn't compromising my beliefs or upset because I couldn't be myself, I was trying to tell you that I'm not in control of how people see me. You can go around acting like yourself and nobody's gonna think you're gay, but all I have to do is laugh a certain way and somebody asks me if I'm gay. I just sit in a chair a certain way and people are asking me about it. I've just accepted that I have to be around people that aren't like that; people who wouldn't care either way."

"So you don't wanna be around me?"

"No! I mean for socializing with people. Or at work or wherever. I can't just go someplace and not act like a faggot for an hour or two. I can't turn it off, whatever it is. And the thing is, I don't want to turn it off. I like who I am."

"You know what, Schoenberg? I like who you are too."

We kissed, long and deeply, the fireplace crackling in the background, the portions of the room outside of the fireplace's glow cloaked in blackness. My body felt exhausted but safe; we'd had sex for an hour or so after we got home from the dinner, and what with my thighs in his hands and his tongue on my asshole, it was nice, but I was drunk and tired and trying to get thoughts of Victor out of my head. I had two competing voices: one telling me to go to London, the other reminding myself that I was not going to London, and because I wasn't able to quiet them, they mercilessly clanged around in my head like two ringing cymbals. I knew the reason they wouldn't quiet down. For all the allure of Johnny Martinez and his celebrity status, my starstruck eyes would not let me forget one thing: he was kind of scary and he wasn't particularly bright.

I was quite sure he had no idea what I meant when I told him about having no control over my image, and I knew he was just agreeing with me because he wanted me to stop thinking about it so that he could go to sleep thinking everything was peachy.

His arms were around me and holding me closely, but as we drifted off to sleep I had a moment of clarity that was my first in almost a month. All of a sudden, everything that was happening in my life made sense to me, and the choices I had made scared me because of their base stupidity. I was scared of being stuck in a nowhere job for the rest of my life, so I accepted Johnny's money. I was terrified that I'd be in love with Victor for the rest of my life, so I had switched my longing toward Ted, because he was close to me, he was connected with the Harley Hutt, and he was gay. I had hooked up with Johnny, a man I didn't know, because he was famous and I thought that fact would make me feel important.

I couldn't believe what an ignorant asshole I had been.

I let my mind drift, and I naturally fantasized about Victor and his arms, and his legs, and his mind. I longed for a conversation with Victor about politics, or gender, or drinking beer, or anything really. The sensation of feeling safe in Johnny's arms was nothing compared to the feeling of exhilaration I had at the Harley Hutt, whether I was in Victor's arms or not.

It had only been a few weeks, but I knew I had to stop seeing Johnny. Every time I said my opinion, he'd take offense and get mad at me for the wrong reasons, because he didn't understand what I was saying.

He didn't want me, personally, he wanted the idea of someone young, and inexperienced. He wanted a younger man to make himself feel younger. He wanted to be able to take the lead and take control. The cash payout was just the first step.

39.

Afternoon arose and I stepped out of bed into bold rays of sunlight, hoping Johnny would be gone. The house was still silent. The only sound I could detect was the subtle blowing of the central air system. I had no idea if it was hot or cold that day. With the climate control, the temperature was so incredibly neutral that the air didn't even really feel like air. I walked into the living room, my feet not making a sound on the floorboards.

I wouldn't have minded owning Johnny's house. It was a veritable bachelor pad. The basement had a rec room with a bar and the living room had an amazing entertainment center, with things I'd never seen before, like DVDs and digital cable, and a video game system that made my childhood Pac-Man games seem like embarrassing relics from an inferior age.

The house was small, one and a half stories, with just two bedrooms, a living room, a kitchen, and a bathroom and a half, but he had clearly put a good deal of work into it. The hardwood floors shone and looked brand new, the counters and appliances in the kitchen sparkled, the living room furniture was all leather and appeared unused. Strangely, though, he had no trophy room, or any indication at all that he was a professional athlete. That didn't figure; he must've had at least one post-season. He had to have kept something.

There were no family photos. The walls held tasteful but clearly unloved art prints. Johnny told me that he'd lived there for five years, but everything looked too untouched. I knew that Roscoe Village hadn't been expensive five years before. He must've bought the house for a steal. I also knew from a little bit of snooping around on Ted's internet that he had earned two million dollars the year before. For that he bought a minuscule frame house in West Lakeview?

I thought maybe he had a second house in the suburbs, a rambling old mansion in Lake Forest, or Winnetka, or Kenilworth, where he kept all the rest of his things. I pulled open a drawer in the kitchen. A pair of chopsticks, a can opener, individually packaged packages of plastic silverware with enclosed napkins. In the cupboard: a plastic cup from a suburban crab shack, a shotglass from Minneapolis-St. Paul, a green coffee mug, and what looked like a holiday glass that fast-food restaurants offer for ninety-nine cents with purchase of a sandwich.

I walked back into the bedroom to get dressed. I pulled on a pair of oversized cargo shorts and a T shirt, an old blue thing with neon Chinese lettering. In my skateboarding shoes, I checked myself out in the mirror and assured myself I still looked young. I didn't want to walk through Roscoe Village looking like I'd been electrocuted, so I went into the bathroom to wet down my hair. On the counter was a note.

August,

I had to be out early today for a charity thing for kids, but come to the game later. There'll be a ticket for you at the box office. Oh, and one thing. Long road trip ahead. I'll be gone for two and a half weeks. So come to this game, because otherwise then I won't see you. I'll be in Montreal and Florida and then St. Louis so you get the idea.

Later bud,

J

p.s. Did you ever have a Cuban boyfriend before? Well, you do now.

I looked into the mirror and saw my face, and it was frowning. On the counter, underneath where the note had been, lay ten one hundred dollar bills, the top one smeared with shaving cream. I picked them up, put them in my cargo pants, and walked out of the house.

40.

The next day I sat in the dining room with the newspaper open, scanning the want ads. A brutal-looking storm was brewing over the lake. Dark grey clouds swirled around to the east and hung so low that it was as dark as night outside. Nevertheless, it was still in the upper eighties and my forehead was sweating as though I were at the beach.

I held a red pen in my hand but had circled nothing. I was determined to find a job the next week, but this time one where I'd actually be doing something useful and hopefully using some of my qualifications. Unfortunately, I didn't seem to posses the qualifications needed for any job I'd seen. I didn't know a thing about using computers. Of course, I had grown up with them, but the computers I used as a kid were out of date by the time I hit junior high school, and then by the time I got to high school the computers were different again, and then in college computers seemed to change twice, so that by the time I sat scanning the want ads, I had little confidence that I'd know how to do anything with them at all. I told Ted as much.

"Be a bartender," he said, good advice coming from someone who had just woken up at five in the afternoon. "At some of these clubs, you can work two or three nights a week and pull in a couple hundred a night. You can live on that."

"No more customer service for me," I said. "I was getting so grouchy at the movie theater that I was scolding little old ladies. But I don't want to work in an office either. Everyone always seems to hate their lives so much but covers it up underneath a caffeine buzz. And the ones who actually enjoy being there: god, keep me away from them. Hmm. Maybe I could get into journalism."

Ted rolled around on the couch, shooting rubber bands at the ceiling. "You could come to the Dong Pipe and work the lights while I DJ."

"Oh, that's nice of you." I imagined myself dressed all in black, passing a joint back and forth with the other employees while I pressed on a board of lit-up buttons that cast a surreal light show around the dance floor. "But I'm sure it doesn't pay enough to cover the rent. I don't want a sugar daddy any longer. If I make any money in this lifetime it's gonna be mine, not some dumb baseball player's."

"Bitter, bitter," Ted said. "Trouble in paradise?"

"Ugh. Something's off. Something is creepy and weird, and it's freaking me out. Who'd have thought you could feel creepy in Roscoe Village? Hey, wait a minute!"

At my outburst, Ted looked up sharply. "What's wrong?"

"The White Sox," I said. I stared at the back page of the paper. "They're still in town."

"So?"

"Johnny," I said, starting to feel even more creepy than I had. "He told me he was going on a road trip and he wouldn't see me after yesterday, for two and a half weeks. They're in town for three more days."

"That's weird," Ted said, losing interest. He got up and started rifling through an old army bag. "So go to the game."

"No, something's fucked up. He always asks me to go to the games. Every time. What could possibly go on this weekend that he wouldn't want me to see?"

"Maybe he's seeing you on the side," Ted said. He cackled. "Maybe you're his part-time lover!"

"Wonderful, something else to freak me out even more. Ugh. Maybe I should have asked Armando Aguilar if he was single."

"Oh, the wild and wacky world of Augie Schoenberg's love life. Will he ever make sense of it?"

"Fuck you. It is weird." A sharp pain shot into the pit of my stomach. "Ow, my stomach hurts now. See, I knew it would come back."

"Boring," Ted said. "Stomach pain is boring....Hey, do you wanna go out tonight? I've got some ecstasy." His eyes lit up, but I couldn't imagine what something like ecstasy would do to my stomach, or for that matter, my brain.

"No," I said, folding up the paper and dropping it on the floor. "I'm going for a drink with Jean-Claude and Roberta. They said they have big news."

"Oooh. Marriage perhaps? Wedding bells?"

I hadn't thought of that. A wave of anxiety passed through me, but I instantly shook it off. "No, you know Roberta's play is at Steppenwolf now, and Jean-Claude's band just played the Metro so it's gotta be career stuff. I'm sure they'll be rich and famous any day now at the rate they're going. Anyway, I'm off to Ukrainian Village. Wish me luck on the CTA."

"You should arrive in perhaps two and a half hours," Ted said. "Now, by car, ten minutes."

I waved and walked into the steaming hall.

The bar was a hole in the wall, but the crowd was interesting. At the billiard table, a bald woman played a game against a beefy truck driver type, and at the video games, a pair of guys in brown and yellow polyester threads drank dollar beers out of cans and exclaimed like kids at each new level that they got to. Jean-Claude and Roberta sat across from me at a table, so close to one another they may as well have been sitting in each other's laps. Their wild grins gave me the idea they were eminently pleased with themselves.

"You're growing a fro," I said to Jean-Claude. He was no longer bald, but had at least an inch and a half of hair topping his head.

"Dude, I'm lettin' it go seventies style. It's gonna be phat."

"Or perhaps just fat," Roberta said. Her hair had become large, too, and was grouped together in two clumps of braids that stood straight up in a V, like an antenna. "So how are things with you?"

"Great," I said, and lit a cigarette. "The screenplay's in the mail, so good things might await. We'll see."

"And," Roberta said, smiling out of the corner of her mouth. "The baseball player?"

"Oh, that," I said, modestly. "Yeah, he's fine. So far so good."

"Dude," Jean-Claude said, too loudly. "I should have known if it would be anybody it'd be Augie. I mean, bangin' one of the White Sox. Holy fuckin' shit!"

"Nah, he's just a guy. Nothing real special. So...what's your news?"

Roberta glanced at Jean-Claude and smirked. "Well, we haven't told anybody yet, but we wanted you to be the first. It was a really hard decision, but after we made it we realized it should have been the easiest one we ever made."

We, we, we. We're getting married.

"We're moving to New York."

I dropped my cigarette on the table. "What? Why on earth do you wanna move there?"

Roberta looked aghast at my lack of congratulations. "Well, things have been going well for us. Like, real well. You know, the play I'm in, the production is going to New York, at Lincoln Center. And Jean-Claude's band just played the Metro and after that one show, they got a record deal. The band's looking at spaces in Brooklyn." She searched my face. I looked back, interestedly, but I was upset. I thought I'd end up with a larger group of friends in Chicago, not start losing people. "There's only so much we can do here. I love Chicago, sort of, but New York just has more. And it's gonna be a necessity for our careers."

"That's wonderful," I said, choking on my cigarette smoke. "God, but how are you gonna afford it? Isn't rent like thousands of dollars per month out there?"

"It'll be tight, but if the record deal pans out, then there shouldn't be a problem. And Roberta's getting paid OK," Jean-Claude said.

"Also," Roberta said, glancing at Jean-Claude again. "We only need a one bedroom; I'm sure we can swing it, especially if we do end up living in Brooklyn." She wiggled her fingers around, nervously.

"Sorry, I'm just shocked. That's the last thing I expected you guys to say. Jesus, it's great. You two are really on your way!"

They managed weak grins. "Augie," Roberta said. "I know you told me that you've always wanted to live in New York. Why don't you come, too? We could be neighbors."

Jean-Claude sat forward. "That'd be awesome, man. Fuck the Windy City. It's for suckers."

"Well, this city of suckers certainly gave you two a pretty good start, I'd say. No, I wanted to live in New York when I was a kid, but that's just cause my mom was always talking about it, and anyway I think I watched *Fame* too many times. So when are you moving?"

"Two weeks," Roberta said. "But we'll be back and forth for a while. You know, moving stuff, and also..."

"We're getting married," Jean-Claude blurted.

"I was supposed to tell him! It's the girl's job to tell people."

"What?" Jean-Claude said. "That's not a rule!"

"That's how it works," Roberta said. "The girl tells everybody and the guy stands there and smiles."

"What?"

"You guys," I said, stubbing out my cigarette. "I think it's a fantastic idea. I mean, look, you're halfway there already. If I didn't know you two, I'd guess you'd been married for years."

"Smart ass," Roberta said, and then she and Jean-Claude kissed.

"All right, I'm gonna vomit. No kissyface tonight, please."

"Can't help it, dude," Jean-Claude said, standing up. "She's the girl I love." Roberta beamed and Jean-Claude sauntered off to the men's room.

"Wow, look at all these changes. You're gonna be a star." I meant it, too. Steppenwolf had produced more Oscar nominees than I could count. "I can't wait to come visit you. I can show you all the nice Jewish delis."

She grabbed my hand. "Augie, I can't wait." She looked down at the table and then back into my eyes. "There's this feeling I have inside of me. It's a warm, enthusiastic feeling and it never leaves. It's centered at the base of my stomach and it leads me around all day on this wave of happiness and optimism that seems to go on forever and ever. I never thought life would feel this easy. Everything is working out for me! I don't know what to do with it. I don't know where to put all these feelings; no one ever tells you what to do when you have that feeling of complete satisfaction. I mean, what do you do?" She stared straight at me, and looked almost helpless, as if she were actually in need of guidance.

"You keep it to yourself," I said.

41.

I got off the L at 35th Street and marched up the escalator to the street as though I were on my way to the boss's office to be laid off. The sun shone so brightly that I could barely see, and my eyes squirmed around recalcitrantly in my head, as if the sun were the enemy and they were its weak, albino victims. Masochistic longing for the winter overtook me: all winter I'd prayed for summer, but by August I longed for cold winds and ice. I thought winter might clear my head.

The White Sox schedule I looked up on the internet made no mistake: the grey, tiny box listed Sunday afternoon's game to start at 1:00 p.m., and beneath that, a small caption of just two words: Wives' Day. It had become eminently clear while I sat staring at the computer why Johnny wanted me to think he was out of town. But I couldn't fathom that he thought I was stupid enough to just go along with what he said, when any newspaper in town could tell me differently.

I thought I should have tried to fuck one of the Cubs.

The park would have been nicer anyway; Comiskey stood grey and unnecessarily vast in the middle of parking lots so wide and free of cars that the sight was almost pathetic. A few dozen fans trotted along near me, doing their best to act like they were enjoying themselves, but with the expressway on one side, housing projects on the other, and the empty parking lots staring us down like gray deserts without the hint of a mirage, I couldn't imagine what joy could come from such a place.

Slowly, and with a stealthy, otherworldly sense of concentration, I wandered around the perimeter of the monstrous park, from entrance gate to entrance gate, where two women in their husband's oversized jerseys stood at each one in front of large green barrels, collecting toys or books or something or other for a children's cause.

The wives' faces were impossible to see: each wore a baseball cap and sunglasses, so that all you could really make out was the hair color of those who had longer hair. Nevertheless, the few fans congregated outside the park were approaching the wives and taking pictures with them, as if they were old friends, no doubt inspired by the celebrity name on the back of each jersey.

From a distance of fifty feet, I stood on a traffic island in the parking lot and watched the nearest gate. Two wives turned around and placed packages in the green barrel and then turned back around and looked for more donors. I moved closer to the gate, pulled in by the prospect of uncovering the solution to a mystery, and the need to know if I'd be single after the next few moments transpired, if I'd be flat broke, if I'd necessarily have to feel like I'd been deceived and used.

The wife nearest me turned to the side, a slight woman with the inklings of short blond hair peeking out of the cap, purple tinted sunglasses decorating her face. The jersey was so large on her that she had tied it below the waist on one side in a knot. I made a half-circle around her, aware of the fact that I was the only person around not in a group, and that I must've looked like a pervert, or a psycho, the way I lurked around the parking lot wearing inappropriately warm clothes for the day and a scowl on my face.

And there it was on the back of her jersey in embroidered white letters: Martinez. I walked quickly up to her. She didn't move.

"Hi," I said, briskly.

After a slight hesitation, and some infinitesimal jerks of the muscles around her mouth, she said, in a falsely happy voice, "Hi, do you have a new, unwrapped toy for a child?"

"I don't," I said, sympathetically, "but I wanted to meet you..."

"Oh!" she said, either surprised or terrified, or perhaps both.

"You see, I'm a friend of Johnny's and I've heard a lot about you."

She opened her mouth slightly, as if unsure of whether I was being friendly or about to take out an uzi and shoot her.

"I've been to the house in Roscoe Village, but I never saw you there." I smiled and hoped she knew about the house in the first place.

"Oh!" And then her voice moved down to a comfortable, sturdy level. "I'm Shari Martinez." She held out her hand and I took it lightly, her scrunched up fingers so small and birdlike that I easily surrounded them. She barely squeezed back. "Yeah, Johnny insists on keeping the house in Chicago, but it's small and he likes it, so I guess it's just as well. What was your name again?"

Augie Schoenberg.

"Michael," I said. "Michael Farinelli."

"Michael. Johnny's never mentioned you before."

"Oh, I guess I'm not a close enough friend yet. It's funny, I could've sworn he said that you live in Chicago."

She cocked her head to the side. I wished I could've seen through the sunglasses. "No, Michael," she said, sounding concerned again. "We live in Florida. We always have."

I nodded. "Well, what do I know? Nice to meet you!"

I walked away, but backwards, staring at her. She looked to the side, almost desperately, as if to rid herself of unease, and disquiet, and the odd, gawking guy who wouldn't take his eyes off of her face. She dropped her hand to the side and wiped it on her jeans.

42.

"Dude, man," Paul Veracruz said. "I think you just made the papers."

We sat in the bar at the Russian bath house, wearing blue cotton wraps and flip flops. The bar was actually in the locker room, and fat, old men with their thingies barely visible below their pot bellies stood around chatting, so that it felt like we were in the midst of a nudist colony instead of on the trendy fringe of Wicker Park.

"Hm?" I asked, dazed. It was the same day. I went directly from Comiskey to the L, where I got off at Chinatown and wandered around the grocery stores looking at fish heads and teapots for a couple hours. Bored with that, I rode up to Wicker Park and dragged Veracruz out of a late-afternoon nap. "Dude," he'd said. "We must bathe." And we had, as nude as we had at the Harley Hutt, but with considerably more people around. Paul looked roughly the same: he was still tattooed, still pierced, and he had added a shiny gold ring to the head of his penis. I'd peered at it in awe, unaware such a thing was possible.

"The Sun-Times," Paul said, offering it to me. "Read the last paragraph of the Around Town column."

I took the paper, exhaling exhaustedly. I hadn't been relaxed at all by the once over from the naked Russian guy with the big sponge.

> **Sox squawk:** Dateline, Rush Street...Which of our city's veteran baseball players was seen dining with a young boy toy over seventy-five dollar steaks at Roselli's last weekend??? Seems one of the boys of summer has found himself a boy for summer of his own, and we don't mean just for male bonding. Our snoopsters heard the whole dish Friday night. How? The not-so-secret lovers had a tiny little spat before the steaks arrived, and the twentysomething Boystown party boy went to the bar to cool off. Problem is, he blabbed all the details into a cell phone. Oops! Wonder if top brass knows that the aging South Sider (oops!) is a little light in the, uh, cleats.

"Oh my God, I'm ruined," I said, tossing the paper on the bar. "Not only will I have an ex-boyfriend wanting to kill me, I'm gonna have a married ex-boyfriend wanting to kill me."

"Augie, this is totally awesome," Paul said. "If this guy fucked you over like you say he did, then you already got your revenge. You should be celebrating!"

"Well, yeah! Fuck him. Ugh! I can't understand it. How on earth could you live like that? I mean, wouldn't you be ashamed? Keeping a house in the city to fuck guys while your wife is at home gardening in Florida. It's gross!"

"Ah, men are slime," Paul said, and put his beer bottle on the bar with a clank. He burped. "Let's get outta here. I've had about all the naked men I can stand."

We walked to our lockers, my face scrunched up, my lips pursed, and my mind utterly confused. I couldn't believe Johnny actually thought he might be able to get away with that kind of lifestyle.

"I need to get out of this town," I told Paul, as I stuck my key in the lock. "And go far, far away."

"Well, do it. I wouldn't mind that so much myself. All I'm doing is waiting tables. There's not much here to stay for." He took off his blue wrap and laid it on the bench. The sight of him nude was so familiar to me it was as natural as seeing him clothed, except for the pierced dick. A glint projected off the hoop, drawing stares from the occasional passing bather.

"Doesn't that hurt?" I asked.

"The inevitable question. It did, it doesn't now. No biggie." He put a white towel on the bench and sat down.

I did the same and then wiped off the bottoms of my feet. The flip flops notwithstanding, I was wary of the treacherous potential for athlete's foot.

Paul put his chin in his hands, his elbows balanced on his thighs. "Look, Augie, I didn't tell you before cause I knew you were upset about that guy, but I went down to Normal last weekend and something happened."

"Happened?" I pulled up my pants and searched in the locker for my shirt.

"I was walking down Cherry Street and there were all these bulldozers. They knocked down the Harley Hutt."

I studied his face, disbelieving him, sure it was a prank.

"They're putting up an apartment building. You should see it, it's horrible."

I turned back toward the locker and sat on the bench. I pulled on socks, and shoes, and then my shirt, but finally I grabbed my towel and put it to my face. I imagined the Harley Hutt, old and awful and about to collapse anyway, being struck down by an army of yellow bulldozers, the property surrounded by a plastic red construction fence. It was as if the town waited for us to leave so they could tell us what they really thought of us. Wipe out all evidence of them. Make it look as though they never existed.

I threw the towel on the floor and got to my feet, staring at the floor. "Jesus, Schoenberg, are you crying?"

I raced toward the exit, embarrassed, my head so full of stress I thought I'd snap if I didn't get outside. I could hear Paul staggering behind me, the clink of the buckles of his overalls, but I didn't wait. I sailed through the hallway and out the doors into the early evening heat, breathless and scared. It seemed that I had no history at all; Victor and I didn't count. Jose and I didn't count. Johnny and I didn't count. The Harley Hutt wasn't worth preserving. I strode down Division toward Damen, going nowhere, and Paul caught up to me, but slowly. He hadn't run.

He put an arm around me and we turned down Damen, going south. As we walked past a trashy bar with a toothless old woman sitting on the stoop, I said, "Maybe if we walk far enough south we'll hit the end of the earth and then we can jump off."

"Ah, I think we'll end up in the Calumet River. And you don't wanna do that.

Look, Schoenberg, what's wrong with you? It was just a house."

"It's just what it represents." We stopped walking and I faced him. "Everything I'm involved in disintegrates after a few months. Nothing ever means anything. There's no permanence to anything."

"Schoenberg, it's not just you. Everyone's life is temporary. Or transient. Permanence is a total illusion."

We walked to the corner and I sat on the curb. Paul lit two cigarettes and gave me one. "I'm sorry, it's just there's something else going on. It's not just the baseball player or the Harley Hutt. Victor's wedding is in a few days. He invited me."

"No shit," Paul said. "He didn't invite me, the bastard. You're going?"

"I hadn't planned to. I don't need another excuse to be unhappy. An arranged marriage, now there's permanence for you. That's a lifetime of permanence."

"Why would you be unhappy? Oh, that's it. You wanna go to the wedding but you won't admit it. Augie, are you jealous of the bride?"

I couldn't help but picture myself standing on a London street wearing a wedding dress. I burst into laughter and ended up choking. "Paul, I am so fucking jealous of that bitch I could scream!"

Paul cackled and said, "Augie, get the fuck out of this town and go to London."

The next day was August 21st. I treated myself to lunch at Marshall Field's, in the basement, for Chinese food. The thousand dollars I'd snatched from underneath Johnny's note was in my pocket, and after lunch I was going to the bank to change them in for British pounds. I'd packed a small bag, just enough clothes for a week, but I couldn't believe how badly I wanted to stay longer. The shrimp stir fry rattled around in my stomach belligerently, taking every last nervous impulse I had as a direct insult. There were messages on my machine; angry messages from Johnny that I'd instantly erased. I couldn't think of any other way to deal with them than to leave, and go to a faraway, unreachable place. I needed a day or a night or any amount of time with Victor so that I could feel like myself again. It's not that I wanted to pull some stunt that stank of fiction bullshit, like disrupt the wedding, but I could ask him if he was sure he wanted to go through with it. Ask him in person. As my meal dissipated, I looked around at the shoppers and felt a small flicker of light that'd been languishing in my head. I knew it could be rekindled. I had to get there.

I broke open the fortune cookie. "Look around," it read. "Happiness is trying to catch you."

43.

The plane landed at Heathrow after circling the airport for an hour. I forced my body to relax, and breathe in: I'd had seven hours of armrest-clutching terror, with turbulence throwing the plane around in the air so violently that I was shocked we didn't plummet into the ocean. The flight attendants fed me bottle after tiny bottle of red wine, but there was a ceiling of fear over my head that refused to lift itself off and leave me in peace. I grabbed my bag and made my way out.

The customs agent looked at me with bored disdain. "And what is your reason for visiting the United Kingdom?"

I was prepared to say, "Vacation," but that word conjured up visions of Florida and white, sandy beaches full of sunshine. From the view I'd witnessed through the airplane window, England offered anything but sun.

"A wedding," I said. He eyed me with such tedium that the monotonous nature of his job became exhaustingly obvious. He stamped my passport and I strode toward the subway.

When I came up from the tube at Bayswater, I stood still, my bag at my feet, and lit a cigarette. Every storefront had a tenant: a bookseller, a Chinese restaurant with whole chickens on spits in the window, an Indian restaurant, countless pubs, a movie theater, currency exchanges. Luxury cars were parked along the streets and masses of people walked past at such a fast clip my head spun. A street sign advised passersby to, "Ensure your pet does not foul the footpath."

I picked up my bag and turned right. I'd no idea if that was the right direction but I had a sudden need to just walk around, and feel what it felt like to be in England. Everything looked old but new, ancient but remodeled. I caught snippets of pedestrians' conversations as they sailed past.

"Well, I might *do* go, but I'm not sure yet."

"And Americans call pubs '*bars*.'"

"We were *knackered* then, weren't we."

A slow mist started to drop down, but no one bothered to pull out an umbrella. I made a turn at the next corner, and wondered if this busy, commercial district would continue on for all of London, and not cease with a dull thud like every neighborhood in Chicago does after a few blocks.

I walked into a small grocery store and tried to find a bottle of water. Apparently, mineral water was all the rage in England. I had absolutely no idea what mineral water might consist of, and thoughts of a slimy, gel-like fluid filled my mind and I almost panicked, thinking they might not even have regular water in England. I rushed to the counter. "Do you have just a bottle of regular old water?" I asked the clerk. She looked at me sharply, as if I may be insane, and then asked, "You want still water, do you?"

I wasn't completely sure if I did. "Yes."

She left the counter and grabbed a bottle out of the cooler. In my jet-lagged panic, I hadn't thought to look for a label that read 'spring water.' All right, Schoenberg, I told myself, you can do this. Chemist means pharmacy. Fags means cigarettes.

The hostel stood on Queensway in an ancient stone building that looked more like an apartment building than anything else. A keypad was attached to the stone exterior, but the door pushed open easily when I leaned on it. Behind the front desk, which was really just the open top half of a split door, a blond guy about my age peered over at me. "Augie Schoenberg?" he called out.

I dropped my bag on the floor, exhausted and relieved. "Yes, I am!"

"We've been expectin' you. My name's Bob. I'm from Oregon."

"Hi!" I said, strangely relieved to see an American after only seven hours' absence.

"Did you have a nice flight?" He was smiling from ear to ear.

"No," I said. "It was the worst. There was so much turbulence. I thought I was going to die!"

"Oh, I'm sorry Augie." He handed me some paperwork to fill out. "Go upstairs and relax for a while." He leaned forward and lowered his voice. "Later tonight we have a DJ coming in, and we sell drinks and stuff, so you can meet some people. I see that you're on your own."

"Am I ever," I said, as though I'd traveled the world alone and hadn't seen a friendly face in years.

He handed me a key. "You're gonna love it here."

I lay on the bed but was too tired to sleep. There were two bunk beds in the room, but my roommates were apparently out enjoying the drizzling day. It was Thursday. The wedding was Saturday. I figured I'd spend the day sightseeing, but hadn't counted on feeling so jet-lagged.

I can't just lay here, I told myself. Big Ben is out there. Buckingham Palace awaits. Victor Radhakrishna is less than a mile away. I had to get out on the streets.

From the map I had, it looked like Notting Hill was the next neighborhood west of Bayswater. I thought I could walk, but the curving streets on the map made me unsure if I'd be able to find my way back. I didn't want to call Victor just yet. I still had that memory of Victor and Isabella laughing together through the wall at my expense, as if my life was a joke, or worse, that the thought of anyone spending his life with me was a joke. I wanted to wait until I wasn't in the midst of a jet lag hangover. I wanted to be sharp when I saw him. Even so, I had to see the house. I wanted to spy on him from the outside.

I walked down Bayswater Road during the evening rush. It was a monstrosity of a street, with muffler-free cars and trucks roaring along at a mad speed, and commuters racing along the sidewalk about as fast. My legs suddenly came to life and I rushed along with the crowd, feeling strangely important. I had no plans that night, but the fact that I'd just crossed an ocean impressed me, and filled me with as much vigor as the jet lag would allow.

I turned on Ladbroke Grove. The street stretched before me in two never-ending rows of white townhouses with tiny little lawns and then wound upwards and disappeared. It was getting dark out, and as the lamps lit up, the white and green vista before me glowed against pools of water in the black road. I found Victor's number and stood across the street, sizing it up. It was a three-story affair, with an unusually tall, black front door. Black luxury cars lined the parkway.

I didn't know what to do, exactly, it seemed sort of dumb to be standing there gawking, so I retreated into a telephone booth and held the receiver to my ear. I supposed I was expecting Victor and Sarita to arrive home at any minute, but the chances of that seemed slim, and anyway Sarita was most likely performing the evening news at that time.

A woman and a girl ran from a townhouse and hailed a taxi. As they piled in the cab, I looked around the elegant block and it finally hit me. *I'm here*. It wasn't a feeling of excitement. I realized that I was totally alone.

While I was gazing at nothing in particular, a black taxi sped away and I turned back to Victor's house. On the steps, two figures in dark clothes clumped up toward the door. I half expected to see Victor in a Bad Religion T shirt and cutoff jeans, but there he was, not fifty feet from me, in black dress pants, black shoes, and a dark blue sweater. Sarita wore a black raincoat and black heels. He held out an arm to her as she made her way up the stairs.

He had gained weight, that was obvious, and in those clothes looked about ten years older. He turned to the side to say something to her and I realized he had cut off his hair. The back of it was tapered as sharply as if he'd just come from the barber, and the front was still parted in the middle but was so short that it didn't hang into his forehead at all. On his left temple there was a white spot. It was getting worse.

Victor pulled out keys and opened the door. Sarita waltzed in gaily and Victor brought up the rear with a stolid swagger that left me utterly cold. I didn't think there was any turning back for those two. They already looked married.

The door closed, a light went on in the front room, but I couldn't see anything through the curtains. I left the phone booth and shivered in the windy drizzle. I hailed a taxi and it pulled to a halt, the exterior as sleek and black as a limousine. When I plopped down inside, I gave the driver the hostel's address and we sped off toward Notting Hill Gate as steadfastly as if we were on rails. Kensington Gardens appeared on the right, a seeming paradise of ponds and roses. I knew if I was going to enjoy myself in London, I needed to get a life.

"Driver," I said, knocking on the plastic divider. "I changed my mind. Take me to Soho."

"Which street do you need, sir?"

"I've no idea. Just take me to the center of it."

We roared down Bayswater Road, past Hyde Park and Marble Arch, and as the lights from Piccadilly glowed brightly in the distance, my face turned unintentionally into a smile.

44.

"*Rock the casbah*," I sang happily to myself. "*Rock the casbah*." Soho was bringing out the early eighties in me and it had come on strong.

The coat check guy looked at me skeptically. "Uh, was that a popular song in the United States?"

"Oh, yeah!" I said, drunk and almost belligerent. "I had the 45. Did you have 45s in England?"

"Yes," he said, handing me my windbreaker. "We did."

I realized quickly that I had turned into an annoying American tourist. But I didn't care at all. The bar had been full of sticks in the mud, who unspeakingly stood along the walls holding pints of beer and staring straight ahead. The music selection, though, was so reminiscent of my childhood that I was catapulted back in time to Evanston, circa 1983, where I bought British pop star magazines and cut out the pictures of Boy George and Sade and Tears for Fears and hung them up on my bedroom wall. As I walked out onto Old Compton Street I entertained the possibility that Boy George himself could come strolling down the street at any moment.

I looked around and inhaled the wet air. The minuscule road was jammed with cars and lights and hordes of revelers, who produced an ear-numbing noise that rang out as loudly as if it were Mardi Gras. I stepped into the cobblestone road and strode down a side street with a market in the middle. The shop windows were full of obnoxiously trendy clothes: outrageous platform shoes, rubber dresses, mannequins wearing dog collars. I passed a peepshow, a Malaysian restaurant, and a bar with a small casino. A brick wall was coated in posters of rap stars.

I looked at my watch. The bartender had called, 'Time, gentlemen,' at 11 p.m. and I almost spit out my beer in surprise. I thought I had heard that clubs in London stayed open 24 hours, but apparently I was at a bar and not a club.

I considered wandering around to look for a nightclub but wasn't sure I'd enjoy being there alone. The streets were so full of confidently overjoyed people in groups, and there I stood, alone and drunk, wishing I had someone to talk to. I devilishly weighed my options for a second, figured what the hell, and caught a cab. I told the driver to take me to Notting Hill.

"Augie Schoenberg," Victor said, mildly, the sound of his voice reassuring me so soundly that I ached with joy through the now-drunken jet lag.

"It's me! I came."

"Where are you?" I could hear his footsteps through the phone. I thought I'd excited him to the point of frantic pacing. I looked out at the row of elaborate townhomes on Ladbroke Grove.

"At a phone booth," I said, coyly, "right across from your house."

"No way. Schoenberg, is this a prank?"

"See for yourself," I said, waving an arm out of the phone booth. "Look out your front window."

The line went dead and I replaced the receiver. I walked out onto the street and watched his house, waiting for the front door to fly open. I was already beginning to laugh, and to rejoice inside, unable to wait for the second I'd see him. No lump formed in my throat.

Endless seconds passed. The door didn't fly open. I finally decided to walk over to the house. After another interminable minute, the enormous black door slowly creaked open, and there were Sarita and Victor looking shined and polished in the gleaming white vestibule, standing next to an antique umbrella stand. They weren't smiling.

"So when did you get in?" Victor asked and held out his hand. Still drunk, I ignored it and threw my arms around him. I grasped a set of love handles that hung over his belt.

"I just got in today. I realized I couldn't let you get married without my supervision." I let go of him and strode into the hall while Victor closed the door. Sarita looked uncomfortably small and urchin-like in a business suit, and the frown on her face would've bothered me had I been sober.

"I thought there was no way in the world you'd come." He cleared his throat, the double chin vibrating. "Augie," he said, motioning protectively toward his betrothed, "This is Sarita. This is my old friend Augie Schoenberg."

Her golden face lit up into a fake smile and she said, while shaking my hand, "Oh, Augie. I've heard so terribly much about you. Sometimes I think the stories from the old university days will never end. Of course, we didn't expect you to call so late."

Her clipped British accent had a deceptively sweet tone that made me instantly defensive. I realized quickly this visit would take place entirely in the foyer. "Well, there's something about Victor that brings out the spontaneous side in me," I said, ready for a cat fight.

Sarita widened her eyes in confusion and Victor shuffled his feet. "God, Augie," he said. "We'd love to have you in, but it's almost midnight and we've got a lot of wedding stuff to do tomorrow."

"Right. Wedding stuff," I said. I would've said more, but the sight of those two in semi-formal clothes looking at me in surprise while they bore mature grins left me feeling wholly immature and scummy.

Sarita smiled at me obnoxiously. "Augie, we are so thrilled to have you at the wedding. And I know Victor has an evening reserved for you this weekend, so you two can catch up on old times. Well! I'm off to bed. But it was nice to meet you!"

"Yeah!" I said, too gruffly, while Sarita pranced off elegantly into a door off the foyer. Once gone, the tension in the hallway was immediately sucked out and Victor hugged me.

"You bastard. I thought you hated my guts."

"God, I wouldn't miss this for the world," I said, inhaling the scent of him, hoping for the smell of graham crackers and beer. Instead, I picked up the faint scent of dry cleaning fluid. "Anyway, how could I say no to free plane tickets?"

He looked right into my eyes and I turned to mush. His brown skin looked so incredibly warm against the backdrop of that cold hallway that I could've kissed him and felt no guilt. As it was, I grabbed his hand for reassurance and saw a white spot on his finger, a teardrop of spilled milk. Unsure of what to do with my grasping hand, he swung his arm back and forth and said, "I am gonna take you out tomorrow and show you the time of your life."

"Great! I have so much to tell you."

"I want to hear every last thing, Schoenberg. I've been wondering what's been going on with you." He laughed a little bit and I let go of his hand. "I don't mean to turn you out into the cold," he continued, motioning to the door, clearly about to turn me out into the cold.

"That's OK! I've got lots of things lined up. There's a party at my hostel tonight and tomorrow I just want to go out and explore."

"Fantastic," he said. He pulled away but kept a hand on my back. "You know, Sarita's ready for bed already, and tomorrow afternoon we've got a lot of wedding stuff to do."

"Right. Wedding stuff."

"Tomorrow night," Victor said, leading me to the door, "we are gonna rock out with our cocks out." I gave him a look and he quickly continued. "There's this great club called Energy that I think you are gonna love. The first time I went there I thought immediately of you."

"Awesome," I said, wanting so badly to stay, and not be alone in a foreign city where I didn't know a soul besides him. "I've got a full day of sightseeing ahead of me but I'll be raring to go. I'll call you."

He patted me on the back and walked me out onto the steps. Under the piercing white porch light, he looked at me with his heavy eyes and hesitated.

"What?"

"Nothing. Well, anyway, get outta here."

Outside, it had started to drizzle again. The front lawn was perfectly green and manicured, and had a tiny stone statue of an angel. It looked uncommonly English. I fully expected to see a hedgehog amble across the grass and then pause in the spotlight coming from the porch light. A sharply-dressed man and woman walked by, the woman looking at us as she talked. "Those guys are cute," she said to the man.

"Victor," I said. "The general public approves."

45.

I rolled out of bed at noon, hung over as hell. The party in the lobby of the hostel had gone till four a.m. and I closed it down. I got to talking with some guys from Switzerland who didn't speak much English but kept saying over and over again, "The Windy City!" I considered responding by yelling, "Lausanne, Switzerland!" but I didn't think that'd have quite the same ring.

My elusive roommates had never materialized. Unfazed and buoyed by the idea that everything I'd see that day would be new, I walked down the hall in boxer shorts and flip flops and took a shower. The bathroom had a tub with no shower curtain. There were no shades on the windows either, and I stepped into the tub, naked except for the flip flops, and took a long, messy shower with my ass hanging out for all of Bayswater to see. When I finished, a half inch of water coated the floor.

Back in the room, I stood naked at the window. The sun shone brilliantly and from the feel of the glass on the window, it was warm outside. Whistling to myself, I got dressed and sailed out onto Queensway. I left the guidebook in the room. I'd spent so much time studying it on the plane that I was sick to death of even the mere thought of the wax museum or the palace or the changing of the guard. All I wanted to see were the streets.

I got a day pass for the tube and rode it till a stop sounded interesting. An electronic female voice announced the stops: Marble Arch, Angel, Old Street, Chancery Lane, Mansion House, Blackfriars, West India Quay. I changed lines because I liked the names: I rode the Bakerloo line and then the Jubilee line and the District line until I exited at Whitechapel. There, wandering around old back alleys, passing decaying pubs and a Kentucky Fried Chicken, I gazed up at luxury condo developments amidst the remnants of Victorian hostels. I tried to avoid looking at the corporate coffee houses and the fast food joints long enough so I could feel utterly lost in an alleyway and so far away in time that the plaques commemorating the Jack the Ripper murders didn't seem so new and the Bengali temple on the corner seemed like it'd been around for centuries. At Camden Town I bought a new pair of combat boots. I was beginning to understand that a thousand dollars did not equal a thousand pounds; it equaled five hundred pounds.

At London Bridge, I marched along the bank of the Thames till I reached Shakespeare's Globe. I took pictures from every angle I could, but had missed the tour. In the end, I didn't mind because I wanted to keep exploring. A ten-minute walk along the side of the river transported me into a Dickens novel, with brick streets, just-lit lamps, tunnels, and the moan of ships sounding their horns. At Borough High Street, plaques outside of inns noted the scenes they appeared in Shakespeare plays. I settled into a Chinese restaurant for a plate of Ma Po Tofu and a Malaysian beer. Everyone in the restaurant was Indian except for me. Guys, young ones, twenty-one at the oldest. I looked at my watch and prayed for seven-thirty to come. I was to meet Victor in Kensington for Thai food and then on to the club. I hadn't seen Big Ben, I hadn't seen a cathedral or a museum, but I was mad with excitement and a strange, solitary sense of joy.

46.

We walked along the dark, empty streets. Victor had dressed up again, elegantly, in black pants and shining black shoes and a purple shirt. I wore jeans and a T shirt and my skateboarding shoes. The signs on the street looked like No Parking signs, but they actually were warnings. "You are in a video surveillance area. Prostitution and drug trafficking will be prosecuted to the fullest extent of the law."

"Like five years ago, nobody lived over here," Victor said.

"Who'd have thunk it," I said, pointing to the sign. "George Orwell's nightmare came true." Victor laughed and I realized how glad I was to hear it. "It's funny. I brought up *1984* in Chicago a while ago and nobody had read it."

"Americans are idiots," Victor said, and winked. "Except for us. What'd you think of the restaurant?"

"I loved it." We'd eaten Thai food and drank several beers from Singapore before heading off to the club. "This area looks pretty run-down, but that was a classy joint. I don't think I could get used to calling shrimp 'prawns,' though."

"You gotta translate from English to English," he said.

"So, tell me about your life in London. You must be liking it. You even look different. You're all dressed up..."

"Oh, whatever. No, it's been really cool, but I haven't had a whole lot to do. I've just been applying to different colleges. And then, you know, wedding stuff."

"Right, wedding stuff. So you're going into the corporate world? I'd have thought you'd end up an overgrown, poor hippie still fighting the power."

He smiled, a little bashfully, and said, "Well, reality set in. I can still work with Amnesty, but I need some sort of career. After grad school, though, I'll probably look into working with a nonprofit."

I eyed the white spot on his temple, the size and shape of a jellybean. I wondered how many others there were around his body, and then figured I would find out later. I stopped walking, almost shocked by my arrogance. I wouldn't find out anything later. He wasn't marrying me. This wasn't a reunion of long-separated lovers, at least not for him. "So you tell me," he continued as we resumed our stride. "What's the deal in Chicago? How's Tony Valentine?"

"God, I really have no idea. He's the only one who moved to the suburbs and no one's really heard from him. I think he's a gym teacher in Schaumburg."

Victor fought back a laugh and put a hand to his mouth. "That's suburban hell. I mean that's really suburban hell!"

We laughed together, a little too hard. "But there is more news. Paul went down to school last week and he saw bulldozers outside the Harley Hutt. They knocked it down."

Victor was underwhelmed. "Well, it was about time. That place had to go."

"I don't know, I thought it was more than that. The parties there were cooler than anything I've seen in Chicago, anyway. I've got a lot of good memories of living there. I mean, six college guys and not one person ever went to a football game!" I watched his eyes carefully, but they didn't reveal much. "Also, Jean-Claude and Roberta are moving to New York. They're on the brink of fame and fortune and could not stay in Chicago anymore, because as Jean-Claude put it, 'the Windy City is for suckers.'"

I was hoping Victor would sympathize and say that that was a horrendous comment to make, but he said, "Well, that is sort of true. New York does make Chicago look like chump change."

I glared at him sideways.

"It's true," he said. "Now Chicago you could master in a couple of afternoons." He puffed out his chest. "London," he pronounced, "takes a lifetime to master."

I opened my mouth in bewilderment. "What guidebook did you read that in?"

"It's a famous saying. It's an old adage."

I rolled my eyes and then looked over at the street. The shops were all closed and we were still the only pedestrians. I burped, patting my stomach.

"How come you're so skinny and I'm so fat?" Victor asked. He pulled up his shirt to reveal a brown roll of flesh sagging over his pants.

"Well, there's more of you to love, I guess. Isn't your wife the lucky one. Yikes."

"You should feel lucky, Augie Schoenberg. Out of everyone at the Harley Hutt, you're the only one I invited."

I looked down at the wet sidewalk. I didn't know what to say.

His voice assumed an almost solemn heaviness that would have made me nervous if I hadn't had beer muscles. "You know, Augie, man, I wanted to tell you. Isabella called me last winter..." He stopped short. "About the thing."

"The thing? Victor, come on."

"About the abortion," he said, resolutely, as if he'd been practicing saying it. "I mean, it wasn't just that she wanted money. She wanted me to know about it, and I was glad she did. But, anyway, I wanted you to know that it wasn't that I went running to her cause I was freaked out about what happened between you and me; it wasn't that I was trying to reassure myself that I'm straight..."

"Yes it was!"

He flinched, and then said, "Well, OK, it was. I mean, God, I didn't even like her, and I think she hated me. I know you must've been upset about it, but I don't want you to think that it was like a rejection of you, cause it wasn't really. It was a mess, that's what it was." He exhaled and put his hands in his pockets. "It meant something, if it means anything to you. As small as it was."

"Did you tell what's her face..."

"Sarita."

"...about the abortion."

"Yeah, I told her. I didn't want to start off with secrets. I also told her about you."

I wasn't expecting that. "And how did she take it?"

"Well, she's got a more European view of these things. Also, I told her it was a once in a lifetime experience."

He smiled at me, the bastard, he was playing Prince Charming.

"I told her there isn't another guy on earth I'd do that kind of stuff with."

"I don't know if that's a compliment or an insult," I said, grinning, almost sure that I had taken it the right way.

"That's a compliment," he said, and while we strode through Kensington and Victor hailed a taxi I smiled inside so hard I thought I might float off the sidewalk.

We walked across Trafalgar Square, an oasis against the massive streets around us, and the calamity of what seemed like the whole city running into each other all at once. We navigated around a flock of pigeons.

"Have you seen Soho?"

"I did," I said, giggling. "I became the ugly American. I actually asked the coat check guy if they had 45s in England while I sang *Rock the Casbah* to him."

"God, Schoenberg, you are awful."

Victor rested a hand on my shoulder. I felt like it was a year earlier and Victor and I were just getting to know each other. As if the past had been full of reckless bliss and I, Augie Schoenberg, had been possessed with carefree youth. "Augie, I have to ask you something."

"Victor, I told you already," I said, giggling. "I can't marry you."

"Oh, please, Schoenberg. No, have you ever done ecstasy?"

My mind filled with awe. That's what he had planned. "No. But I'd love to try it."

"Dude, that is so awesome. You are going to love it!" We walked under an arch and came to a line of people. After a quick stroll through a metal detector and a brief stop at the admission window, we were in. I didn't even have to show ID.

I stood on the third floor watching the dance floor. Victor had taken out two twenty pound notes and was on a mission to find the drugs. He assured me he could buy it easily, which I hoped was true. I was wondering why everyone at the club was walking around with bottles of water and Victor said, "It's because they're all on ecstasy, stupid."

The crowd was awfully young. I was getting used to only seeing the over-21s at clubs, but apparently in the rest of the world, the teenage contingent could go out dancing, too. A couple of people bumped into me roughly, but I didn't look at them. I leaned against the bar and gazed out at the vast dance floor, full of insanely active people jumping around like their lives depended on it. I knew the night with Victor was going to end up with him going home to his fiancee and me going home to my hostel alone, but the offer of an ecstasy trip made everything in the world seem right. We wouldn't have sex, but we'd have the next best thing.

Two hands rubbed my shoulders. I turned around and Victor stood in front of me, looking pleased. "Did you get it?"

"Yeah," he said. "Really easily, too. It's all over the place."

"Aren't you worried you'll be in bad shape for your wedding?"

"Augie, this is so incredibly worth it. I don't care if I puke through the whole ceremony."

I wanted to throw my arms around him and smother him with sloppy kisses, but I opted instead for the wise choice and restrained myself.

"Ready?" he asked. "Open your mouth." He placed a tablet on my tongue, two of his fingers pressing against my lips. "Let it dissolve in your mouth for a while and then swallow it."

"You sound like an expert."

"I've had my moments," he said.

The pill tasted like aspirin. I let it get wet and chalky and then moved it to a place between my cheek and my teeth. "By the way, is this club gay? I can't tell."

"It is," he said, "but I think some nights are gayer than others."

If it was gay I was impressed. There were three levels of dance floors and twice as many bars. The club must have been an entire city block long.

"How long will this take to work?"

Victor shrugged and then I pushed him out to the dance floor. We danced around obnoxiously, neither of us talented enough to attempt to look good dancing to the absurdly fast techno that was playing. We chased around laser beams and jumped up and down and doubled over laughing for no reason. I felt nothing but mild happiness. I told Victor I wanted to sit down.

We walked to a set of chairs near the bathroom and the instant before we sat, Victor grabbed my arm and said, "Oh, shit."

I glanced over, terrified. "What's wrong?"

"Did you just feel that?"

"What?"

"Oh, shit, Augie, I think we got some really good stuff." He guffawed and then sat on a chair and ran his hand through his hair.

I didn't feel a thing. I went to sit down and then it hit me: the lights in front of me started to move and left long, sperm-like trails behind them and the people walking by seemed to bounce as they went past. The music sped up and became so loud it felt like a stereo was playing it from inside my brain. A wide, all-encompassing feeling of heavy pleasure overtook me and plowed through me, from my spine to my toes to my head. I couldn't feel any muscle in my body at all. I walked a few steps and could not even feel the weight of myself on top of my feet. My breathing slowed and thoughts shot through my head like rockets.

I sat down and looked at Victor. He had a enormous smile on his face and was sweating profusely. "Holy shit!" he said. "Do you feel it?"

I grabbed his arm for support. "Fuck yeah I feel it. Jesus Christ what's in this shit?"

"A whole lotta love!" he cried and then cackled and rubbed his hands together. "Touch yourself!" he called over to me, even though I was four inches from his face. "It feels so awesome!"

I ran my hand along my head. The feel of my palm on my hair was as gorgeous as a deep and lasting orgasm. I pressed my hands together and rubbed them slowly and carefully against one another. My lips curled upwards and I sat in the chair involuntarily smiling as wide as the Cheshire Cat, my teeth clenched together, grinding away, hoping for some sensation themselves.

"I can't believe I've never done this before! It's better than sex!"

Victor put a hand on my neck and massaged it. I leaned back into the chair, far back, and felt nothing but gut-wrenching pleasure and the strong, confident hand on my neck.

"If you stop doing that I'll kill you," I said. "Victor I'm getting incredibly stoned." I sat up and grabbed his arm. "You can't leave me alone tonight; I'll totally freak out. Just stay with me until this shit wears off." There was a longing inside of me for security and affection that defied reason. I thought if Victor even went to the bathroom I might lose my mind. "Victor, you don't understand, you have to stay by me!"

He put his face directly in mine and took my hand. "Augie, I'm not going anywhere. I'll be with you through this whole thing."

"Promise me you won't leave. I'm not a big drug person and I don't know what'll happen. Just stay close to me, cause otherwise I'll totally lose it."

He put his arm around me and I rested my head on his shoulder. "I'm not going anywhere. I'm here only with you. Just us. I promise."

"Talk," I said, sitting up, "just keep talking. Victor, I'm flying to a different planet right now. Just keep talking!"

"Dude, it's amazing! Feel this. Just feel this feeling! You can't beat it. I've done this like four times since I've been here and it's absolutely amazing. Don't you feel like everything is just speeding past you and you're watching as if you're inside of a music video and the rest of the world isn't reality anymore?"

I clutched his shoulder. "It is like a music video. That's exactly it!"

"It's crazy. It feels so fucking good! I love everyone right now! Everyone!"

"That's not true!" I said. "On ecstasy you only love one person. Even I know that!"

"All right, I love you Schoenberg! I really do!"

"That's just the drug talking. But I love you, Victor, and I mean that seriously! Like I really love you!" We clutched each other for dear life. The most amazingly awful need to express my feelings was brewing up inside of me so rampantly that I was afraid of what might come out of my mouth next. But I didn't care if I seemed like a fool to Victor. All the cramped anxieties about seeing him again slid off my brain and I finally knew that what I felt about him was right, and that I was entitled to feel it, and entitled to him.

Victor wiped a stream of sweat off his forehead. He looked as if he'd just run a marathon. "Schoenberg, it's not the drug. All right it is. Who gives a shit. I fuckin' love you so fuckin' much."

"You're amazing. You're so absolutely amazing it's made me sick for months. Victor, I don't think about anything else but you. I can't date anyone. I dated one of the motherfucking White Sox for Christ's sake and all I could do was dream of you. I even dated a frat boy, Jose Rubenstein, and he fucked me over, too! The baseball player had a wife! And Jose Rubenstein was evil! You don't know how absolutely wonderful you are compared to those assholes! No one knows but me. You are amazing!"

People walked past us but paid no attention. I grabbed onto Victor's shirt and wouldn't let go. "Schoenberg, you are the coolest guy on the whole motherfuckin' planet. I'm so glad you're here."

"Did you hear me! I said I dated one of the White Sox and all I did was dream of you! That's how much I love you!" I watched his sweating face as he bent over laughing hysterically. "You are beautiful!"

"Augie, you have no idea how much that means to me! You're in Chicago fucking the White Sox? You're like the coolest fag ever!"

"Thanks!" I said, proudly. I stared at his gorgeous eyes, his unbelievably intelligent face, the tiny sideburns. "You're so fucking beautiful!"

He shook his head. "You have no idea how much that means to me. No one ever told me that!"

"Not even what's her face?"

"Not even her. Dude, you have absolutely no clue how excited I was about tonight. It's undescribable."

I pressed my face up to his. "Victor you have to tell me that's the truth because that bitch Isabella told me that after we slept together you barfed for two days! Tell me that's not true! It's been killing me!"

Victor held my face in his hands. They felt as warm and wet and soft as bath sponges. "Augie," he said calmly, staring into my eyes with deep concentration. "There is no truth to that whatsoever. You made me the happiest guy around."

"You're lying!" I cried. "I love you to death but you're lying!"

"Augie," he said. I collapsed back into the chair. I didn't have the strength to sit up. "That is total bullshit. She was just jealous. Augie, I wanted to be with you more than you wanted to be with me!"

"Then how come you didn't go the PJ Harvey show? Victor, I sat outside the Metro like the biggest loser on the planet. I can't believe you didn't come!"

"I'm sorry about that! I really am! I had too much shit to do, that's all. It wasn't personal!"

"But do you know that I love you!"

He grabbed me around the shoulders and we sat quietly for a moment. I pressed my ear against his chest and listened to the sound of his heartbeat, its subterranean rhythm reassuringly steady compared to the music polluting my other ear. "Don't leave me alone," I said. "This drug is too strong."

He rubbed my head. "This is really strong shit."

I made my way to the bathroom. The bottoms of my shoes felt like they had been inflated with helium. I was desperately thirsty and so high I couldn't feel any pain at all. My muscles moved as easily as the thoughts in my head, the need I had to tell Victor what he meant to me, and the knowledge I had that he'd tell me something wonderful back.

I looked in the mirror after I peed. My curly hair stood on end, solidified by so much sweat. I touched my head, my arm, and breathed in. *I'm still here.*

Outside, I tried to regain a little sanity. I walked to the bar and paid five pounds for a bottle of water. My face felt so hot it was as though I'd been sunbathing at Hollywood Beach for hours. The water cascaded down my throat and filled another need. The need to cool off.

Victor was where I left him. I sat down and rubbed my hands together. I wanted things to be more sane and more real. I wanted to know that everything he said was true.

"Do you love London?" Victor asked.

"I love it so much. Every street is so fucking cute. And the people's accents are amazing. They make English sound so good!"

"I know! They invented it!"

"I don't wanna go home." I looked into Victor's eyes, reassuring myself that I had his complete confidence. "You know the White Sox guy I dated? It got out in the papers that we were dating. They didn't name him, but they kind of alluded to who it was..."

"Yeah..."

"And he left angry messages on my machine. I don't wanna go home at all!"

"Stay here!" Victor said. "Wouldn't you love it! What do you have to go home to anyway?"

"Nothing, I guess! God, I could become one of those permanent hostel residents that works there for their room and board and does nothing but party!"

"You can!"

"Victor!" I cried, still feeling the need to attach myself to him. "I love you!"

"Stay here! Don't go home!"

I wrapped my arm around his sweaty back and rested my cheek against his shoulder. We were both so clearly on drugs I was surprised we hadn't been arrested. I wouldn't have minded if we were, so long as Victor was there with me.

We walked under the arch. A mad dash of people swarmed by, pouring out of clubs and taxis and alleys, shouting and whistling. We ran across to Trafalgar Square, the air outside as light and warm as a summer night on the plains, but with an edge to it. The cars and trucks blew past us with such loud arrogance that it seemed they were all diesel-fueled stock cars. I relished the sight of the city before me, three hundred and sixty degrees around the plaza, but a safe distance from us: the square itself was nearly empty and gave Victor and I our own, private space. With Victor silently walking beside me and the soft feel of the air, the most serene feeling came over me, full of peace and affection. Victor pointed to a statue on a stone riser in the center of the square. "Let's hop up there." We hiked ourselves up and sat on the stone covered in darkness and looked around in awe at the lit panoramic view around us. In the distance, but on every side of us, crowds poured out of Piccadilly Circus and Covent Garden and Soho with a persistent, muffled roar, peppered with honks and screeches and the sound of happy calamity. "Listen to that crowd," I said. "Is it like this every night?"

Victor nodded. "It's party central, but this is for tourists. You need to go south of the river and hang in Brixton."

"Is that where London's Harley Hutt crowd goes?"

"Totally," he said. "That's exactly right. Check it out sometime this weekend if you can."

A soft breeze blew over us and cooled the sweat all over my body. "You were right about coming down. It is light as a feather. I feel absolutely at peace."

He looked over at me with a grin of affection that still lingered from the ecstasy. "That trip was a complete release. Don't you feel better?"

"It cured a lot of things," I said, feeling quite wise. It seemed that all the anxieties I had about my love life came to an absolute, sharp point at the height of the drug's powers and then slowly drained out of me. "I feel really at ease and happy with myself."

Victor put an arm around me, doubtlessly assured by the dark, private spot we shared. "That's all I could ask for."

I was so content and placid amidst the chaos that I could have fallen asleep in his arms.

The voice of Arundhati Singh was in my head, softly and gently, repeating over and over again the sage and powerful words she'd spoken in her lectures. Victor was next to me on the stone riser talking about his insecurities and anxieties. Family life was ahead of him, and I gathered he wasn't sure if he was up to it. Arundhati Singh's voice became softer and softer until there was just the faintest trace of noise.

The words and the ideas didn't cease, though, but sounded off in my head in a different voice, and this time it was mine. *Participating in a system that orders the world.* So what's up with this trip, Augie? he asked. I have a feeling you wanna take me back home with you. *Fiction orchestrates the social voices of the era.* If this was a movie, I said, you'd leave her at the altar and race to Heathrow to gather me up in your arms. *Challenging the division between magic and reality.* You could talk me into almost anything, Augie. But this ain't a movie. *The visible power structures. The capacity to connect.* Of all the people in London tonight, I said, I'm the one who loves you. *Narrating a dream, constructing a myth.* This feeling I have tonight, he said. I don't have any pretensions that it's an accident. I'm only happy now because of you. *The colonizing impulse.* You could walk away, I said. Chicago ain't far. You and me, an apartment in Rogers Park, rock shows on the weekends.... *The land or the person in relation to the land.* I don't want to lose this, Victor said, motioning around. It's the future for me. *The romantic view: things are getting better all the time.*

I couldn't say anything, I clutched his arm. *History and violent circumstances that divide them also connect them.* The wind blew against my skin, its touch was like the gentle touch of lips. In a different world, he said, it'd be you tomorrow instead of her. *Desexualization as a form of colonization. Us vs. them.* I don't wanna hear that, I said, cause I wanna hear it so bad. *We must exclude someone or we'll be left with nothing.* You, he said. Are gonna turn this world on its head. The screenplay, the creative powers in your mind. You're making it your world. *The imperialist creates a place. People become texts—what do they mean?* I'm not there yet, I said. I can't even find a boyfriend. *Love and marriage constructed on the backs of slavery. Racism, etc. Europe used to be a place of darkness.* Your last year wasn't a failure, Augie Schoenberg. You didn't have a boyfriend, you had three. *Truth is a story, you make it up.* Victor, I think you just saved my life.

We moved closer, arms around each other, the crowd in the distance still roaring, but to them we were invisible, and safe. *The narrative conceals as it reveals.* Victor pulled a camera from his jacket pocket and held it out in front of us, his arm extended so far that the camera seemed to dangle precariously over the edge of the stone column. If he dropped it, it'd smash. Smile, Augie, we'll remember this one forever. I rested my head against his and grinned like I never had, absorbing every ounce of warmth he gave off. *Humanity dwarfed down below.* The bulb went off and left me blind. *Illusion as reality vs. illusion dissolving.* I'll send it to you, he said. Keep it in a safe place. *The Westernized syntax; the ending.*

47.

I didn't go to the wedding. When I woke, it was three o'clock in the afternoon. I looked at my watch and felt a terrible sense of relief. I was in no condition to be at a wedding. My mouth was dry as paper, and my bowels were filled with streaking pains that had me in the bathroom after I returned from Trafalgar Square. I rose from the bed, my head oddly heavy and not functioning well: thoughts seemed to have an oppressive weight to them that slowed them down. I couldn't make any decisions.

I slept again and when I woke up it was dark and my shirt was covered in sweat.

I left Bayswater and roamed through Covent Garden. I ate a breast and a wing at Kentucky Fried Chicken but with my drug hangover it tasted like cardboard. It was hard to swallow. I thought of dropping in on the reception, but I didn't know where Kings Street was. There was only one thought I had in my head. Alcohol.

I traced the Thames and wandered along slowly, and endlessly, but with a purpose. I would go to the other side of the river and finally get away from the tourists and the commerce and the insatiable need that London had to stride through the curving, ancient streets with a determined, arrogant importance. I wanted to be alone.

The Radhakrishna Temple stood before me. Outside of it, a plaque told the story of Radha, the milkmaid, and Krishna, the deity. Their erotic and sexual love represented the idea of love in its innocent soul form, unlike worldly love motivated by selfish desire. The two were separated and though they were reunited once, they would never again be together as lovers.

Two teenaged girls walked by, openly talking about me. "Do you think that guy's gay?" one said. "Oh, well," the other responded. "He'd be cuter anyway if he didn't look like he was going to cry."

In Brixton, in the darkness, solitary and full of whiskey and ale, I walked past Electric Avenue. I got on buses and then got off. I wandered in and out of unfriendly pubs, where mean, fat men sat alone at the bar grimacing at me. I was followed by a group of teenagers and then lost them by hopping down into the tube. I found myself in Elephant and Castle, drunk at 3 in the morning and thirsty for more. I woke up on the Mile End bus the next morning, stinking of piss.

That night in Trafalgar Square, the ecstasy slowly dissolving, the crowds becoming thinner, Victor and I jumped down and walked toward the road. I was high that night, and not just stoned, but higher than I'd ever felt, because I was there.

We strode along toward the street in front of us, the wind blowing at us perfectly. And then I remembered something. "Victor, I'm turning 23 next week. The year's almost over."

"So you tell me. Good year or bad year?"

"It had its highlights." And then I laughed. "Especially one guy who somehow made Normal, Illinois seem like the most gorgeous place on earth."

Victor's eyes were on the pavement, but his face looked pleased. "So what are you gonna do when you get back to Chicago?"

We picked up our pace and I said, "When I get back to Chicago, that plane is gonna fly over the city..."

"Yes?"

"And I'm gonna soar through those skyscrapers like the...like the..."

"Yes?"

"Like the falcons that nest in them and the world can kiss my ass!"

"That's perfect!"

We came to the street and a taxi stopped. Victor must have hailed one, but I didn't see him do it. "Be happy, Schoenberg," he said, getting into the cab. "Do it for me."

And then he was off, and I wasn't, and I stood in Trafalgar Square with the whole world spinning in circles around me and my mouth compulsively grinning and my heart beating so hard I felt like I was about to rise.

Book Five

I'll tell you how the Sun rose—
A Ribbon at a time—

>   -Emily Dickinson

48.

In the future, the thousand dollars will run out and I'll go back to the hostel to pack my bag, glad to be going home. The sound of the people will cease to sound cute, and airy, and full of intelligence but will ring in my ears as snappish, and bitter, and deceptively sinister. It won't take long to pack, just five minutes, and then I'll make a final check of my passport and my plane ticket and the few pounds that I have left in the pocket of my jeans.

On the tube, the train will rise up from the tunnel so quickly that not ten minutes from Bayswater we'll be above ground and coasting through suburban-like neighborhoods, the cottages with their brick fences and tiny backyards rolling past my eyes as if they're fictional, and made up, and will cease to exist as soon as I can no longer see them.

At Heathrow the line will be long, but when I make it up to the counter the ticket agent, short, blond, trying to sound more official than she thinks she can get away with, will ask me what my destination is. Chicago, I'll say, proudly and she'll move her head slightly, as if she's marginally impressed.

I'll think of the life that waits for me in Chicago, and the hot, steamy apartment and the smile on Ted's face when I walk through the door. No one in the airport will have any idea what I've been through in London or what awaits me at home, the story belongs exclusively to me.

The plane will take off at noon and the whole flight will be incredibly sunny and so smooth that the pilot will never turn on the seatbelt light, but will let us roam the cabin as we see fit. When I recline back in my chair, thoughts of the past will pour through my head and I'll close my eyes and watch them, as though they're playing in a movie on the screen in front of me. Slowly, with the projector and its reels moving in slow motion, the past year will play itself out in translucent celluloid frames, flicker by flicker, and Victor and Jose and Johnny will appear, staring at me, in mugshots. For some odd reason that I'll be eternally and madly grateful for, those pictures and the memories they bring with them will become lit from behind, and a searing chemical in my brain will tell me that I will be in charge of the past. That I don't need to be afraid of the future or of being alone. That this story, these stupid scribblings of Augie Schoenberg, will mean something—that I'm not just some gay Jew from Evanston that people want to push around—that I'm a force that will matter, because this story happened, and it will have this ending, where Chicago will arise outside the windows and the cabin will fall silent as everyone gazes out at the unbelievable spread of skyscrapers and water below us. The Hancock building will stretch into the sky in such an agonizingly beautiful, official way, presiding over the other buildings and the lake as though they're its children, and then the woman next to me will call out, "Now that's a city!"

The plane will make a sharp turn over Evanston and while I try to locate my parents' house, the plane will almost fall into a nosedive and the sound of the engines will stop, and we'll glide over the suburbs as if we need no fuel, no machinery to do it.

Too soon, we'll touch the asphalt at O'Hare and everything will become a blur. The familiar American voices and the familiar signs and the familiar cars, everything regular, and homey, the feeling of belonging will be humbling. I'll almost jump up in the air with joy, but really will just walk faster, breathing hard and fast. On the L, the rustling of trash on the floor, the screeching wheels of the train, and the unintelligible call from the PA system will blend together into a recognizable din that won't hurt my ears.

In Edgewater, late at night, the air so hot that whole families will be out on stoops, staring at me, I'll breeze past, under the L tracks, past the old Chinese place, up the elevator of our building until I see Ted, lounging on the sofa, airy, electronic music bouncing off the walls.

Hey world traveler, he'll say, rising to hug me. Your baseball player finally stopped calling. He said to tell you he's moving to Florida for good, all because of you, or something like that. There was quite a little controversy here. Also, there's another message for you. I left it on the machine, but it's from Hollywood.

My arms will grasp on to his back and I'll kiss him on the cheek.

How was the wedding?

I didn't go.

Wasn't that the point?

No. It wasn't the point at all.

At the window, if I turn just right, I'll be able to make out just a little bit of the street and the black void of water beyond it. I'll know I'm home.

This is where I belong.

No kidding. You live here.

I longed for things for so long. I longed for everything.

Don't you anymore?

I do. But that feeling, that incredible sense of urgent need, it's gonna make me so incredibly happy.

Why?

It makes me feel alive.

Acknowledgments

I must thank the Prince of Woodlawn for putting me up in high ghetto style while I wrote this book. No amount of vermin, rodents, or friendly neighborhood gunfire can take away from his generosity. Melissa Banks, Peter Liebman, and Caroline Bilicki were my first readers and copy editors. Laverne Street offered help when I most needed it. Chris Baugher provided software and Rauscher Systems, Inc. helped with health insurance. Emily Teiken inspired the original idea for this, which I don't think she knows. She also sold me a car when I was desperate. Zohreh Sullivan's class 'The Literature of Imperialism' at the University of Illinois was also an inspiration for this novel. Mark Costello told me I could write. Meryl kept me company when I was holed up writing. Janice Goodman connected me to a job where I could work from home, and I'm probably most grateful for that. Without the above-named people, I wouldn't have been able to write this book.

> Matt Rauscher
> Chicago
> April, 2005

LaVergne, TN USA
10 February 2010

172667LV00003B/169/A